MW00779337

Bentonsport:
A CHRISTMAS STORY

Enjoy the "journey" to Bentonsport!

BY LISA SCHNEDLER

Merry Christmas!
Lisa Schnedler
Psalm 37:5

Scrivenings
PRESS
Quench your thirst for story.
www.ScriveningsPress.com

To my parents, George and Patricia Wagner, for the legacy of faith they have shared with all of us!

Copyright © 2022 Lisa Schnedler (Emunah LLC)

Published by Scrivenings Press LLC
15 Lucky Lane
Morrilton, Arkansas 72110
https://ScriveningsPress.com

Printed in the United States of America

All rights reserved. No part of this publication may be reproduced, stored in a retrieval system, or transmitted in any form or by any means—for example, electronic, photocopy and recording— without the prior written permission of the publisher. The only exception is brief quotation in printed reviews.

Paperback ISBN 978-1-64917-236-5

eBook ISBN 978-1-64917-237-2

Editors: Shannon Taylor Vannatter and K. Banks

Cover design by Linda Fulkerson - www.bookmarketinggraphics.com

Cover background photo by Cassandra Louise Coffin

This is a work of fiction. Unless otherwise indicated, all names, characters, businesses, events, and incidents are either the product of the author's imagination or used in a fictitious manner. Any resemblance to actual persons, living or dead, or actual events is purely coincidental.

Acknowledgments

Thanks to Harold Schnedler and Deirdre Lockhart for editing my manuscript and to Cassandra Louise Coffin for her lovely photography.

Bentonsport, Iowa
1869

"Well, ladies, we can all agree upon one thing—this simply has gone on too long. Too long!" Virginia Carrington slammed her palms on the table and stared at the other three women sitting around it. They nodded, almost in unison.

"And," she continued, her curls bobbing on her forehead, "we've been entirely too patient. Much too patient."

Annabelle Manning patted Virginia's hand. "Oh, Virginia, dear, you tried so hard."

"Twice." Virginia lowered her voice in a harsh whisper, her green eyes glistening. "Yes, twice, I imposed upon dear friendships, first begging Mercy Paine and then Emmalou Barnes to turn their precious daughters over to me to present them to Mr. Barton in the most captivating and intriguing way."

After pushing back from the table, she walked to the center of the room, her dress swishing against the broad floor planks.

Within this setting, the winter's fire cast a glow on her stout frame. She strutted as if she were performing on stage.

"'Mr. Barton,' I said." She curtsied. "'I would like you to meet Miss Paine. You two have a great deal in common.' Yes—I emphasized this. And then I said, 'Miss Paine is highly educated and attending college in Mount Pleasant. She is musical too.'

"And what did he say?" Her tone changed from pleasant to stern.

She deepened her voice. "'A pleasure to meet you, Miss Paine.' And then he walked away, chatting with Pastor Lockhardt. Not a glance back. Not a pause. Nothing. I was humiliated—hu–mil–i–ated!" She pulled a handkerchief from her skirt pocket, dabbed her forehead, and returned the lace-trimmed cloth to its place.

"Did I give up, ladies?"

The three women shook their heads, nearly in unison.

"No, I did not. I regathered my pride, and then I visited Emmalou, requesting permission to introduce her daughter to Mr. Barton. Lovely, kind, demure Eleanora was returning home from a year in New York. She's cultured. Yes, cultured! How could this not be the perfect match? So, I stopped by and asked Eleanora to accompany me on a walk."

Virginia strolled across the floor. "And we reached the academy just as school was ending for the day. So, I led Eleanora by the arm, and we made the ascent up the hill to the academy."

She marched in place as though climbing a steep hill and fanned herself, her elbow crooked, arm and arm with the invisible Eleanora.

"I paused, of course, to catch my breath. But, as soon as I had full control of my voice, I smiled at our headmaster and said, 'Mr. Barton, I imagine you've not yet met Miss Eleanora Barnes. Miss Barnes'—yes, I emphasized *Miss*—'has been in New York for a year to study art. She just returned home, here only briefly before she begins college.'

"I stepped away from Eleanora and placed my hand on his arm. 'Eleanora,' I said, 'I'd like you to meet Thomas Barton. Mr.

Barton is the headmaster of our academy. This is his second year, and we're so glad he joined us.'"

Turning, bracing her hands on her generous hips, her lips clamped in a straight line, she nearly shouted, "Well, ladies, does Thomas Barton take my cue to converse with this young lady? Does he inquire about her time in New York? Does he ask what college she will be attending?"

She paused for a dramatic silence.

"No, no. He humiliates me once again. He smiles at Eleanora, tells her it is a pleasure to meet her, comments on the lovely day, and slips back into the academy."

With this, Virginia walked to her chair and resumed her position at the head of the table.

"So, ladies, this is absolutely it. If we want Thomas to remain as the headmaster of our academy, he must find a wife. And, because Bentonsport has few eligible young women, we must make this our moment."

Suella Thompson interjected, "What is special about this moment?"

"As you surely know, Elizabeth Miner is coming home—completely unattached." Virginia folded her hands on the tabletop. "This time, we're not going to rely on simple introductions. No, never that again. This time, I am throwing Elizabeth Miner a welcome home party, and I'm inviting the whole town."

"Oh, we'd be happy to help you," Annabelle chirped.

"Well, yes, I will need help with the party. But I need your help before the party. That's why I asked you to come over today. Ladies, we will create excitement the likes of which Bentonsport has never experienced. If Queen Victoria herself were coming, it wouldn't outdo the excitement we will create throughout the town about the arrival—yes, I said *arrival*—of Miss Elizabeth Miner. I want Thomas to hear her name in every store, in every street conversation, until he hears the name in his dreams. I want him to not only desire but yearn to meet this divine woman."

"Well, Elizabeth is pretty and nice, but ..."

"Anabelle, it doesn't matter what she is. It only matters what he thinks she will be. This won't be an introduction. It will be an anticipated event. And this time—"

A knock on the door interrupted. When Virginia rose and answered it, there stood Thomas Barton. She took two steps back, unable to choke out even a greeting.

"Ladies." Thomas nodded to the women and held out a book to Virginia. "Mrs. Waters said it was fine for me to interrupt. I'm returning this. I read several sections to the children, and they enjoyed it very much."

"Why, Thomas, do come in."

"I can't stay right now. I'm running errands. But it's nice to see you ladies. Good day."

He closed the door and left.

Virginia returned to her seat and lowered her voice to a whisper. The women leaned in. "This time, ladies, we will not fail."

Chapter One

There was talk of a pending storm.

After sealing the envelope addressed to his parents, Thomas Barton drummed his fingers on the well-worn walnut desktop and stared out the windows at the gray sky. They would be saddened by its message. His family was hoping he'd travel the nearly one thousand miles from Iowa to Pennsylvania for the holidays—a trip of two and a half days by train.

But if the rumored storm were true, he couldn't risk being stranded in Pennsylvania, even for Christmas. In his second year of teaching at the Bentonsport Academy, he felt responsible for his twenty-six students. No one could take his place.

His gaze wandered over the few furnishings in his second-floor living quarters—the cannonball bed, chest of drawers, and bedside table with the lamp he carefully carried when he moved to Bentonsport. In the center of the room stood a round walnut table. It could accommodate two people only, which suited him well. He nearly always ate alone. Now he would be alone at Christmas.

As he descended the stairs, Thomas's steps echoed in the narrow stairwell. Then he slid on his coat and stepped out the door, locking it behind him. A slate-gray sky hung overhead. He strode to the post office, hoping the walk would rid him of the creeping sadness. The dirt roads were hard from the long months of cold. Trees stood unmoving, armlike branches stretched up high.

As he turned the corner, Virginia Carrington, Bentonsport's most prominent busybody, left her house. She didn't look in his direction but stood on her walkway, rooting through her cranberry drawstring purse. She drew the bag shut and hustled toward the road. He'd have to watch what he said, as it would no doubt be repeated.

"Good day, Mr. Barton." She secured her pale green bonnet.

He smiled back. "Good day, Mrs. Carrington."

She approached and took his arm. "You won't mind if I walk with you into town, will you? I'm on my way to have tea with Luella."

"I'd be delighted," he lied and prepared to engage in a skirmish of small talk.

Two carriages passed, their horses decorated with red bows and brass bells. Young couples walked arm in arm with each other, enjoying the brisk day. Would he ever have someone special to take on a stroll about town? Someone besides Mrs. Carrington?

"I was going to visit you today, Mr. Barton. You're invited to the welcome home party Mr. Carrington and I are hosting this Saturday evening for Elizabeth Miner."

He couldn't match a face with the name.

A wave of her free hand saved him the trouble. "You probably haven't heard much about her. She's William's daughter. She's been away at school for three years. A lovely young woman."

He hesitated. Normally, he would make excuses—do anything other than be subjected to her matchmaking skills. But, with the dark winter days and the empty holiday season ahead, he knew he needed to be with people. He grinned, then cleared his throat. "Your event sounds like a nice way to enter the holiday season."

"Oh, it will be. Mark my word."

Virginia Carrington lacked all subtlety in her pairing

attempts. Twice before, she'd tried to set him up with women he had no interest in. But a party might just be what he needed.

When they reached Front Street, she released his arm. She pointed toward an elderly woman dressed in a navy skirt with a red sash, using a tapered black cane. "There's Annabelle Manning. I need to extend an invitation to her as well. Good to see you, Thomas." She patted his arm. "Don't forget Saturday evening!"

On Front Street, the five-story brick building across the way blocked his view of the river. To his left, cedar boughs and ribbon decorated the brick stores. A merry fiddle played *Good Christian Men Rejoice*. Ernst Gentry, a retired farmer, entertained shoppers at Christmastime by playing carols.

Another Christmas season and he remained alone. Disquietude crept through him. Why were times of joy always laced with melancholy? His yearning and loneliness seemed to frame even the happiest of events. Nevertheless, the season also brought hope—and now, his hope focused on Miss Miner.

Virginia Carrington called her lovely.

He shook off his thoughts.

Early expectations of romance rarely led anywhere other than disappointment and sadness.

He proceeded to the post office, and when he tugged the door open, the bells hanging beneath its framed window jingled.

"Hello, Thomas." Benjamin Ross, the postmaster, stared over wire-rimmed glasses far down his nose as he set aside a pile of letters. Tall and lanky in his early fifties, with his stiff turned-up collar and carefully knotted tie, he'd have appeared equally at home in a courtroom.

Thomas slid his letter across the marred wooden counter. "Good morning, Benjamin. What's new in town?"

"Most talk today concerns Elizabeth Miner coming home. No one thought she would return home without a husband, but according to her parents, she's unattached. Seems no one back East measured up to her standards." Benjamin shot him an

7

amused glance. "I imagine all the young gents in town'll be finding reasons to stop by the Miners' place."

Thomas steadied his expressionless gaze. This Elizabeth Miner must be quite something to create such a stir.

"I'm sure her parents will be glad to have her back." He tapped his envelope. "I wish I could send similar news to my family—about coming home, I mean. But with this forecasted storm, I can't consider going to Pennsylvania for the holidays."

"Oh? I'm sorry, Thomas—for you and your family." Benjamin glanced down at the letter. "Well, Beulah and I would enjoy having you for a meal sometime during the holidays."

"I'd appreciate it."

"Let me know when you're available. We'll set the date."

"I will." When a stout man in a long woolen coat came to the counter, package in hand, Thomas thanked Benjamin and left the warm post office for the chilly air. Two invitations in one morning? The holidays looked better already. And the intriguing prospect of meeting Miss Elizabeth Miner—intriguing because it seemed he'd have to vie with other single men for the chance.

Chapter Two

C laaang!

Sarah Peterson had slid the last batch of cranberry orange bread into the oven when she jolted, startled by the loud bell on her back door. After two years, the bell still made her jump. Caroline Murphy, her neighbor and best friend, entered the room, boots clopping against the wooden floor. Sarah closed the oven door and switched off her iPod.

"So, how was it?" Caroline hung her coat, scarf, and cap on the hooks beside the door. She slipped off her boots and placed them under her jacket

"How was what?" Sarah did her best to hold back a smile.

"Don't give me that." Caroline wagged a finger. "You know what I'm talking about."

"It was okay." Pulling a stool out from under the counter, she motioned for her friend to sit and then hugged her arms about herself, letting the buttercup-yellow walls cheer her. "It's always pleasant to have an evening out. Mark and I went to Mount

Hamil and ate fried chicken. Kind of a loud place but a cozy environment. And the food was good."

Settling in, Caroline unfolded some sewing from her flowered satchel, her straight brown hair blocking her face. "Do you think you'll see him again?"

"I don't know. We didn't talk about future dates. We discussed his work in logging and mine here, baking—that type of thing." Sarah put the blue sugar bowl and spoons on the counter—how nice they looked against the cherry wood top. "He's a nice man who likes to have fun." With luck, the subject would end there.

Caroline leaned in, her brown eyes flashing. "You could do a lot worse."

"Don't I know it." Sarah laughed. She'd had her share of miserable dates. Nice was better than terrible, but wonderful would be even better.

Her kitchen remained Sarah's favorite place to hang out, one of the reasons she'd decided to become a professional baker. Here, in her domain, she could always find peace. The center island, cabinets framing the back, and display cases surrounding the front comprised her home-based bakery.

Warm today as the ovens steamed the windows, blurring the snowy scene outside but allowing the light through the fine lace curtains. With Christmas less than two weeks away, the days were short—and daylight precious.

She brought out two China cups and saucers and poured tea. "On to more important subjects. How's business?"

The fragrance of jasmine rose with the steam from the cups.

"We're busy. Bill's been working hard getting online orders shipped out. His new tin lamps are popular." She held up a half-completed tree skirt. "I've been finishing several tablecloths and quite a few personalized Christmas stockings and these too. How about you?"

"Scads of bread, Christmas cookies, and pastries. Did you see the kids clustering in here yesterday? I invited Barbara's third-grade class to decorate cookies with me. We were up to our earlobes in powdered sugar." She tucked a lock of her hair behind her ear, then sipped her tea, its sweet warmth a familiar comfort. "Speaking of kids, how's the baby?"

"Moving and getting big. See?" Caroline smoothed her jumper against the growing bulge. Though both in their thirties, Sarah marveled how her friend could still pass for twenty. With her brown hair parted straight down the middle, smooth round face, and peppy demeanor, she seemed like a young college girl. "I'm over the awful tiredness and have so much energy now—kind of proportional to my weight."

"We should all be so lucky." Sarah giggled as she measured her sourdough starter. Then she added sugar, corn oil, salt, and water, stirring the batter with sweeping strokes. "I love easy recipes, especially this time of year. The holidays get too busy." She kneaded the mixture and then placed the dough in an oiled bowl, allowing it to rest. She smirked. The deep sink filled lip-high with dishes loomed before her. "And now for my least favorite task—washing dishes."

"Ah." Caroline flattened the lace on the tree skirt. "But think what a great wife you'll make someone. Baking and cleaning up too."

"We can hope. Someday."

Filling the sink with steamy water, Sarah peered through the misted window. She would find the right man—someone educated who enjoyed conversations long into the night and loved to laugh. The combination just hadn't come together yet.

"Hey." Caroline's cheerful voice broke into her thoughts. "Bill and I are going to the jazz festival in Burlington next weekend. You should come. You'll meet a few of his old high school buddies and hear some great music."

Sarah stiffened. Yes, getting out and meeting people would be good for her. But she never liked being set up. She dipped her ringless left hand into the suds.

Clenching her fingers under the water, she fibbed, "I'd love to."

Chapter Three

T homas paced the room, stopping at each cluster of students, surveying their work for their upcoming staged version of Charles Dickens's *A Christmas Carol*.

Some students painted scenery and assembled costumes while others rehearsed their parts. Against the walls stood finished backdrops of various scenes: Scrooge's office, his bedroom of ghostly visits, and Tiny Tim's cozy home.

Art class was dedicated to building sets, English class to writing the script, history class to learning about England and its customs, and math class to plotting the actors' locations on the stage. By matching the lessons to components of the play, he kept the students focused on their studies and created an escape valve for their holiday excitement.

He pulled the long loop of a paint-splattered apron over his head. "All right, boys, let's lay out Scrooge's street. Girls, could you get the paints? All the shades of black, gray, and brown you can find. And both cans of brushes—the broad flat ones and the thinner ones."

After the boys laid canvas on the floor and spread newspapers to catch spills, he motioned the girls to join him. "Now, several of you sit over here on the left. Use the smaller brushes to outline each object in the scene. Then shade them in with the broader brushes."

"How do we know what color to use?" David Saltzer, a boy with round glasses, cocked his head like a robin.

"Good question." Thomas pointed to the words penciled in each section. "The scene designers have labeled each section with a color."

David squinted at the lettering, his lips moving as he mouthed each one he read.

"Over here on the right"—Thomas moved to the top-right corner—"I need those of you who like to paint skies."

Three of the older girls walked over and stood.

"This canvas will be used for the predawn scenes and late at night, so we want a dark but moonlit sky. The moon will reflect off the clouds, so this area will be silver." He gestured toward the middle. "The other sections will be shades of dark gray, dark blue, and black."

The room buzzed while Scrooge's neighborhood came to life. As sections of the sky were painted and repainted until the moon cast an eerie glow on patches of rippling clouds, the streetlamps glowed against the foggy background.

He'd just crouched on the floor to help Joe, his youngest student, paint the cobbled street when Abigail, seated across from him, stood and waved. Thomas looked over his shoulder. A group of mothers clustered at the door, watching the children—and him. He'd heard the parents, particularly the mothers, were curious about the play, but he hadn't expected them to show up at the academy. Abigail's wave alerted the other children, who stood and ran to their parents.

"All right, everyone," Thomas called above their chattering voices. "After you clean up, you're free to go. Paintbrushes in the buckets to soak. We'll let the scene dry overnight, so walk around it for now."

The students clattered away the painting supplies, some of them discussing the predicted snow.

As he ensured the last of the brushes went into the buckets, soft voices drifted his way.

"He's so good with them," one mother said, her voice just above a whisper. "He would make such a good father."

"Well," answered her companion, "there may be a better chance of that with Elizabeth's return."

As the women laughed, his face flushed. Elizabeth again. Regaining his composure, he greeted the women as if he hadn't heard their remarks. He wiped his long fingers against his apron. "It's always good to hear laughter in the academy. And especially pleasing to hear the laughter of you fine ladies." He bowed, hopefully leaving the women embarrassed but pleased.

The boys and girls raced to get their coats and lunch boxes. With the last child's departure, he closed the door, and the room fell silent. He cleaned the chalkboards, the swoosh of his cloth accompanying the wall clock's steady tick. After extinguishing the lamps, he climbed the wooden stairs to his apartment.

As he sat and removed his highly polished black leather shoes, his thoughts returned again and again to Elizabeth Miner. Out of all the eligible bachelors in town, his name seemed to be on the shortlist, at least in some matchmakers' eyes. A smile pulled at his lips. Some still deemed him "eligible," even ten years after he had become so.

On Saturday, Thomas laid out his finest wear for the Carrington event the following evening. As he rummaged through a dresser drawer for the gold cufflinks his grandfather had given him, he considered what topics he might raise in his conversation with Miss Miner. He could ask about her schooling. He could discuss the play his students were planning and invite her to attend. He could tell her he was the most intelligent man in the county. He grinned. Being a liar and braggart was probably not the best first approach.

Once satisfied with his planned attire, he left the school building and headed to Greef General Store. Breathing in the ever-present smell of spices, leather, and coffee, he chose a box of chocolates for the Carringtons, a bag of candy canes for the children to place on the tree at the church, and assorted hard candies as a treat for them at the hanging of the greens.

He shifted his weight while joining the line of customers at the cash register. The hum of chatter offered bits of shared holiday plans, a promised exchange of cookie recipes, and snippets of the latest local news. Elizabeth Miner topped the list of topics.

As he entered the academy, his purchases in hand, thoughts of Elizabeth Miner swirled in his head. He spent the remainder of the day gathering evergreen branches to decorate the church sanctuary windowsills and then hauled the branches to the church in an old wagon one of the children abandoned at the school. The church, a stately brick structure with a tall white steeple, stood dark and shuttered. He stacked the branches in a neat pile outside the door.

Home again, he dressed in his formal attire, tucked the bags of candy in his coat pockets, grabbed the box of chocolates, and headed for the church. The hanging of the greens brought back fond childhood memories when the event meant Christmas Day lay just around the corner. This church, too, became a place of festivity, filled with the smells of cedar, pine, cinnamon, oranges, and clove.

Carriages passed him as he walked up the hill. He quickened his pace as a buggy pulled alongside him.

"Greetings, Mr. Barton," a student's voice sang out.

"Shouldn't you be in school?" another chimed in.

Thomas and their parents joined in the laughter as the buggy continued its climb.

Near the church, William Miner's carriage and horse overtook him. He glimpsed a young woman inside. Tendrils of hair the color of sunflowers curled about her face beneath her blue bonnet. This elegant beauty had to be Elizabeth.

Picking up his pace, Thomas arrived as the carriage rolled before the church door.

William climbed out and went to the other side to open the carriage door, offering his hand to the young woman.

Thomas rushed to follow them up the stone steps. Gaining the entryway, he positioned himself in William's line of sight, hoping to be introduced.

But before Thomas could make eye contact, Pastor Lockhardt clasped his hand. "Good evening. You certainly look dapper tonight."

Normally, Thomas would have greeted the jaunty pastor's warm handshake in kind. But tonight, as the Miners passed through the door and away, he wished his friend were not so attentive. His shoulders slumping, he focused on Pastor Lockhardt.

A short man, solidly built, Pastor Lockhardt smoothed his abundance of white hair. "Your children are about to start singing, Thomas. Won't you join me up front?"

"Of course." The enthusiasm he tried to infuse into his voice seemed to lodge in his throat, the words coming out flat. This would further delay his introduction.

Pastor Lockhardt sat just left of the center aisle, and Thomas took the spot next to him, placing his box of chocolates under the pew.

The children formed a semicircle behind the communion table. Whitewashed walls and dark windows framed them.

Pastor Lockhardt rose, strode onto the platform, and faced the congregation. "Welcome to God's house." His voice boomed over the packed pews. "We'll begin this celebration of our Lord's birth with some carols."

The twenty or so children sang "The First Noel," "Silent Night," and "Joy to the World." The younger ones swayed back and forth to the melody while most of the older ones self-consciously stood stiff. Rambunctious children who had shouted to him from carriages now, in front of their elders, avoided eye

17

contact. Their confidence had better return for *A Christmas Carol*.

After concluding their performance, the whispering and giggling children scrambled to their pews. Pastor Lockhardt read the account of Jesus's birth from the gospel according to Luke. Closing the Bible, he said, "Let us pray. Heavenly Father, we thank You for Your Word. We thank You also for the children's gift of song and ask You to bless us now as we gather to decorate Your home for this holy season, amen."

He stepped from the platform and raised his arms, his black robe flowing. "I invite you all to assist in decorating the church, enjoy some refreshments, and join in the caroling."

Elizabeth also rose, engaged in conversation with Lucinda Carrington, the Carringtons' oldest daughter. They ambled to the back of the church, lifted some of the cedar branches Thomas had brought earlier, and began placing them in the deep windowsills. He moved toward them, but Joe Miner, Elizabeth's uncle, intercepted him.

"Thomas." The man slapped him on the back. "We need another strong fellow to help us move the pump organ aside to make room for the tree. How about lending a hand?"

"Certainly." And thus, yet another chance for an introduction to Elizabeth slipped past.

As he straightened his jacket after they'd pushed the organ over beside the communion table, a tap brushed his shoulder. Virginia Carrington's catlike eyes gleamed up at him. "The children are nearly finished decorating their tree in the vestibule. Could you help them with the star?"

He rubbed his forehead. "Of course."

Thomas followed her to the foyer, walking past Elizabeth and Lucinda hanging ribbons on the pews. On the way, he retrieved the bags of candy from his coat. In the vestibule, he placed the tin star atop the children's tree, his frock coat bushing against garlands of cranberries, popcorn strings, orange slices studded with cloves, and frolicking gingerbread men they'd made in Sunday school.

"You did a great job with your performance this evening." He crouched to eye level with the smaller children. "I have a surprise for you."

As he distributed candy sweets from two bags, the younger children shrieked in delight, and the older ones held out their hands with a polite thank you.

"Hang these on the tree in the front of the church." He opened the candy cane bag. With a candy cane in one hand and their own candy in the other, the children ran to do as he instructed. Thomas followed, stuffing the empty bags into his pockets, and a smile spread across his face. The church transformed into a magical place of light and color.

Mamie Huntington, the church accompanist, had taken her place at the piano. She was thumbing through a booklet of Christmas hymns as thirty or so adults, including Elizabeth, formed three half-circles around her. Thomas, Joe Miner, and a few others tidied up, sweeping up pieces of greenery and ribbon. Thomas kept glancing at Elizabeth. She was one of the loveliest women he'd seen in Bentonsport. Or in Pennsylvania, for that matter.

He needed an opening, an inroad to an introduction. But, as Mamie played the beginning notes, his shoulders stiffened. Timing continued to work against him.

When the last song concluded, parents gathered their children and belongings to hurry home and prepare for the Carringtons' event. He joined the minister near the church entrance as the others departed. Elizabeth Miner was with her brother and Samuel Wright, a friend of his. As they reached the front door, she smiled and thanked Pastor Lockhardt for "the nice service" but took no notice of Thomas. Surely, this evening wouldn't end without even an opportunity to say hello to this beautiful woman?

He and Pastor Lockhardt extinguished the candles and kerosene lamps, engaging in light conversation as they moved through the sanctuary. Then Thomas retrieved from under the pew the box of chocolates he'd brought for Mrs. Carrington. The two men put on their overcoats and headed outdoors. They chatted as they walked the two blocks, their breath lingering in the frigid air. The flare of oil lamps washed the exterior of the Carringtons' brick house. Carriages lined both sides of the street and continued around the corners.

At the front door, the two men wiped their shoes on the horsehair mat, and as soon as Pastor Lockhardt turned the crank on the ornate doorbell, the Carringtons' housemaid, Merrie Waters, opened the door. Dressed in a starched white apron and pleated cap, she curtsied.

Thomas gave her his warmest smile. "We're all dressed to the nines tonight, Merrie."

She laughed and shook her head. "Quite a night, yes, and quite an affair."

Carols, this time played on a piano accompanied by a harp, softened the air. The scents of spiced punch and evergreen branches joined the aroma of a rich variety of hors d'oeuvres.

"Smells like Christmas," Pastor Lockhardt said as he removed his gloves, scarf, and coat.

Thomas shed his outerwear as well and gave it and the box of chocolates to Merrie, who took them to an adjoining room.

Pastor Lockhardt walked toward the dining room, but Thomas entered the parlor, where Elizabeth sat on a chair in a far corner, punch cup and saucer in hand, engaged in discussion with Lucinda Carrington.

Elizabeth's skin appeared as delicate as china, her figure willowy. When she spoke, her sapphire eyes sparkled and flashed. Transfixed, Thomas didn't notice Virginia Carrington until her skirt brushed his leg.

"Mrs. Carrington." He cleared his throat. "I was—admiring that painting." He pointed to a landscape hung behind Elizabeth's chair. "Who is the artist?"

Virginia laughed. "My father painted it. Come, have a closer look." She led him past a table heavy with crystal goblets over to where the women were chatting. "The landscape is the view he had from the front porch of his boyhood home."

He nodded, his whole body stiff. If he lowered his hand even slightly, he would brush Elizabeth's nape.

The young women continued their hushed discussion as he breathed in the rose water Elizabeth wore.

"Thomas," Virginia said, "have you been introduced to Miss Miner?"

"No," he said as casually as he could. "I don't believe I've had the honor."

At the mention of her name, Elizabeth looked up. Her blue eyes met his.

"Elizabeth, this is Mr. Thomas Barton, headmaster of the Bentonsport Academy. Thomas, Miss Miner."

"A pleasure to meet you, Mr. Barton." Elizabeth placed her punch cup and saucer on the table next to her and extended a gloved hand, fingers pointed downward.

He grasped her fingertips. "How do you do?"

"Help me greet our other guests, Lucinda," Virginia cooed, taking her daughter by the arm.

Lucinda rose, and the two women walked toward the front hall, Virginia pulling her daughter along.

"Won't you sit down?" Elizabeth gestured toward the chair Lucinda had vacated.

"Thank you." He tried to remember the opening lines of the conversation he'd been rehearsing. His heartbeat quickened —*What* were they?

"Mrs. Carrington tells me the town is pleased with your work at the academy."

She had heard of him. He sat straight in his chair. With his palms moist, he tried not to wiggle like a child on the first day of school. "I'm glad t–to be here." Had he actually stammered? How awkward.

"When I graduated from teaching school, I considered coming back and working at the academy. But of course, you already had the position, and Bonaparte is a short ride down the road. It has a fine academy as well, and fortunately, they had an opening for me."

He steadied his breathing. "I've heard good things about the school."

"As this is my first year of teaching, I would be grateful for any assistance you can provide."

"It would be my—"

"From the moment I learned I'd been selected for the position, I began outlining my lesson plans, and I believe I have a strong start. However, I'll need to refine them as I go along."

Should he try to offer his assistance again?

She picked up her punch. "I plan to start the year with the theme of nature, beginning with the life cycle of animals and insects. I've incorporated the writing of short stories, the drawing of illustrations, and direct nature studies to extend the theme to each of the disciplines—literature, math, science—to create unity of thought."

"I'm working on a similar effort. For our Christmas play—"

"Oh, I don't mean to give the impression this is *my* original idea." She waved a hand. "It's a well-established method of instruction and quite effective from what I've heard. This teaching structure is popular back East, and I'm certain it will soon become the standard in this part of the country."

He opened his mouth, but not fast enough.

"I apologize. I must be boring you with all this talk of instruction. But I'm so excited by the thought of having my own class. I have wonderful ideas of how I shall structure the room to stimulate the children's imagination and, at the same time, facilitate learning. First, I plan to—"

Little wonder Elizabeth Miner hadn't found a husband back East. She couldn't stop talking. His heart sank. He realized—*felt* —how much he had staked in this encounter. The loneliness at once began to creep in. Would he be a bachelor for the rest of his life?

Giving up trying to speak, he nodded often as this woman talked. If he turned his back on her and started a conversation with someone else, several minutes would likely elapse before she realized he was no longer paying attention. Too polite to end the monologue, he let his focus wander.

Many older women stared at them, smiling their satisfaction, no doubt calculating the number of months until he proposed, as they exchanged I-told-you-so looks. While Thomas again watched Elizabeth's lips move, her brother intervened. "Liz, I have someone who'd like to meet you."

Smoothing her cornflower-blue dress, she stood. "I have so enjoyed our conversation, Mr. Barton. I do hope we'll have the opportunity to speak more about our classwork in the future."

Exhaling, his shoulders loosening, Thomas stood and went to make a plate for himself in the dining room. He then joined the men gathered in Mr. Carrington's study, where the heavy cigar aroma centered him in male company.

In time, the pastor suggested everyone adjourn to the parlor to sing carols. Though he didn't feel drawn to more singing, Thomas would agree to any activity that didn't include Elizabeth Miner's chatter. He followed the others, taking care to position himself at the opposite end of the room from her. Nearly an hour into the entertainment, he excused himself, collected his belongings from Merrie Waters, and escaped.

The sky had cleared. Around the corner and up the hill, the academy cast a square silhouette against the starry sky. Home had never looked so good. Loneliness. Sadness. The awful but familiar conviction he'd never find the right woman stirred a raw space in his heart. But better he spent time in only his own company than with a woman who could see, discuss, and be absorbed in only one person—herself. He had himself, but he longed for more.

Chapter Four

Thomas woke early on Sunday, attended worship service, and spent the rest of the morning tidying his living quarters. It didn't take much time because he kept his three rooms in order throughout the week. His thoughts moved from the night before to tomorrow night's play and back again. Was he being too harsh in his judgment of Elizabeth? She was beautiful. But no. For most people, a conversation required two people; for Elizabeth, it took only one.

Rather than dwell on his disappointment, he headed into the timber behind the academy to chop more firewood. Perhaps the exertion would lift his spirits.

He found several fallen trees and began chopping firewood and kindling. The strenuous activity helped him focus. After two hours, it came to him—he would go home to Pennsylvania for the holidays, despite the bad-weather threat. He wouldn't telegraph his change of plans but rather surprise his family.

Straightening, he threw the wood into the wagon. While Elizabeth Miner had been a disappointment, he wouldn't allow it to dampen his holiday spirit. A beautiful woman, Elizabeth would make a lovely wife—for any man hard of hearing or hopelessly introverted.

25

He carried half the load into the schoolroom, stacking enough logs there to keep it warm through the following night. Then he carted all the remaining wood to his living quarters and set some by each of his two stoves. He'd spend the evening preparing the schoolroom for the play, but for now, he went for a walk.

Why couldn't women be more like Pastor Lockhardt, engaging in brief straightforward conversations? Or Benjamin Ross? Or even himself? Why did Elizabeth have to be such a talker?

He stopped and shook out his shoulders. No more dwelling on the night before. He'd focus on the good ahead, including his students' play. He wouldn't give up hope. Who knew? Someone's eligible aunt or maybe a cousin from a neighboring community could be in attendance.

CHAIRS CREAKED, BOOTS CLOMPED, AND VOICES murmured as parents, grandparents, and other community members crowded the large classroom. Thomas peered behind the backdrop, making sure the children in the first scene were ready. As the last audience members sat, he walked out and stood before Scrooge's office backdrop.

"Welcome, everyone. We're grateful you've joined us tonight as the children bring to life *A Christmas Carol* by Charles Dickens. In the twenty-six years since he wrote the story, it has become a classic tale of the season. The children have worked hard to bring you this performance, and we invite you to enjoy it."

He took his front-row seat and placed the stack of cue cards on his lap. The children entered the stage from the left, and the cold-hearted Ebenezer Scrooge lectured the mild and meek Bob Cratchit. The children stayed in character, as he had directed them, and didn't stare into the audience.

The second act flowed smoothly, with each child delivering a nearly flawless performance. As the play neared an end, he glanced to his left. Two women were blotting tears as Scrooge vowed he'd be a changed man. Then Scrooge, now called "Uncle Scrooge" by Tiny Tim, patted a dog on the road, waved to passersby, and followed Tiny Tim down the lane—and off the stage.

The remaining cast members left the scene, and the curtain closed. After a brief delay, the students came out in groups and bowed to hearty applause. Thomas placed his cue cards under his seat, stood with a deep satisfied breath, and shared the children's joy at a performance well done. Following the cast members' bows, he took one himself as the audience applauded.

Laughing, the children pushed their desks back in rows and gathered their belongings. He said goodbye to everyone as they departed, receiving warm wishes for a merry Christmas and continued praise for the production. He smiled to himself as Elizabeth Miner passed, deep in conversation with her brother.

When the last of the crowd had gone, he stowed the smaller props in trunks under the stairs and stacked the remaining rolled-up backdrops on the closet shelves. He surveyed the classroom, clean and ready to receive the students after the holiday recess.

By half-past eleven, his energy subsiding, he climbed the stairs and boiled two stockpots for bathing and a pot for tea. As he packed, he mulled over what gifts he might take home. He'd have to buy them before purchasing his tickets.

Having drunk some chamomile tea and bathed, he forewent his usual nightly Bible reading and dropped into his bed, drifting off as soon as his head hit the pillow.

BANG. BANG. BANG.

Thomas shuddered at the knocking rattling the academy's front door. He lit his bedside candle and stared at his ticking clock. Three fifteen. Why would anyone arouse him now?

Could there be a fire? Wide awake, heart pounding, he picked up the candleholder and hurried toward the stairs. Had he neglected to dampen the classroom fire or extinguish one of the lamps?

The banging continued.

At the bottom of the stairs, everything appeared to be in order. No fire. No smoke. Barefoot and dressed only in his nightshirt, he flung open the door. The rush of cold air and falling snow struck him.

On his porch, out of breath but smiling, stood Pastor Lockhardt.

"Pastor?" Thomas wiped his face with his sleeve. "What's happening? Are you all right?"

"Not to worry, Thomas." His friend stepped inside, shut the door behind him, and handed over his hat and scarf.

Thomas shivered as Pastor Lockhardt took off his glasses and wiped the fog from each lens with his handkerchief.

"I must speak with you. I'm sorry for waking you, but this couldn't wait until sunrise."

What could the pastor need to discuss at this hour? Thomas dropped the scarf and hat on the nearby desk and gestured toward the staircase. "Let's go up to my rooms where it's warm."

His friend's footsteps echoed against the high ceiling as they ascended. Thomas lit a lamp, blew out the candle, and placed the candle holder on the table. He found his slippers and robe, and then positioned two chairs near the stove while Pastor Lockhardt removed his coat.

The man wore an eager expression, no trace of fear or concern. His eyes held an extra twinkle as a growing smile crinkled his face. "I have great news."

Great news? At three in the morning? Thomas tried to think of a response.

"Do you believe some things cannot be explained?"

I feel that way right now. He nodded.

"Do you believe in miracles?"

How was he supposed to answer? Particularly to a minister.

At *three* in the morning. The pastor better get to the point. Thomas slumped into the chair.

The ticking of the clock seemed to grow louder.

Pastor Lockhardt rubbed his hands together, scooting his chair closer. "Sometimes, we can't understand things with our minds. We can only believe them with our hearts."

Again, Thomas nodded, the words little more than a buzz. Why such an abstract conversation in the middle of the night?

But Pastor Lockhardt didn't wait for him to speak. "Tonight, as I was in bed, I was thinking about how wonderful the play was. How blessed Scrooge was to be able to step outside his world, so he could see his life clearly and find the real person inside himself. Perhaps falling asleep with those thoughts on my mind opened the door for me to receive word of this opportunity for you."

The wood in the stove crackled, followed by a loud thump as a piece of wood fell hard against the stove's chamber.

Thomas cleared his throat. Opportunity? "For what?"

"For discovery." Pastor Lockhardt shifted closer, elbows on his knees, hands clasped before him. "You see, you are about to go on a bit of a journey."

He stifled a yawn. "You know of my plans to visit my family back East?"

The pastor's eyebrows arched. "Back East?" He shook his head. "No. You're going on a journey—to Bentonsport."

Either the pastor had a vivid dream or taken leave of his senses. Thomas flexed his hands between his knees and stared at them, trying not to shake his head.

A cold hand capped his shoulder. "I don't know what you'll discover on this adventure. That will be for you to find out."

This made no sense. Exhaustion taking over, Thomas rubbed his forehead. Something was wrong with this man, and he shouldn't be alone. Perhaps he should suggest the pastor spend the night. Thomas could sleep on the sofa. His guest could take the bed.

"I am not confused." The pastor gave Thomas's shoulder a brief squeeze. "You are to be given a tremendous gift."

Thomas tried to focus, but—at present, putting his head on his pillow would be his gift of choice.

Pastor Lockhardt stared back at the floor as though searching for the right words. "I realize this is all vague, but what I know isn't complete."

"And what *do* you know?" Thomas winced. He hadn't meant to sound so short.

"Simply this." The man's voice changed to a staccato pace, seemingly reciting a series of statistics. "You will go to sleep after I leave, and when you awaken, you will be here, in Bentonsport, but in the future. The journey you will take is of time, not distance."

Thomas said nothing. What could he say to something so crazy?

"I don't know how much time will have passed, but you'll discover something special, meant just for you. You might come back a changed man."

"Like in *A Christmas Carol*?"

The pastor laughed. "Oh, you are no Scrooge. And I wouldn't want you to be much different from how you are now." His face tightened. "But you will be different. Of that, I am certain."

Right. Thomas smiled as if this all made perfect sense. He wanted to get back to sleep.

Standing, his friend warmed his hands at the stove. "You'll go to bed tonight and wake up here, in Bentonsport, at some point in the future. You'll come back to our time on Christmas Eve, ten days from now. Once you return, you won't be able to go back." He stepped forward once again and squeezed Thomas's shoulder. "Do you understand what I've said?"

No. But only by playing along would he be able to go back to bed, so Thomas nodded. "I have to go to some future Bentonsport and discover why I'm there. And I have only until Christmas Eve to do it."

Pastor Lockhardt clapped. "Yes." He settled back in his chair. "What a gift you're being given. Why, if someone from fifty years ago came here and saw our town's growth, they'd be shocked. Imagine how large and prosperous Bentonsport will be in the future. But don't get caught up in the changes, Thomas."

Thomas stood and stretched. Taking this chance to end the conversation, he said, "I noticed the snow is kicking up. Won't you stay here tonight?"

"No." His friend straightened his shoulders. "I can walk two blocks. Besides, I'll need some brisk exercise to help me sleep."

When the two men reached the front door, Pastor Lockhardt gave Thomas's shoulders a shake. "Godspeed, Thomas." He then grasped his hand. "There is nothing to fear."

No. He'd never been afraid of other people's dreams. He picked up the pastor's hat and scarf from the desk and handed them to him.

Pastor Lockhardt bundled up, then opened the door. Nearly an inch of snow rested on the front step. The wind had died down, but the snowfall continued.

After Pastor Lockhardt set off down the academy's walk, Thomas closed the door and headed upstairs. Traveling through time? He'd better check on the pastor tomorrow. He put two more logs in the stove near his bed and watched them take flame. Why a man with Pastor Lockhardt's intellect and education would think such a statement made sense … made no sense.

Removing his robe and slippers, Thomas extinguished the lamp and climbed back into bed. The sheets were cold. The clock, lit by moonlight, revealed ten till four. With the long-forecasted storm now a reality, the train would be delayed or service canceled.

His plans to return home for the holidays vanished. Perhaps there had been little hope in any case, but it had seen him through the last days. He didn't know what the holidays would hold, but he'd worry about that tomorrow.

Chapter Five

T he morning sun cast warm rays across his face. Thomas stretched. The storm must have passed. He would be home for Christmas after all.

Two knocks sounded at the door. *Not Pastor Lockhardt again.* These knocks were softer than the pounding that awakened him hours earlier. And much closer. Could someone have gotten into the academy and come upstairs without waking him?

"Good morning." A somewhat plump, slightly stooped woman entered, carrying a breakfast tray. Wisps of gray threaded through the hair she'd smoothed up in a twist at the back of her head. A white apron shielded her calf-length navy dress.

He tugged the blanket up to his chest. Who was this? He'd never had a woman—any woman—in his private quarters, at least not as an adult.

He lifted his fingers. The quilt covering the bed wasn't his. Nor was the bed.

"My, how you've slept." She carried the tray to the table near a window draped in fine lace. Where did that table come from? And those curtains? "Guess you must have needed it."

He closed his eyes and opened them again. He must still be sleeping or in a hazy state of shock. When he leaned back, his head hit something hard. A high, ornately carved headboard. Where was he?

"Breakfast comes with the room. Dinner too, but not lunch." She raised the shade a few inches.

Where was his robe? He generally draped it across the walnut nightstand. But the table beside his bed, painted white with pink flowers, held a clock and a lamp—a strange paper-like shade rested on a glass globe.

He folded his arms across his chest. What was he to make of this? *Any* of this.

"What a lovely day." The woman fluffed the two embroidered pillows on a high-back chair.

Finally, he saw something familiar: His bags stacked neatly against the wall. But why here? The last he remembered, they were waiting at the top of the stairs, ready for him to take to the station.

"I'm glad you found the key and let yourself in last night. The owners weren't sure what time you'd be arriving. Have you been here before?"

He cleared his throat. "Um, no. I don't believe I have."

"Well, it is quiet around here this time of year." She removed a stack of cream-colored towels and washcloths from the trunk at the end of the bed and, after closing it, set them on a chair next to the window. The towels looked fluffy, almost cloudlike, different from the flat linen towels he used. "You should visit again when the weather's warmer. That's when most of the tourists pass through."

Tourists? He must be at an inn or hotel. But how did he get here? And *where* was *here*?

"We only have one other guest right now." The woman adjusted the shade again, allowing more light in. "The owners left for the holidays, so I'm in charge. The guest book says you're paid up through Christmas Eve."

He tried to remember signing a guest book. Had he completely lost his memory of the night before?

"If you don't mind my asking, what brings you to Bentonsport right before Christmas?"

His shoulders fell back. He was still in Bentonsport. If he could find out where he was, he could make his way back to the academy. "I ... well, I'm here to relax."

"Sounds nice." She moved toward the door. "Just make yourself at home. If you need anything, I'll be in the living quarters off the dining room. My name's Lani."

Lani? He hadn't heard that name before. It sounded Polynesian.

"I serve dinner at six every evening. If you don't make it, I'll put a plate for you in the fridge."

Fridge? He'd better not ask.

Before leaving the room, she turned back. "You look tired. Nothing on the tray will spoil. Why don't you get some more sleep?"

"That would be nice, but I'll get up." He gave her a pleasant smile.

As soon as she shut the door, he leaped out of bed and went to the window to get his bearings. Across the road, a structure like a rectangular tent with open sides housed four tables. Beyond it, the partially frozen river ran the full length of his view. He could dress, leave the inn, and follow the river. When he reached the stores, he'd find the academy. He wanted to go home.

He opened his largest bag, unearthing clothes he'd packed the night before. As he was dressing, he tried to come up with a reasonable explanation for his presence here. He remembered his friend's visit. He remembered going back to bed. But he couldn't remember anything after.

Knees buckling, he sat down. Details of the pastor's late visit, his strange behavior, and their discussion came back. His spine tingled—could it ...? No, he'd focus on getting ready and sort out what had happened as he made his way home.

Razor and shaving soap and their leather pouch in hand, he walked across the room, picked up the white pitcher with the rose-colored flowers, and found it empty. He'd have to ask Lani for some water. He set the items on his bedside table, unearthed his cologne and splashed some on his cheeks, removed his comb from the compartment in the trunk and combed his hair, then left the room. The hallway, papered in a floral pattern, led to a narrow staircase.

At the top of the steps, he called out, "Lani?"

She emerged from the room to the left, drying her hands on her apron. "Ah, you're up. Just doing a bit of cleaning in the kitchen before starting lunch."

"I need to shave, but the pitcher is empty."

She laughed. "We keep to the period as best we can, but we do offer our guests all the conveniences of home. There's running water in the bathroom off your room."

He swallowed hard. There was water running in his room? He hadn't noticed any. His confusion must have shown, for she headed up the stairs and motioned him to his room.

"Come with me."

She opened a door he'd assumed was a closet. Inside, a basin on a pedestal stood across from a gleaming white tub and something like a porcelain chair. At the basin, she twisted a shiny knob, and water poured from a faucet. "I can fill the pitcher if you'd like."

How in the world could water come out without a pump?

"We have all the modern conveniences. No outhouses or chamber pots. We even treat you with an indoor potty, although we do have an old-fashioned chain pull to flush." She patted the toilet and gestured to the chain hanging from a wooden box above it.

His face warming, he looked away, even more confused.

"There's soap in the soap dish at the sink and an extra bar at the tub. Anything else you need?"

"No, but thank you." He rubbed his hands through his hair.

Lani stood back and scrutinized him. "Love the period dress."

She chuckled. "It's a great way to experience Bentonsport's historical flavor."

After she left, he tried the knob on the sink. As before, water spilled out. He placed his hand under the stream, then wiggled it back and forth, palm up, palm down. It wasn't ice-cold. In fact, it became warmer and warmer until it was so hot he had to pull back his hand.

He cranked the knob in the opposite direction, and the water stopped flowing. Amazing! He tried the other knob. Even after he'd held his hands under the faucet for quite some time, the water remained cold. When he twisted both knobs at the same time, warm water streamed out. He'd love to have this contraption at the academy. No more heating the stove and waiting for the water to warm. He moved on to the chamber pot, deducing its function and putting it to use.

Though he'd heard about these luxuries, he didn't know any had been installed in Bentonsport. He dampened his brush and used the soap in the cup to create a rich lather. Then he brushed in a circular motion over his lower cheeks and chin. With his razor, he shaved in clean, short lines, rinsing the foam off the razor as he went. The familiar act was soothing, a bit of normalcy amid all these strange things.

When he searched the room for his coat, he found it on a hook behind the door. He slipped it on and crept down the stairs so as not to alert Lani of his departure.

A brisk wind blew, so he shoved his hands deep into his pockets. Finding his scarf in his right pocket, he wrapped it around his neck. The sun gave everything a haloed effect. Snow covered the ground, but the walkways were clear, the slush having been melted by something like salt.

Hands buried deep in his pockets, he looked left and right but didn't recognize anything. He pivoted and stared at the building he'd exited. The winter air caught in his throat. Although a sign near the front door identified it as The Bentonsport Inn, this was the Phoenix Hotel. He walked by it on his errands at least once each week. Greenery hung around the entrance, adding a festive touch with red bows .

The river flowed past the inn, a stable force amid all this change. But an iron bridge spanned it feet from where he stood. When had that been constructed?

He started his walk up the main street, hoping to see a familiar face, recognizable buildings. The whole scene seemed desolate. No mills along the riverbank. No people on the sidewalk. Not even a stray dog. But someone had been taking care of the remaining old buildings bedecked with greenery, ribbons, and shiny ornaments.

A half a block down the road, he came to the Greef General Store. A white wooden sign with black lettering stood in front of the building. It stated the building had been constructed by Mr. Julius Greef in 1853 and was purchased by the Van Buren County Conservation Board in 1983.

Wait—1983? That couldn't be right. The tingling sensation crept up his spine, and memories of Pastor Lockhardt's prediction made his head hurt. Time travel? The whole idea was unnerving. Preposterous. Incomprehensible.

He walked to the wooden bench before the Greef Store and sat. Resting his head against the window behind him, he tried to clear his mind. The sweet scent of dried orange slices and cloves wafted from a ball of cheesecloth someone had attached to the boughs draped over the store window. He breathed in and exhaled.

As much as he tried, he couldn't remember anything between the time he laid his head on his pillow and the moment he awoke at the inn.

He was in Bentonsport. That much he knew. According to the sign, the year was sometime after 1983. And if Pastor Lockhardt had been right about the dream—or vision, as it was now beginning to seem—he would be in this town until Christmas Eve

What in the world had happened to this place? The entire three blocks on the side of the street close to the river were bare of the mills he knew, cleared except for a few ornamental trees around a gazebo and a stone foundation. The only building he could see down that side of the road—the furniture factory, a two-story brick edifice with floor-to-ceiling storefront windows—stood beyond those three blocks.

Could a fire have destroyed nearly the entire town? When?

Whenever he pondered Bentonsport's future, he envisioned bigger, grander buildings along the river, more people, more prosperity. But now, after at least a hundred years, few buildings remained standing, and vacant lots lay as reminders of where hope had been.

Lani had said the town drew tourists. What would anyone come here to see?

Footsteps passed beside him. A man about his age, dressed in a well-worn jacket and faded work pants, walked down the brick sidewalk, smoking a pipe. Salt-and-pepper hair brushed his collar, and a trimmed beard framed the pipe hanging from his lips. "Morning." He removed the pipe and studied Thomas.

"Good morning." Thomas stood to greet him.

"Pretty cold to be sitting outside." Pipe back to his lips, the man took several slow puffs. "You're here visiting?"

"Yes."

The man lowered his pipe, removed his hand from his pocket, and held it out. He had a powerful grip. "I'm Bill Murphy. My wife and I live in the old Greef house." He pointed down the street to the right.

No, that couldn't be. Thomas looked up and down the road. "I thought the Greef house was behind us to the left."

"That's the Herman Greef house. We live in the Julius Greef house. You must be familiar with this town to make that connection. Have you been here before?"

Um ... Thomas cleared his throat. "Many years ago."

Bill took two short puffs on his pipe. "Not much open till the weekend. You could visit the print shop and the weaving shop. They're in the old Odd Fellows building, straight down this road.

Our baker, Sarah, sells pastries, coffee, and tea out of her home. She lives in the old Montgomery house, which used to be the Carrington place, next to our house."

Greef house. Montgomery house. The Carringtons' place. These names were familiar. At least something of the town remained.

"Sarah's bakery isn't open for business today, but if you mention that I sent you, I'm sure she'll be happy to serve you coffee and some of her goodies." A short puff of his pipe followed this information. "I'd better get going. Hope to see you around." With a friendly wave, Bill continued down the brick sidewalk.

Thomas walked down the riverbank. The only thing left of John Brown's five-story gristmill was the foundation. It now, according to another sign, housed a butterfly garden.

At the familiar furniture building, Thomas stopped to peer through the plate-glass window. A loom stood in the middle of the floor, and behind it were several printing presses. Another white sign described it as the former Odd Fellows Building, now housing a weaving and printing store.

He walked back up the street to the road where the pipe-smoker had said he lived. The one leading to the academy, if it was still standing.

As he neared the Carringtons' house, the smell of fresh baking bread made his mouth water until he regretted ignoring that laden breakfast tray. He thought of stopping to purchase some pastry but strode on, anxious to see if the academy still existed.

Once he rounded the corner, the Methodist church and its parsonage stood there just the same, only newly tuck-pointed and painted. The buildings looked cared for. He continued along a road covered in a hard black surface like poured slate.

He increased his pace, relieved to find the academy looked as it had when he walked into it last night. Or was it a hundred years ago? Not one of the neighboring houses remained.

In simple block letters, as with the other signs in town, this sign stated the building had been constructed in 1851 and functioned as a school for grades kindergarten through twelve until 1951. In 1959, the Bentonsport Ladies Aid acquired the building, but the Bentonsport Improvement Association took the deed of the site in 1975 and held it until 1992.

Thomas aged with each line.

The sign concluded that the building was now privately owned, and the academy's classrooms were used for seminars and retreats.

He thrust his hand in his trouser pocket and found his key. His thumb rubbed across the metal surface. Oh, how much he wanted to unlock the door, climb the stairs to his bed, go back to sleep, and try to start this day fresh. Back in *his* Bentonsport. But the key probably wouldn't work. Even if it did, the building was now someone's home. He couldn't barge in.

A rumbling interrupted him. A bright-blue vehicle, rather like a square buggy, traveled toward him on the smooth road. He stepped back from the curb onto the academy lawn. People sat inside it, but it traveled much faster than a buggy and had no animals in front. How in the world was it moving? Was something inside pulling it along?

As the vehicle rounded the corner and left his view, he heard Pastor Lockhardt's words—*Don't get caught up in the changes.*

But how could he not?

A gust of wind kicked up and, chilled inside and out, Thomas tugged his overcoat tighter. Maybe what he needed was a warm roll and a cup of hot coffee.

But how would he pay for it?

He jiggled the coins in his coat pocket. They wouldn't last him long. In a trouser pocket, he found several dollar notes. Would this currency be accepted?

Lani had said his room was paid up. He had no idea how, but she'd said it. She also told him two meals a day came with his room. If he watched his spending, the money he had should last a few days ... unless prices had risen over the last hundred-plus years.

If Pastor Lockhardt's premonition were correct, he would be here until Christmas Eve But was his time the same as the time in this place? He didn't know what year it was and wasn't sure of the exact month, although the Christmas decorations indicated it was late November or December. He had no idea how long he'd spend in this strange place and time. Nor did he know when—or even if —he'd get home.

Chapter Six

S arah had been baking since seven that morning, and by ten o'clock, the ovens left her sunny kitchen sultry. Water droplets streamed down the windowpanes like tears. The radio, tuned to her favorite classical station, played the happy music of Vivaldi. Caroline perched on her chair at the center island, was engrossed in her knitting.

"Why don't you put on Christmas songs?" Caroline asked. "You won't be able to play them much longer, you know. Less than two weeks now until Christmas. Oh, my. I'm not nearly ready yet, are you?"

"No. But I've mailed all of my out-of-town presents, and I finished making jelly for my local gifts. I still need to purchase several more baskets. I thought I'd fill them with homemade bread and cookies, tea bags, and mugs and deliver them around town on Christmas Eve."

Keeping busy and upbeat during this season was best. Loneliness and sadness lurked beneath the festivities—she'd experienced them more than once in her life. "But I do have gifts for a particular friend—and godchild."

Her needles stilling, Caroline shook her head. "I wasn't fishing for that, you goose."

The kitchen door opened, clanging the sleigh bells on it. A tall man, head down, entered the room, closed the door behind him, and wiped his feet on the mat.

"Can I help you?" Sarah asked.

He glanced up, his cheeks red with cold. Despite their ruddiness, he was quite handsome. His chiseled face was framed with long dark waves of hair, which he tucked behind his ear. His eyes were dark and warm, like coffee with a scant bit of cream.

"I hope I'm not intruding." He offered a tentative smile. "Bill Murphy said I could purchase some baked goods and a cup of coffee if I mentioned his name."

Caroline laughed. "My husband, the self-appointed town welcomer. Doesn't know a stranger and never will. Come on in and join us."

The man took a hesitant step.

"I'm Caroline Murphy, and this is my best friend, Sarah Peterson."

"I'm Thomas Barton. Pleased to meet you—both of you."

Sarah dried her hands and set aside her baking utensils to wait on him. Having customers in the middle of the week in winter—unusual. Having her customer be a good-looking man—even more uncommon.

UPON OPENING THE DOOR, THOMAS SOUGHT THE MUSIC filling the room but couldn't determine its source. It sounded as if the musicians were right in the room, but the two women weren't playing anything. The one standing behind the counter, staring at him, was quite beautiful, in a cute but boyish sort of way. The other sat on a stool and glanced his way, though not with the first woman's intensity as she set her needlework on the counter.

The young woman, Sarah Peterson, approached a small box and turned a knob, which lowered the music's volume. He planted his feet to resist walking over and examining the box as he

BENTONSPORT: A CHRISTMAS STORY

remembered Pastor Lockhardt's warning not to focus on the changes. Nonetheless, it intrigued him.

He removed his overcoat.

Mrs. Murphy labored down from her stool. "My, my." She hung his coat on a rack by the door. "You do have the spirit of Bentonsport."

Averting his eyes from Mrs. Murphy's obvious condition, he suddenly thought that indeed, his clothes might no longer be in fashion. "I–I thought I would dress for the occasion."

"Bentonsport is almost tourist-free during weekdays this time of year," Miss Peterson said. "What brings you to our little piece of heaven?"

Piece of heaven? Bentonsport had kept its natural beauty—the hilly landscape, the river. But it looked a lot less heavenly. "I was here a number of years ago. I came back to do some ... exploring."

Mrs. Murphy beamed. "How long ago were you here?"

Stalling, he cleared his throat.

"Let me get you that coffee." As Miss Peterson poured steaming coffee, she gestured to a chair adjacent to the long counter in the middle of the kitchen. "Have a seat. Many of us wear period costumes when the tourists are here. You'll fit right in on the weekend."

She really was lovely, with her short blonde hair that just brushed her shoulder and her eyes the color of springtime grass—green but of a lighter shade.

"I'm afraid I brought mainly clothes from this period. I'll remember to pack differently next time." If he had his way, there wouldn't be a next time.

"Cream or sugar?"

"No, thank you. Black is fine." He diverted his eyes, not wanting to gawk. How could a woman dressed in pants like a man, with short hair sheared in layers, have such a softness?

"Where are you staying?"

45

"At the inn by the river. It's comfortable, and the woman in charge is kind."

"Lani is the best." Mrs. Murphy folded her knitting. "She helps at the Greef Store from time to time too."

Had he stood there only days ago with his students staring at toys in the shop window?

"Do you mind if I continue my baking as we chat?" Miss Peterson walked toward the counter to retrieve her baking items.

"No, not at all—that is, if you don't mind my sitting here while I drink my coffee."

"It's nice to have visitors," Mrs. Murphy interjected. "We get lonely out here on the prairie during these winter months." She laughed, but he didn't know why. He imagined he would be lonely in this town any time of year.

Miss Peterson rolled out long smooth ovals of dough on a marble slab. "So, where are you from?"

Sipping his coffee, he considered his answer. "Pennsylvania. I teach school, and we're on recess now."

"I'm guessing you teach history." Mrs. Murphy picked up the teapot.

"I teach a variety of subjects, including history."

Returning to the island, she filled her cup and set the teapot next to it.

He held his coffee mug with both hands, warming his fingers, and turned the questions from himself. "Speaking of history, I am curious. What happened to Bentonsport between the 1870s and now?"

Mrs. Murphy waved a hand toward Miss Peterson and then back at him. "How many hours do you have to spend?"

"I tend to rattle on when it comes to this town's history." Miss Peterson rolled her eyes.

"I'd enjoy hearing all about it."

She selected cookie cutters from a drawer. As she spoke, she cut out wreaths, Christmas trees, candy canes, and stars.

"Well, Bentonsport began to decline around 1873 ..."

Incredible. Just four years.

Bracing his elbows on the counter, he leaned forward. While he wanted to hear the story, he couldn't prevent a shudder. Part of him feared learning how his prosperous, growing town would begin to deteriorate.

"But the story of Bentonsport's development is a much happier one." She described the town's growth along the Des Moines River, detailing the mills and factories that cropped up at the river's edge.

Thomas sat still as Miss Peterson described his home—his world. She didn't have all the facts correct, misplacing a few buildings and transposing names, but she created a vivid sketch of the Bentonsport he knew and loved, not the shell of a town that remained.

As she spoke, she gazed out the steamy window as though she could see the areas she was describing, clearly charmed by the town in her mind. Wanting to fill in the details for her, he felt as if he were watching an artist roughing out the first lines of a painting but not knowing how to add the color. She brushed the flecks of dough from her long fingers.

He took a few sips of coffee, stopping himself from correcting minor points, describing the dust of the streets, the hollow sound the wooden sidewalks as you walked the main street, and introducing her to the townspeople ...

"But things began to change in 1873." With a spatula, she transferred the dough cutouts onto two cookie sheets. "The Greene brothers decided to move their paper mill from Bentonsport to Blue Rapids, Kansas. That was the first domino."

The Greenes? His shoulders stiffening, he sat up straight. The Greenes had been concerned about the recent decline in river traffic, but surely, they wouldn't move their mill from Bentonsport?

She slid the cookie sheets into the oven. After closing the door, she twisted the knob on a round dial, and it began to click.

"Twelve minutes until cookies." She stacked her bowls and

cooking utensils beside the sink, then filled it with steamy water. "The next domino fell when John Brown's woolen mill caught fire," she said over her shoulder.

He swallowed hard. John Brown was a member of his church. His children attended the academy.

"According to local historians, John Brown planned to rebuild but died before he had a chance."

He stared into his coffee mug. When his throat tightened, he cleared it, trying to swallow his sadness.

"So, Thomas," Mrs. Murphy said, "do you want the mill-by-mill account of the demise of Bentonsport or the abbreviated version?"

"Oh." He jerked his head up. "I'd like the unabridged version."

Miss Peterson cranked off the water, turned and smirked at her friend, then, looking straight into Thomas's eyes, said, "There isn't a great deal more I know in terms of details. They say bad news comes in threes, and for Bentonsport, the third bad event came after the mill fire."

She refilled his cup, picked up the ticking dial, glanced at it, and set it down.

"I have to watch the timer closely. One minute, these cookies are golden, and the next minute, if you don't get them out of the oven, they are burnt black."

Torn, he pushed his knees into the cabinet to steady himself. He hoped the baking would distract Miss Peterson from her tale of Bentonsport's decline. But he also wanted to find out more of the specifics. How his prosperous town could fall into ruins ... It was almost unthinkable. And yet here it was—right in front of him.

The timer buzzed. Miss Peterson wiped her hands on her apron, opened the stove door, and removed two cookie trays.

"Goodness, those smell good." Mrs. Murphy leaned over the counter and took a deep whiff. "Gingerbread?"

"Close. They're spice cookies. Three more trays and I should be done." Miss Peterson set the cookie sheets on the white marble slab, then moved each cookie to a cooling rack.

At home in Pennsylvania this time of year, his mother and sisters would also be baking for their neighbors, family, and church members. He could be halfway home by now if he hadn't been so detoured. His chest tightened. One day at a time ... one moment at a time ... he had to find his way home.

Miss Peterson began to roll out another oval of coffee-colored cookie dough. "Let's see, where was I? Oh yes. Shortly after the fire, an ice jam damaged the dam supplying water for the gristmill. The mill owners repaired it, but when the high water receded, the gristmill had been damaged. The company went out of business. Not long afterward, it burned down, just like John Brown's woolen mill."

Fires, flood ... what next? In the Bible, all those stories of towns being destroyed ... But that was ancient history. How could something like that occur to his town? He brushed his hand through his hair.

Miss Peterson was still talking, describing the river traffic's decline, replaced first by the railroads and then by cars.

Thomas filtered out the unknown words like *cars* to understand her gist. With the mills and the river traffic gone, Bentonsport declined.

"The town probably would've become a ghost town were it not for a few people who could see the potential within the ruins. Folks started moving here to resettle the area in the early sixties, and they're still coming. Gradually, the old buildings are being restored, and new ones are being built."

"What of the commercial buildings—other than the mills?"

"All gone." Miss Peterson sighed. "Decay, fire, floods. Finally, the county had to bulldoze the remains to control rats and other vermin. Thankfully, we are beyond that phase of Bentonsport's history. A few more people move in each year, mostly artists and craftspeople. New shops open, which draws tourists like you."

Doubtful any other visitors came in the way he did.

"But what brings them here?" This barren town held no charm for him.

Miss Peterson and her friend smiled at each other. "Many come here to see the remnants of a historic town. And while they're here, they find their hearts."

He sipped his coffee to avoid speaking. *People find their hearts here? Amid these empty lots?*

After selecting new cookie cutters, Miss Peterson pressed the shapes into the dough. "There is a magic about Bentonsport. I don't know its source. It may come from the old buildings themselves. You look at them and realize, over a hundred years ago, people like you stood in this spot. They dreamed dreams and went about their lives, raising children, doing what they could to make this a better town."

She swiped away wisps of hair with the back of her hand, her wistful words hanging in the air. "They didn't fail. Time just marched through Bentonsport and left it worse for the wear, much as it does each of us."

What did this lovely woman see here? Why did she find magic where he saw only decay?

Her blue countertops reflected the light shining through the curtains, creating patterns of light and shadow on the surface. She sifted white powder into a bowl, then added water, making a shiny thin paste. Caroline looked from him to her, then back as she put away her knitting and retrieved her tatting, smiling.

"Personally, I think the magic may rest in the loveliness of the scenery—the same thing that attracted the original settlers." She continued speaking, her dreamy voice soft like the frosting. "The winding river cutting through the hills, the shapely cedar trees, the prairie grass and wildflowers. It's a perfect setting for a quaint town." After spooning the paste into smaller bowls, she added drops of deep-colored liquid to each, creating shiny colors.

"The stillness forces me to reflect on myself and my life. There aren't distractions preventing me from focusing on what's important. The beauty here makes reflection a pleasant experience. I feel sorry for the visitors who come here, hurry through the shops, and leave with their bags of treasures without taking the time to acquire the one thing Bentonsport gives best— the space, time, and beauty to understand who you are."

Hmm ... He stirred his coffee. Outside the window, he first heard, then saw, one of the modern moving carriages pass by.

He couldn't tell her he understood her feelings for this place. Not this Bentonsport. She could talk about the town at its pinnacle, but it wasn't part of her. The heavy smell of woodsmoke, the laughter of children. As evening fell, lamplight would dot the hillsides. This was the town he loved.

Where was the romance in ... emptiness?

"Sarah has always seen this town in poetic terms." Caroline Murphy held up her work and studied the stitches, smoothing a few loops. "Since she isn't from here, she sees it with fresh eyes. Bill and I aren't from Bentonsport either, but we grew up close by.

"For us, Bentonsport represented a place to try out our talents. But what Sarah says is true. When people visit our town, they walk the streets, scope out the shops, and stroll across the pedestrian bridge. We don't have all the distractions of large towns."

Dusting some loose sugar from the counter into her hand, Sarah rinsed her hands. "Families come here and discover togetherness and play. We don't have movie theaters, malls, or arcades, so they find pleasure in what we do have—outdoor games, picnics, bonfires, bike rides. Kids who start out thinking this place is boring end up wanting to come back when their weekend is through—that is, if they take time to relax."

He sipped his remaining coffee. Movie theaters? Arcades? Warmed by cups of hot coffee and the heat of the oven, he was ready to return to the inn and rest. He was still tired from having his sleep interrupted the night before. And trying to adjust to the changes in this world further exhausted him.

"Well." He stood and stretched. "Thank you for sharing the

51

town's history and a few of your own stories. You've given me a lot to think about. But for now, I'd better be going. I've stayed too long already."

"Come by anytime." Miss Peterson wiped the counter, pushing crumbs of dough into her hand at the island's edge. "It's always fun to chat with visitors, especially now, when we have so few. And, with just ten days until Christmas, soon the shops will be closed for the season."

Ten days. Just ten days. He walked to the shelves of baked goods lining two of the room's walls. After selecting a package of cookies and a loaf of fruit bread, he reached into his pocket and withdrew a one-dollar note and handed it to Miss Peterson.

She wiped her hands on a dishcloth and studied the money. Then her eyes widened. "Where did you find this?"

He fingered the dollar bill, engraved with an image of two men in a canoe.

"Caroline, come look at this. It's one of the original notes from the Bentonsport bank."

The two women surveyed the bill as they would a rare jewel. When he gave it to them, they turned it over, examining it.

"This is a treasure," Sarah said. "Do you have any idea what it's worth?"

Mrs. Murphy passed the bill back to him. "Richard Tarrant bought two of these at an auction last year, and they went for over three hundred dollars apiece."

Thomas swallowed hard. It was hard to imagine. When he felt around in his pocket, he had at least five bills, maybe more. If he sold even one of them, he'd have more than enough money for the remaining ten days of his visit.

Miss Peterson's shoulders sloped. "I wish I could buy this from you, but I don't have that kind of money to spare."

His brows furrowed. He wanted to give each of these women a bill. But that would seem peculiar.

"I have a proposition for you. If you ladies let me join you for tea or coffee every day while I'm here, and if you'll let me trouble you with my questions about the town and join you for some conversation ..." He extracted another one-dollar note. "I'll give each of you one of these as a token of appreciation."

Sarah laughed as she shook her. "You don't need to buy our company."

He raised his hands in the air, palms up, as he often did when he wanted to make a point to his students. "I want to be able to drop in on you without feeling I'm intruding. I promise not to come more than once or twice a day. As pleasant as the inn is, I will feel closed in if I don't break free of it once in a while. And it's too cold to spend the whole day outdoors."

"You have a deal." Mrs. Murphy snagged a bill from his hand. "I can't wait to show this to Bill." Grabbing her coat, she headed for the door. "I'll be back later this evening, Sarah. It was lovely meeting you, Thomas ... what's your last name again?"

"Barton. Very nice to meet you, Mrs. Murphy."

"Oh, and please, call me Caroline." The door banged shut behind her.

"I'm sorry. Caroline is almost too eager at times."

"Her enthusiasm is refreshing." He gave Miss Peterson the second bill.

"Are you sure you can part with this?"

"I have a few more." He fingered the fold of bills in his pocket.

She smiled as she slipped it from his fingers. "I will accept it as a gift of friendship. I may even have it framed."

"Thank you, Miss Peterson ... or is it Mrs.?"

"Definitely not Mrs. But you should call me Sarah." She laughed. "I wouldn't answer to anything else."

"Very well, Sarah." Taken aback by the informality, he nodded. It was quite pleasant. He bowed slightly. "Then, with your permission, I will return tomorrow."

"Please do." She walked to the door with him and offered him his overcoat.

The sun reflected white against the snow. Carrying his baked

53

goods under one arm, he trudged back to the inn by way of the academy. His emptiness and fear had subsided. Bentonsport had not worked its promised magic, but perhaps the two ladies had.

As he approached the academy, he wished he could go inside, climb the stairs, and slip into his room. But that couldn't happen for ten more days—that is, if Pastor Lockhardt was correct.

Jamming his hands into his pockets, Thomas fingered the key and finished his walk to the inn. Then he slipped inside the familiar hotel. Exhausted, he lay on the bed, intending to take a short nap, and fell into a peaceful dreamless sleep.

Thomas awoke in a dim room, lit only by the streetlight outside, his head heavy from a deep sleep. He felt for his bedside clock, then let his hand fall idle over the edge of the bed. He was some time in the future, at the inn. The round windup clock at his bedside showed it was after ten.

He found a tray of sandwiches, apple slices, and sponge cake on the table between the windows. Hungry and grateful, he polished off the sandwiches and tart apples. He lingered over the cake. It reminded him of the cake Mrs. Ross had served at dinner just before the school play.

Setting the book down, he walked to the window. Street lamps burned with a steady glow. Homesick for the real Bentonsport, exhaustion tugged at him, despite his nap. He drew the shade, switched off the lamp, and lay across the bed.

Only ten more days, and he'd be home.

He hoped.

Chapter Seven

T homas arose fully awake. The aroma of frying bacon and coffee caused him to descend the inn's staircase two steps at a time. In the kitchen, music similar to Sarah's filled the room. Another box rested on the counter. Lani stood at the stove, humming as she flipped bacon strips.

The oval oak table held three place settings, and he took a seat.

"Well, look who's all bright-eyed and bushy-tailed this morning." She removed a pitcher of orange juice from something like a large white icebox.

"I am rather hungry." He spread the napkin in his lap.

"I didn't want to wake you for dinner last night. Did you find the tray I left you?"

"Yes, thank you."

Lani poured him a mug of coffee. "And what are your plans for this sunny day?"

After breathing in the invigorating aroma, he tested a sip. "I went to see Sarah yesterday—"

"Our baker girl?" Eyes twinkling, she patted his shoulder, then returned to the stove and began cracking eggs into a bowl. "Sweet girl. Always has a smile on her face."

He warmed his hands on the cup. "Her friend Mrs. Murphy

—Caroline—was there too. She mentioned a gentleman who might want to buy some of the old currency I have."

"That'd be Richard Tarrant. He's always buying up bits and pieces of Bentonsport's history. Maps, money, books, photos— just about anything he can lay his hands on."

"What does he do with it all?"

Butter sizzling in the skillet, she poured in the eggs. "He plans on setting up a museum."

Thomas's possessions now were museum-worthy. His mouth curved downward. Right. He was a relic.

"If you have old things to sell, he's the one to see." She brought the pan toward him and loaded his plate with bacon strips. Then she brought the smaller skillet to the table and scooped a portion of hot scrambled eggs onto his plate. "That should hold you. A good hot breakfast is just the trick for a cold winter morning."

"Thank you, Lani. It looks wonderful." He bowed his head in prayer, silently thanking God for the food and the strength for another day in this strange place.

"Looks like our other guest might sleep through his meal like you did last night." Lani picked up the third table setting and arranged it on a tray.

With a wink at Thomas, she added a bowl of sliced strawberries and bananas from the rectangular box, two muffins, a glass of orange juice, and a red napkin to the wooden tray.

He ate his breakfast slowly, savoring each bite of soft scrambled eggs and salty, crisp bacon. If he closed his eyes, he could be back in Pennsylvania, sitting in his mother's kitchen. Strange how some things changed so dramatically, yet others were so familiar.

"Did Sarah tell you how to find Richard's home?"

"No. Does he live close?"

"Not too far, over in Vernon, across the river. You can get there by taking the walking bridge. Richard lives in a brick house just down from the Vernon schoolhouse."

Thomas had seen the schoolhouse, but he'd never noticed a brick house nearby. It was probably new ... at least from his perspective.

Lani carried the breakfast tray away. Thomas wondered if he'd have a chance to meet the other guest. So far, they seemed to be on opposite schedules.

When she returned, she brought the empty plate to the stove. "Time to feed me," she said over her shoulder as she moved the last two strips of bacon from the pan and scraped the remaining eggs to her plate.

As he finished his coffee, she pressed a button on a black box on the countertop. The box opened. She put the plate of food inside, closed the door, and pressed some buttons on the side.

It hummed.

When she removed her plate, the eggs were steaming. Somehow that box quick-heated food. A cold box and a hot box —both beyond his ability to understand.

If only he could take the good things of this world back to his —and vice versa.

He bowed his head to give her time to say grace, but she began eating without even a pause. Apparently, prayer before meals was no longer common here. Well, it was not a custom he'd give up— no matter how archaic it made him seem.

She tore off a piece of toast and used it to scoop up a chunk of the egg. "What big adventures do you have in mind for today?"

"I'd like to visit Mr. Tarrant this morning. If you think he's available."

"Wouldn't be a bad idea to call to make sure he's home." She stood. "I can do that for you."

She walked to the countertop and picked up a slim black rectangular object. She poked at its face, then lifted the device to her ear. "Richard, it's Lani. I have a guest who has some old Bentonsport money he'd like to sell. Sarah thought you might be interested."

How was she speaking to Richard Tarrant?

"No, I haven't seen the money."

If the man lived on the other side of the river, how could he hear what she was saying and communicate back?

"He's ready to come up now." She raised her eyebrows at Thomas in a questioning manner, so he nodded, stood, and retrieved his coat from a hook in the hallway. He reentered the room in time to hear Lani say, "Okay. See you later."

She set the object on the counter, sank back in her chair, and scooped a bite of her egg. Then she pointed out the window. "He says you can come right over. If you look over to the right, you'll see the bridge. It used to be a car bridge, but it wasn't maintained for the weight of vehicles, so they converted it to a walking bridge."

Thomas didn't understand cars, but walking he understood.

"Cross the bridge and walk up the hill, and before you reach the Vernon schoolhouse, Richard's house is to the right."

Sounded easy enough. "Thank you for the help."

PATCHES OF SNOW DOTTED THE GROUND. THE FAMILIAR river flowing under ice shimmered as he crossed the bridge. In his town, people ferried to Vernon, which now consisted of three houses and the schoolhouse, the effects of time appearing even more severe than in Bentonsport.

He walked up the flagstone path to a brick house. Within seconds of Thomas's knock, a burly gray-haired man greeted him, wearing a white shirt and gray trousers.

"You must be Thomas," he said warmly. "I'm Richard Tarrant. Please come in."

Thomas followed him into a parlor, sparsely furnished but neat and orderly. Shelves holding old books and various items—baby spoons, railroad lanterns, coins displayed in frames—lined the wall to his right. Though the pieces were commonplace, he didn't recognize any particular object.

His host held out his hands. "Would you like me to take your coat?"

After Thomas handed him his coat and scarf, the man gestured toward a chair. Even as Thomas sat, he surveyed the shelves. He'd never seen such a wide variety of objects in one room.

"What brings you to Bentonsport?"

"I'm visiting the area," Thomas said, almost comfortable with this now-familiar question. "How long have you been in this town, Mr. Tarrant?"

"Call me Richard."

Did anyone go by their surnames in this place? Everyone was so casual about introductions.

Richard lowered himself into his chair. "I've been privileged to live in Vernon my whole life, except for two years. It's a great place."

"I appreciate your willingness to see me on such short notice."

"Lani said you have some old Bentonsport money you're hoping to sell." Richard laced his hands in his lap and leaned back in his chair. "I enjoy anything from the past, but I'm especially fond of the currency. The artwork has much more detail than anything we have on our money today. But more than that, when I hold old currency in my hand, I can't help but think of how many people have handled that bill."

Thomas reached into his pocket and took out two banknotes.

"It's like reaching out and touching the past." Richard cradled the currency in one palm.

Thomas felt like a well-preserved corpse. He shook off the feeling. He needed money he could spend to get through the next ten days.

"You're offering to sell these?"

"I have a number of them. And since I came on this trip with little spending money, I thought it best to sell one or two."

"What are you asking for them?"

Trying not to let his voice reflect his discomfort over quoting the price Sarah mentioned, Thomas swallowed. "I was thinking of two hundred fifty dollars apiece."

"Sold!" The older man beamed. "I'll purchase them both, but I don't have that much cash on me. Do you mind an e-Transfer?" At Thomas's frown, the man waved the question away. "What do you say we ride to Bonaparte bank together?"

What they would ride on or in, but he knew better than to ask. "I'd like that." What, if anything, of Bonaparte would he recognize?

"How about a cup of coffee before we set out?" Richard stood.

"Thank you." Relieved the negotiations had gone smoothly, Thomas could relax and enjoy some easy conversation.

Richard returned with two mugs and a platter of cookies. "I got these from Sarah's bakery across the river. You've been there, I assume?" He offered Thomas a mug, then lowered the plate, offering him a cookie.

Thomas selected a Christmas star outlined in yellow frosting. "I had coffee there yesterday with her and her friend, Caroline."

"Nice people." Richard, a tree-shaped cookie in hand, the mug on the table beside him, scooted back in his chair and crossed his legs. "Folks around here are hoping Sarah finds a beau and settles down. It's probably the only way we'll keep her long-term." His cookie crumbled when he bit into it, leaving little specks on his tie. "Not right for someone to be all alone in this world."

"She doesn't have any family?"

Richard shook his head. "Her parents were killed in an accident when she was young. Her grandmother raised her, but she's gone now too."

Though Thomas had lived without family nearby for years, he could always visit them. To be all alone, with no one to go home to—he couldn't fathom it.

"Sarah's a great baker and a real honey. If I were thirty years younger, I'd be on her front step with my courting outfit on."

Well, that was one thing he didn't need to bother with. Ten

days wasn't long enough to make a friend, let alone have a romance.

"But we are good friends. She comes over here every couple of weeks to chat about the town, history, art, music, all sorts of things. I go to her place at least once a week to have coffee and tease her and Caroline."

Richard rummaged in an open wooden box on the table next to his chair and then gave Thomas a folded paper printed with tiny Christmas trees. He took one for himself and wiped his mouth. Thomas did the same, having never held a paper napkin.

"Caroline will have her hands full in another couple of months with the new baby. We're all pretty tickled, though. You'd think we were all going to be grandparents or aunts or uncles, which we almost are in a community like ours."

In his Bentonsport, when a new baby arrived, all the women gathered at the new mother's house, bringing gifts and advice. "Babies always stir up excitement."

The men finished their coffee. "Ready to head out?"

Richard flashed a wink as he removed a tan jacket and tweed cap from the coat rack and handed Thomas his scarf and coat. "I like that you wear historical garb just to go visiting."

"Well, that has been a problem, actually. Sarah and Caroline told me folks only dress this way during the tourist season. I need to find something more ... casual."

"I don't wear period clothes, but I always dress up more than the others around town." Richard grabbed his keys off the hook. "That's how I feel most comfortable. Guess I'm from a different era."

Thomas couldn't help but smile. They had that in common.

They went to the bank in Bonaparte in Richard's vehicle. It was fascinating—and loud. The seats were made of some type of smooth leather-like material. The front of this carriage-like contraption had holes with levers that blew warm air throughout the inside. There were all sorts of knobs Thomas would love to try. He didn't.

Richard pulled up to the bank and went inside. Returning, he deposited six crisp bills in Thomas's hands. Four were marked as one-hundred-dollar bills and two as fifty-dollar bills. They looked like counterfeits, but surely they weren't. He could see why Richard and others liked to look at the older, more artistic paper money.

As they drove back to Vernon, Richard pointed out homes and farms sitting back from the road. They drove through Bentonsport, crossed the river on a high bridge upstream from the town, and entered Vernon. But, oh, how easy it was to cross the river!

At his house, Richard drove into the side building and switched off the loud roar. The men got out, and Thomas shook Richard's hand.

"Thank you. For seeing me so promptly, for purchasing the currency, for the coffee and cookies, and for the trip to Bonaparte."

"My pleasure. Come back again if you have time."

"Thank you. I will try."

Away from the warmth of the amazing vehicle, Thomas shivered as he headed toward the bridge. At the foot of the bridge, he saw a hand-painted sign he'd missed going in the other direction—General Store: Fresh Eggs, Baked Goods, Beverages. Perhaps they also sold clothes. He followed the arrow about a quarter mile down a gravel road to a cozy farmhouse tucked behind trees and overgrown bushes. Adjacent to the house was a field about an acre in size.

As he walked up the drive, he saw two black buggies parked in front of a slant-roof shed next to the house. So, trucks had not entirely replaced the horse and buggy.

He knocked on the front door. A young woman, dressed in a plain mid-length dress, her brown hair tucked in a white cap, answered with a pleasant "Good day."

"Good afternoon. I saw the sign for a general store. Is it nearby?"

"You are almost there. It's in that building." She gestured to a cheery yellow cottage with a long addition on the back. "I was just heading there myself. My parents own the store, and I work there. I'll walk you over."

As they crossed to the store, he asked, "I was wondering if the store sells men's clothing?"

"We do." She led him to the porch and opened the door.

Entering the store, he smelled the familiar scent of spices, herbs, and breads, much like the Greef Store. The young woman walked behind the counter and stood by the cash register.

Across from the door, jars, cans, and sacks of fruits and vegetables crammed the shelves. Wooden barrels near the counter held various grains—barley, wheat, flour—the same as at the Greef Store. Shelf upon shelf of clothing stacked the wall to his right. Black work pants. A nice selection of colored shirts. Hanging on hooks at the end of the shelves were pairs of suspenders.

He lifted a pair of black pants off the shelf. "Are these everyday work clothes?"

The young woman kept dusting the counters. "Our men wear them. However, I don't believe they are for the English."

He didn't care what folks from England wore. He merely wanted to blend in with the men in Bentonsport. He had only seen two men since he'd come to the town. He couldn't remember what Bill was wearing—he'd been too stunned. Richard had worn a white shirt and pants but admitted he dressed formally. Thomas would have to take the young clerk's word. He selected a pair of black pants and suspenders and a white shirt.

The young woman wrapped each piece of clothing in paper and stacked them in a brown bag. "That will be ninety-two dollars and fifty cents."

He flinched. It would take him a year back home to earn so much. He'd have a hard time getting used to these prices. He took out a hundred-dollar bill. The young woman handed him the change—similar-looking currency and some coins. He recognized

Washington on the quarter, Jefferson on the five-cent piece, but had no idea whose portrait was on the smaller coin.

As he started to leave the store, he paused by several tin holiday cookie cutters in various shapes. He selected a few to give as gifts to Sarah. He also found baby toys, rattles, and chewing rings for Caroline's expected baby. After paying, he thanked the young clerk and left.

The air was warming, though the sky had faded to gray. Back in his room, he changed into his new clothing, connected the delicate hooks on the shirt, then threaded on the suspenders. The pants were roomy and comfortable.

After he admired the new clothes in the mirror, he noticed it was already after three in the afternoon. He wanted to visit Sarah and Caroline before supper and give them their gifts. Placing them in his overcoat's deep pockets, he headed to Sarah's house.

When he reached her front walk, the yeasty fragrance of freshly baked pastries wafted through the air, and hunger twisted his stomach. He clanked the door knocker, a brass half-ring that had dented the plate where visitors had been too aggressive.

"Come in," Sarah called out.

As he opened the door, he savored the aroma heavy in the warm room. Then he removed his coat and scarf, folding them over his arm.

Sarah, facing the sink, submerging pans in the dishwater, turned to greet him. "Thomas." Her lips parted as she surveyed him.

Not able to discern Sarah's thoughts, he could tell that she certainly noticed his new clothes.

Caroline emerged from the adjacent room. "Well, aren't you a strange bird?" She bit her lower lip. "First, you arrive dressed in period costume. Now you look like a—"

"Like a what?" His face flushed.

Sarah approached. "You look like an Amish man. A fine Amish man, at that."

What were they talking about? "I just wanted to purchase

some clothing less formal than my period clothes. I found a store on the other side of the bridge and—"

Sarah held up a hand. "You won't find any casual clothing for sale in Bentonsport. The town isn't big enough to support such a store."

Eyes narrowing, Caroline peered at him. "You look like you're pretty near Bill's size, perhaps a tad thinner. He has lots of old blue jeans and work shirts. I'll run home and pick up a few things for you. Lani does laundry for guests if they request it. Just ask her to wash your clothes sometime during the weekend, and that should get you through to the end of your visit."

"I don't want to trouble you." He couldn't imagine wearing another man's clothes.

"No bother or I wouldn't have offered." Caroline strode toward the door. "I'll be back in a jiffy."

Frowning, Sarah looked him up and down. "Aren't you familiar with the Amish?"

"Not entirely. I have heard of the sect, but there are no communities near my town."

She removed two cups and saucers and lifted the teapot from the drying rack.

As she cluttered around, he wondered what her silence meant. He shifted his weight and straightened his left suspender, feeling like a fool. How would he get through the remaining days without giving himself away? If only he could tell Sarah and Caroline who he was and how he got there. But that would seem too preposterous. Better to be quiet.

The bell over the door rang, and Caroline came in, arms laden with neatly folded clothes. "Go in the back room and change into these."

He thanked her, somewhat relieved despite his reticence to accept the clothing.

"This way. You can change in my guest room." Sarah moved from the counter, still seemingly in her own thoughts.

He followed her down the hall. Framed photos of a child and

a much older woman graced the right side. The photos were crisp, clear, unlike the rather murky ones he was used to. Was the child Sarah? With her grandmother, perhaps?

She opened a door to a room papered in a floral pattern with red and pink peonies. Lace curtains draped the windows. A mounted needlework sampler hung beside a dark mahogany bed with an ornately carved headboard.

Never in his life had he been in a bedroom with any woman who wasn't part of his family. Well, other than with Lani.

"Is something wrong?" Head cocked to one side, hand still on the doorknob, she studied him.

"Not at all." He forced a smile. "It just reminds me of my sisters' rooms back home."

The tenderest of smiles curled her pink lips, her expression softened, and her shoulders loosened. "They must like antiques."

"They would certainly like this."

"Well, make yourself at home. Here." She handed him a paper bag. "You can put the clothes you're wearing in here. If you need anything, just call."

Once she eased the door shut behind her, he unhooked the eyes on his shirt, then placed the 'Amish' apparel in the bag. He then slid into the soft denim pants and work shirt. The outfit would be considered work clothes in his town, something one would wear to do hard labor. Nothing a gentleman would ever wear—even to garden. But it would feel good to fit in.

SARAH SHIFTED HER WEIGHT ON THE STOOL WHILE Caroline poured the jasmine-scented tea Sarah had prepared. She stroked her forehead and spoke low so he couldn't hear. "There's something strange about him, don't you think?"

"Maybe he's just a bookish guy. One of those professor types who's brilliant but has trouble getting dressed in the morning."

No, she knew bookish people. There was something strange

about his behavior. "He seems sweet in some ways, but also kind of ... well, different. I can't put my finger on it."

"Maybe he came here to get away from something or someone —or to think. He's probably bored. There is so little to do here this time of year. If I went somewhere to escape a situation or to think about something, I'd—"

He walked into the kitchen, arms folded across his chest, shirtsleeves pushed up on his forearms. His shoulders looked more square in the casual shirt, his arms muscular.

No doubt about it, he was tall, dark, and handsome. It was a trite expression, but it fit. Like the clothes.

He stood beside Caroline but fixed his eyes on Sarah. "They seem the right size."

"You look ... fine. I mean, just fine." She swallowed. She'd better not be blushing

"Thomas, Sarah and I were just discussing how bored you must be." Caroline rescued her. "Visiting here this time of year."

"Well, that's not the term I would use ..."

"Seeing you in Bill's work clothes gives me an idea. How would you like to have a series of brief internships during your time here? You could go to Bill's tin shop for one or two days and help him out. You could spend a day or two helping Sarah with her baking. Then maybe work with some of our local artists."

He unfolded his arms and looked down, apparently mulling over the idea. Then his face broke into a broad smile. "What a wonderful idea."

Caroline faced her. "Sarah, what do you think?"

"With Christmas coming, folks around here will work him to death if he gives them a chance." Sarah slid him a cup of tea and a plate of cookies. "Several of the artists around here—like Bill and Caroline—are finishing up last-minute orders. If I were you, I'd set some boundaries. Work only the hours you want to, so this is still a vacation."

"Bill won't care what time you show up, and you can leave whenever you want." Caroline brushed crumbs off the island into her cupped hand and poured them into the sink. "He'll be grateful for whatever help you can give. But with the other artists, if you let me know how much time you'd like to spend, I can take care of the arrangements."

"My time is pretty free, so whatever works for them will work for me." He quickly finished his tea and two cookies. The parlor clock chimed the half-hour, and he began to edge away. "I should head back to the inn for dinner."

Sarah got his coat and scarf, which had a distinct spicy, smokey smell, like slightly singed clove. My, he was a good sport. How many men would let strange women dress them—and plan their vacations?

He turned to Caroline as he slipped on his coat. "What would be a good time to start with Bill tomorrow?"

"He's an early bird, so any time after six would be fine."

As he reached into his coat pocket, his face lit up. "With all the focus on my clothing, I forgot about these." He pulled out two handfuls of items. "I brought you each a little something to thank you for the hospitality you have shown this stranger."

He gave Sarah a bag holding three cookie cutters and handed a bag of baby toys and rattles to Caroline.

Handsome and thoughtful. Perhaps that could compensate for odd? "Thank you, Thomas. But you aren't a stranger anymore. Starting tomorrow, you are one of the Bentonsport artists."

"Artist's apprentice—I wouldn't presume to be more. After you see my work, you'll agree." Thomas bade the two women goodbye and stepped into the cold air.

Chapter Eight

T homas spent the next day with Bill, learning bits and pieces of tinsmithing. When the day neared an end, long shadows fell across the room, causing the silver streaks in Bill's hair to glisten, almost like tinsel. Caroline came with a tray of tea, cookies, and apple slices. She asked Bill to pull a bench deeper into the room and placed three chairs around it, then invited the men to join her.

"So"—she raised her eyebrows at Bill as she poured the tea—"do we have another tinsmith in the making?"

"We just might." Bill moved his chair closer to her. "You're a quick study and a good worker, Thomas." He took a long sip of the hot tea. "You can help me any day you'd like."

"I'd enjoy that." Thomas couldn't help breaking out in a big smile. He missed his friends, his community. But the sense of panic, estrangement, and isolation was gone. He was feeling more at home in this new town and especially with these people.

Bentonsport was working its magic once again.

"If it's okay with you, Thomas," Caroline said, "Sarah would like your next apprenticeship. A group of nursing home residents is coming to her shop tomorrow as part of their holiday outing. She can use all the help she can get."

A nursing home? It must have to do with ill or frail people.

"Honey"—Bill touched his wife's hand—"I doubt Thomas wants to work in the kitchen. I'm sure he'd rather help in the blacksmith shop or the—"

"You sound downright chauvinistic." A sly smirk moved across her face.

"I don't mind working in a kitchen." Thomas finished tidying his work area and then sat at the end of the bench. "In fact, I enjoy it. I grew up with two sisters. So, it wouldn't take as much time to teach me to bake as it would to show me how to smith."

"Then it's settled." The big grin she gave her husband somehow reminded Thomas of his sisters sticking their tongues out at him.

Stiffening his fingers, Bill put his hands up in surrender.

She waved her white napkin back and pointed at him. "Sarah goes all out for her visitors. So, it might be best for you to wear those period clothes. She'll have an apron for you, so you won't have to worry about messing them up."

"Apron," Bill murmured under his breath.

While Bill stacked their plates on the tray, Thomas gathered their cups, all the while wondering why he felt so happy yet nervous about the prospects of working with Sarah. While he finished, Caroline watched with a knowing smile.

THE NEXT MORNING, AFTER ENJOYING A CUP OF COFFEE and fruit, along with some small talk with Lani, Thomas headed to Sarah's place. As he approached her house, smoke curled up from her chimney and dissipated into the blue sky.

After he clanked the door knocker, her voice called out, "It's unlocked. Come on in."

He hesitated. For the first time in his life, he'd be alone all day with a woman he was not related to. In her home.

Taking a deep breath, he stepped inside, and the warmth of

the woodstove and the smell of something sweet baking greeted him. He hung his overcoat on a peg.

"It's me," he called out.

"I'm in the summer kitchen—through the door."

He glanced at the front hall mirror. His hair had dried and hung in curls near the base of his neck. His cheeks and nose were bright pink from the cold air. Yet dressed in a white shirt, tailored rust-brown woolen pants, and a button-up tan vest, he looked much more like himself. Felt more like himself too.

Considering he'd aged more than a hundred years in less than one day, he looked pretty good too. Chuckling to himself, he went to greet Sarah.

Inside the summer kitchen, he found a young woman, her hair pulled back in long blonde tendrils, with a curl hanging toward her face. She wore a light blue dress gathered at her waist, with tatted lace edging the sleeves.

When the woman turned around, he gasped. *Sarah?*

She grinned. "It's old-fashioned, I know. But I like this look."

"So do I." The words tumbled out of his mouth with no thought, or he would have stopped them. At least, he wouldn't have been so abrupt.

She blushed under his gaze.

He couldn't help staring. "The transformation is amazing. You look as if you stepped back in time." *And I should know.*

Head down, she sorted through her mixing bowls. "You look rather dashing yourself. And quite ready to help in my 1870s kitchen."

"So, what can I do?"

"The aprons are over there." She pointed to a row of hooks.

After rolling up his sleeves, he hooked the loop of the white apron over his head and turned so she could tie the strings around his waist.

He didn't have to close his eyes to imagine being at home. Even better, he'd be spending the whole day with a beautiful woman whose presence didn't fill him with anxiety.

71

Sarah led him back to the main kitchen. "I'm afraid, even with the apron, you're going to get quite the flour dusting today." She laughed, and the curls on her blonde hairpiece bobbed.

"A little flour won't bother me." He stood on the opposite side of her counter. "It brushes off easily, and these clothes are old." *Really old.*

"Even more reason to keep them nice."

"Well, I'm not concerned about it, so I hope you won't be either. I'm here to help, learn, and enjoy my day."

"Sounds good to me." She peered inside the oven. "I've started a batch of shortbread cookies. I like baking for the seniors. It brightens my whole day."

She patted the brick wall of the bustle oven. "We're going to use the bustle oven to bake the cookies when they're here." As she described how to bake with a period oven—so similar to the one at his grandmother's house—he let his mind wander again. She was so beautiful and kind ...

"When I serve them, I don't tell them which cookies come from my modern oven and which are made the old-fashioned way. But I always use the bustle oven for demonstrations of period baking."

After returning to her modern kitchen, she used colorful quilted hot pads to remove a tray of lightly browned cookies, cut in varying shapes, from the newer oven. She motioned him closer.

"We'll let them cool for just a couple of minutes, and then you can use the spatula to place them on the cooling rack." She passed him a wooden-handled spatula.

He eased the browned cookies to the rack while she rolled dough out on the marble slab nearby.

"Would you like to listen to some music?" With the back of her arm, she brushed a long blonde tendril off her forehead. "I can turn on the radio."

"Yes, music would be nice."

She rotated the circle on the black cube on the counter. Soft music filled the room.

Of all the things Thomas had seen in this Bentonsport, he most wished he could take that box back. To possess the ability to have music fill the room at the turn of a dial? Remarkable.

"I usually listen to internet channels, but this particular station has a good selection. The DJ sneaks in new songs or international pieces. It's nice to hear new carols."

He wanted to pick up the box, investigate it, and find out what it contained and how it worked. But that would seem odd. Perhaps, if Sarah ever left the room ...

The music stopped, and a man spoke. "Santa will feel right at home here in southeastern Iowa in one short week because a big blast of snow should be hitting us Monday night. Here's Tina with the full forecast."

Who were these people? How were they speaking through the box?

"That's right, Don." A perky woman's voice followed. "The next three days will be sunny and cold, with a high of thirty degrees. But then bundle up and get out those snow shovels. Monday will start out cloudy. In the early evening, the snow will move in and could stay with us through midday Wednesday. The weather bureau is estimating an accumulation of up to a foot of snow. So, get your—"

Twisting the knob, Sarah cut off the woman's words. "I was hoping for a white Christmas, but not a blizzard."

Thomas, realizing he'd stopped working, resumed placing cookies on the rack. The weather sounded much like the weather he'd left behind.

She turned on the water at the sink. "Well, at least the weekend should be pleasant, and that'll be good for business. With a bit of luck, the roads will be clear for your travel home. Did you drive or fly?"

He jolted. The cookie on his spatula clomped onto the rack. Crumbs littered the counter. Did folks here fly? He hadn't seen anyone flying, but he'd start looking more carefully at the sky. He took a deep breath, remembering Pastor Lockhardt's warning to not get caught up in things in this world. But it was hard!

"I always take the train when I travel long distances." He walked to the sink and stood close to her as he washed the cookie sheets. He noticed she smelled sweet, of vanilla.

"Really? I've only been on two train trips, years ago. But whenever I'm in Fairfield, and I hear the train whistle blowing and watch it whiz past, I always think how pleasant it would be to sit in the passenger car, drink tea, and watch the scenery go by."

The tightness in his neck relaxed. People still traveled by train, but she seemed almost sentimental about it. Travel by 'truck' on smooth roads as he had done with Richard must've taken over.

"I don't get to travel often." She took the cookie sheet from him and dried it with a white towel, then set it near her rolled-out dough and cut out the cookies with the tin shapes. "I lived with my grandmother in St. Louis, and we didn't have a lot of money for luxuries."

She was using the cookie cutter he'd given her.

"We still have some serious baking to do." She looked up at the clock. "I need sixteen loaves of bread and at least three dozen more cookies."

"You lead. I'll follow."

"Why don't you finish cutting out this batch?" She clattered a pile of cookie cutters on the counter. "Use whichever ones you like. Place the unbaked cookies here." She pointed to the cookie sheet she'd just dried. "Then sprinkle them lightly with colored sugar." She slid over three bottles of sugar—green, red, and blue. "I'll put together a batch of dough to use when our guests arrive. Then we'll focus on bread. Deal?"

"Deal."

After he finished cutting out the dough, Thomas began spooning sugar on top.

The soft whoosh of her wooden spoon through dough lent a rhythmic pattern to their work. Then it stilled as she sifted in more flour. "Caroline and I expected you to have left Bentonsport by now. With everything closed up and a storm on its way, we figured you'd want to get out of here."

"I might have wanted to leave." He grinned. "But two fair maidens had pity on this sojourner and allowed him to enter their world, thus saving his vacation ... and their poor old visitor's mind."

She shook her head, and her ringlets bobbed against her cheeks. "Hey, we never said you were old. You can't be much older than Caroline or me."

"Thirty-seven." He stiffened. *Give or take a hundred years.*

"Well, I'm thirty-four, so let's not talk about being old, okay?"

The conversation continued, light, free, and easy, as though they'd been friends for years. This was a new experience, enjoying the company of a beautiful woman, in her home, with no one around. It felt a bit naughty, but he liked it.

She mixed a bowl of frosting and taught him how to decorate the cookies using a bag of frosting and a variety of tips.

From under the counter, she lifted a bowl with a big hook inside attached to a black metal contraption. "I know folks didn't use a mixer to make bread in the eighteen hundreds. But this machine can make dough faster than I can by hand. And it gives the bread a lighter texture."

Surely, something so clunky couldn't make bread lighter?

"I'll whip up the first batch to show you how. Then, if you take over the mixing, I can grease and flour the pans."

The people who'd lived between his generation and hers found amazing ways of making life more pleasant, mixers turning themselves, music coming out of a box, hot water coming out of faucets. It was all unbelievable.

She showed him how to add ingredients to the mixing bowl a little at a time. As he added them, she set sixteen bread pans on the counter, sprayed each with something that misted out of a can, and floured them. Another nice invention. He was losing count of them all.

After they slid the bread into the oven and washed the mixer, utensils, and bowls, they returned to the summer kitchen. She put her hand in front of the bustle oven. "Still hot." She peered inside.

He walked over and warmed his hands in front of the oven.

She smiled at him, flashing one deep dimple. "When the visitors arrive, I'll give them a brief summary of baking from the mid-eighteen hundreds. Would you like to help me with the demonstration?"

"I'll do what I can."

"You seem to have a good grasp on history. I'm sure you'll do just fine."

As she spoke, she retrieved a soup pan and poured apple cider into it. They returned to the modern kitchen, where she added cinnamon sticks, nutmeg, and a few spices he couldn't identify into a piece of cheesecloth, tied it together, then floated it in the cider.

"That should do it. We have just enough time to tidy up."

They washed at the sink, dusted off their clothing, and wiped down all the countertops. They had just finished when a vehicle, something like a railway coach, pulled up in front of her house. Fifteen elderly men and women scuffled up the front steps.

"Come in, come in," Sarah greeted.

The two of them helped their guests off with their coats, and he carried the items to a table in the summer kitchen.

Several of the older women chatted with her, asking about the sales of her Christmas products or about Caroline's health, before migrating to the kitchen.

One older woman turned to Sarah, her eyes twinkling. "Oh, I'm so glad you found a beau. We've been praying the right one would come along."

Sarah blushed and opened her mouth

"And so handsome," a second elderly woman said in a low but clear voice. "Definitely worth the wait."

Amused over Sarah's predicament, Thomas stayed silent.

"He's not a beau." She cocked her head and grinned. "Thomas and I are friends."

"All the same, I'm happy for you."

Sarah shrugged at him, so he winked, letting her know he was fine with the misunderstanding. Fine? He enjoyed the thought of being this beautiful woman's beau, though it would be impossible. One couldn't build a relationship in less than two weeks—or could one?

Together, they walked into the modern kitchen and stood behind the long counter that stood in the middle of the room. They accompanied their guests into the summer kitchen where the demonstration would begin.

"Welcome to the Montgomery House," Sarah began. "For those of you who haven't been to my home, this building is believed to be one of the first homes built in Bentonsport and dates back to the 1840s.

"This kitchen is all original, including the fireplace, which was used for cooking and heating, and the bustle oven used for baking."

Although tempted to add details to the story, how, with the windows open, the street would be filled with the aroma of baking, he didn't. He didn't want to interrupt or draw attention to himself.

Instead, he clasped his hands before him as Sarah used the poker to nudge the logs in the fireplace. "Mrs. Montgomery would stoke the fire in the open hearth. It would still have hot embers from the day before, so she just needed to add logs and kindling to create a new fire." With her mitt, she lifted the hook hanging from within the chimney over the fire. "She would hang a pan of water on this hook for hot tea and coffee. Then she turned her attention to the day's baking, which on this day includes vanilla spice bread.

"Let's head back to the modern kitchen, and we can check on the bread." They headed into the adjacent room. "Thomas, why don't you see how our bread is progressing?"

He opened the door to one of the modern ovens. A light came on inside, bathing the golden-brown loaves. "They look ready." He shut the door, and the light went off. Automatic lights?

Sarah came to his side. "Since looks can be deceiving, we'll test them to make sure."

Glad she took over, he stepped back. He had no idea how to test bread. Plus, having her standing so close was delightful. Perhaps all this baking gave her the scent of vanilla which always seemed to follow her.

She plucked a piece of thin straw from a narrow pewter vase next to the oven and poked the straw in the middle of one loaf. "Yep. Completely clean. It's ready."

The warmth of the open oven heated his face, and the scent of vanilla intensified the warmth.

"Mrs. Montgomery would carry the pot of water upstairs to fill pitchers for her husband and children, waking them so they could wash, dress, and begin their chores. She then returned to her kitchen and made breakfast, which usually consisted of porridge, bread, and butter."

And, in his house, eggs, bacon, ham, rolls. His mouth watered.

"I didn't bake our bread in the bustle oven today, but Thomas and I have mixed a batch of Christmas cookie dough. So, if you stand here at the countertop across from me, you can cut the dough into shapes. I'll bake the cookies you cut in the bustle oven.

"Thomas and I already baked a batch to share with you as soon as you finish cutting out your cookies and decorating them. Oh, and I have spiced apple cider on the stove."

As their visitors walked up to the counter and began sorting through the basket of cookie cutters, Sarah rolled out a slab of dough. Thomas helped the guests decorate their cookies with colored sugar. When one woman's hand shook as she tried to shake the sugar onto a cookie, he steadied her. Helping out felt natural—like teaching. When he sensed Sarah's eyes on him, they shared a smile.

Once the cookies were ready, she slid them into the bustle

oven. Then he passed around the plates of cookies and slices of the vanilla spice bread, and she distributed the mugs.

After each guest had been served, she asked him to help her pour the hot cider.

"At your service, Mrs. Montgomery," he replied with a grin. How lovely she looked. Why didn't she dress like this every day? Her boyish look was cute, but like this, she was stunning.

THE WOODEN-HANDLED LADLE SMOOTH BENEATH HER fingers, Sarah stirred the steaming cider. Warm spices teasing her nostrils and hope nipping her heart, she savored this moment. The handsome man at her side helping serve her houseful of guests. The cookies baking in the oven. The stoves heating the house. She captured a picture in her mind and tucked it into her mental treasure box.

Thomas handed her a mug.

"Tell them to be careful." She filled it and handed it back. "This is hot."

"One of the visitors has a bit of a tremble. I'll set her cup aside to cool."

How good of him to notice. Kind to the elderly.

She checked the nearly done cookies. "What do you think?" she asked as Thomas joined her. That scent of smokey clove seemed to trail him, subtle but nice.

"This has been my finest morning since coming to Bentonsport."

Mine too. But she didn't say it as she fit the metal door back over the opening.

"Your home reminds me so much of my parents' place this time of year, with all the holiday baking, the house filled with friends. I almost feel as if I were there ..." Homesickness echoed in his tone.

"Pennsylvania, right?"

"Um … yes. That's where my hometown is."

One of the male guests walked over to where they stood, his cane thumping against the hardwood floor. "Sarah, how about playing us some carols on your piano like you did last year?"

"Well, if you'll sing loud enough to cover my playing, you've got a deal."

The gentleman gave her a thumbs-up.

THOMAS SANK INTO A STUFFED CHAIR NEAR THE PIANO, listening to Sarah play Christmas carols while her elderly guests sang. The music itself was enjoyable. And watching her—even more so. Her soft, delicate features. Her upturned nose, long lashes. Her long neck. She was lovely, from the front and from the side.

Sarah ended with one of his favorites, "O Come, All Ye Faithful," then stood and curtsied to the applause. Everyone returned to the kitchen for the cookies they'd made.

After saying goodbye to the residents, Sarah and Thomas returned to the parlor. "How about sitting for a few minutes before lunch?" She plopped on the couch, her skirt puffing and then settling around her.

"Sounds like a good idea." He sat on a chair across from her.

"We need to package up the bread. And I thought we'd make kringles this afternoon—if you're up for another round of baking?"

"I'm yours for the whole day." How pleasant that sounded. He was spending the whole day with a lovely, charming woman. "You play beautifully."

She smoothed her skirt. "I was a music major in college, and I taught music at the elementary school for eight years. But I enjoy it more now since I play for pleasure instead of work."

"Why did you—?"

A loud knock interrupted. The kitchen door opened, and Caroline called out a cheery hello.

"We're in the parlor," Sarah replied.

Caroline appeared in the doorway and held up a paper bag. "I brought sandwiches and chips."

"You are the best."

Thomas helped Sarah pull the table to the center of the parlor and arranged three chairs around it. She set the table while Caroline laid out their lunch. When she tore open a bag and poured its contents onto a plate, he recognized them: Saratoga Chips. He'd only tasted them once at a lodge near Sarasota Springs.

"So, what have you been up to today?" Sarah bit into her sandwich.

"Frantically finishing Christmas orders. How'd the baking go?"

"I wasn't much help," Thomas said between bites. "But I certainly enjoyed it. Sarah was magnificent."

"Why don't you two come over for dinner tonight? My sister-in-law sent us a huge smoked salmon from her trip out West. I could cook up some green beans and a salad to go with it."

An evening with these new friends sounded wonderful, but he already had a commitment. "I told Lani I'd be eating at the inn tonight."

"Call her and let her know you won't be there. She'll be fine."

Sarah's face was bright, and she nodded approval. "I'll call Lani and tell her our plans."

"Then it's a date," Caroline concluded, reaching for another chip.

How blessed he was to have encountered Caroline. His unexpected trip would have been much different if she hadn't taken charge to ensure his time was memorable. Every town needed a Caroline. And a Sarah.

Chapter Nine

T homas stood at the sink with his sleeves rolled up, washing Sarah's dishes and placing them in the rinsing rack—thoroughly enjoying the many experiences this place had brought him. The comfort of friends. The openness of people. The convenience of so many new inventions.

As he was mulling these thoughts, Sarah walked in and stood next to him, towel in hand. "Caroline suggested we have dinner at her place around seven thirty. Is that too late for you?"

He chuckled. "At home, I eat whenever I choose. There's only me at the academy at night, so I cook when I get hungry."

"You live in an academy building?" She put the plate away.

Not again. When would he learn not to trip over things, bringing his world into this one? "Unusual, right?"

"Well ..." She raised an eyebrow. "Not if this were a hundred years ago. But for today, yes."

Why did everything have to be so different?

She picked up a bowl. "Do you get tired of living where you work?"

"Um ..." Thomas stalled, measuring each word. "Well, my living quarters are part of my compensation. I don't have to pay for a place to live."

"I taught music for eight years, and by the end of the day, I was so anxious to get home you couldn't have locked me in that school."

"You didn't enjoy teaching music?"

"It wasn't a bad job." She rinsed another plate. "It just wasn't right for me. I like having more control over my hours. Here, I can work early in the morning or late into the night if I want. And as much as I like people, especially children, I prefer not to be surrounded by them for seven hours a day."

This he understood. There *were* days he wished he could lock the door and just be by himself. But he welcomed the children's voices as they broke the overwhelming solitude of the high-ceilinged academy. "Wouldn't it be nice to have a bit of both—the silence of baking and the laughter of children?"

"That's why I invite groups in. I'd go stir-crazy by myself all the time. Having folks visit, then having the place to myself, is heavenly. I don't make as much as when I taught. But I work for myself, and I have more control over my time."

Summers and winter break were the only times he had control over his time. And those days flew by.

She hugged a dried platter to her chest and braced a hip against the counter. "How about you? Do you enjoy your work?"

"I do." His hands warmed in the soapy water as he peered through the foggy window. "I like teaching the children. And, since I don't have responsibility for a family, my income is sufficient." He thought about this situation off and on. If he were fortunate enough to get married, he'd need to begin tutoring or doing something in addition to teaching to support a family.

Turning away from the counter, she stacked the platter with another. "Could you put these up there? I have to use a footstool when I need those." She nodded to the top shelf. "So, do you like living in Pennsylvania?"

Careful, watch what you say. "I like where I live. Do you?"

A sudsy cloth in hand, Sarah began wiping the center counter down. "I'm smitten with Bentonsport. It sounds odd, but here, it felt like I was coming home. Unless something dramatic happens, I'll be here the rest of my life."

It was rather sad that a beautiful unmarried woman lived in a town with only a few dozen people. Only through chance, or through grace, would she ever find a man who could love this place enough to stay.

"So, you ready to make some kringles?"

"Just show me what to do."

THEY FINISHED THE FIRST ROUND OF BAKING.

"Do you ever get tired of doing dishes?" Thomas asked as he headed to the sink with another armload.

"Do you ever get tired of grading papers?" She winked.

He playfully flung a cluster of bubbles from the dishwater toward her cheek.

Sarah wiped her face, grinned, and scooped up the bottle with a handle and sprayed him.

"Oh, a weapon?" Grinning, moving closer, he held out his hand. "Let me have it."

"Uh-uh."

The bottle behind her, she stepped back.

Two more steps brought him to her. "I am not about to let you win a water fight."

"You started this." She scooted around the counter toward the back door.

"We aren't even yet." His outstretched hand nearly touched her.

Sarah reached for the doorknob behind her, opened the door, and sprinted. She ran around a large tank with rounded ends. Bending down, he scooped up a handful of snow and packed it into a ball. Just as she raised her head to find out what he was up to, he hurled the snowball at the side of her head. She dodged it, and it grazed her hair. An intense snow fight ensued.

"What is that thing you are hiding behind?"

"You are such a city boy!" Sarah shouted from the oval cylinder's other side. "It's a propane tank."

What 'propane' was, he had no idea, but his question distracted her. So, he sneaked around to her side of the tank. Just as she stood to hurl another snowball, he grabbed her.

She squealed as he seized her snowball and rubbed it against her hair for the final victory.

"Unfair," she said, struggling but then laughing. When he let her go, she brushed the snow from her hair and retrieved the plant mister.

"Your weapon, please, madam."

She handed it to him. "I concede ... for now."

Chapter Ten

J ust after six, Thomas returned to the inn to change into Bill's work clothes. He wished they could stay dressed in the period attire—she looking so beautiful, he feeling much more like himself. Dressed like this, he almost could believe he was back in his Bentonsport. But the outfit would seem out of place to his hosts.

Surprising how clothing had become more casual, not more elegant. Even more surprising how the women felt comfortable appearing like men. He preferred the way women dressed in his town—with beauty, modesty, and elegance.

He arrived at Sarah's home, wearing his heavy topcoat and scarf. After knocking at the door, he heard the now-familiar "Come in ... it's open," this time from the top of the stairs. In the hallway, he stomped his boots on the mat.

"I'm nearly ready," she called down.

Loosening his scarf, he waited to see the modern pixie-like Sarah with shorter hair and men's pants.

Instead, she came down wearing a short black suede skirt, a white beaded sweater, black stockings, and black pumps.

His neck warming, he lowered his gaze. Never had he seen a woman's legs—at least not to such a degree.

"Is something wrong? "

"Um, no." He couldn't look up. He further loosened his scarf as the warmth of his neck tingled up his cheeks. "I just was thinking you might be ... cold."

Sarah laughed as she opened the closet. "That's why I'm getting a coat."

Helping her on with the ankle-length coat, he was relieved he no longer needed to divert his eyes. When she faced him, a new softness added light to her penetrating eyes. Could it be she was developing a fondness for him? His heart beat hard.

As she picked up the bottle on the hall bench, he wiped his palms against his coat. Might he have misinterpreted what he saw in her glance?

"I'm starving," she said.

"Me too."

They strolled next door. Thomas had to remind himself Virginia Carrington would not be answering his knock. He tapped three times.

Caroline answered, wearing an apron that revealed her growing bulge. "Well, come on in." She took their outer garments. "Bill's in the family room, building up the fire. Why don't you join him while I get us something to drink? I have hot punch on the stove."

"Sounds great." Sarah handed her the bottle.

"Sparkling juice." Caroline turned it over in her hands, then started toward the kitchen. "Just perfect."

Down the hall, tables, overstuffed chairs, and couches divided a large room into smaller areas. Glass panes, like a greenhouse, formed the entire back wall. Thomas surveyed the room, impressed by what had been done to the old Carrington place.

Bill knelt before the fireplace, repositioning the logs. When Sarah entered the room, he stood and gave her a quick hug. He didn't even seem to notice the length of her skirt.

"Welcome, Thomas, make yourself at home." Bill firmly shook his hand. "I'm just finishing tending this fire."

Sarah gestured to the couch, so Thomas sat beside her. The warm light cast a golden glow on her skin. She was so pretty.

I'm leaving here in seven days. He had to get rid of these thoughts. They led straight to sadness. He couldn't make time stand still, even if he wanted to. And he wasn't at all sure that he did.

Setting the poker next to the fireplace, Bill stood again. "So, you two have been baking all day, I hear."

"Thomas was a tremendous help. We entertained our visitors and still managed to make bread and kringles for tomorrow."

And wash a million dishes.

"Okay—virgin or non-virgin punch?" Caroline asked as she entered the room.

Huh? What did she mean?

She flashed a playful wink. "Doctor's orders—no alcohol while I'm preggers."

Preggers? The only place he could imagine saying the word *virgin* was in church, and even there, the term made him feel awkward. But *preggers*—never. Not even in all-male company.

Bill and Sarah asked for virgin punch. Thomas nodded in agreement. Caroline soon returned with four steaming mugs.

Thomas sipped the warm drink. This world was a different place. He shifted, the colored lights glowing on the Christmas tree mesmerizing him.

The constant light from the ceiling fixtures and lamps was a nice improvement, especially on long winter nights. And the ease with which light was available: a flick of a switch, a turn of a knob, a pull of a chain—amazing.

"Caroline," Sarah said, "your flowers are gorgeous."

Leafy plants heavy with bloom tucked in the greens on the mantle. Somehow, in this era, plants bloomed in winter. Perhaps it was all this light?

"After the holidays, I'm going to get spring fever," she continued. "Happens to me every year."

"I can't wait for the seed catalogs to start coming in the mail."

Wistfulness edged Caroline's voice as she warmed her hands on the mug. "That's when I start gardening in my head, picturing what I'm going to plant where."

Now, *this* was familiar. Just after the new year, his parents started making plans for the spring garden as if talking about warmer weather ushered it in sooner.

Stretching an arm past her middle, Caroline set her mug on the table. "You should return for a visit in the spring. Not that winter isn't beautiful here. But during the cold months, we all retreat inside, working on crafts and planning for the next year. The snowbirds head south and shut down their homes, which makes this place even more like a ghost town."

Caroline paused and pushed a strand of hair behind her ear. "But come spring, we open the doors and let the warm breezes blow through. The bulbs start to bloom, and the trees turn a gorgeous lime green. Next, the stores all open, and tourists start flocking in. It's a different place."

In Thomas's Bentonsport, spring meant children becoming restless at school, anxious to ride their scooters, fly kites, and play ball. Women cleaning, airing linens, dusting and sweeping, and beating carpets. Men and women sitting on benches in front of stores, enjoying the gentle breezes, and exchanging the latest news. And farmers getting fields ready, tending to livestock and their new broods.

Bill cleared his throat. "Perhaps we should let Thomas complete his first visit before planning his next stay."

They all chuckled.

"I'm certain it's lovely," Thomas said.

"So, on the topic of plans ..." Mug back in hand, Caroline sipped her punch. "What would you like to do this weekend, Thomas?"

He rested his mug on a coaster. "I thought I'd go look at the stores in the morning. I'd like to pick up a few last-minute gifts. I also would like to attend church on Sunday. What time does the service start?"

"There's only one functioning church in Bentonsport," Sarah said. "It's the old Presbyterian one up on the hill. Service begins at nine."

"Do you all go?"

"Sarah does," Caroline answered. "Bill and I attend a Catholic church in Houghton. It's a bit of a drive, but Bill's grandparents and all of his family and friends go there, so it feels like home."

The Catholic church in his Houghton was a large structure with two towers standing high above the town. Was it the same?

"Oh, and Sunday afternoon, we're holding our annual Bentonsport Christmas get-together." She rose to stir the fire. "Did Lani tell you about it?"

"I haven't been around the inn much lately."

She jabbed the logs with the poker. "Every year, on the last weekend before the stores close for winter, the merchants and residents meet at the inn and share a potluck. Since you've been a part of our community, you should come enjoy the festivities."

Caroline was amazing. From one activity to another, she would make sure his visit was a pleasant one. "Sounds like fun."

"By the time the stores open in the spring, the baby will be here." Sarah fluffed a pillow and tucked it behind Caroline's back as she sat down.

"I hope so. Dr. Ahern says my due date is April twentieth, which is about two weeks after the stores open." Caroline sighed. "That seems so far away."

Amazing this ease of the women's conversation in mixed company. They didn't seem to mind the men in the room—even one who was practically a stranger.

"So, what are your plans, Sarah?"

"I need to pick up a few more baking goods. I'm always needing more baking powder, cinnamon, cloves. I go through a lot of spices this time of year. And I have to get some more salt. I don't want anyone falling in this weather, and my walks get slick."

"If you want help clearing them, just let me know," Thomas offered.

"Oh, thanks." She nodded. "I will."

"It is wonderful to have a man around the house," Caroline said, repositioning her pillow.

Bill cleared his throat and shot Caroline a sharp glance. "With that big snow coming in on Monday and lasting through Wednesday, everyone's going to be finishing up some shopping this weekend." He winked at Thomas. "You'll have a chance to see the old town hopping."

This town? Hopping? He couldn't imagine it.

"Yes." Sarah crossed her legs and sipped her punch. "I guess I'd better go to Keosauqua first thing tomorrow and stock up before there's nothing left." She plunked her mug down. "I'm never prepared for these storms. Last year, when we got eighteen inches of snow in one day, I couldn't find a single battery for my flashlight."

Bill laughed. "Yeah, you ended up camping out over here until the power came back on. That old stove downstairs does a pretty good job of heating the house in a pinch. We installed a firebox upstairs, but it takes electricity to power the blower. So, it's useless when the lines are down."

Electricity must have something to do with quick light and heat. Easy to see how their lives would change without it. More like his world.

"We're getting soft." Bill stretched one arm across the back of his couch, cupping his hand on his wife's shoulder while unfolding his legs and scooting toward her. "People who lived in our homes a hundred and fifty years ago would laugh at our dependence on electricity."

Laugh, no. More like envy.

Caroline stood. "I'm starving."

"Amen," Sarah agreed.

As they ate, Bill discussed the work he had to complete before the week's end to ship his orders in time for the holidays. Sarah and Caroline listed everything they needed to finish.

If he were back home in Pennsylvania, he'd be helping his

father chop wood, enjoying playing endless card games at the dining room table, with conversation as the real entertainment.

Caroline dropped her napkin on her plate. "And don't think we've left you out, Thomas. I lined up a special project for you to help with on Monday, if you're game. Richard Tarrant is putting together a museum on historic Bentonsport. He's leased the Greef Building's upper floor to display his artifacts—photos, pottery, books, postcards—nearly his entire collection. I promised I'd ask if you'd like to help."

He enjoyed Richard's company. He wiped his mouth and folded his napkin on his plate as well. "I'd love to."

"You'll need to paint the upstairs." Bill crumpled his napkin. "Last time I was up there, the place was a mess, full of cobwebs and peeling paint."

"Bill has several coveralls hanging by the back door," Caroline added. "Why don't you take one with you before you leave tonight? Then you won't have to worry about soiling your clothes."

Coveralls? Must be some type of overalls. "I appreciate that."

"Who's ready for dessert?" Caroline stood. "I baked an apple crisp today, and we can top it with vanilla ice cream."

"Yum." Sarah helped Caroline clear the table.

The food never stopped here. It seemed more like Thanksgiving than a normal meal.

Bill leaned across the table. "You don't need to let Caroline plan your whole time off, you know. If you want to kick back for a while, get some rest, read a book, don't let her schedule all your days."

"No, I appreciate it." Thomas sipped his crisp juice. "She's done a much better job planning my vacation than I could have. And I do relax in the evenings. Truth to tell, it would be depressing to sit around the inn all day, and it's too cold to stay outside long."

"Well, Caroline can get carried away. I mean, her heart's in the right place, but she tends to look ahead and plan backward."

The men laughed.

Bill lit his pipe, and Thomas stared into his glass. How would Caroline plan if she had to go backward more than a hundred years?

The women entered, each carrying two dessert bowls. The warm apple crisp paired nicely with the vanilla ice cream. Tart and sweet. Warm and cold.

"This is heavenly," Sarah said. "The perfect winter dessert."

The gentle click of spoons against china accompanied their silence. Then, finished, Caroline stretched and stifled a yawn.

"We all have a big day tomorrow." Sarah stood and picked up her bowl. "Let me help you clean up."

"No, there isn't much to do, really." Caroline took the bowl from her hand. "Why not stay a bit and play a game or two? Bill and I can finish the dishes later."

The games Thomas played may have become obsolete. Sarah glanced at him, one brow raised.

He swallowed hard. "What games do you like?"

"Oh, hearts, gin rummy, canasta ..."

"Gin," he said, recognizing at least one of the games.

Bill left and returned with a deck of cards. Sarah divided the cards, handing half of them to Bill. Caroline reentered with a teapot, sugar, and creamer on a tray.

When Caroline sat, Bill handed her the deck, and she asked Thomas to cut the cards.

As Sarah sorted through her cards, Bill drew the first one and studied it. Then Sarah sat back in her chair, keeping her cards close to her chest. Thomas folded his cards in a neat pile and leaned forward to keep track of the cards played.

"Ah, an intense player," Sarah ribbed and gave his shoulder a playful shake. "Don't trust him," she said. "He seems like the quiet type, but he's competitive in battle—especially those pertaining to water and snow."

"Only those I don't start." He winked at her.

"What?" Caroline asked.

She was answered only with smiles. The conversation and game continued.

After five rounds, he fanned his hand across the table. "Gin."

Sarah tossed her cards onto the discard pile. "I wasn't even close."

After six rounds, Thomas said gin again and displayed his hand. Caroline and Bill threw in their cards. Sarah thumped Thomas with hers before tossing them on the pile.

"We need to go." She sighed.

Stretching his arms in front of him, Thomas stood while Caroline retrieved their coats and Thomas's scarf. It had been such an enjoyable evening.

Bill shook his hand while the two women hugged each other. If Bill lived in Thomas's world, Thomas would've liked to get to know him better.

Thomas retrieved the coveralls, and he and Sarah stepped out together into the brisk night.

"Look up." Her breath hung white in the cold air. "The stars are amazing."

They didn't shine quite as brightly here as in his Bentonsport, probably due to the light from the windows. But the sky was still beautiful.

They strolled side by side. How many times had he walked down this street, on his way to the academy, wishing he had a woman at his side? Now, he walked beside a beautiful woman hundred years too late.

At her back doorstep, he took her hand. "Thank you for a wonderful day. For the baking and the snow fight. And a lovely evening. You and Caroline have taken what could have been a trip full of loneliness and dreariness and filled it with experiences and friendship." He kissed her hand and then walked away.

Chapter Eleven

Thomas entered the kitchen as Lani flipped flapjacks at the stove.

"Well, this getting up early is becoming a habit with you."

"You're to blame," he teased as he took his seat. "One whiff of breakfast sent me rushing to get dressed and downstairs."

The other guest was in the chair across from Thomas, reading a newspaper. Finally, they met.

"So, how is the eagle watching going?" Lani said. "This is Steve Wright. Steve—Thomas Barton. Steve is quite the eagle watcher."

He doubled up his paper and shook Thomas's hand. "Good to meet you." Steve turned to Lani, "I saw another six yesterday. Not nearly as many as you can see downstream around the big dam at Keokuk. But I prefer this more natural setting. It sounds like it's a good thing I came this weekend, though. The forecast's calling for quite a snowstorm Monday night. The eagles don't come out in that kind of weather."

"Steve's decided to head out early," Lani chimed in from the stove. "He's leaving tomorrow before the bad weather hits. Are you likely to do the same?"

"No." Thomas folded his arms across his chest and leaned back in his chair. "You'll have my company, if it is agreeable with you, until early Saturday morning."

"Well, I'm thankful you're staying." She filled his coffee cup to the brim. "These storms can cause quite a ruckus, and being here by myself, I appreciate having a man in the house who's handy. You are handy, right?"

"It all depends on what I need to be handy with. But I can get us through a storm. I've survived them so far." Thomas picked up the robin's-egg blue pitcher from the table and stirred cream into his coffee. Deliciously strong, it was almost too hot to drink.

Lani brought them two plates stacked high with pancakes. "I suppose you have. Pennsylvania is always gray and raining or snowing, something to do with being between the mountains and the ocean, right?"

"Mmm-hmm," Thomas replied. "The weather is usually mild, but when it snows, we can get feet, not inches, of snow. Still, Iowa weather isn't terribly different, in most respects."

"Ah." Lani slapped her hands on her ample hips. "An expert on Iowa weather as well now?"

"Well, at least that's what I have heard."

After the men finished breakfast, Steve excused himself and went upstairs. Thomas said goodbye to Lani and stepped outside. As he walked down Main Street, he noticed the town was strangely busy. Vehicles lined the street on both sides, and people were carrying packages.

He entered the Greef Building. Two wooden sleds and one old toboggan were placed against a wall. Did children still use them, or had they become decorative items from the past?

Further down the room, past the tables displaying children's toys, were the cases the Greef family had displayed food items in. They contained jewelry and items such as pipes, logbooks, shaving cups, and ladies' hair ornaments. Thomas bent over it, wondering if anything would be familiar.

"May I help you?"

Straightening, he smiled and nodded to a woman who appeared to be in her early fifties, her graying hair pulled up in a bun. Delicate red flowers peppered the gray skirt flowing to her ankles, and she'd buttoned her long-sleeved, high-collared white shirt to the collar. In those garments from his time, she could have been one of his students' grandmothers.

"I'm just admiring the items you have for sale." He swept his right hand toward the case. "Quite a collection."

"Oh, they aren't mine." She looped a stray piece of hair behind her ear. "I just work here. We rent space to antique dealers." Pointing, she moved closer to the case. "If you notice, we have items from many periods, starting from the 1850s all the way through the 1960s, if you can call those antiques."

Thomas swallowed hard. The 1960s items were antiques? He would be classified as ancient. He shook off the thought. "Do you have any items from early Bentonsport?"

"I doubt it. Anytime we get anything in here from early Bentonsport, we let Richard Tarrant know. We tend to favor him because he's developing a museum. Have you heard about it?"

"Caroline asked if I would help Richard get the room ready for his display cases."

"Oh?" She folded her hands just below her waist. "So, you're a friend of Caroline and Bill."

"Well, Caroline offered to help when I arrived with little planned to occupy my time." *Actually, no plans at all.*

"No surprise. Caroline is a people person, always makes everyone feel welcomed and at home. With her help, you are likely in for a wonderful stay. Please let me know if I can help you in any way."

As she turned to assist another customer, Thomas surveyed the shelves and then crossed to the back of the store where books lined the wall.

Not recognizing any of the titles, he scanned the spines, pausing at a familiar one, its cloth cover flaking and crinkled. He eased it, a book of Christmas hymns, off the shelf and opened the crackly cover—Thomas Barton 1857.

His face warmed and his heart raced. This was his book. He'd taken it to the Christmas sing-along at the Presbyterian Church just a week—just a ... time—ago. A yellow sticker listed its price at one dollar. Compelled to purchase it, he wondered if he could take it back with him. How strange that thought was! The book was already back there, waiting for his return. But, for some reason, he couldn't bear the thought of his book sitting on the shelf, collecting dust.

As he reviewed the other titles, his eye caught something familiar. On the second shelf, he found a black book with a leather binding, a royal blue bookmark draped over the cover—Pastor Lockhardt's Bible.

His heart sank. Why would something as precious as a man's Bible end up on a shelf in a store where any person could pick it up? And it was for sale for how much? He opened the front cover. Two dollars. He'd give it as a gift to one of his new friends. At least it would be in good hands.

Holding the two books, he scrutinized the shelves for additional treasures. Finding no other books he recognized, he selected a book of children's stories and nursery rhymes with carefully etched illustrations. It would be a good gift for Caroline. He didn't know who he would give the Bible to, but he'd give the book of hymns, and perhaps one or two other gifts, to Sarah—of course, he would change its inscription.

After purchasing his books, he stepped outside. The wind, blowing in short, sharp gusts, fought his closing the door. It took him three tries. He turned up his collar. What a day for shopping.

He sprinted to the next store—a one-room shop selling jewelry made with semiprecious stones. On a stool in one corner, a gentleman sat behind a large table. The man greeted Thomas before refocusing on untangling a length of chain. A couple at the store's far end scrutinized a display of rings.

Having little interest in jewelry, Thomas walked through the room so as not to be rude, glancing at the various gems and settings. Preparing to exit, he paused by a display of glass and pewter items, and discovered a pewter pipe holder, a particularly fitting gift for Bill. He selected some Christmas ornaments to complete Caroline's gift and purchased a long-stemmed rose, hand-forged by the blacksmith, for Lani. With most of his purchases completed, he'd visit Sarah before returning to the inn for supper.

The wind had died down. Several cars were parked along her street. As a customer was leaving, Thomas didn't bother knocking. He wiped his feet on the mat and entered her warm kitchen.

Sarah placed baked goods in paper bags as she rang up each purchase for four other customers. She wished them a merry Christmas as they left the store.

"Whew." She smiled and straightened rows of baked goodies.

How lovely she was! "I finished my shopping this morning."

"Well, it looks like you were successful." She gestured toward his bags.

"How about you? Are you nearly done?" He slid into a seat at the counter.

"Close. After the stores close, I am going to run to Keosauqua to pick up the baskets to complete my gifts. And tonight, I'll discipline myself to finish putting together my presents. Then I'm done. Would you like some coffee?"

"I'd love some if you have it made."

"Right here." As she lifted two mugs out of the cupboard, the bells on the door jingled.

Lani wiped her feet and shut the door. "Not as cold as it was earlier, but still not gardening weather."

"Hey, Lani," Sarah added a third mug. "What are you up to today?"

Lani sank onto the seat next to Thomas and stirred cream into her coffee. "This is just what I needed." She took a long sip. "I thought I'd run over here for some thick sliced bread. I am planning to make Thomas French toast for breakfast one of these days since he's decided to rise with the sun and have breakfast."

He just shook his head, stirring his coffee. Of all the people he'd met in Bentonsport, Lani was one of his favorites. He had never met a woman who could be so direct and, at the same time, lovable.

"And I want a package of your rolls if you have any left. Richard brought by some of the turkey he cooked in his smoker, so I'm going to serve Thomas turkey with rolls for dinner. Sound good, Thomas?"

He nodded. Indeed. He couldn't remember the last time he'd had smoked turkey.

"Over there, on the top shelf, Lani," Sarah gestured above Lani's head to the display. "I have two packages left. Thomas, would you get one down?"

"I'll take both and freeze one, so I have an extra on hand." When Thomas handed them to her, Lani thanked him and placed them to her left on the counter. "Say, why don't you join us for dinner tonight, Sarah? I have plenty of food. Richard brought by enough turkey to feed an army. We can eat and then join the carolers."

"Carolers?" Sarah inclined her head and wrinkled her brows.

"Richard thought up the idea this morning. With the bad weather coming so early in the week, he's getting a group together tonight to go caroling for the shut-ins and then on to his house afterward for hot chocolate. You'll have to eat anyway, Sarah, so how about joining Thomas and me for dinner? And you, Mr. Thomas, should join us for caroling. We could use another strong male voice."

"Well ..." He saluted with his coffee cup. "I'm a male voice, if nothing else."

"Sounds like fun." Sarah brought cookie trays to the island and set biscuit tins next to them. "Will I have time to run to Keo before we eat?"

"Sure." Lani finished her coffee. "Richard wants everyone to meet at the inn at seven, so we could eat as late as six fifteen and still have plenty of time. I'll see you both then." She paid for her goods and headed out, the bells jingling as she shut the door behind her.

Alone with Sarah once again, Thomas rested against the counter. "Can I help you do anything? I got used to standing on that side of the counter, not just sitting here watching."

"No, I just have some packaging to do. Later tonight, I'll need to bake a bit more." Surveying the store, she said, "Things moved off the shelves this morning, thanks to the bleak forecast."

"What do you do with the products that don't sell?"

She refilled his cup. "I take some to people around town who can't afford to buy treats. I freeze some for myself for later, and if I have a fair number left, I sell them at the grocery stores in Keosauqua and Bonaparte as day-old products at a reduced price."

The bells jingled again, and Richard Tarrant entered, removed his gloves, and stomped his feet.

"Sarah, dear," he bellowed, "and, say there, Thomas, good to see you. Good to see both of you." He claimed a seat next to Thomas, rubbing his large hands together. "I came for two purposes. First, I want to invite you to join a group of carolers I've put together, impromptu."

Sarah got down a mug for him. "Lani was here not more than five minutes ago and invited us." She filled a red coffee mug to the brim and slid it over.

"Well." Exhaling, Richard lifted the mug for a long drink. "I don't have the energy to do everything you young people are doing to rebuild this village. But I am going to help as much as I can. To be honest, there was a time when I thought I'd die alone in a ghost town."

Thomas stretched his hands and then rubbed his palms on his thighs. He swallowed back his thoughts that this town was not far from a ghost town. But he admired Richard's optimism.

Richard drummed his fingertips on the countertop. "And I

need to purchase refreshments for tonight—you know, cookies, whatever you have available."

"Let's see, I have two packages of iced cookies I just finished decorating. I have three kringles and several loaves of bread. That's about it. I'm packaging these cookies up for a customer who is picking them up tomorrow."

"I'll have your cookies and kringles. If we don't eat them all, Thomas and I can nibble away on them while we start at the museum on Monday. Are we still on, Thomas? I was just relying on what Caroline said."

"I plan on helping you. Caroline even provided work clothes for painting."

"I'll provide lunch," Richard added. "Have you ever had an Iowa tenderloin sandwich?"

"Noooo?" Thomas straightened in his chair, intrigued and somewhat repulsed. He had never heard of such a thing.

"Well, you and I will have the best tenderloin sandwiches in this corner of the state. Remember the old mill restaurant I drove you past in Bonaparte? They're served right there, with chips and a drink. It's quite a meal."

"You'll be full for the rest of the day, trust me." Sarah braced her elbows on the counter and planted her chin in her hands. "When Caroline and I split one of those, we're both full."

The bells on the door rang again, and six customers clattered in. "Nice in here," one of the women said as they tucked gloves in their pockets and unbuttoned their coats.

"I'd best be going, Sarah." Richard pushed back from the counter after drumming his hands on it one more time. "If you could just tally these things up."

"And I should head back to the inn." Thomas rose and put on his coat.

While Richard paid for his baked goods, Sarah placed them in two large sacks, telling the other customers she'd be right with them.

"I'll see you tonight." Thomas tipped his hat and left.

Chapter Twelve

Sarah turned the Open sign around on her front door and went upstairs to change clothes before leaving for Keosauqua. Having forgotten to ask if the caroling was in period-style clothing, she phoned the inn.

"Bentonsport Inn." Lani sounded out of breath.

"Lani, sorry to bother you, but I forgot—is this period dress for tonight's caroling, or should I wear warm pants and a sweater?"

"You know, Richard never did say. But knowing him, he'd be tickled if we showed up in our period outfits. Or at least period coats. But, since he said nothing, I'm sure there will be a variety of dress. So that's a long way of saying either way is fine."

Sarah changed into jeans and a sweatshirt for her shopping. She hung a period-appropriate, green-and-red striped woolen skirt on a hook attached to the back of her bedroom door. Then she grabbed her purse.

The air was becoming bitter. She warmed up her truck, thinking of gifts and what food she needed to buy to get through the next few days. And into those thoughts, one thing kept intruding: Thomas.

Something *was* unusual about him—his preference for

dressing in period clothes, his carrying old money and arriving with no plans and nothing to do. Many things about him appealed to her—his good looks and manners, his willingness to help and ease of conversation, his intelligence and snappy sense of humor. He was leaving after Friday, but Pennsylvania wasn't too far away. Right?

She drove slowly, keeping an eye out for deer. The sun had set, leaving only a strip of orange light across the horizon. Strange, he seemed attracted to her and appeared to enjoy her company, but he gave the impression that, after Friday, he intended not just to leave but to never return.

It reminded her of her brief teenage romances at summer camps. Going in, everyone knew the relationships would be short-lived, lasting only until the final day of camp. Then everyone would gather up their gear, give hugs, and promise to write, knowing no one would.

She tightened her clenched grip on the steering wheel, both angry and sad. Angry that, at her age, she should be involved in anything even remotely like a summer teenage romance. And sad that she felt so sure this wouldn't last.

Why was she such a failure with men? Those who were attracted to her were never a good match, and those she liked were not eligible. She was attracted to Thomas, and he seemed attracted to her. And they were both eligible. But the feeling of temporary remained as solid as his gentlemanly ways. She sighed. What would make him want to stay in touch or, even possibly, return?

She parked in front of the corner drugstore. Christmas carols playing from loudspeakers hanging on the streetlamps lifted her mood.

Inside, she slipped past the line stretching back into the first aisle and headed to the household section, then selected batteries for her radios and flashlights. She stacked together twenty deep wicker baskets, ten per group, planning to use them to hold her Christmas breads and jellies. She tucked the batteries in one of the top baskets, then stepped into the checkout line. Near the cashier's table, brightly wrapped packages sat on a table offering last-minute gifts.

Next year, would she have a godson or a goddaughter to shop for? The line edged forward. Now she was just a few shoppers away from the checkout person—Mrs. Baxter. An elegant petite woman with a thick English accent, Mrs. Baxter had married a Keosauqua native who was stationed overseas and had returned with him when he elected not to re-up.

Alongside the gift table now, she set down her baskets to inspect the remaining music boxes, two with glass lids and two with inlaid wooden lids. The first was of a church with a tall spire, much like the one she attended in Bentonsport. When she lifted the lid, it played "Angels We Have Heard on High." The second box depicted a shepherd boy looking up at a dazzling star. Not surprisingly, it played "The Little Drummer Boy."

The person in front of her finished checking out. No one stood in line behind her, so one of the young clerks flipped the Open sign on the door to Closed and began tidying the store.

Sarah spread out her items on the counter.

"Say, I heard some good news about you this week from Mona Story." Mrs. Baxter's still-thick English accent added lilt to her words.

Sarah, searching for her credit card, replied, "Oh yes. Mrs. Story came to my place with the nursing home group."

"A few of the residents were in here during their outing. She shared your news as soon as she got to the cash register. And I was delighted to learn of it, Sarah, just so delighted."

"Um, news?" Sarah hesitated, then took out her credit card, inserted it, and tapped OK. "Which piece of news would that be?"

"Why, your new beau, of course. What news? My word." The woman grinned. "She said he is quite nice looking and handy in the kitchen, to boot."

"Oh." Sarah shook her head. "She's talking about Thomas,

and he is no beau. He's a visitor to Bentonsport, and he'll be leaving early Saturday. Caroline and I wanted to make his stay more memorable, with all the stores being closed, so we planned his days working with each of us. That day was his day with me."

Mrs. Baxter, not looking at Sarah, stacked her items in two bags. "Mona said the two of you made quite a pair, a fine-looking couple. Everyone in the room thought him quite taken with you."

Her cheeks heated under the woman's sudden scrutiny. Sarah turned her attention to her purse, replacing her credit card in her wallet and clicking it shut.

"You know, Sarah, I'll tell you something I haven't discussed in years." Mrs. Baxter leaned forward, her elbows on the counter, her voice lowered so Sarah, too, had to lean forward.

"When I was a young woman, even younger than you, there weren't any local boys I had taken a fancy to. But, when I was about eighteen, several American soldiers arrived in my village, who had been stationed in Germany. They were there to take part in some short-term training drills offered at a base just outside our town. My, I was glad to see them!"

She paused, waiting for a young sales clerk to walk by. "I knew those young men wouldn't be staying in our town long. There was this one soldier, a tall, blond-haired American I was interested in. He came to one of our dances, and he and I talked and danced. And we just seemed like, well, like an item. We spent a few days together when he was off duty. But after two weeks, he had to return to his base in Germany."

The lights in the back of the store dimmed. Emma Baxter stopped her story. "Oh, Sarah, let's finish up here before we're talking in the dark. I'll finish my story on the way to the car."

Sam Simpson, the pharmacist, called from the back of the store, "Are you ready to call it a day, Emma?"

"Nearly so." She placed the receipt in one of the bags and handed both to Sarah. Emma took off her blue smock, folded it in half, and laid it on a shelf under the counter. Then, picking up her purse, coat, scarf, and gloves, she called out, "Have a good rest of the weekend, everyone."

Then, with her arm around Sarah, they exited the store.

The air was damp and cold. Emma tugged on her coat and gloves and wrapped the scarf around her neck. She gestured toward the bench.

"We'll talk here." She took a seat. "Harry was to be transferred. And what were we to each other? We had only known each other for two weeks. But what a glorious two weeks it had been."

Oh, how she understood how the young Emma must have felt!

"My older sister could see I was interested in this young man, and on the day before he was scheduled to depart, she gave me a piece of invaluable advice. She said, 'Emma, don't let that boy leave without taking some mementos to remind him of your time together. If he is as interested as he seems, these items will become treasures. He'll think of you and the good times when he sees them. Make them small items, something easy to carry. Emma, use your head.'

"Well, I thought long and hard to come up with just the right thing. I was young, and money was short, so I couldn't afford to buy him a watch or a ring, something expensive and elegant. But then I thought of just the right parting gift. Harry had taken up smoking in the military. The climate in Britain is quite damp and often rainy, drizzly, you know, and Harry complained that his 'smokes,' as he called them, were getting damp."

She paused and tucked her scarf closer to her neck. "So, I walked down to the local store and bought a leather case to hold his cigarettes. I brought it home and, before wrapping it, tucked several personal items in the case's side pocket, where the matches were to go. I slipped in the dance card from our first dance, a photo of myself, and a calling card with my name and address.

"We had one last, glorious day together, and then Harry left." She patted Sarah's hand. "But the gift worked like a charm.

Within two weeks, he wrote me a nice long letter and sent his photo in the envelope. I wrote back, and we corresponded for more than two years. When his military commitment was over, he made one stop back in my hometown before returning to America. That was to propose. I came over here for my wedding."

She grasped Sarah's hand between her two gloved ones. "Sarah, too many people let wonderful opportunities pass them by simply because they seem impossible or risky. I could have let Harry go back to Germany and seen it as a passing moment. But, with prodding from my sister, I followed my dream and have had a wonderful life."

Sarah squeezed her friend's hand. "Emma, I hardly know this man. He's only been in Bentonsport since Tuesday. But I'll tell you—and please say nothing to anyone about this, promise me?"

The little woman's chin tipped up, her eyes sparkling. "I never share what I'm specifically told not to."

Sarah's heart beat hard, and her throat closed slightly. "I don't know how to describe it. I enjoy being with him, you know? I look forward to his visits, and when we're together, we just, well, 'click.' But there just isn't enough time left to even know if this could work."

"Nonsense." Emma shook her head so hard her scarf loosened. "There's only a limited time if you want it that way or if you stop breathing. Heavens, in this day and age, you're seconds away by phone or email and hours apart by plane. It isn't as though your friend is going to fall off the face of the earth."

She gave Sarah a motherly smile. "Just take my advice, Sarah, or I should say my sister's advice. Don't let him leave without taking something with him that will remind him of you, a token, a memento. Something he can hold and remember you by. And, for heaven's sake, make sure he has your email address, phone number, and home address. If it's meant to be, then it will be."

With that, Emma rose and gave Sarah a quick hug. "Enjoy these few days with your friend, dear. Even if the relationship doesn't last, you're making memories you will always treasure."

Sarah stood and hugged back tight, then returned to her truck. She glanced at her watch. Forty-five minutes past five. Just fifteen minutes until the grocery store closed and thirty minutes until dinner at the inn.

Her conversation with Emma—and her new goal of getting a gift for Thomas to help him remember their time together—absorbed her thoughts. But ... what? She slowed as two deer crossed in front of her truck. Frustrated, she put aside the problem. No wonder Caroline believed she'd become an old maid.

Chapter Thirteen

Thomas entered the kitchen as Lani clattered at the stove, stirring gravy, checking the rolls, and warming turkey in the oven. The table, set with a bright red tablecloth, white china plates, and water glasses rimmed in gold, seemed to match his period attire. Happy and rested, he stepped into the hallway to adjust his black tie in the mirror. "Smells good."

"Thank Richard and Sarah," Lani called out. "I only take credit for the trimmings."

Thomas removed his coat from the hall tree. "I thought someone should walk Sarah over for the meal."

"Thomas." Lani smiled over her shoulder, her spoon dripping gravy on the stovetop. "After all these years, Sarah knows the way."

"I'm not afraid of her getting lost. But it wouldn't be right for her to walk here unaccompanied."

When she shrugged, he went out the front door and walked up the brick sidewalk past Greef Store. Frigid air chilled the abandoned streets. The river churning between the pieces of floating ice offered the night's only sound. As he turned the corner, a figure in a long flowing skirt approached.

"Hark, who goes there?" Sarah called out in a cheery voice.

"The same stranger who has walked these barren streets now these many nights," he answered, "seeking a damsel in distress, in need of a chaperon to see her safely to her destination."

He met up with her, and they stood face to face. Then he offered his arm, which she accepted with a curtsy.

"I'm sorry I'm running a few minutes late," she said as they began their stroll. "I was talking with an old friend, and time just got away from me."

"You're right on time. Lani was just finishing up at the stove when I left. Dinner will be ready when we arrive."

As they approached the inn, Lani puttered beyond the window, lighting candles. Inside, they wiped their feet on the mat. Thomas helped Sarah with her coat. What a pleasure it would be to take her, dressed just as she was, back to Bentonsport and introduce her to the town. He grinned. She'd cause quite the stir with the townswomen determined to find out everything they could.

"Come, come eat," Lani urged, "before everything here gets cold and I have to put it back in the oven."

Thomas pulled out Sarah's chair and, after seating her, seated Lani, then himself. Bowls of smoked turkey, whipped potatoes, gravy, green beans, and rolls steamed from the center of the table as Thomas bowed his head and said grace.

Lani passed the bowls to her guests.

"This smells heavenly, Lani," Sarah gushed. "Almost like Thanksgiving."

"Well, thank Richard for the turkey and yourself for the rolls. All I did was whip up potatoes and gravy and heat green beans."

"All the same," Sarah said, scooping potatoes on her plate, "there is an art to putting together a meal. And the potatoes and gravy are such a treat." Turning to Thomas, she added, "This is the only time of year when we natives get to sample Lani's good cooking. I keep telling her she should open a restaurant here."

"Who knows, maybe when I retire from the inn. Mr. and Mrs. Moss, the owners here, have been too nice for me to just walk out the door. Maybe in a few years, when I have more money set aside, I'll try opening a little place just for fun. But, for now, I'm content. The life I have here is more than I thought I'd ever have when I arrived in Bentonsport."

Thomas cut into his turkey, the succulent scent ascending on the steam. "What did bring you to this place, Lani?"

"Oh, it's a rather sad story, not in holiday keeping. But it does have a happy ending, so perhaps I will tell it." She sipped her tea, then swept a curl from her cheek. "I met a man at a dance in Fairfield who was from this area. He was tall and handsome, and well, he just swept me off my feet.

"We dated for just a few months, and then we married and moved here, to the shack of a house near the main road. You've seen it, haven't you, just behind the inn? More like a chicken coop than a home. But, my, we were happy there."

Thomas didn't remember seeing such a building. And it certainly didn't exist in his Bentonsport.

"Well, it was late November, and just two weeks after we settled here, Frank, that was my husband's name, went in the woods behind the academy to hunt for meat—deer, turkey, rabbit, it didn't matter what type. We needed food and had little money between us. Frank worked in construction, and winter was his slow season. I hadn't found a job in this area yet."

Lani stared at her hands as she played with her wedding ring. "He was gone nearly five hours when there was a banging at my door. And who was there but the county sheriff, standing there with this sad look. He put his hands on my shoulders and told me Frank had fallen out of a tree stand he was sitting in and had broken his neck. Dr. Nollie, who lived across from the academy, had gone to chop wood and found Frank. But it was too late. Nothing could be done."

As Lani's eyes misted over, Thomas and Sarah looked down at their plates, Thomas toying with his potatoes, Sarah poking at her beans, waiting for Lani to continue.

"Well, there I was, a widow, living in a tiny chicken coop with no money, no job, no husband, and all welled up inside with grief. I hardly remember the funeral, really. Members of the church somehow gathered the money to have him buried. I never did find out how much the burial was or who gave the money. Imagine that. Here, I had been in town just two weeks—and Frank was not well known—and the town chipped in. But that's just how this town is."

Lani ate a bite of turkey. Thomas and Sarah ate silently.

Up till now, Thomas had seen Lani as a carefree woman. She managed this burden well.

"Well," Lanie resumed, "I promised you this story had a happy ending. About a week after the funeral, Mr. and Mrs. Carter came to visit and made me quite an offer—they owned the inn back then."

She scooted back in her chair, and her face brightened. "They wanted to do some traveling and be less tied down. They couldn't pay me much, but if I would come and live at the inn, cook and clean, and serve as hostess, they'd give me free room and board, a monthly stipend, and money in an account for my retirement. Now, how could I resist? It was so perfect for me. And I've been here now for more than thirty years through three sets of owners."

After pausing to eat, Lani pointed her fork at them. "Some people ask if I regret coming to Bentonsport, and I don't—not a moment of it. I'm a lucky person who followed her heart and ended up just where I should be."

A knock interrupted. She pushed back her chair and fussed at Thomas and Sarah. "See, you get me talking, and the next thing you know, our guests are at the door. My, my." She opened the door. "Come in, Richard, before you freeze. How about having some of your own turkey?"

He wiped his feet on the mat and handed Lani his coat, scarf, and hat. "No, no, you go ahead and finish your dinner. I've already eaten, and I see by your clock, I'm a bit early. I will have a cup of tea with you though, if you have any made." He was dressed in period clothing, a short jacket, red vest, and bow tie. "Thomas, Sarah, good to see you both again."

"Likewise," Thomas said while Sarah gave him a quick wave as she chewed.

He sat across from Thomas as Lani set his place with a cup and saucer and filled his cup.

"So," Lani began, directing the conversation to Richard, "do you think we'll have a large group tonight?"

"Oh, I'd say there might be ten or so of us. We'll sing out so people will think there are more. I thought we'd circle around Bentonsport, carol across the bridge to Vernon, and then end up at my place for coffee and cookies. I had these booklets copied, so we're all singing the same words."

"It also helps to know the tune." Lani patted his shoulder. "But we'll cock our heads in your direction if we need to find the note."

Smiling at them, Thomas wondered if Richard had a good voice or if she was just poking fun.

As Lani began to clear the table, Bill and Caroline arrived, followed by the other guests.

Caroline stomped her boots on the mat. "I think this is all of us. We may pick up a few more along the way."

Lani put on her period coat, which was gathered at the waist and spread out around her ankles. She pinned a hat to her head. Caroline said she thought Sarah, Thomas, Richard, and Lani— the only ones who'd dressed in period clothes—should stand in the front of the group as they went door to door. Richard distributed the carol booklets. Lani took battery-powered candles from the windows for the carolers to carry, and they headed out.

Making their way through the town, they stopped at each house showing any signs of life and sang their way through the booklet of carols. Richard and Lani walked arm in arm in front. Thomas and Sarah followed.

The group finished the caroling in Bentonsport and made a candle-lit procession across the bridge to Vernon. As the wind

whipped up from the cold water, they hummed "The First Noel."
After crossing the bridge, they walked to the Amish farm where
Thomas had purchased his clothing.

The Amish family came out and stood on the front porch,
wearing warm coats and shawls. Two boys held oil lamps. The
mother snuggled a baby in her arms, who sucked his clenched fist
as they sang. Slowly, one by one, the rest of the group stopped
singing and hummed as Thomas and Sarah continued the song.

At the refrain, Thomas and Sarah smiled at each other. They
harmonized the remaining two verses, and when they were
finished, the Amish family and the others applauded. He
squeezed her hand. They did complement each other well.

The final stop was Richard Tarrant's house for cookies,
kringles, coffee, and conversation. Lani reminded everyone of the
annual Bentonsport Christmas party scheduled at the inn the
next day. Well-warmed from the fire and coffee, the carolers said
their goodbyes and left. Except for Lani, Thomas and Sarah were
the last two to leave.

Humming some of the carols, they meandered to the bridge
and paused midway across. Ice chunks, white with moonlight,
floated under them, and a frigid wind whipped around them.
Sarah snugged her coat tighter. In elevated spirits, Thomas took in
the scene, knowing he would remember this moment for a long
time.

He braced his elbows on the iron railing. "It's hard to believe,
isn't it, that in just a few nights, this whole scene will change with
everything blanketed in snow?"

"It will be hard going for a couple of days, but then things will
settle down. It should be pretty, just in time for"—she swallowed
—"the holidays and your trip home."

Thomas pushed away from the rail, the mood beginning to
dampen. "Say, you never told me you're quite the songbird."

"Well, neither did you." She gave him a broad smile.

They continued their walk to town, which showed no signs of
life. When he offered his arm, she placed hers in his. *A stroll with a*

single woman along the river at night. This may never happen again in my lifetime. He imprinted the sights, sounds, and scents in his memory—the starry sky, the churning water, the faint hint of woodsmoke and cinnamon, this beautiful woman.

As they walked down the main street, Sarah hugged his arm close. "How about one more. Let's see—do you know ...?" And she began the first verse of "Good Christian Men, Rejoice."

Thomas joined in, and the mood livened. They turned down Sarah's street and arrived at her door as they finished the final refrain, "Christ was born to save! Christ was born to save!"

Slightly out of breath, Sarah leaned back against her door, fumbling in her pockets for her key. "Are you planning to be at church tomorrow?" She found the key.

"Yes, and you'll be there too?"

Sarah nodded. "We won't be a duet then."

"Ah, but I'll be listening for your voice." He bent down and kissed her hand. As he stood up, he looked into her eyes. And they drew him in. There was no thought. No turning back.

He moved his head down toward her and closed his eyes. He brushed his lips against hers and felt their softness, their warmth. Drawn deeper, deeper, he held her now and kissed her firmly. As her arms tightened around his back, he stopped, took slow breaths, and rubbed his cheek against her hair. He managed to let go, stand straight, and steady himself. In the moonlight, he could see her eyes were moist, her cheeks red. Truly, she was stunning.

"Sleep well." He kissed her forehead and walked back to the street.

He would remember this moment all his life. He had kissed other women, but never one in the moonlight. And not this one.

Chapter Fourteen

T homas awoke to the smell of hot-spiced meat and the sound of Lani slamming oven doors. He showered and dressed, choosing his tailored pants, white shirt, and jacket, foregoing the tie in an attempt to appear formal but not outdated. Still, he might stand out, as men seemed to wear their pants somewhat lower and their shirts less starched.

He walked down the stairs, through the hallway, and into the kitchen, where Lani stood peering into the oven. Her blue-jacketed dress fell just below her knee. She'd curled her hair and secured it in a ponytail. Nice to see women still dressed up for church.

"Whatever you're cooking smells good." He sat at the breakfast table.

"Well, I'm glad, but don't get yourself too eager. This is for the party tonight. I'm making three shepherd pies for our guests. For this morning, I thought we'd stick to something lighter, like fruit compote and one of Sarah's kringles, since we'll be eating so well this afternoon. Is that okay?"

"Anything is fine, Lani. Remember, I live alone. I do all the cooking myself. So, having someone else cook and clean up is a treat in itself." *And ... not as lonely.*

"Well ..." She carried the cream and sugar to the table. "Tonight's party is a potluck, and our group is known for its love of eating and good dishes."

She placed a wedge of the kringle on his plate and poured his coffee. At a knock at the door, she walked to the adjacent room, then returned with Richard, who was taking off his coat and hat.

"I thought I'd walk with the two of you to church. Afraid I'm running about fifteen minutes early, though. Can't seem to break the early habit. Just restless, I think." He hung his coat and hat on the hall tree.

"Well, you aren't too early for a hot cup of coffee."

Something in Lani's tone drew Thomas's attention. It lacked the teasing scolding she used with everyone else. With the youthful ring to it, almost like that of a schoolgirl, he arched a brow. Did the two of them have feelings for one another? No one had hinted at it before.

"Sounds good." Richard seated himself across from Thomas. "You must think I'm a terrible nuisance, Thomas. Really, I'm just a bit lonely, and I take ruthless advantage of Lani's hospitality and conversation. It gets quiet on that side of the river with no one else in the house."

"You're never in the way here, Richard." She refilled her cup of coffee. "Besides, how else would I stay on top of all the local news?"

"That's a kind way of saying I'm a busybody?"

"That's a nice way of saying you're a true friend of everyone in town, and everyone keeps you posted on what's happening."

Richard added sugar and cream to his coffee and took a slow sip while Lani checked on her casseroles.

"You know, Thomas," Richard said, "I never had many friends before I retired. I have found friendships take time, time just to be there for a person, even when nothing in particular is happening. If you're there during the ordinary times, people will want you there in the important times of their lives. That's why so few people today have many true friends. People fill their time with work and activities and don't allow themselves the casual time to develop friendships."

Too busy for friends? Hard to imagine. It seemed he was always with friends and acquaintances, whether in stores, at church, during school activities. But loneliness—this he understood. In the winter months, people stayed in their homes, and on many long winter nights, the ticking clock offered his only company.

Lani added a wedge of kringle to a plate in front of Richard.

"Well, that's another advantage of living right here." Lani gathered up the plates, cups, and saucers. "Most of us have time to plan the get-togethers, and those who are too busy find ways to attend. Not like the big cities. But we take advantage of the retirees, like Richard. I'm sure you know everyone here better since you've had a chance to slow down and get to know us as people instead of insurance policies."

Was Thomas again eavesdropping on a conversation behind a conversation? Was Lani saying Richard was getting to know her better? Thomas was beginning to feel like the matchmaking Mrs. Carrington. What a disturbing thought. He pushed back his chair with too much force, causing Richard to raise his eyebrows.

Lani, turning off the oven, didn't seem to notice. "Speaking of knowing people, everyone will wonder if we plumb forgot about church if we don't get moving."

In the hallway, Thomas retrieved his coat, scarf, and gloves. Several wrapped gifts glistened on the table beneath the stairs. Lani gestured toward the packages. "Oh, I forgot to mention. As part of our end-of-the-year potluck, we draw names and give gag gifts to each other—you know, a small item that reminds us of a funny story about that person."

She placed her hands on her hips. "The only rules are that it cannot be a nice gift—it has to be a gag gift—and it has to cost less than five dollars. I drew two names because we had an odd number of guests, and one of those names just happens to be Miss Sarah, so if you'd like to take her name, that would be fine."

"I'll try to think of something." But for the moment, he couldn't think of anything.

AFTER CHURCH, HE WALKED TO THE MAIN STREET, wondering if any stores would be open. He hoped to find a suitable gag gift—something funny he had shared with Sarah. But all he could think of was the snow fight. He couldn't exactly give her snow. And five dollars seemed like a whole lot of money for a gift that wasn't 'nice.'

With Main Street bustling, vehicles lined up against the boardwalk. A gaggle of young girls stood outside of the Greef Building, huddling to keep warm. They giggled and jumped up and down, holding signs—*Annual Used Toys Sale ~ Support Brownie Troop 915*. As he stopped in front of the building, two girls grabbed his arms. "Wouldn't your children love a toy for Christmas?"

"I don't have any children." He paused and looked at each of their faces. They let go, their glowing expressions disappointed. "But there may be something I'd like to buy. Why don't you show me what you have?"

They again took his arms and, skipping beside him, led him into the Greef Store. On his left stood three tables, each piled with used toys. Three more girls followed them into the store. Three other girls stood behind the tables. Seeing a potential customer, they cried out, "May we help you?"

"Let's see." Thomas rubbed the back of his neck. "I'm not sure what I'm looking for, but I'll know it when I see it. I may need to look around for a few minutes."

The girls clustered behind one of the tables, talking amongst themselves. Nestled among the familiar stuffed bears, toy guns, and cloth dolls were strange-looking objects with wings, men with bubble hats coming down to their necks, and vehicles like Richard's truck.

At the back of the second table, he found what he thought was an ice cream scoop. He picked it up. It was different from the ones he used. This had two separate scoops attached to one handle. Thomas turned it over in his hand, wondering if, somehow, it made balls of ice cream. It was priced at three dollars.

"Do you know what that is?" one of the girls asked.

He lifted his head. "An ice cream scoop of some sort, I think?"

"Well, it could be used for that, maybe, I guess." Her strange squishy shoes making squeaky noises, she walked over to Thomas. "But that's not what it's for. You use it to make the perfect snowball, like this." The girl took the contraption from Thomas and led him outside. She scooped up snow in her two gloved hands from the ground and pressed some into each scoop. Then she squeezed the handgrip, much like one squeezes a nutcracker, and the two scoops came together forming a perfectly round snowball.

"It makes the snowball hard, like a rock. Watch." She hurled the snowball across the street at the wooden gazebo. It hit with a *thuuud* and shattered.

This was the perfect gift for Sarah. "I'll take it."

The girl led him back inside. Bending over the table, she took a piece of red paper and neatly printed instructions on making a perfect snowball. She tied the instructions to the scooper with a green ribbon, impressing him with how she took care of her customers. Two other girls wrapped the present and handed it to him as if it were a king's scepter.

After paying for the item, he thanked them. Then he placed two more dollars in a jar marked Donations before heading back to the inn, satisfied he was now prepared for the party.

Chapter Fifteen

The potluck was a livelier meal than most parties—more like a big family reunion. Thomas sat with Bill on his left, and the gentleman on his right introduced himself as John, the watercolor artist from across the river, who lived in the old Vernon Academy building. According to Bill, John came to Bentonsport in the early seventies, meaning the 1970s.

"He'd never tell you," Bill added between bites, "but he's more than just a local artist. John's known throughout art circles nationwide. He's won several awards in New York for his work."

John continued to eat, shaking his head and smiling. "Hard for anyone to have a casual conversation after such an introduction. Fleeting fame and little money at those events. I make a living teaching art classes and selling prints. But I love the art shows. They're the spice of life, kind of the icing on the cake. And, speaking of cake ..."

When John headed to the dessert table, Thomas followed but stopped as Sarah approached from the kitchen, carrying a silver coffee pitcher.

"I saw you when I came in," she said. "But you were engrossed in conversation, and I was needed in the kitchen. Did you get to try the dish I brought? The knishes?"

"The what?"

"Knishes." She laughed. "You're from the East Coast, but clearly not from New York. Knishes are a kosher dish. It is a crisp roll filled with a spicy meat paste. Did you get to try one?"

"I don't think so. I must have thought it was another roll, and ..."

"Oh, don't apologize." She waved her free hand. "I was just hoping you had a chance to try one. Do you like ethnic foods?"

She moved toward the kitchen, and Thomas was on her heels, feeling he was back on the teeter-totter of careful conversation. "I eat fairly standard foods, you know, roasts, vegetables ..."

"Ah, not an adventurer?" she asked, her eyes wide.

The comment didn't seem quite fair, especially after what he'd been through during the past week. "Well ..." Selecting each word, he leaned against the counter and folded his arms. "I can be if I'm prodded."

"I'm too adventurous." She took a step toward him. "I tend to try things in hopes—or I guess, with faith—that I'll like them. Most of the time, I haven't been too disappointed. You know, I'm afraid sometimes that, if I don't try something, the chance won't come around again and I'll have to think back and say to myself, 'Now why didn't you do that when you could?' I guess I'm more afraid of missing out on something wonderful than I am afraid of trying something I won't like."

"It's probably a better way to be." He glanced down at his feet until she took another step closer, and their toes were nearly touching. He looked up. The warmth of the kitchen had created a sheen on her cheeks. She was lovely.

"You've sufficiently shamed me into trying the knish." He shrugged.

"Oh, you don't need to eat one now. You were just getting ready for dessert, weren't you?"

"Yes, but ..."

"I'll give Lani the leftovers to share with you this week, and you can tell me what you think. But no fibbing. Deal?"

"Deal."

After he served himself a slice of the pecan pie and she took a slice of cherry pie, they claimed the two armchairs positioned alongside a low table. A table lamp cast a glow over the chairs, warming the darkness entering the windows.

"We're ready for our gift exchange, about five minutes, okay?" As they nodded, she pointed to couches and chairs clustered by the fireplace. "We'll have everyone gather over there."

Sarah and Thomas finished their desserts as the guests began to find their seats.

They retrieved their gifts and returned just as Lani walked over to Richard with his gift. "He already knows I drew his name. But he doesn't know what's inside."

A big red bow tied up the silver-wrapped package. Richard withdrew a pair of gently worn ice skates and held them up high so everyone could see them. He deadpanned Lani. "I have no idea what this gift means."

She jumped up and grabbed the dust broom from over the fireplace to swat him. "Oh, you. You know what this is all about!"

Richard dodged the broom. "You tell us, and I'll see if I can remember."

Standing in the middle of the room, she propped one hand on her hip and clanked the broom handle against the floor. Richard obviously enjoyed her drama.

"Well," she began, "I was in the Greef Store last April—and it was one of *those* Aprils, I'm sure you all remember, when we still had a few icy mornings? Well, I made my way down to the store carefully because it was slick, and as I was browsing, I came upon a stack of photographs of Bentonsport from the older days. Of course, I thought of Richard and rang him up."

She placed the broom against the wall and folded her arms across her chest. "Well, how was I to know that little buzzard would get so excited that he raced across the bridge, fell, and wrenched his back? Bill, out for his morning walk, found poor Richard trying to get up and brought him to the inn to recuperate. And guess who his nurse was?" She raised her eyebrows with great drama and pointed to herself.

"And he was a wonderful patient, I'll grant you, but I told him, if he was going to be a dang fool and get so charged up that he comes running across an icy bridge, then I wouldn't tell him about the little treasures I find. That put him into quite a pout, so, in compromise, I suggested he wear skates next time. He smartly said he didn't have skates. And, now, he does." She took a deep bow to the applause.

Richard rose to his feet, giving her a standing ovation. "Ah, but what a gift this is, my Lani, because when that pond behind the Amish store freezes up this year, you and I are going skating." Even as Lani waved him off, he winked. "I always put my gifts to use."

When Lani reclaimed her seat, Caroline gave her a sign saying Lani's—Open for Business for her kitchen door.

"You can use it now to let Richard know he can have a meal." Caroline winked at Richard. "And use it later when you open your restaurant."

Perhaps others in the room suspected a budding romance between Lani and Richard.

During gift exchanges among people Thomas didn't know and stories he didn't understand, he sat back, watching everyone's enjoyment. To be brought into all this joy with unfamiliar people was indescribable. Perhaps a bit like heaven?

After about an hour, the game came down to two last gifts, Bill's and Thomas's. When Bill handed Thomas a heavy box wrapped in newsprint, Thomas unearthed three pairs of well-worn jeans and three work shirts. A note on top said, "Don't leave home without these." He held up the clothes, thanking both Bill and Caroline for dressing him.

Finally, Thomas stood and asked Lani to help him read the name on the package. People snickered, glancing over at Sarah, who glanced downward. "Ah, yes." He brought it to her.

As Sarah removed the wrapping paper and studied the gadget, Pastor Turner ventured, "A snow cone maker?"

Thomas snickered with the group, though he had no idea what that was.

Twisting it back and forth in her hand, Sarah's eyes glowed and her lips curved into the softest of smiles. "I have just been challenged to a rematch, having narrowly lost to my opponent last week. And you know, with this, I just may win."

Thomas shook his head. "I don't think it improves aim ... but your snowballs will at least look nice."

She jabbed his arm rather sharply.

Everyone picked up the colorful wrapping paper and stuffed it into the trash bag Lani passed around. Then they began gathering their things.

"A wonderful ending to another great year for the shopkeepers and a terrific lead-up to Christmas," Pastor Turner said.

The guests left in clusters, chatting.

Sarah was putting on her coat and scarf when Thomas approached. "If you promise you won't use your new weapon on me, I'd like to walk you home."

"No promises, but I'd like your company."

Lani and Richard carried dishes to the kitchen while Thomas bundled up and met Sarah at the door. "Thanks again, Lani," Sarah called toward the kitchen, and Lani waved them on their way.

The frigid air, such a severe contrast to the inn's warmth, made Thomas's eyes water. With the sky clear except for a few patchy clouds, the moonlight reflected against the snow. Bentonsport was still.

They walked side by side, avoiding ice patches. He offered his arm, which she accepted.

"It's hard to believe my time here is already at the halfway mark." Wistfulness was one of his favorite states. Perhaps all the years of living alone made it just too familiar. "It's also hard to believe how accustomed I am to all of you and this area. It seems ages ago, not just five days, when I sat on a bench and wondered what I was to do here for ten days."

"You did seem uncomfortable your first day, but you fit in fast." Her deep breaths created small clouds in the night air. "You know, we'll all miss you. We've had such fun including you in everything we do."

At her house, he walked her up to the front door. When she fumbled for her key, he bent down and kissed her. Once. Twice. Thrice. He stepped back.

"I'll see you tomorrow." Then he pivoted and strode down her walkway.

How strange this had all become! His feelings for Sarah had grown so intense. And yet in five days—*five* short days—he'd be gone.

A dull ache lodged in his chest. For the first time, he realized he didn't want to leave.

Chapter Sixteen

As Thomas warmed his hands on his cup and gazed out the window, Lani came up behind him, clucking her tongue, and steadied her hand against his back while looking out the window with him.

"You can't stare the storm away." She squeezed his shoulder, then stepped back. "You can't see it on the horizon yet. But it's coming. The weatherman said Omaha already has a foot of snow and it's still coming down. So, it's best we buck up and be prepared, that's all."

Richard stepped into the entryway. "I've come to collect my helper. I wouldn't call this painting weather, but we don't have the luxury of painting in the good weather when the shops are all open, so we better get started now."

"Well"—Lani pointed toward the table—"I haven't finished setting out breakfast yet, so just hold your horses, come in and eat with us."

"Don't mind if I do."

Bundled in a topcoat, hat, and scarf, Richard peeled off his outer clothes layer by layer, handing each piece to Lani to hang up. He was the type of person who could drop in on anyone and have them pleased to see him. It was quite a gift.

"Thomas, I'd say you look like you're ready to work, coveralls and all."

"I have Caroline to thank for that. I have her to thank for many things."

"That's the way we men feel about all the women here." Richard grinned at Lani, who carried bowls of steaming oatmeal and a plate of French toast to the table. "But the women will have us to thank over the next few days with all this snow. We'll be busy shoveling walkways and keeping track of everyone. Awfully good of you to stay for all this, Thomas. Not many young men here."

Flattered to be called 'young,' Thomas sugared his oatmeal, stirring as steam escaped in upward streams. In his world, with so many truly young men in town, he wouldn't be counted among them.

"Well, my travel plans are several days off, so there's no need to thank me." He saluted Richard with his coffee mug. "Besides, it's just another part of the adventure. Each day's brought new things. I expect this day will be no different."

"Speaking of what the day brings, let's try to paint the room before lunch. I promised I'd take you to the old gristmill for lunch, and I hope to invite Lani, seeing as I owe her a meal or two." Richard winked at his hostess as he poured syrup on his French toast. "Of course, Sarah is welcome to join us for one last meal out before the storm."

"That sounds like the last meal before the execution," Lani said. "But I never turn down a meal out, so count me in. Would you like me to call Sarah, or do you two gents want to extend the invitation?"

"It might be best if you call her." Richard's fork clinked the edge of his plate. "Our time is short, and we have a lot to do."

The men finished their oatmeal and slabs of French toast and carried their plates and bowls to the sink. Then, handing Thomas his coat, Richard turned to Lani. "We'll meet you here at noon, okay? And we'll stop by and pick up Sarah on the way unless you call to tell us she's busy."

The wind had begun to gust. A slate-gray sky hung over them, but the snow hadn't arrived. They walked side by side. Lani and Richard had to sense his attraction. Why else would they continue to pair them? But he didn't mind. It seemed there were Mrs. Carringtons in every community, and the single people around them benefited from their intrusions.

SARAH AWOKE LATER THAN USUAL, STILL STRUGGLING to come up with the right gift for Thomas. Something small. Something useful. Something special he could carry with him. But what?

An item or two to make him laugh and remember their fun together. Something to remind him of their baking? Their talks over morning coffee? Thomas enjoyed her piano playing and their caroling. Perhaps music was the answer.

She also needed to slip him her phone number, address, and email address.

Pausing to sip her morning coffee, she then continued cleaning, sweeping, dusting off countertops, and thinking of possibilities, then dismissing them. A book of poetry? A bit sappy, especially since they hadn't discussed poets. A book on Iowa? Bentonsport? No, not personal enough. A one-way ticket from Pennsylvania to Iowa? Expensive and forward.

Her cell phone rang, Lani's number lighting up the screen before Sarah swiped to answer. "Hi, there Miss Sarah," the peppy voice said. "And what would you be doing this fine day?"

"Deciding on last-minute gifts and tidying up," Sarah sighed.

"Now, that is no way to spend your Christmas break. I have a better offer. Richard and Thomas just left for their painting day, but Richard invited you and me to be his guests, with Thomas of course, at lunch this noon at Ben's. Now, isn't that a better plan?"

"Much." She leaned up against the counter, repositioning one foot over the other. "I'll need a break by then."

After Lani explained the details, Sarah clicked off her phone and set it on the counter. She finished up and changed for town. She had settled on music for one gift. It would be perfect if she could find a CD of hymns with the ones they'd sung together. It would need to be a fine recording—one he would want to listen to over and over. But she also wanted to give him some kind of more personal music. Maybe she should make a digital recording of her own playing?

She paused midway up the stairs. Earlier, when talking to Emma, she discounted giving him cookies because they'd be gone by the beginning of the year. But what if she baked up a batch of her best chocolate chip cookies and then tucked a note inside, saying, "For future orders, call or visit ..." Then she could attach her business card giving him all her contact information.

Two gifts decided, she needed to think of something fun. Having changed and freshened her makeup, she hurried downstairs. As she put on her coat, she glimpsed the snowball maker. Where had he bought it? Perhaps she could locate an identical one—"his and her snowball makers" might work.

THOMAS AND RICHARD ENTERED THE GREEF BUILDING. Gray light drifted through the front windows. Their footsteps echoed in the abandoned room as they crossed to the stairs.

"Kind of sad in here, isn't it? Seems so hollow and lifeless when the old girl is closed up for the season. At least it's warm upstairs."

His classroom had the same feeling when school was over. Old wooden boards squeaked on the narrow staircase before they entered a rectangular room. Boxes stacked in neat piles sat in the room's center, and sheets of canvas lay on the floor.

A flip of a switch bathed the space in light. Richard pointed at a round object on the wall. "I got a head start this morning when I turned the heat up here and spread the drop cloths to protect the floors. I don't know about you, but I can get pretty messy with a can of paint."

Smiling, Thomas remembered his students painting their backdrops. They could be messy too.

"I also boxed up my favorite artifacts and photos. While we're still clean, would you like to have a look at some of the memorabilia we've gathered?"

With a nod, he settled in a chair and wondered if he might recognize anything in that box.

Richard eased open a slim box with pictures of cookies on it, smiling as he lifted out a stack of photos.

He cradled them in his left hand. "This is the collection of photographs we have of Bentonsport and Vernon. Most of these, dating from the thirties and forties, are photos of the homes and businesses." His finger slid up and down the sides of the photo. "Many were in disrepair even back then."

Bending closer, Thomas squinted. The post office, the newspaper building—how quickly Bentonsport deteriorated. All that happened in just sixty years from when he knew the town?

"Pretty sad, huh?" Richard stooped to another box. "But, now, look here. These are the real gems. Taken just at or just after Bentonsport's prime. We don't know the exact date of the photos, but look. See this one."

The north side of Bentonsport, facing the Presbyterian Church and the academy. Thomas took the photo and tried to conceal his emotions. This—*this*—was Bentonsport. *His* Bentonsport, with houses lining the hillside.

He felt as though he could close his eyes and somehow just slip back, back into time, to his home. His hand shook as he struggled to put the photo away and turn to the next one.

Richard extended his hand, taking his precious portal to the past. "Amazing, isn't it really? I would've loved to have seen this town then."

"Yes," Thomas replied. And he stopped. If even one more

word slipped free, he'd say too much. Richard would love his Bentonsport.

"Now," Richard continued, "this next one here is a view of Bentonsport from the Vernon side." He pointed to the center. "Mills and the other buildings lined the river. And, notice, no bridge. People back then had to take a primitive ferry back and forth to get from one side of the river to the other."

"Umm-hmm." Hopefully, the sound passed for a response. Thomas bent closer, mesmerized by the photograph, caught between two worlds. Homesickness—as strong as he'd experienced his first day here—twisted his insides. Yes, he missed his Bentonsport, its bustling riverfront, Pastor Lockhardt and Benjamin Ross, and even Mrs. Carrington. They all seemed so far away, lost in a dream world. But here they were. He held them in his hands.

A long low breath left Richard's lungs. "We've lost so much of this town. I could look at these all day, but just one more photo before we get to work. See this one?"

Thomas cupped an old, grainy photograph in his palm. The main street of Bentonsport, looking down the street toward the hotel. Though he recognized the buildings, the photo had aged so severely he couldn't discern much detail.

"Now, here is the amazing part." Richard rubbed his hands together, scooting to the edge of his chair. "I took this old photo —and several more just like it—to a good friend in Des Moines. This computer geek just loves to mess around with scanners and software. Anyway, he loaded them through his scanner. Then, with this fancy software program, he was able to clean up the photo and zoom in on the detail. Just look here."

With no idea what any of that meant, Thomas accepted the new photograph from Richard. It had been cleaned and enlarged and copied, with detail so fine, you could see the hitching posts in front of the Greef Store and the road's hard dirt surface.

A man stood in front of the post office, smoking a pipe, and although Thomas couldn't make out the face, he looked much like Mr. Carrington. He wished he could tell Richard what the town was like. What the people were like—how different, yet wonderful, his life was. More wonderful than he'd realized.

"All of these will be displayed in the museum here for everyone to enjoy. I hope to have the whole thing ready by the time the stores open this spring." Richard returned the photographs to their boxes. "But there is so much to be done before then. Enough here to keep an old man busy all winter, wouldn't you say?"

Thomas nodded. His world had seemed so far away, and now here it was, close at hand. He strode to the window, unable to conceal his emotions.

"As much as we've lost, we've had a few gains, like that beautiful walking bridge. Always something positive out there, right? If you just look for it." Richard walked over to him and clapped a hand on his shoulder. "Well, we best be getting to work. I brought this tape player and some of my favorite old Christmas music to keep our spirits bright. I don't own one of those fancy iPods or Pads or whatever you call them. I'm old-fashioned in that way. I give the past up a little at a time."

Give the past up. That's what he needed to do right now. He'd think about his home later.

Richard switched on the machine, and the sound of harps filled the air. As the carols played, they stood at opposite sides of the room, each alone in his thoughts.

SARAH TOOK A QUICK STEP OVER THE CURB AND ONTO the sidewalk, avoiding a patch of ice, and pulled her coat against her chest as she passed shoppers on her way to the drugstore.

Inside, she located a CD of Christmas hymns they'd sung while caroling. She scoured the toy aisle. Then, seeing no snowball makers, she sought out Ted, the owner and pharmacist.

At the pharmacy counter, she handed over the object, and Ted turned it in his hands. "I haven't ever carried these. At least, it doesn't look at all familiar."

As she sighed and slid it into her bag, he walked around the counter and pointed to the left. "Have you seen my latest toy? A salesman brought this in here yesterday and set it up. I thought I'd keep it through the holidays to see how popular it is. It's one of those photo machines, you know? Like they had when I was a kid, probably when you were a child too.

"You put a dollar in the slot and sit on the chair, and it takes a strand of four photos." He pointed at the opening on the machine. "Only, these machines have much better technology than when we were young. With this one, you can select a background."

He drew back the curtain. "You can type a one- or two-line caption to go with each photo. You have to type pretty fast, but customers have had a real kick with this machine. One of the backgrounds is Santa, and you can pose in such a way it looks like you're sitting on his lap." He shrugged, lowering the curtain. "Seems there's always something new. But sorry, Sarah, I can't say I've ever had one of those snowball makers. I sure hope you find something you like."

Alone, she opened the curtain, sat, and studied the backgrounds. One with four gorgeous women, another with four handsome men. A beach scene, the Santa scene, a dude ranch— bull included—and finally, a white winter scene, piled high with snow, complete with a snowman. Perhaps a photo was just the trick.

She dashed down to the grocery store and purchased a sack of zip-top bags. As she returned to the drugstore, she scooped up a handful of snow from under a tree and packed it in one of the sandwich bags. Placing the snow baggy in her purse, she reentered the store and headed to the photo booth. She stopped when she saw two sets of legs underneath the curtain.

Inside the booth, two young girls squealed their delight,

crying out, "No, make this face, like this!" and "Lean over, you're blocking my face!" Then came a flash and more laughter.

Normally, she would've enjoyed listening to them. But her snow was melting. Finally, the girls emerged and stood to the side, waiting for their photos to fall into the wire bin. A sign on the booth promised just five minutes for development—*five* minutes?

The girls leaned against the machine, giggling with hushed voices. They wouldn't move until their photos dropped into the bin, and by then, her snow would be reduced to a puddle.

So, she entered the booth and read the instructions.

She followed all the instructions until she read the section on 'action shot.' Time was critical, and her snow was melting. But ...

"Excuse me?" She glanced around the curtain.

When she asked about it, the peppy preteens poked their heads into the booth and explained how each of the scenes had optional 'action shots' matching the scene.

The redhead's ponytail bobbed. "The beach shot has three optional action shots." She pointed to the screen with her short red nails. "One where a wave bursts across the photo, showing your face through the wave. Another has a shark, and your face appears in the shark's jaws. The third one is a crab pinching whatever body part you position its pincers on."

"How about the snow scene?" Sarah squinted at the screen. "What action shots come with that background?"

"Oh, that one only has two options." The taller girl popped her bubble gum. "The first one is an avalanche, so you look like your head is sticking out of a huge mound of snow. The second one is a big white blob on the screen with the word *splat!*, so it looks like you threw a snowball at the camera, and your face shows up behind the splat."

"Oh, thanks," Sarah said, trying not to sound hurried. "I'll give it a try."

When the girls removed their heads from the booth, Sarah giggled. The second action shot—icing on the cake.

Fumbling a bit, she used the gadget to form her wet snow into a soggy, but perfectly round snowball, which she left in one of the device's cups, and then rested the device on the seat next to her.

She dropped her dollar bill in the slot and positioned her hands on the keyboard ready to type. Soon, the options came up for the background scenes and Sarah selected Option 6, the snow scene. The light began to flash for the first photo, and she gave the camera a sly expression. It flashed, and she typed in the caption, "When you lose a battle, you either give up or get a better weapon."

The light again began to flash, and she smiled at the camera, removing the snowball, placing it in her left hand. She brandished the snowball maker in her right hand. As soon as the camera flashed, she dropped both and typed in, "Even better when the weapon comes as a peace offering from the other side."

In the next seconds, she scooped up the snowball and cupped it in her right hand as if she were preparing to hurl it at the camera. She flashed a wicked grin. The camera blinked, and holding her breath, she typed in, "Ah, but I wouldn't fight when you're not fairly armed." She jammed the melting snowball back in the plastic bag and prepared for the final shot.

The next screen popped up, and she selected the Splat shot. She grinned wide, the camera flashed, and she typed in, "Or would I? Tag, you're it."

Then she struggled. How should she sign off? Love? Sincerely?

Her heart started pounding as the seconds ticked away. She leaned forward, her fingers dancing over the keyboard. "Fondly, Sara ..."

The shot closed before she could type in the *H*. "Great," she huffed, her shoulders hunching as she toyed with the idea of redoing the shots, getting the spelling of her name right. *How* could she not have planned an appropriate closing? What was she thinking? Was *fondly* too familiar? Too formal? Perhaps she should change it.

Shaking her head, she grabbed her purse and snowball maker.

If the photos turned out—if she didn't look haggard, ancient, or fat—she'd leave her name as Sara. It was correct phonetically, and she could always add an *H*.

She exited the booth just as the girls' photos dropped into the wire rack. Carefully, just touching the sides of the photo strip, like an old pro, the taller girl removed it and walked to the corner of the store, with her shorter friend charging behind her on tiptoe, trying to get a look.

Sarah stood next to the photo booth, hoping no one would come over to see the photos.

What would she say? "No, you can't see my photos?" That would be rude. Besides, people would wonder what she was hiding. The photos dropped into the bin. She scooped them up, careful to touch only the sides, paid for her CD, and strode out to her truck.

She checked her watch. Just under two hours before Richard and Thomas would be by to pick her up for lunch—plenty of time to wrap some gifts and prepare her baskets, except for the loaves of bread. She'd bake those the morning of Christmas Eve, so they'd still be fresh for Christmas. At least her Christmas shopping was done. She switched on the carols and headed home.

"Perfect," she released the word on a sigh, hoping she was right.

Chapter Seventeen

B y midmorning, Thomas had the first coat of paint on one wall. As Richard finished a last swipe on his wall, he called for a break. He retrieved his coat and removed a metal cylinder topped with two cups from one pocket. From the other, he withdrew a pouch containing slices of pastry and a few cookies.

"I promised you a treat and tenderloin today for all your help, Thomas, and I don't break my promises, especially those pertaining to food. So first, let's have our treat." They pulled together three crates to create a table and chairs.

Thomas surveyed the walls. "Well, we may have the first coat done before lunch. What do you think?"

"You're right." Richard stirred white powder into his coffee, turning it the color of light caramel. "My, this place will look spiffy when it's all done." He slanted Thomas a knowing glance. "Maybe you'll even come back to see it sometime."

"I'd like that." He would. He drank his coffee black most days. "I admire you for taking on a project like this. Not many people would invest so much time and money to create a museum for a small town."

Richard shifted his gaze to the window, his jaw tightening. He took a long sip. "You know, I'm not a man who shares his thoughts and desires easily. Maybe because your time with us is so short and we've become friends so quickly, I feel I can confide in you. Or maybe you're the type of person people feel comfortable with. In any case, I'll tell you I'm creating this museum for two reasons—one selfish and one somewhat altruistic. But the driving force is the more selfish motivation."

Intrigued by his honesty, Thomas set his cup on the crate, braced his elbows on his knees, and laced his fingers together.

"You see"—Richard divided the remaining coffee between their cups—"for most of my life, I was concerned with building wealth. Maybe it had to do with how I grew up knowing what true poverty was and never wanted to fall victim to it again. Or maybe I felt money made me secure, you know, not vulnerable."

He took a short sip of the coffee. "In any case, when I started working, I kept busy from early morning until late at night selling insurance policies, handling claims, and attending company meetings. I wasn't concerned with contributing to the world around me. I took but rarely gave. Now that I'm much older"—he chuckled and shook his head—"yes, much older, I've come to believe I missed out on an awful lot in life. In many ways, I missed the mark."

Richard bit into the kringle. "You know, I just started to realize this about five years ago. The turning point came when people I knew well passed away. I got involved in burials, funerals, and other such matters. John Schaffer, an acquaintance of mine, died. Nearly three years ago now." He wiped crumbs from his hands and watched the flecks fall to the floor. "Hard to believe it's been that long ago."

Thomas held his cup in both hands. Men in his Bentonsport didn't share feelings. It just wasn't done.

"Anyway," Richard continued, "he named me executor of his estate, and I was charged with dividing his things among his friends and relatives, then disposing of the rest. The whole year I was working on this, I kept having the sense I was giving John away. And I kept thinking to myself, I wished John had somehow given himself away. He would've enjoyed it."

Turning the cup around in his hands, Thomas leaned forward. He'd never thought of death quite like that, but he could see how Richard might feel that way, giving away another man's possessions.

"People would've been thrilled to have John give them little gifts, his time, his service. But now, each time I met with someone listed in the will and handed them the things they were to receive ... it was so businesslike, with the release of possession forms and other documents. And ... it was sad, because the gift was shrouded with John's death, not his life.

He shook his head. "I'm not saying he should've given everything away and become a monk. But he should have given away much of what he'd stopped wanting. And he should've given more of himself to these people I met. They all liked John but had few memories of times with him."

Mulling the thoughts over, Thomas popped a chunk of the kringle into his mouth and chewed slowly. Yes, he knew something of what Richard meant. He'd been to estate auctions when the deceased's possessions were spread on tables and blankets across the yard. And seeing family items going to someone who never knew the person or the stories behind them saddened him.

Richard sipped his coffee. "I sound like I'm being overly critical of John. And truly, that's not how I mean this. Because, you see, these feelings were a much greater indictment of me than of him. Here, I had collections upon collections of items, like all these Bentonsport artifacts." He pointed at the boxes. "I had no room to display them and only took time to look at them and enjoy them once or twice each year."

Glancing around the room, he turned and laid his palms on

his knees. "Hence my museum idea. I wanted to enjoy giving and, of course, needed to do so while I was still alive. And as a side benefit, this way I can enjoy them more often myself."

"Well, I'd say it's quite a gift to the community."

Richard nodded, the movement ruffling his gray hair. "But again, I am doing it for me. Years ago, I decided if life offered me a lesson, I'd learn it quickly and not go through the pain of being taught twice. John's death benefited me in that way, and in a sense, that was his gift to me. I didn't just learn about giving away things. I learned about giving away myself, about becoming involved in my community and embracing it, with all its wrinkles and its glories."

He smiled broadly. "So I started the annual caroling to our shut-in residents, our telephone tree to ensure everyone has all they need during a storm or a power outage. And I'm not done— no, I still want to come up with ways to make a difference right here. I share this with you not to show how good I am but what I've learned."

A gust of wind rattled the window. Thomas glanced up, still ruminating over this story. He had few material items to worry about giving away. But how much did he give away of himself? In his loneliness, was he becoming focused on himself? Richard picked up the conversation again.

"From John's death and the death of other friends, I learned this is not my final home. No matter how much I choose not to think about death, it will come. And if, as I believe, I'm going to spend the rest of the time with my Lord, I need to get to know Him better while I'm here. And now, enough of that sermon. I leave the preaching to Pastor Turner. That is, when he's not down south. During the winter months, the amateurs fill in—including me."

Thomas laughed. "I thought it a pretty good sermon."

Richard pushed to his feet. "I've dominated our snack time. I'll give you the floor at lunch. And speaking of lunch, we'd better get back to our painting so we can finish the other two walls before picking up Sarah and Lani."

HAVING WRAPPED HER GIFTS, SARAH PUT TOGETHER the Christmas baskets to deliver on Friday. Perhaps she'd talk Thomas into going with her, giving them additional time together on his last day. She set the twenty brightly colored baskets on the kitchen countertop, lining each with a green and white checkered placemat. She then covered each with lace doilies, ensuring the edges of both fell over the basket rims.

From her highest cabinet shelf, she took down boxes of homemade jelly jars, each with one of her labels imprinted with her shop logo. Under the logo on each jar, she printed the type of jelly the jar contained, followed with her greeting, "For a joyous Christmas morning! Sarah."

Though she couldn't afford expensive gifts, her neighbors would know she cared.

Leaving room in the middle for the loaf of bread she'd bake early Friday morning, she placed two jelly jars in each basket. Then she added two individual tea bags. A cup of hot tea and warm bread topped with jelly—the perfect way to start Christmas morning.

By the time she nestled the baskets on the shelves lining the kitchen island's backside, so any friends who might drop by wouldn't see them, a glance at the clock revealed she had just under a half hour to tidy up and change.

When her phone rang, she answered it. "This is Sarah Peterson."

"Thank heaven," the unfamiliar female voice rushed on. "This is Michelle Barkley, and I live in Fairfield. Emma Baxter—she's in my gardening club and says she's a friend of yours—gave me your number. Well, I'm afraid I need your help."

Sarah opened her mouth to respond.

"Each year, I place a big order of iced cookies with the local nursing home. The nursing home's cook makes the cookies and decorates them with the residents. The money I pay them goes toward the nursing home's activity program. It's been a good arrangement. I benefit because there is just no way I could bake so many cookies, and my husband benefits because he gives them as gifts, a dozen to each of his employees, along with their Christmas bonuses."

"Sounds great." Sarah eyed the clock. Where was this conversation going?

"As I said, the order I place is rather large." A deep breath seemingly pushed the words through the speakers. "Four hundred and fifty dozen, to be exact."

Sarah knitted her brows. Large? That was a *huge* order.

Michelle sighed. "Well, I just received a call from the nursing home. Their delivery truck, with all the ingredients, is stuck in the blizzard in Nebraska. The woman in charge of the kitchen has called all the grocery stores, and none—that is, not one—has ingredients in the quantity she needs.

"With this storm, everyone's stocking up, and none of the stores can commit to getting shipments. On top of that, last night, the cook learned her mother in Chicago is ill, and so, with the ingredients now unavailable, she's canceling my order and leaving for Chicago today, hoping to outdrive the storm."

Sarah estimated the ingredients and the time necessary to make 450 dozen cookies.

"Are you still there?"

"Yes," she said, focusing on the conversation.

"Well, when Emma heard the situation, she suggested I see if you could help."

Could she? Sarah tapped the phone as she surveyed her kitchen. This was a dream order. *If* she had enough ingredients and time. "Let me see what I can do. Can you hold on for a moment?"

"Oh, of course." An airy hint of hope came through as

though the woman had just waved her hand shooing Sarah off to look at her inventory of baking supplies.

Sarah checked her flour and sugar bins. Her delivery had just arrived on Saturday, so she had enough dry goods to complete the order. If she hurried, she could drive to the Amish store in Vernon for butter. She double-checked her supply of green and red sugar.

To bake and decorate 450 dozen cookies? Moving at a fast pace, it would take her at least twenty-two hours over three days. It was doable.

Michelle interrupted her thoughts. "I should add that I spoke with my husband. As we've had a good year, we both agreed to give our annual two-thousand-dollar donation to the nursing home and pay the same for the cookies."

Sarah plopped on one of the kitchen stools. Two thousand dollars? This one order would give her the boost she needed to get through the slow winter months until the stores reopened. *And* the nursing home would be receiving its usual donation. She'd feel bad getting the order at their expense.

"I'll do my best. I need to confirm that I can purchase enough butter at this late date, but I'm confident I can. How would you like the cookies decorated, and when do you need them?"

"Decorate them as you please." Laughter bubbled into the words. "We will hand out the Christmas bonuses first thing Friday morning, so as long as I have them by then, I'll be thrilled. You can deliver them to my house. Are you familiar with Fairfield?"

"Pretty much." Her heart rate picking up, she moved the phone to the other hand and wiped her sweaty palm against her top. As the reality of the order's size began to sink in, Sarah forced herself to draw in a few deep breaths.

"I live in the large Queen Anne home on Main Street, the one that used to be a funeral parlor. The house is kind of a lilac color."

She knew the house. "Okay, if you don't hear back from me today, you can assume I have everything under control and will deliver the cookies to you no later than Friday morning—hopefully by Thursday night. Is this the number I should call?"

Michelle confirmed her phone number and provided the business phone number. She thanked Sarah again for tackling such a large last-minute project.

As she clicked off the phone, the time on the phone's screen jolted her. She had five minutes remaining.

She raced upstairs and changed into a white turtleneck and a black ankle-length jumper with a slit up the side to her knee. She eased on a pair of warm black tights, brushed her hair, and centered her gold and red hairband, allowing tendrils to fall about her face. She was just sliding into her black patent leather low-heeled shoes when the doorbell rang.

I could use some lipstick, maybe some mascara. But there just wasn't time. At the bottom of the stairs, she breathed in deeply and opened the door.

On the doorstep stood Thomas and Richard red-cheeked and smiling. "Come in." She waved them into the hallway. "I just have to grab my coat."

"Dress warmly," Richard called after her. "We're walking over to the inn to pick up Lani, and the wind is kicking up."

"Any sign of the snow yet?" Sarah called from the closet.

"None, yet. But don't get your hopes up. The storm isn't supposed to get to us before evening. And the wind says it's coming. We won't dodge this one, but at least it held off until the stores closed."

She struggled to get her arm inside her coat sleeve. "Well, I'll have my hands pretty full until Friday."

Thomas assisted her. "So, what do you have planned?"

"I had an unexpected phone call this morning." She slipped on her gloves as she walked into the biting cold. "A woman phoned with what I guess you could call an emergency cookie order."

HOW, EXACTLY, COULD THE DESIRE FOR COOKIES EVEN approach an 'emergency'? Thomas scuffed his foot on the pavement. Perhaps they were for a funeral? But even that wouldn't be an 'emergency.' Even so, he was grateful to have something to discuss to get his mind off what he would soon be eating. *Tender Loin*? His stomach turned. Better to think of cookies.

"I'd be happy to help," he offered. "I don't believe Caroline has lined up any plans for me after Richard and I finish painting. My only other commitment is to clear snow around the inn after the storm."

"That would be great." Relief slowed her voice. "Caroline will have her hands full finishing up her last-minute orders, so any help would be wonderful. And, if the storm keeps you busy, I'll just keep baking away until someone can dig me out."

At the inn, Lani, dressed and waiting, suggested they take her car since she'd warmed it up. Conflicted, Thomas slid into his seat, looking forward to being with friends, especially Sarah, but worrying about the looming meal. What if he just couldn't eat it?

When they reached the old gristmill, a woman with gray hair curling out from a white cap led them to a table with a river view, then brought them the hot tea they ordered.

"Order whatever you'd like," Richard said as they surveyed the menu. "Lunch is on me, but I would like Thomas to have the tenderloin sandwich, seeing as he has never had one before."

There was no way out of it. He couldn't hurt Richard's feelings. He'd have to order the tenderloin—and somehow eat it.

When the waitress came, Thomas couldn't choke out the words. But Richard ordered tenderloin sandwiches for them, while Sarah and Lani chose the spiced chicken sandwich. Spiced chicken sounded really good.

"Well, missy." Lani frowned at Sarah. "If you aren't deep in thought. I don't remember having a lunch where you sat so quiet."

Attempting to be attentive, Thomas kept staring at the other diners, trying to discover if any one of them had this tenderloin.

"My mind is just going in a hundred directions." Sarah stirred her tea. "I texted Caroline to see if she could help me with the new order I have to fill. Bill texted back that she's feeling under the weather. Have you talked with her today?"

"No, but she's probably just worn out. Between getting her Christmas orders nearly completed and mailed, then going to the Christmas parties and events, she likely overdid it and needs to spend a good day in bed."

"I shouldn't have bothered her with the baking. It's just ... time always passes much faster when she's at hand."

"Well, if it's another set of hands you need"—Lani was kicking her crossed leg back and forth—"count me in. I'm not as entertaining as Caroline, but I may be of some use."

"You are great company, and I may take you up on that."

The food arrived, and the tenderloin sandwich had the appearance of thin fried fish and the taste of pork, only chewier. He tasted it again for, indeed, it was delicious!

The meal continued with small talk and praise for the food. When they left, the clouds were now a darker shade of gray, foreboding. Thomas shivered, tugging his coat closed and, for the first time, believing their odd forecasts of snow. Still, no flurries speckled the air.

Lani parked beside the inn and headed inside while Sarah walked with them as far as the bridge. A frown marred her forehead, her thoughts obviously consumed with her baking. Her steps slowed. "I need to run over to the Amish store while the weather is still good. I'll see you both later. Thanks again for lunch, Richard."

Thomas stepped toward her but then stopped. He smiled, trying to appear more casual, his hands loosely in his pockets. "Is it still okay if I stop by for tea when we're finished?"

"Of course." She flashed a smile, and his breath caught in his chest. What was happening here?

Richard continued on to the Greef Building, and Thomas turned from watching her leave. "That Sarah." Richard puffed before him. "I'd say she's a keeper. For your sake, Thomas, I hope they make them this sweet and pretty back in Pennsylvania."

"Well, if they do"—Thomas thrust his hands deeper into his pockets—"they keep them well hidden."

Chapter Eighteen

Approaching the Amish store, she chuckled, thinking of Thomas decked out in Amish attire. Such a hard man to understand—polite, kind, and humorous. All of this, and good looks too.

Yet he was different, somehow out of place with his formal way of speaking and his old-fashioned manners. These little quirks made him more mysterious and interesting.

He wasn't the type of person to reveal his thoughts readily. No, with someone like Thomas, that would take a great deal of time. And they had very little left.

THOMAS WAS RETRIEVING THE PAINT CAN BY THE window to replenish his roller tray when he glimpsed someone burdened with packages attempting to cross the bridge. Sarah? He squinted, shaking his head. What was she thinking?

"Richard." He set down the paint can and grabbed his coat. "Sarah's about to take a tumble on the bridge. I'll help her home and be right back."

He sprinted across the street, up the bridge approach, and

onto the bridge. He was nearing her, just ready to take the boxes, when he stepped on an icy patch, slid forward feet first, and landed hard on the bridge deck.

"Thomas!"

Her boxes clattered to the wooden boards. She ran forward and knelt next to him, placing her hand under his head.

He squinted, bringing her into focus. "Uh." With one hand, he probed the back of his head. He couldn't stay spread out on the bridge, but his head throbbed.

"I'm okay now." He tried to sit up. Pain shot through his head.

"Whoa, there, Thomas." Richard jogged up. "I'll help you up." He wedged his shoulder under Thomas's arm and eased him to a sitting position.

"He hit his head," Sarah whispered as the two men attempted to stand.

"I think I'm okay." Thomas blinked as he tested a smile. "My head and ankle hurt, but otherwise, I'm fine."

The men stood up, Thomas with his arm around Richard's shoulder for support. He stood on one foot and his injured ankle up. "If I can just go to the inn and put my foot up, I should be fine."

"I'm responsible for this whole thing." Sarah's voice trembled. "I shouldn't have tried to carry so many things across the bridge when it's so slick."

She shouldn't have. "No, it's my fault," he politely insisted. "I should have watched where I was going and—"

"Okay," Richard interrupted. "Let's not argue about who's at fault. These things happen, even to old fools like me. Sarah, if you wouldn't mind letting Lani know, we'll limp along and meet you there."

By the time Richard helped him hobble there, Lani and Sarah were standing outside to meet them.

"Thomas, Thomas." Lani clicked her tongue against her teeth. "Something about that bridge must make men feel they can charge across it, even in this cold weather. Perhaps he should see a doctor."

"I agree. I think—"

"No, no," this time, Thomas interrupted Sarah. "Let me elevate my foot, and I'll be fine. But I do feel like a fool." The throb in his head was reduced to a dull ache. The pain in his ankle was intensifying.

Chuckling, Richard helped Thomas into the armchair across from the fireplace. "Well, if you're a fool, I'm a bigger one. Let's hope it's nothing but a sprain, and you'll be back on your feet in no time at all. There's nothing they can do for a concussion, but we'll have to watch you to make sure you're okay."

"I'm sorry I ended our painting session. Perhaps, if this all clears up, I might be able to help out Wednesday or Thursday."

"If you're up for it, Sarah will need your help more than I will. My project will go on for months. Though I do enjoy your company, Sarah does too."

Reaching down, Sarah brushed the hair back from his forehead. She still looked shaken.

He caught her hand against his cheek. "I am fine, Sarah, truly."

Lani ran up the stairs and returned with a roll of brown cloth. The three of them assisted Thomas in removing Bill's coveralls and helped him slide back into the chair. Lani lifted his foot, positioning it on the upholstered footstool.

Sitting beside him, she removed his mud-splattered shoe and sock and began wrapping his ankle.

"I can do that." Thomas tried to stop her, embarrassed to have someone taking such care of him, almost as if he were a small boy.

"You'd better keep this ankle propped up for the rest of the day," Lani scolded. "If you're feeling less pain tomorrow, you can do some walking. But just in case, I'll get you a crutch to use. I have an old one upstairs from when Richard stayed here after his fall. I also should get you some aspirin. How does your head feel?"

"It seems better. Just an ache back here." He touched the back of his head.

Richard excused himself to retrieve Sarah's boxes and butter. "I'll take your butter over to your house."

"No." She headed toward the door as well. "I'll go with you. I learned that's too much for one person to carry."

After the two of them left, Lani returned with the crutch. "And now we have our own Tiny Tim here for this Christmas season," she teased.

Thomas laughed. At last, a joke he understood.

As he rested in the stuffed chair, Lani made him tea and added a log to the fire. She placed an ice bag on his swollen ankle and draped a wool wrap around his shoulders. The warm wrap and hot fire masked the cold ice pack. His ankle grew numb, and the pain subsided. His eyelids felt heavy. The fire, tea, and wool wrap lulled him into a heavy sleep.

THE MANTLE CLOCK AWAKENED HIM CHIMING SEVEN. Out of instinct, he stood. As a pang shot from his sore ankle and his head throbbed, he collapsed into the chair. The ice bag was gone. Lani had propped a crutch against the table. He positioned it under his arm, then pushed up out of the chair and stood, leaning on the crutch.

He tried a careful step forward, then another. After several more, he made a circle around the room.

Lani stood in the doorway, her arms crossed and her head tilted to one side. "I heard the crutch tapping the floorboards and wanted to see how you were doing." Motherly concern warmed her tone. "Can I get you anything?"

"No. Thanks for everything, Lani," he said, still shaking off the heavy sleep.

"I was just going to awaken you to make sure you were okay. Sarah phoned just after four to see how you were getting along. I told her you were fine. Why don't I ask if she would like to come for tea? I'll prepare a full English tea for the two of you, then go to my apartment. I have some Christmas cards to get out."

She returned five minutes later. "All set. She's finishing up a few things in her kitchen, and she'll leave at eight o'clock sharp. I'll get the tea tray ready. You stay put and read or something until eight."

He paged through a book on Iowa barns and fidgeted until a quarter of eight, anxious to see Sarah again.

Nearly half an hour later, Lani returned to the parlor, she fluffed the couch pillows, stoked the fire, and added two logs. "And where have you gone to now?" She stood still, her hands on her hips, watching him stare into the fire.

"Just thinking things through. I don't like the thought of her walking over here in the dark by herself. I should at least sit on the bench outside and watch for her."

"Well, if you insist, Well, if you insist, let me get the tea tray and help you with your coat. But first, let's wrap that foot so you stay warm." After she tied a long rag several times around his foot, she went to the kitchen. When she returned, she was carrying a tray complete with a silver teapot, two blue teacups and saucers, a pitcher of cream and a matching bowl filled with sugar cubes, and a plate of assorted cookies and chocolates. She eased the tray onto the end table and moved another chair to its side.

When Thomas stood, she helped him with his coat. "I'd say you were a darn fool if I didn't think you were so smart. Young women like Sarah don't fall into your lap every day." She tugged the shoulders of his coat, smoothing the lapels. "In my thinking—and I have given this quite a bit of thought, mind you—there are two reasons she wasn't swept off her feet years ago."

Looking at him directly, she continued. "The first is because of her old-fashioned ways. Being raised by a grandmother, she picked up values and even manners that don't necessarily match today's ways." She pushed aside the throw rug so he wouldn't trip. "Now, those of us around here find her charming and sweet.

But I can see why some men might find her too old-fashioned and maybe even too mature."

As she helped him to the door, he asked, "And the second reason?"

"The company she keeps, the place she lives. Just look around you. How many eligible young men have you seen since you've been here? The answer is none. No, Richard and I have discussed this many times. We both often said that, one day, someone is going to visit this town—just fall down from the heavens!—and discover the jewel we have. And I'm not talking about our buildings." Flashing a white-toothed smile, she opened the door.

The wind had died down, and the snow floated in delicate flakes. Nearly an inch now dusted the walk. Filling the air, it appeared like fog out in the distance. He brushed off the bench.

He could see only halfway up the block. He decided to walk down the street so he'd be able to see Sarah when she rounded the corner. But as he rose, the shadow of a woman wearing a hooded coat and holding something emerged from the blur. As she drew near, she kept her face down to shelter her eyes from the falling snow.

Not wanting to frighten her, he called out, "Who is this that appears, like a spirit in the mist?"

Her head jerked up, and a smile curved her soft lips. "And who is this?" she teased. "My wounded protector, watching and waiting, prepared to defend me with his crutch?"

As they entered the inn, the fire blazed in the sitting room they had to themselves. He positioned himself in the chair, setting the crutch to one side, while Sarah headed to the kitchen and returned with a plate of sliced bread.

"I made you fruit bread," she said. "I'll do the honors."

She filled their teacups and added a sugar cube to each along with a cookie and a slice of bread to their saucers. As she was setting his on the end table, she nodded to the book face down on the table. "*Old Barns of Iowa?*" She raised her eyes. "Are you interested in barns?"

"I'm interested in most things." He entwined his hands on his lap. "At least I like to think I am. I can't say I've ever read a book on the design features of barns, but it was this or old recipe books. Between the hot tea and the fire, I fell straight to sleep and didn't awaken until seven."

Her lips pressed white in the center. "I shouldn't have tried to carry so much. I'm sorry you got hurt so close to your trip home and so close to Christmas." She set her cup on its saucer, positioning it so the pattern lined up, and straightened in her chair. "Speaking of Christmas, I was thinking today ... if you leave late Friday or early Saturday, whenever it is you're leaving, you'll spend Christmas on the train. You can't possibly make it to Pennsylvania in under twenty-four hours, can you?"

"I'm not quite certain of my arrival time, but Christmas will begin for me whenever I make it home."

Her expression suggested she wasn't pleased with his response. She pursed her lips and moved them from side to side. Flipping the book over in her hand, she stared at the cover.

"I'm sure," he teased, "if you're anxious to read that book, Lani would be happy to loan it to you."

She replaced it on the table with a weak smile. "I have nothing against barns, but I can't say this is on my current reading list." Silence stretched. "So, other than those on old barns, what types of books do you like to read?"

Trying to look contemplative, he stared into the fire. Again, this was one of those moments where he had to choose his answer carefully. He didn't know any authors of her era. But if he said an ancient author she would know, like Shakespeare, he'd sound archaic. So, he took a chance. "Well, recently, I have read several of Dickens's books. And, with the older children I teach, I often read books by spirited authors, like Mark Twain, for example."

"Ah, the good old classics. I love *The Adventures of Huck Finn*, *Tom Sawyer*, all those books," she said, her voice warming. "When I was a girl, our class would take an annual field trip to Hannibal and visit the cave and Becky Thatcher's house. It's been years since I've visited those places."

He exhaled and picked up his cup. "And what types of books do you like to read?"

"You know ..." Firelight caressed her face as she leaned forward, clasping her hands between her knees. "There was a time, not long ago, when I read little other than fiction. But, for the past year, when I can eke out time, I've found my interests have switched to biographies or autobiographies, usually about women."

A log shifted in the fireplace, and for a moment, the crackling fire filled their silence.

"Earlier this fall, I read a book about a woman who lived in the late 1800s. She was single and raised by her father to be determined and headstrong. She never married, and then sometime in her thirties, she sold everything she owned to purchase a small orchard."

Sarah lifted her teacup and, with her other hand, traced the gold-embossed rim. "I just loved that book. She detailed her struggles to make the orchard into a business that could produce a real income for her. In the end, a series of droughts brought about the orchard's demise, and the woman sold everything and went back to teaching."

She took a long sip of tea. "Sad, you know, but I enjoyed reading about her tenacity, and she did to try to make the orchard work. And now, I'm reading about a woman who started beekeeping. It's such a pleasure to read how she's tending her business *and*, through that effort, is caring for her soul." She replaced her teacup. "I'm sorry, I'm talking too much."

"No." Thomas rubbed his palms against his pant legs, then entwined them with his palms flat against his chest. "I was just thinking about what you were saying—about your taste in literature. It sounds like you're reading about women much like yourself."

Sarah laughed, wisps of her hair bobbing. "These women are

truly courageous. They each left everything familiar and plunged headfirst into new lives."

"But"—he tented his fingers and tapped them together—"isn't that what you did? You left teaching and your life in the city and moved here to begin a business and help rebuild this town. That had to take courage."

She stared at her lap. "The difference is I'm not courageous. In fact, I'm too careful. I take change slowly. When I decided I wanted this lifestyle, I went to baking conferences. I studied as an apprentice. No, I think a better comparison would be Caroline. She had faith and jumped right in." She grinned at him, blonde tendrils falling against her cheek.

"But ..." He lowered his voice as if his words could frighten this courageous woman. "She also had Bill."

Sarah glanced back to the fire, its light creating a golden outline of her profile. "I'm certain that did make a difference. Just knowing someone else is there can make jumping into any new venture much easier."

A long low breath escaped her lips, and her shoulders straightened. She curved her hands around her cup. "The good thing about Bentonsport is I have people I can go to for help, even when I'm in over my head. And speaking of over my head, I've done it again with this cookie order."

"You've taken orders this large before, haven't you?"

A thin smile lifted her cheek, deepening her dimple. "And," he added, "You'll have me there to help for the next two days, and—"

But she was shaking her head. "I've caused you enough grief. You stay here, off that ankle. I'll stop in—after the men have cleared a path, that is—and have tea."

"Not a chance," he countered. "I would go stir-crazy just sitting around. Besides, I'll be able to walk on it more tomorrow as long as I'm careful. I can sit and cut out the cookies, decorate them, wash dishes from a chair—"

"Do *what?*" She giggled, then waved a hand with a laugh. "Okay, okay, I've got the picture. And I can use all the help I can get. The weatherman says this storm is supposed to continue all day tomorrow and into early Wednesday morning. Wednesday and Thursday, everyone will be busy digging out, and that takes us to Christmas Eve. And, in all this flurry of cookie baking, my best friend is sick in bed, and I should be over helping her."

"How is she?"

"I dropped by there after I heard you were fine." Concern deepened the creases between her brows. "Bill's certain she has the stomach flu because she is achy and doesn't want to eat. When I peeked in on her, she was resting, so I didn't wake her. I'll take some soup over tomorrow. He plans to drive her in to see the doctor after this storm blows over if she isn't feeling any better."

"Let Bill know that if there is anything I can do to help, I'm happy to." He picked up his tea, cinnamon steam warming his face.

"I'll tell him, but he's got things under control. Caroline was nearly caught up on all her last-minute orders."

After finishing her tea, Sarah clinked the cup onto the saucer. "I hate to say it because it's so nice here by the fire, but I should get home before the storm picks up."

His heart sank. Each goodbye at the end of the evening brought the final goodbye that much closer.

He set his cup down. "Just give me a minute to get my coat on, and I'll walk you to the end of the street and watch you until you get to your house." When she started to voice an objection, he cut her off. "And don't protest. I'll take my crutch and walk slowly. If you complain, I'll walk you all the way home."

"Well, we can compromise." She threaded her arms through her strangely puffy coat, then fluffed her hair free of the collar. "You can sit on the bench outside the side door. It's pretty much in line with my driveway. I'll flash the headlights on my truck off and on a couple of times, and you'll know I made it. I can't risk you getting injured again. I need all the help I can get tomorrow."

He conceded, and they walked together to the side door. The snow was falling in clumps. Everything was gray and white. He sat on the bench and reached for her hand. "I hate for you to walk in this alone."

After tucking her hair deep under her hood, she squeezed his hand and bent over so he could hear her say, "I'll be fine. I've walked in this type of weather many times. And it's only a couple of blocks."

She leaned toward him, her hand in his, her fluttering hood framing her full face. How pretty she was, her cheeks flushed from the cold, her lashes damp. Letting go of her hand to reach up to her shoulder, he pulled her closer. Her movement was fluid with his own, with no resistance, no pause for thought. He slid his hand behind her head, through her silky hair.

The warmth of her breath reached his face, and his heart quickened as he pulled her near and closed his eyes. His lips found hers, and he kissed her, gently at first, then more firmly—for how long? He didn't know. There, in the darkness, shrouded in the falling snow, he thought not of his world or her world but just of them. The warmth of her lips, the softness of her hair, the pressure of her hand on his shoulder.

It must have lasted the briefest moment, but he knew, even years later, he would remember every detail and savor it over and again. As he already had their first kiss. And their second. He slid his hand from her shoulder and clasped hers in both of his.

She stood, more flushed and misty-eyed than before, and said, "I'll see you tomorrow."

Chapter Nineteen

His mind filled with thoughts of Sarah, Thomas struggled to fall asleep. His ankle throbbed when he rolled over, but the pain had dulled. When he slumbered, it was a dreamless, heavy, deep blanket of sleep. He didn't know how long he had dozed when a pounding on a door awakened him.

The noise came from somewhere downstairs, perhaps the front door? He couldn't tell. And, for just a moment, as he struggled to escape from his fog, he wondered if he had somehow slipped back in time, back to his room, and if he would find Pastor Lockhardt, again, on the door's other side. As he became aware of his surroundings, he knew he was not at the academy.

In his wakening state, he questioned if somehow Pastor Lockhardt had found his way through the door of time and come looking for him. He sprang out of bed, shed his nightshirt, and put on the jeans and work shirt he'd placed on the chair near his bed. Pain from his ankle tingled up his leg, but it was greatly reduced from the previous evening. With his crutch, he headed out of the bedroom just as Lani was coming down the hall.

"Coming, I'm coming," she called toward the front door, and seeing Thomas, she said, "What time is it?" She glanced at the

169

clock. "Five fifteen. *Who* would come at this time—and in a storm?"

"I—I don't know."

A gust of wind blew the door back from her hand, and a drift of snow fell through. In the swirling snow stood Sarah.

"My dear! Come in, Sarah, come in." Lani grasped her by the wrist, drawing her into the front hallway.

Thomas pushed the snow outside with his crutch handle and shoved against the door with his shoulder, shutting it with great effort. Then he engaged the latch to ensure it would not blow open.

Sarah unwrapped the scarf from her face, revealing the tears streaming down her cheeks. "Oh, Lani, Thomas!"

As he pulled Sarah to his chest, Lani rested a hand on Sarah's back and, in a motherly tone, said, "Sarah, ... what is it, dear? Tell us so we can help you."

Sarah wiped her face with the back of her hand and lifted her head from Thomas's shirt. "Lani, it's Caroline. Caroline and Bill. Caroline is h-having terrible pains, and Bill has lost his mind!" She covered her eyes with her hands, crying again.

"Come, Thomas, Sarah." Lani ushered them along. "Let's go into the kitchen and sit down." While he helped Sarah to a chair, Lani brought a box of tissues, tightened her robe, and sat on Sarah's other side. "Okay, honey. Now start at the beginning and tell us what has happened."

Sarah shuddered in a deep breath while he sat next to her, his hand on her back, not saying a word. But his chest tightened.

"What's wrong with Caroline and Bill?" Lani asked. "And *how* did you manage to get over here in these conditions?"

Tears continued rolling down Sarah's cheeks. Sniffling, she wiped her face with a tissue. "Bill banged on my door and woke up me around four thirty. He was—*is*—in a complete panic. Caroline was in terrible pain. His truck wouldn't start, so he wanted the keys to mine to get her to the hospital."

Sarah blew her nose, then crunched the tissue in her hand. "I didn't know what to do. With this whiteout, they'd never make it across the bridge, let alone to Keosauqua. He wouldn't let me see Caroline but insisted I give him the keys." Shuddering, she shoved the wadded tissue into her pocket. "So, to stall, I lied, told him I left them here when I visited Thomas last night. I told him I'd run over and look."

She tugged out another tissue and blotted her eyes. "I kept my left hand outstretched against the buildings and groped my way to the inn. What should I do? There is no way they can make it to Keosauqua. There is just no way!"

"Why, we'll call the hospital and get their advice." Lani squeezed Sarah's shoulder. "They'll have a way of getting someone to us."

"The phone lines are down." Sarah ran her hands through the hair clinging to her face. "I got through on my cell phone. The hospital said they could send an ambulance out at some point, but they have two of their ambulances north of town at an accident and another on the way to Iowa City. Bill. Won't. Wait."

Thomas rubbed his chin. "What about someone riding out?"

Sarah shook her head. "No vehicle could make it in these conditions. You can't see six inches in front of you, and the roads are snow- and ice-covered. You'd never even make it out of Bentonsport."

Lips pressed tight, he weighed his next comment. But really, he had nothing to lose. "I meant, why doesn't someone take a sleigh to town?"

When the two women gawked at him, he cleared his throat. "It would take time, and the horses might not stay on track. But your chances are much better, especially if you have horses used to making the trip."

Lani and Sarah just sat there, quiet as students during a test. *What* were they thinking?

"You know, Sarah ..." A lilt lifted Lani's voice. "He just may be on to something here. The only horses that would pretty much know their way are the Zimmermans' team. You have met the family, right, Thomas? The Amish family with the store over in Vernon? Heavens, those horses have made the trip hundreds of times. They *could* do it blindfolded."

Sarah, her nose red and her eyes brimming, smiled. "It might work."

He rose. "I'll go ask them."

"Heavens, no," Lani scolded. "You cannot get by on your bum ankle."

"My ankle isn't nearly as sore." He rested his weight on the crutch.

"I'll go with him." Sarah snapped to her feet. "If Bill comes looking for me, you can tell him we went to get help."

Lani stared at both of them. "Well, really, there is no choice. But don't go to the Zimmermans' house. Go to Richard's. He's good friends with everyone. Let him ask for horses and a sleigh."

"Good idea." Sarah helped Thomas with the coat sleeve. "We'd better go."

As they walked to the door, Lani ducked into the closet and emerged, holding a cane. "You'll find this easier than that crutch."

He grasped Sarah's arm with one hand and the cane in the other. When Lani opened the door, snow blasted through the doorway.

AND SO THEY WALKED, HUDDLED TOGETHER. UNDER any other circumstance, Sarah would have been swept away by this moment—Thomas's arm around her waist, his cheek brushing against her head, his warm breath on her face. But all she could feel was an overwhelming sadness.

With Thomas's arm around her, she allowed herself to face her worst fears. What if Caroline lost the baby, the baby that meant so much to her and so much to everyone in town? The tears welling up in her eyes spilled over, freezing onto her cheeks.

Her thoughts went beyond this horror to a darker level. What if Caroline didn't make it?

THOMAS COULD FEEL SARAH SHAKING. AT FIRST, HE thought she was getting chilled, and he held her closer to him. But her shaking only intensified. She was crying. He reached for her chin and tipped her face toward him. Even with her puffy eyes, she was beautiful. She was everything he wanted. He knew it with such certainty that, for a moment, he struggled to breathe.

He drew her close again as the ice-laden wind swept around them. "We'll get through this, Sarah." He infusedwarmth and certainty into those words. "You have to trust me. We'll all come through this just fine."

As Sarah wiped her face with her gloved hand, they approached the bridge walkway, and she used her silver rod device to sweep the pathway with light. "I should warn you, this bridge gets pretty slick."

Cheeky grin in place, she looked up, and they laughed. Holding on to each other, they crossed the bridge and struggled onto Richard's driveway. Light illuminated several of his rooms despite the early morning hour.

Within seconds of their knocking, Richard, dressed in padded bib overalls and a work shirt, motioned them inside.

"Lani called. My scanner's been going off all morning with accident reports. All the ambulances are out."

He scratched the back of his neck. "The Zimmermans will lend us their horses. They're good people."

"Do they have a sleigh?" Thomas asked.

Richard's face brightened. "We're thinking along the same lines. They don't, but I do. I store it over at the Whites' barn, back behind the Bentonsport cemetery. We can borrow two horses from the Zimmermans, but we need to find someone who knows how to hook up the sleigh and drive it. I've never used it."

"I can do that." At their puzzled looks, Thomas shrugged. "I've taken my students on sleigh rides."

Richard clapped him on the back. "God did send you to us. Let's get going."

SARAH'S PHONE RANG, LANI'S VOICE SCREECHING INTO the night as soon as Sarah swiped to answer. "Bill was here. He was frantic for the keys. I tried to calm him, but I didn't get far. He kept pacing the room saying he couldn't wait. I don't know, Sarah ... If he found anyone in town to loan him a truck, they are on their way."

The sky was beginning to lighten, turning the landscape a murky gray. In the dim light, Sarah parted from Thomas and Richard and trudged through the slick deep snow toward Caroline's house.

"Dear God," she prayed, "let them still be there."

An older model car was running in Caroline's driveway. The house lights were on. With a deep breath and a second quick prayer, she knocked.

Bill glared at her with the eyes of a madman. His hair unkempt, his face unshaven, he let her inside. "We don't need your truck. Tony lent me his car. I'd rather we end up in a ditch than stay in this house and watch her and ..." He buried his face in his hands. His shoulders slumped.

She wrapped him in her arms, and he leaned his head against her shoulder. "It's going to be okay now—you hear me?" She lifted his head with her hands and, looking him in the eyes, smiled. "Really. Thomas has a plan."

Like a tired child, soothed by his mother's voice, Bill led Sarah to Caroline. One look at Caroline, curled up on a couch, and Sarah cringed as the outstretched fingers of fear squeezed her heart.

"Hey, sweetie, it's me." Sarah crouched by her friend.

Caroline's eyes opened, and her lips formed a faint smile. She reached for Sarah's hand.

"How are you feeling?" Sarah clasped her sweaty hand.

"Hurts." Her eyes closing, Caroline clung to Sarah's hand.

"So, are you having contractions? Does the pain come and go?"

Caroline's whole body shuddered. "It isn't what the doctor described. This h–hurts—*really* hurts—th–then goes away. N–no pattern. And, when it gets b–bad, I throw up."

"We're going to get you to the hospital soon, now," Sarah promised.

When Sarah explained how, the slightest of smiles curved Caroline's tremulous lips. "Only in Bentonsport." She held her stomach, winced, and moaned.

Rubbing her back, Sarah sat by her side. No wonder Bill had been so frantic. If it made any difference, Sarah would've stood on the front porch and screamed for help. But there was no point. And she had to be calm for her friends.

"I'll be right back." She brushed Caroline's cheek with her hand, stood, and left the room.

Bill was standing in the family room, staring out the window. Sarah walked up behind him. "Any sign yet?"

"Sarah, look, I can't do this anymore. I'll give them five more minutes, and then I'm carrying her to the car. We'll take our chances."

Moaning came from the family room. Bill squinted out the window.

Sarah cupped her hand on his shoulder. She wouldn't be able to convince him to give Thomas and Richard more time. She'd have to distract him instead.

"I'll sit with Caroline. Can you get the things we'll need together?" She squeezed his shoulder. "We'll need a hot water bottle, warm blankets, and soft pillows. Can you think of anything else?"

"I'll start with that."

As he left the room, Sarah glanced out the window. Still no sign of them. The snow seemed to fall harder now. She returned to Caroline. Her eyes were scrunched shut, and she was biting her bottom lip. Sarah kneeled beside her, "Worse, uh?"

Caroline nodded, her eyes still shut.

"Have you been able to sleep at all?"

She shook her head.

"Thomas and Richard should be here soon." Sarah brushed Caroline's hair from her face and straightened her pillow. "I so wish I could do something more."

"Pray."

Her eyes misting over and her throat beginning to close, Sarah swallowed several times. "I pray for you each day. I'm just praying harder now."

Bill clamored around in the front hall. Fearful he might have gathered everything she sent him after, she kissed Caroline's closed hand and headed to where he was rummaging through the front closet, searching for Caroline's coat and hat.

"Are you looking for Caroline's coat?" She poked her head in the closet, just behind him.

"I have all the things you suggested, and now we're heading out of here." He backed out of the closet, his arms draped with Caroline's outer garments. "It's not that I don't appreciate all you, Thomas, and Richard have done, but we could be standing here an hour from now waiting for the two of them. And that's an hour Caroline could spend in the hospital with people who know how to help her. You and I don't, Sarah."

She was tempted to say, 'Or you could spend an hour in the ditch before we find you and add frostbite and hypothermia to Caroline's problems.'

But Bill's face revealed the rage behind it. All she could do was stall.

"Okay," she said, trying to sound as though she were conceding. "I'll help in any way I can, but let's do this right. If you're taking the car, at least pack everything you need if you did end up in a ditch. Do you have flares?"

"What?" He set the items in his arms on the chair.

"Flares," she continued. "You know, roadside flares you set up on the highway if you have an accident so people can see you. I have some in the emergency kit in my garage."

"I'll get the flares, and then we're leaving." He headed out.

Sarah paced in front of the window, fisting her hands. "Come on, Thomas, please come on. God, bring them here." She was trying to think of other distractions—a Thermos of water? Cat litter for traction? What else did they recommend for driving in storms? As she was developing her mental list, Bill returned, holding her emergency kit.

"Why didn't you put that in the car?" she asked.

"Because they're here." His lips turned up in a half smile. "You won."

For a few seconds, she absorbed what he said. Then she hugged Bill, put on her coat, picked up her scarf and gloves, and headed outside.

To ensure Bill wouldn't take the car, she pocketed the key.

Thomas stayed in the driver's seat as Richard climbed out and walked toward her. "I'm sorry it took us longer than we planned, but Thomas had a masterful idea of creating two canopies of sorts out of the protective blankets I had covering the sleigh. We used the tops of two old arbors to create frames over the front and back seat. It will keep most of the snow and wind off you guys."

Ingenious! The sleigh looked like a covered wagon with two small humps.

"But," Richard continued, "it's going to be a long trip. Even this sleigh can't go fast in these conditions. Climb up here next to Thomas." He steadied her with his hand. "I'll help Bill get Caroline situated and then head over to the inn to settle Lani down. The two of us may venture out in a while to see if any of our older residents need assistance." Once she was seated, he glanced toward the house. "How is she doing?"

Suppressing a shudder, Sarah spoke first to Thomas and then to Richard. "I don't know. She's so pale and in tremendous pain. But she's aware of everything going on and even teases a bit."

Bill, wearing a thick jacket, stocking cap, and heavy gloves, carrying an armload of blankets and pillows, sprinted over to the sleigh. He shielded his face from the blowing snow and piled his load on the back seat. "Thank you—both of you. If we're ready, I'll get Caroline."

As he carried a bundle wrapped in blankets, nothing of Caroline was exposed. Richard lifted the canopy so he could position Caroline onto the back seat.

The wind blew in sharp stabbing gusts, creating a dizzying stir of snowflakes and prickly ice crystals.

Sarah held up the blanket separating her seat from the back as Bill uncovered Caroline's face. Richard held his part of the canopy back and, upon seeing Caroline, said, "There's our girl."

Caroline, pale, moved over so Bill could climb in next to her. Covered up again, she curled up, her head on Bill's lap and an arm against her stomach.

"Just try to rest," Sarah murmured. "We'll get you there soon."

Then she touched Thomas's arm. "We're all set."

"Godspeed." Richard stepped back. "We'll be praying for you here."

Thomas clicked his tongue at the horses and gently slapped the reins against them, and they were off down the main street, past the Greef Store and shops. At the inn, Lani stood at the bay window, rubbing the fog from the glass with her palm. When she waved, he tipped his hat. They reached the highway—indistinguishable from the rest of the terrain—and turned west toward Keosauqua.

The horses kept a steady pace, and Sarah shivered, realizing, for the first time, the dangers they faced, even with the sleigh. Everything was white. When the winds gusted, she could see only as far as the horses. As the gusts subsided, her view was only a few yards beyond the horses. The road, gravel shoulders, and embankments blended into a wide long stretch of white.

She snuggled close to Thomas so Caroline couldn't overhear. "How can you see?"

"I can't," he replied, looking at her with a serious expression, and then his lips turned up. "I just aim for the middle of what I think is the road and hope for the best. I also am trusting that you have a better sense of this road than I do."

Unnerved by the thought of being the navigator, she shivered. What he said was true. She'd driven this road hundreds of times. Leaning forward, she searched for landmarks.

"Okay, just up ahead, a wide bend will end over there, at the bridge."

As they rounded the curve, she lifted the blanket behind them and glanced at the backseat. Bill gave her a quick thumbs-up, so she lowered the blanket and pivoted back. "She's quiet, and he seems much more relaxed."

"The burden is now ours." The muscles in his neck were taut.

She cupped a gloved hand over his. "I can see where we need to go. There's a steep hill ahead just as soon as you cross the bridge, followed by a wide right-hand turn."

Nodding, he focused on the road.

"How do these sleighs handle slick hills?"

"The sleigh will do fine if the horses can make it up. I'm more concerned with how we manage going down. It will be safest if you give me some warning before we start downhill so I can climb out and guide them."

"The only hill we need to worry about is into Keosauqua. The road to Keo is full of ups and downs, but mostly gentle descents."

They crossed the bridge and began the steady climb up the steep, curving hill. The horses kept their footing, making the climb seem effortless. The road leveled out for a long stretch, and the snow blew across the flat plain in steady streams. This was followed by a second hill, then a long stretch of road sloping downhill. The pattern repeated several times.

"How did you learn to drive a sleigh?" She didn't want to distract Thomas, but breaking the tension might be good.

"From my grandfather. He took us for rides when we were children, and when I was about ten or so, he let me take the reins."

"You never know what God is training you for, do you?"

Thomas laughed. "I'd say that is true."

While he kept the horses at a slow steady pace, Sarah stared ahead, trying to locate familiar landmarks: an old abandoned barn, the white homestead farmhouse on the hill, the dip in the road with a frozen creek at the bottom. They'd been traveling for more than an hour when they reached the larger highway. Thomas turned the horses to the right, toward Keosauqua.

She rested her hand on his arm. "This is the steep downhill stretch into Keosauqua. It ends at the bridge."

After letting the horses continue a few yards farther, Thomas brought the sleigh to a stop.

Bill stuck his head through the draped blankets. "Is there a problem?"

"No." Thomas relinquished the reins to Sarah. "I'll guide the horses down the hill. I don't want any trouble when we're so close."

Bill lifted the canopy and climbed out of the sleigh. "Let me help."

"We need to keep them slow and steady," Thomas said to him. "I'm mainly concerned they'll lose their footing and pull the sleigh into the ditch."

They each took the lead for one horse, Thomas to the left, Bill to the right.

"Hold the reins with a little slack," Thomas called back to Sarah. "We'll steer. Use the reins to keep them pointed straight ahead."

"You left your cane." She reached for it.

"I won't need it. I'll use the horse to steady myself."

Grateful there were no other vehicles on the road, Sarah

shrugged her shoulders a few times to release the tension. She'd never commanded horses before. The men walked slowly, their feet sliding occasionally.

At the steepest part of the descent, the horses tried to take the lead, but Thomas got between the two mares, his head in between theirs, and held their bridles.

"That's right. Easy does it now," he said to them. "Slowly now, slowly. That's it."

The horses stayed in close step with him. At the bridge, the two men climbed back in, and Thomas waited until Bill was situated in the back.

"See," he said as Sarah scooted over and surrendered the reins, "you didn't even need my help. You took charge of those horses like a seasoned farm girl." He pecked her cheek as she smiled.

They moved faster through Keosauqua since some sand had been spread on the roads.

"Let's go around to the emergency entrance." She pointed to the driveway. They made the turn, but two ambulances blocked their way.

"You can pull over here—to the side."

Thomas did as she suggested and stopped the sleigh. He climbed out, but before he had a chance to assist Bill, Bill was outside, gathering Caroline into his arms. Sarah took Thomas's hand as they walked through the automatic doors, where a nurse led them to the emergency bay and settled Caroline on a cot.

"She's been in tremendous pain for more than six hours, and we don't know if she is having contractions or not," Sarah said, still holding on to his hand.

"Richard called about an hour or so ago. I'm so glad you made it." Sherrie, a nurse who frequented Sarah's bakery, pointed to a room behind her. "Let's wheel her into the procedure room."

Caroline turned onto her side, holding her middle, her eyes shut tight. Bill rolled the cart into the room, and Sherrie pulled a curtain around it.

"I'll wait out here," Thomas said.

"I'll be right back." Sarah let herself through the curtain and squatted by Caroline's side. She kissed Caroline's cheek. "You're safe now. We're all here, and they'll find out what's wrong now, okay?"

Caroline took Sarah's hand and gave it a limp squeeze. Sarah stood up, blinking back the heat behind her eyes. She walked to the hallway with Bill—haggard, tired, and weak—behind her.

He enveloped her and Thomas each in a strong hug, then stepped back. "Thanks, both of you."

Trying not to cry, Sarah nodded. "We'll be in the lobby over by the chapel. Let us know when you know something, okay?"

She and Thomas joined about ten people in the lobby, some resting with their heads against the wall, others, their chairs forming a circle, speaking in low tones. Two toddlers sat on the floor, crashing their plastic cars into each other and laughing each time.

Thomas brushed his shoulder to hers as he rubbed his hands together. "So, what do you think?"

"Well," she began, "we're so blessed to have made it, and Caroline is in good hands." She looked deep into his eyes. "We've all been blessed by an angel that brought you to us."

He bent forward, his hands clasped between his open legs. At length, he shook his head. "Well, if an angel brought me here, he blessed me as well."

They sat, watching the children play while the hospital staff came and went. A man with a large silver belt buckle introduced himself as an ambulance driver and offered them steaming coffee cups.

When nearly an hour had passed, Bill entered the lobby, accompanied by Sherrie. Thomas and Sarah stood, and she asked, "How is she?"

Bill glanced at Sherrie. "Well, it seems to all be good news. She isn't having contractions. The pain seems to be from her gallbladder flaring up. They've given her something for the pain, and they're getting ready to admit her to get it under control. It's fine for you to go back and visit. But Sherrie wanted to speak with both of you."

The nurse gestured toward the chapel. "Let's step in there. It will be more private." Once they sat in chairs clustered in one corner, Sherrie smiled. "We were all impressed with your cleverness in finding a way to get here. We have several patients who we know need to be seen—no real emergencies—but, still, they should come in. With our ambulances overworked already, we were wondering if you mind transporting some of our patients this afternoon and evening?"

Thomas glanced toward Sarah. "I wouldn't mind. In fact, I'd enjoy helping. But I should take Sarah home first so she can start her baking project."

"No." She held up her hands in a Stop motion. "I'll bake day and night if I have to, but right now, I'd like to visit Caroline and then help you. Just give us a moment, and then we're all yours."

SARAH TAPPED ON THE DOOR AND THEN OPENED IT, peering around the side. Caroline lay on the bed, the side rails up, covered with a sheet and a blanket.

When Sarah padded in, Caroline gave her a weak smile and gestured to her IV. "I'm all juiced up."

"No pain?" Sarah squeezed her hands together.

"None now. They put the monitor on me, and the baby is doing great. Sarah, I thought I was losing the baby."

"We wouldn't let that happen." Sarah raised her hands for emphasis. "Even if we had to take the sleigh all the way to University Hospital. I'm going to let you rest now."

Caroline reached for her hand. "You came through for me again. I'd also like to thank Thomas. Could you get him?"

"Sure thing." Sarah stepped outside the door and motioned Thomas in.

When they approached her bedside, Caroline said, "Sarah,

could you do me a favor? Could you find my nurse and see if I can have some ice water or a soda? There's a soda machine downstairs, and Bill should have some money."

"I have money, you goose." Sarah rolled her eyes. "I'll find out and be right back."

Chapter Twenty

Thomas glanced around the room, where only the chair looked normal amidst the oddities and contraptions. Long metal rods framed the bed. Poles with lit boxes and hanging bags stood nearby. He followed the cord from the bag across the bed to where it was taped to Caroline's arm. She opened her hand to him.

"Bill told me I owe my getting here to you."

He stepped forward and held her hand. "I'm just glad you're feeling better and you and the baby are well. It's nice that, for once, I can help you. You've done so much to make my visit memorable, Caroline."

She crooked her free arm under her head. "I have one more favor to ask, if I may. I may not be home before you leave, and I want you to promise me something."

Puzzled, he nodded.

"Sarah is my best friend. Bill and I have introduced her to several of Bill's friends in hopes one of them would be the right man for her. Sarah doesn't fall for men easily, and we've always said just the right person would have to come along and sweep her off her feet."

He took a deep breath, unprepared for this. His heart began

LISA SCHNEDLER

to beat faster. He was already far beyond his limits in talking to a woman by himself, let alone chatting with a woman in a bed about his most intimate feelings.

"You've only been here a short while. And Sarah's connected with you in a way I've never seen her do. I realize this is a strange conversation, and I'm embarrassed even to say it, but please, Thomas, talk to her. If you are going to stay in touch with her—or even come back for another visit—*tell* her. If this is it, if you're leaving with no plans of continuing to get to know her, let her know that too. But don't wait until you're ready to leave, okay? Promise me one way or another, you'll tell her and tell her soon?"

His face flushing, he studied the shiny gray squares making up the floor. He'd never had such frank discussions with anyone, let alone a woman.

"Yes, Caroline." He lifted his face. "I will talk to her."

Sarah entered, carrying a tray with a glass of ice and a can.

"The nurse says you can sip on this." She placed it on the metal stand next to Caroline's bed. She opened the can and poured. "They'll move you to your room in a few minutes." As she straightened and dried her hands on a tissue from the box on the stand, she frowned between them. "Is there something wrong?"

"No, no," Caroline said. "I was just telling Thomas I didn't know if I'd be home before Christmas. Can you imagine spending Christmas in a hospital?"

"Don't think of that, now," Sarah scolded. "Besides, if you're in here at Christmas, we'll bring Christmas to you. Isn't that right, Thomas?"

Her eyebrows rose as she realized no, he wouldn't be here on Christmas Day. She swallowed and faked a laugh. "Well, Bill and I won't let Christmas pass you by. But we won't think about that now. We'll plan to have you home by then."

As a thin, dark-haired nurse entered, Sarah kissed Caroline's cheek. "We'd better get our taxi service underway. We'll stop in before heading home, okay?"

At the nurses' station, they gathered directions to the patients they'd pick up.

Before dark, they embarked on six trips and returned each patient to their homes.

"What do you say," Sarah said as they pulled up to the hospital doors, "we go check in with Caroline and Bill and then head home? The horses are tired, and I'm exhausted."

Anxiety about getting Caroline to the hospital had energized him. But now, he was tired, and just thinking of returning to Bentonsport brought relief. He stretched, shook out his shoulders, and followed her through doors that opened as they approached. If only he could ask questions.

After finding their friends sleeping, they walked to the nurses' station, and Sarah jotted a note for when Caroline awoke. Then hand in hand, they strolled back outside. Swinging her up high, Thomas placed Sarah on the front seat and climbed in next to her. The snow was now a light mist.

"It's so pretty, really, isn't it?" She rested her head against his chest as they started out.

The night was perfect. The streetlamps glowed through the white mist. He bent down and kissed the top of her head, unable to imagine leaving her in three short days. And *what* would he say to her?

He snuggled his arm around her and let the horses go forward at their own pace. The sleigh rocked back and forth, and the horses' hoofs made soft thuds against the thick snow. Just as they were crossing the bridge out of town, Sarah went limp, asleep against his chest.

He leaned back in the seat, enfolding her waist with his arm. He'd never been in such an intimate position with any woman. Two weeks ago, this whole scene would have been unspeakable, unimaginable. But so much had changed. His breath quickened.

In the quiet night, with the weight of this beautiful, sweet woman against his chest, he allowed himself to realize something he'd been pushing aside for days. He wanted to stay with Sarah.

He wanted a chance to let their relationship deepen and grow. He'd be willing to stay or to take her with him. It didn't matter which Bentonsport they were in. He just wanted them together.

They passed the old Erickson farmhouse halfway to Bentonsport. If it were possible to take her to his Bentonsport, she could set up a bakery near the Greef Store. The town would embrace her. But then his spine sagged—he had come to Bentonsport for a purpose, not a person. Wasn't that how Pastor Lockhardt had put it?

Kissing the top of her head, he lingered. Her hair smelled of vanilla, warm and sweet. This wasn't baking vanilla, but some type of perfume, with a musky undertone. He breathed it in. How would he tell her he couldn't return? He tugged back on the reins as the horses began their first slow descent.

Tell her the truth—she'd think he was touched. Be factual and say he wasn't coming back—she'd think him cruel and caddish.

And yet Caroline was correct. He had to say something. He couldn't just disappear.

The sleigh glided through the mounds and tracks in the snow. Sarah stirred, repositioning herself against his chest, but never fully awakened. Tenderness gripped his chest, nearly stilling his breathing, his heartbeat.

Whatever he said, it would have to be honest, simple, and straightforward. He'd plead for her understanding and, somehow, describe his feelings. But, first, he needed to come to grips with them himself.

He now had two Bentonsports where he felt at home, where he had friends. Of course, he was much more comfortable in his Bentonsport. There, he fit in. He could be himself, without watching every word or pretending. But *that* Bentonsport didn't have Sarah. How could he wake up in a world where Sarah didn't exist? Had not yet been born. And how long would it take to fill the void, or could it ever be filled?

One of the horses blew long snorts of steam into the air. He clicked his tongue to reassure it and move them along.

He glanced down at her. Their relationship was still too new to define. What their relationship would be like if they were back in his community, if he had met her there ... he couldn't imagine. His feelings for her had deepened much more quickly than circumstances permitted in his time. He gently brushed back a lock of her hair from her cheek.

In his world, he and Sarah wouldn't have spent time alone, discussing their lives, playing, and getting to know each other so early in the relationship. Under the town's watchful eyes, they would've been given only brief times to sit alone and talk, in someone's parlor or on someone's porch.

They crossed the bridge into Bentonsport. He slowed the horses in front of her house. He opened the sleigh door and eased her head to the seat before climbing out. He trudged through the snow to the front door to be sure it was unlocked, opened it, and left it ajar. Then returned to the sleigh and slid Sarah into his arms. She stirred, awakening as they approached the house.

"Where are we?" Her drowsy voice was almost musical.

"We're at your house." He carried her into the doorway and clicked on the kitchen light.

"Ah." She yawned, and her lips eased into a sleepy-sweet smile. "Caroline is safe, and we are home."

As he carried her, she didn't protest but rather curled into him. In the parlor, he eased her onto the couch. She switched on the lamp to her right. Soft yellow light flooded the room.

After covering her with the blanket that draped the sofa arm, he then nestled an embroidered pillow under her head. Slowly, he sat next to her.

She smiled up at him, yawned, and closed her eyes, snuggling into the blanket. "I can only rest here for a minute. I need to start baking. I have so many cookies to bake before Thursday, and I have to visit Caroline, and ..."

When she dropped off to sleep again, he kissed her cheek and headed back to the inn.

Lani and Richard were sitting in the kitchen when Thomas entered. They both stood up.

"Oh, Thomas," Lani said. "Did Caroline take a turn for the worse? You've been gone so long."

He squeezed her in a quick hug. "The news is all good. Caroline is doing well. The doctors believe the baby is fine. They mentioned it might be a flare-up of her, um, gall bladder, I believe." Thomas shifted his feet, uncomfortable talking about Caroline's specific health conditions, and ended the explanation.

The moment quickly passed as Lani picked up the conversation. "Bill called and told us that news ages ago, but where have you been?"

"Give the young man some tea or something warm." Richard motioned them toward the kitchen. "He's been out in the cold."

Thomas reviewed the day, recounting their trips to and from the hospital. When he finished, he asked about their day. Richard described how he and Lani made the rounds to all the shut-ins, ensuring each was well.

Lani returned from the stove with a tray of teacups. She set it down and pointed her spoon at Thomas. "Fifteen more minutes —just fifteen more—and I would've called."

"You must be exhausted." Richard winked at Thomas.

Thomas hadn't realized how tired he was, but as he sat in the chair, in the warmth, sipping hot tea, a sudden exhaustion overcame him.

"I'm afraid I am." He stifled a yawn.

"With your permission, Lani." Richard rose. "I'll leave the sleigh in front of the inn tonight and lead the horses back to the Zimmermans on my way home. We can borrow the horses again sometime tomorrow and take the sleigh back up to the Whites' storage barn."

As Richard put on his coat, Lani stood and wagged a plump finger. "Now, don't you go tripping on that bridge. We don't need two men with bad legs around here."

Laughing, Thomas shook his head. "That would be just one,

Lani. The crisis has been good medicine for my ankle. I've hardly thought of it."

"Well"—the solidly built woman jammed her hands on her hips—"don't be surprised if it thinks of you tomorrow when everything settles down."

"We'll just have to come up with another distraction for him," Richard said. "Perhaps a female distraction?"

Lani pretended to swat Richard on the shoulder, both laughing.

"That female has ideas of her own, all centered on cookies," Thomas said.

"Ah yes," Richard said. "You two will be busy for the better part of two days, I'd say, trying to get that project done. I may stop by tomorrow if you don't mind. Keep you company and offer encouragement."

"Notice he didn't say the word *bake*," Lani teased.

"No." His brown eyes twinkling, Richard tugged on his gloves. "I know my strengths, and that isn't one. But I also didn't say the word *eat*, so I won't be nibbling away your accomplishments."

"Speaking of strengths," Lani interrupted, "you better get some sleep, Thomas, or you'll be no help at all."

After Richard said his goodbyes and Thomas and Lani retired, Thomas readied himself for bed, rehearsing his talk with Sarah. But the bed was warm, and his eyes heavy.

Tomorrow ... Tomorrow, I'll figure out exactly what to say.

Chapter Twenty-One

Thomas carried the weight of the day on his shoulders as he walked down the stairs and into the kitchen.

"Well, here I thought we'd see you all bright and cheerful this morning, after yesterday's glorious success," Lani teased, pouring his coffee. "My, I thought you'd come down for breakfast humming and feeling good. But, look at you, your brows all knotted up like you're trying to solve all the world's problems."

The cream turned the dark liquid of his coffee the color of caramel.

She placed the carafe in the middle of the table and sat next to him. Then she added cream to her coffee and cupped the mug in both hands.

He glanced up and found her staring at him. He buttered his toast.

"This puzzlement wouldn't happen to have anything at all to do with the fact that you're leaving us in just three short days, would it?"

He cast a smile her way but didn't reply. Instead, he took a deep sip of his coffee.

"Now, I don't flatter myself when I say you might miss us. My real thinking is that, while it may be true that you'll remember us, there's one of us you truly might miss."

He nibbled a corner of his toast. Normally, he appreciated Lani's chatter. But not today. "You could say that, in some way, yes." He didn't want to seem evasive, but she wouldn't be satisfied without some type of reply.

"Well." She huffed. "The simple solution is to stay in touch. You young people have so many advantages today—you can phone, fly, drive, email, text, chat, or do something completely old-fashioned like write to each other. Look at this as a beginning, not an ending. That road you leave on runs both ways, and you can always come back. Why, I might even want to put up with you again."

She stood, tousled his hair, and went to the island to get two napkins.

"Thanks, Lani." But the words filled no hollow inside him. His dread of this day was mounting. It couldn't end any way but badly.

"So ..." She set a napkin at each of their places. "You and Sarah have a big day ahead, trying to get that order together."

"She was hoping to have everything delivered by tomorrow night." He picked up his coffee, inhaled the invigorating aroma, then drank the warm liquid. A perfect cup of coffee. Although he usually drank it black, for some reason, here, he was beginning to like it more with cream.

"But we will be fortunate to have everything baked and delivered by Friday morning."

Lani dropped into the chair beside him again. "I offered to help in any way I can, so if I can be a help and not a hindrance, just give me a call. Otherwise, I don't want to take away from your last three days together."

Few women in his town would give up the chance to witness a couple's remaining time together. Such privileged insight would guarantee them invitations to teas and gatherings for days ahead.

He straightened his slumped form. Lost in his thoughts, he'd been terrible company. He stood and kissed Lani on the cheek. "We'll let you know if you can help."

He made his way down the street, almost wishing to fall—anything to prevent his talk with Sarah. But she needed his help—and needed the truth. He reached her stoop, knocked, and stomped his feet.

As Sarah answered the door, the heat of the ovens whooshed out. The room smelled sweet, like warm vanilla. Much like her hair. Dusted here and there with flour, she looked like a bespeckled angel in her crisp white bakers' outfit, her nape-length hair pulled up and twisted in the back with a gold clip. Clunky black shoes lifted her two inches taller.

"You could've slept in, you know," she teased.

"From the looks of things," he said, nodding toward six trays of freshly baked cookies on drying racks along the counter, "I should have come earlier."

She laughed and hung his coat on a hook. "Don't become neurotic like me. I couldn't sleep late—I kept thinking about all the baking. I finally gave in around four, got up, and started the ovens."

SARAH DIDN'T MENTION HOW SURROUNDING AND overflowing her thoughts was her deep sadness in knowing he was leaving in three short days. Upon waking, she'd decided she could take no more of his silence on the subject. Even if he'd only agree to stay in touch, she'd have hope.

But her determination faded as he entered the kitchen. She ached to put her arms around him, smell the sweet-spicy scent that seemed to infuse his clothing, tell him how much she enjoyed being with him, even doing the mundane chores of life. Yet she sensed such forwardness wouldn't work with Thomas.

As she handed him a steaming mug of coffee, a smile lifted his lips. "Well, you look no worse from lack of sleep."

"If you mean no worse than yesterday morning"—she swiped at her hair—"well, it doesn't get much worse. At least, I hope it doesn't."

"I thought at some point, before heading home, I'd like to visit everyone one last time to say goodbye."

Sarah swallowed hard. How she hated that word! 'See you later,' 'Talk soon,' anything but the word *goodbye*.

"I didn't come over here to drink coffee and watch you work." He walked to the other side of the counter. "I want to help. As you've seen, we make quite a team."

She scanned his face to see what he had meant. "Quite a team." Her throat tightened on the words. As she searched his face, she could see his comment was lightly made, just conversational. But it was too late. The words burned deep, deeper. She struggled to breathe but could only take in short gasps of air. She gripped the counter.

"Just ignore me," she said. "It's been a hard couple of days, and I imagine I'm tired, and ..." She hurried to the parlor, wiping a tear as it snaked down her cheek. Though she gestured for him to remain behind, he stayed in step with her.

When she curled up against a couch cushion, he sat apart from her, his feet planted on the ground, hands clasped between his knees. He stared at the patterned carpet.

"We have to talk, Sarah."

Each heavy word struck a blow.

"I promised Caroline I wouldn't leave without discussing the future. It's a conversation I didn't want to start because I enjoy your company so much, and I wanted to convince myself we could continue in this way."

This was not a conversation she wanted to have. This must be how it felt to be terribly sick, go to the doctor, and know, from the moment the doctor sat down, the news wouldn't be good. No wonder so many people waited so long to go for help. No, she never could've started this conversation on her own.

"I don't even know where to start." He moved his fingers up

like a tent, then back down again. "I came to Bentonsport thinking I was here to discover something. I didn't come looking for a relationship—my stay would be too short to form friendships. But here I am, and in just over a week, I have more friends here than I do back home. And then there's you."

She brushed a lock of hair from her face, the clock ticking away the time. Strange how she usually didn't hear it ticking since it was such a part of the background sounds. But, in moments of intensity, the clock took on a life of its own, ticking louder and louder just when things grew still.

"I had just left a disappointing situation back home regarding a woman. I was reconciling myself to not thinking about her when I met you. And, Sarah, you are so different from other women I have known. When I'm with you, I feel like I'm back home, with my mother and my sisters."

His mother? His sisters?

"I don't mean that the way it sounds. What I mean is I am so comfortable in your presence, and it is so refreshing. I can't imagine giving this up."

"But ... why do you—do *we*—need to give it up?" Desperation—terrible, despicable desperation—pushed the words out. "I understand you have to go back home to teach, but that doesn't mean you have to give all this up. You could always come back. There's spring break, right? And summers and, I don't know, maybe I could even go out there for a visit?"

Thomas shook his head. "Trust me, Sarah, it just can't work. It's just—"

"Another woman?"

"No."

"Money?"

"No."

"You don't want to come back, and—"

"Heavens, of course, I do." He thrust his hands forward, his voice revealing his frustration.

"What the ..." Sarah rose to her feet. "Thomas, what is this?"

Rising as well, he placed his hands on her shoulders. "I can't explain this. I'm sorry. I can't."

Heat tingled up her neck and cheeks, scorching her ears, and she could think of nothing to say. He made no sense. She removed his hands from her shoulders and pivoted toward the kitchen. She couldn't look at him without her heart aching. How could he lead her on while knowing he was leaving and not coming back? "You'd better go now."

He approached her, stepping around in front of her. "Go?"

He was so handsome. So completely wonderful. And her heart felt the sharp cut of broken glass. "Because, you see, Thomas, I have no trouble explaining how this is for me." Her voice shook as she swallowed, fighting to hold back—what? Anger? Tears? "I could easily fall in love with you. It's that simple. I don't know how this happened so fast.

"You fell into my life, and now I think of you—of *us*—all the time. When I'm baking. When I'm running errands. When I'm getting ready for bed at night. It doesn't matter where I am, I remember the wonderful simple times we've shared over the past week, where this could lead if you were to feel the same way." Not in control of her movements, she stepped toward him. "This could be so wonderful, but not if you don't want this to work—"

"Don't want?" He pushed his fingers against his forehead. "What in the world would lead you to think I don't want this to work?"

He paced back and forth in short strides like a caged lion. But then he snapped around and faced her. "It has nothing to do with what I want."

"Then what does it have to do with?" She held her ground. "Please"—her voice dropped to a plea—"help me understand. I could handle it if I could make sense of what you're saying."

He wasn't going to respond.

Shoulders slumping, her heart breaking. She averted her gaze. "Just go then, please. No more games, no more pretending. I can't fool myself into thinking this is going anywhere, and it hurts too much to have you here now."

He couldn't move, couldn't think. He had nothing to say, nowhere to go, and the only person who connected him to the life he wanted was now shutting him out. Her profile tight with pain, she stood there unmoving. Not looking at him. Unable to imagine leaving her like this, he somehow found himself putting on his coat and scarf, taking his hat, and reaching for the door.

Cold air stung his face. He looked toward her, one last time, but her back was still to him. He eased the door closed between them.

Hollowness carved out his insides. Three more days. Three long days. Was this what he came to learn? That a wonderful woman who brought him such joy and pleasure existed, but she was born over a hundred years too late? That this middle-aged bachelor was capable of feeling love, just not with anyone in his century? That a broken heart hurts, but watching the heartbreak of the person you care about hurts even more?

What sort of exciting adventure was this? This was no memorable journey. This was Hell, plain and simple.

He somehow ended up back at the inn, cold and wanting to bury himself in sleep. Sleep for three long days, if possible. As he opened the door, a newspaper rustled as Lani folded it. Then the soft shuffle of her house slippers whispered against the hardwood floor.

"Why, Thomas"—she helped him with his coat and scarf—"don't tell me you've finished your baking. I may not ..." She stopped when she saw his face. "No"—the word came—"no, it's not that. What, Thomas, a quarrel? You and Sarah?"

When he hobbled into the sitting room and collapsed into one of the large overstuffed chairs, she pulled a chair next to his.

"I think ..." He rubbed the bridge of his nose. "I think, if you can, you should go to her."

Neither said a word as they sat side by side.

Lani pressed her hands to her thighs. "You're right."

She left the room and went to her apartment. After several minutes, she entered the front hallway and put on her coat and hat. He looked up as she came to the doorway.

"I don't know what time I'll be back. If I don't get back before noon, there's a casserole in the refrigerator. Just heat it up and help yourself. I don't sound like much of a hostess, but you'd probably rather have me out of the inn for now."

The hollow sound of the closing door echoed deep in his chest.

SARAH LAY CRUMPLED UP ON THE COUCH WHEN THE bell over the door jangled. Thomas wouldn't come back unasked. He was a gentleman, if nothing else. And any customer, well, they could just go away. Footsteps approached the kitchen. Someone poured coffee. Then the acrid scent neared, and the couch cushions shifted as Lani sat next to her.

Without a word, the woman rubbed her back, her hand moving across Sarah's shoulders. They sat there in silence. Lani sipping her coffee and rubbing Sarah's back, Sarah making sniffling noises, keeping her face covered in the crook of her arm.

"He said h–he's never coming back." Never. Coming. Back. Never ... the words were a refrain she couldn't stop playing.

"Sarah." Tender scolding—oh-so-familiar and welcome—deepened Lani's voice. "Nonsense. How could he possibly *know*?"

Sarah raised her arm enough to peek at this kindhearted woman, absorb that tenderness, that motherly concern she ached for.

Misted eyes gleamed back at her. "How can either of you know with any certainty what tomorrow will bring? He may *think* he's not coming back here, but he cannot *know*—not for certain. I know you've lost people. This is harder on you than others. But, honey, think about this. When your parents took off in the car the day they died, did they know they weren't coming back? When my husband went hunting on the day he died, did he know he wouldn't be coming home? Or did I?"

Sarah sat up, wiped her eyes on the back of her hand, and hugged the pillow against her hollow heart.

"Of course not. These things just aren't known. Now, I'm not saying you should be planning your future as if he were coming back. I'm simply saying you're borrowing trouble and getting yourself all worked up over something no one—except God, that is—even knows about."

Sarah fumbled in her apron pocket for a tissue and blew her nose.

Lani patted her leg. "My mother always said to me. 'Learn from your past, hope for your future, but live today, making it all you can.' Don't you see, Sarah? You're throwing away precious time—time you can't get back."

Time! How could she talk about time when they only had three days left? Sarah wiped her nose and sat up. "But that's just it, Lani. Knowing what will happen tomorrow makes today so painful. It's like knowing someone is dying and having to put on a brave face. I know he's leaving and—"

"All you know, Sarah, is he's going back home. Right now, that's all you know. Just like you said, when someone is dying, you don't know when or how. Heavens, you might be the one to go first. You hold tight to your memories. But you don't regret the good times spent together, right?"

"I suppose not." She fluffed the fringe of the pillow, letting it land smoothly against her fingers.

Lani drained her coffee and stood up. "Let's get to work on those cookies. After a bit, when you feel stronger and your face isn't quite so red, if you'd like, I'll fetch Mr. Thomas, and you two can salvage what will be left of this day and quit talking nonsense about what you do and don't know about the future. You'll just enjoy today, or should I say this afternoon?"

Hope. Her heart began to warm with the sweet breath of hope. Sarah hugged Lani. "You're just like a mom to me."

"And you're like a daughter."

Chapter Twenty-Two

Thomas had just settled in the parlor armchair, intending to sort out what had just taken place, when someone knocked and opened the door. "Anybody home?" Richard called inside.

"In here. I'm the only one here."

Richard shuffled his boots back and forth on the mat, clattered his outerwear on the coat rack, and strode across the hall toward the parlor.

"Thomas? I thought you'd be at Sarah's all day."

He dropped into the chair next to Thomas. Thomas kept his gaze fixed on the fire now reduced to mere tongues of flames and embers. One thing he liked about most men was their comfort with silence.

Richard stood up and added a log. He stirred the fire with the poker. "Is there something wrong? Something perhaps I could help with?"

"I have succeeded in ending my stay here on a sour note. Sarah is crying, Lani is helping her, and I'm sitting here, not knowing how this all happened or what to do."

As flames curled around the new log, Richard returned to his chair. "Do you know why Sarah is crying?"

Thomas picked up a coaster from the side table and tapped it against his palm with a rhythmic thudding. "I won't be returning."

Silence again. Just the fire filling the room with warmth and sound.

"I had promised Caroline I would be forthright with Sarah. Not allow her to misunderstand our future together." He tapped the coaster again, rapid-fire.

"And you felt you needed to tell her right away, today?"

No. What *had* he felt? Thud. Thud. Thud. He matched the taps to his thumping heartbeat. "I went over to help her with the baking. The conversation led toward our relationship." Thud. Thud. Thud-thud. "And I had no choice but to tell her the truth."

"And she ...?"

His lips formed a humorless grin. "Asked me to leave."

Thud. Thud. Thud.

Richard scooted back in his chair and laced his hands behind his head. "I'd say she has the right person with her right now. Lani has been through an awful lot in her time. People with that sort of history can help put anything in perspective, including this. If I were in your place, I'd wait for Lani to come back and take your cue from her. She might even convince Sarah to set this aside and see you for your last days here. You never know."

Thomas scowled at the fire, tapping the coaster against his palm.

"In the meantime." Richard pushed to his feet. "If you'd like to join me, I was just on my way to take my sleigh back. I borrowed the Zimmermans' horses, so I'll need to bring them back too. The outside air might do you good."

"The only thing I could think of doing, when I left Sarah's, was crawling in bed and sleeping until Saturday." Thomas set the obnoxious coaster aside. "But I'm not tired. A walk would be better. Thanks, Richard."

As they stepped out, the sun shone on the snow. More than

its glare made it hard to see. Short gusts of wind blew snow and ice crystals against his cheeks and eyes. He wrapped his scarf across his face and squinted against the glare as they hitched the horses. When they climbed in, Richard handed over the reins.

"You're the pro, I hear."

In few things, and not at all in love. A wry twist pinched his lips. "I have had experience, recently." He tried to sound jovial, but the attempt fell flat.

He eased the horses onto the main road and gave them a great deal of rein, allowing them to maneuver the drifts. Now and then, when they headed toward the roadside ditches, he pulled back and steered them into the center of the road.

"Head toward the church," Richard shouted over the gusting wind. "You remember the old barn, right? Just beyond the church?"

The horses traveled slowly as they approached the steep hill. The snow was slick, and the horses lifted their heads, reluctant to pull the sleigh on the icy surface. After several attempts to get them to move, Thomas shook his head. "It's no use. We're going to have to guide them up."

In front of the horses, each took one lead. They trudged the hill, stopping from time to time to allow the horses to find their footing. The wind stilled, making their climb more pleasant.

"There, girl." Thomas stroked the quarter horse's muzzle. "Up we go, just a ways more." Uphill from the church, the road began to level. Thomas shifted his gaze between the ground, the snowdrifts, and the horizon for the best path. At one point, Richard positioned his head across the horse's neck and pointed toward the adjacent land. "Over there is the old Bentonsport cemetery. We have stones there dating all the way back to the 1840s. Not many burials there today. If it weren't for the snow, I'd show you some of the older stones. Quite a bit of history right here."

Thomas stopped as the passage of time once again became real to him. In his Bentonsport, the cemetery was only a few decades old. There were just a smattering of stones, but here, the cemetery, though small, contained perhaps as many as a hundred stones of various heights and sizes. The snow had covered the smaller ones.

As they trudged past, he was torn between wanting to read the stones for names he might recognize and not wanting to face the reality that many of his friends and neighbors had long ago been buried there. They had nearly passed the cemetery when Thomas, against his better judgment, glimpsed two names—two familiar names—and his heart sank.

In the last row, three stones from the end, stood a monument carved in marble. Atop it was an open Bible and just under it, within a frame of intricate scrollwork, was the name *Ross*. Thomas couldn't make out the Scripture verse that followed, and the first names must have been further down on the stone, now covered with the snow.

His gaze slipped to a stone two down. An angel atop the stone looked down on those who lay beneath. Worn and cracked through the years, the writing was still intact. Written just under the angel, in soft scrolling letters, was the word *Barton*. Thomas tripped, causing the horse to snort and stomp.

Don't read on. Do not read on. Don't ...

But he read down as far as he could before the snow rendered the writing illegible. On the stone's left-hand side, just below the Barton in smaller lettering was the name *Thomas* and, to the right, the word *Sara*. He had trouble making out the writing under the two names. The words under his name were worn and cracked. But he could, after just a moment, read those under Sara —*Cherished Wife, Devoted Mother, now home.*

"It may sound strange," Richard interrupted Thomas's trance. "But it is a fascinating place. So many of the names you read in the early history of Bentonsport, you'll find here."

The two men continued up the winding road to the barn. One step after another, holding the reins, Thomas scuffled through the snow in a daze. To think that, within three feet of where he was walking, lay his body and those of his family, at least that of his wife—Sara?

"Here we are," Richard shouted out as the wind picked up again. They led the horses into the shed, and Thomas unhitched them. They covered the sleigh with old burlap sacks left heaped where they had tossed them aside—was that yesterday morning? They placed the arbors against the far wall.

"As musty as this old barn is," Richard continued, "I must admit it's sure nice to be out of the wind." He picked up an old horse brush and began brushing down the Zimmermans' horses. "I wish I had some oats and water to give you, old girl. But I will get you home in a jiffy and back to your warm stall."

He must be dull company if Richard had to resort to talking to the horses. But how could he make small talk—chat and joke? Not after that stone in the cemetery, one he didn't want to talk about. He needed time to walk and think. He needed to be by himself. Again, they each took one horse's lead. Thomas helped Richard shove the creaking barn door closed and notch the plank back in place.

As they approached the cemetery, Thomas positioned himself for a better view of the stone. He didn't want to see the dates. He had no desire to know the year of his death. The thought chilled him in a way the wind couldn't. But he wanted to see if anything in the writing under his name could confirm the stone was his.

It would be a tremendous coincidence if there were another Thomas Barton who lived and died in Bentonsport with a stone of such apparent age. Still, Barton is not an uncommon name. But he knew of no other Bartons in Bentonsport. Or Vernon. Or Bonaparte.

As the back of the stone came into view, his heart beat hard. They passed the back of the cemetery, and he turned his head to read the inscription. He stopped and squinted hard at the writing under Thomas, making out the four words underneath—*Teacher, Father, Husband, and Friend.*

He matched his pace to Richard's. Teacher? The stone had to

be his. How many other teachers with his name would reside and die in Bentonsport many years ago?

"A group of us got together to try to restore some of those old stones in the cemetery."

Richard again began to pass the time in small talk. "We had a bad incident there a few years back. Some teenage boys wreaked havoc, knocking over stones and tearing the place up. No reason why, just to be destructive. So, we got together and borrowed the Whites' tractor and put the stones back up."

He gave the horse a gentle pat. "We're trying to raise money now to repair those that were damaged. It's hard, though." At this point, he was nearly shouting against the wind. "Because there are so many needs in the county for the living, let alone the dead. Still, out of honor and respect, we need to do what we can. Don't you think so, Thomas?"

Of course, he would want the cemetery where he was—would be—buried to be kept up. No one wants to be forgotten, with even his final resting place desecrated. But he tempered his response, saying only, "You did the right thing."

They neared the end of the steep hill beneath the old church, and Thomas looked over at Richard. The cold and exertion were taking a toll on him. Perhaps he could accomplish several things at once.

"Richard, I'll take the horses back over to the Zimmermans. I'd like some time to think things through, and it would be wonderful if you could drop in on Sarah and Lani and find out how things are going."

"Well, I can't say I'd miss the walk." Richard didn't hesitate. "If you're certain it's okay, I'll take you up on your offer. And I'll bring back what little information two women will share."

Richard turned right toward Sarah's house, then called back, "Hey, be careful on that bridge. I hear it can be slick."

Grinning, Thomas nodded, then continued straight ahead, the thud of the horses' hoofs against the snow and the whipping wind the only sounds to distract his thoughts.

It was so strange to see, in one glance, the end of one's life on earth. Yet, in one glance, he saw not only the end but also the middle. His wife and mother of his children, Sara? He knew no Sara in his Bentonsport. But perhaps she hadn't yet arrived. There was always a steady stream of new residents. Few eligible women moved to town, but it wasn't out of the question.

Or maybe he would move out of town, marry this Sara, and return. But that seemed improbable. The stone described him as a teacher. It seemed unlikely that he would leave town and return to his teaching job.

In all likelihood, the stone meant he would remain in Bentonsport, remain at the academy. And that thought did not displease him.

He had come to love the town and its people. But his loneliness troubled him. And now, he beheld a promise of an end to the loneliness. Was this what he traveled here to learn? Was this his gift? That there was an end to his loneliness, that the future would be bright? That he would no longer feel the sense of longing when he saw couples pass by hand in hand? He would now live with hope and expectation, knowing his turn was coming.

Then a thought seemed somehow to come from outside of himself. Perhaps he had not come here just for himself but for someone else. If the Sara on the stone were this Sarah, perhaps he had come for her. But she'd asked him to leave her home.

As he struggled within himself, with the horses, and with the weather, his mind swirled and gusted like the snow about him. He tried to ease the horses across the bridge without falling again. He tried to bring clarity to his muddled thinking. He tried to focus on this one sliver of hope.

There were only two choices. Either this Sarah was the Sara on the stone, or she was not. If this were the case, he could do nothing but wait—expectantly. He shook his head and smiled at the thought of himself scouring rooms at each social occasion, attempting to locate any Sara. No, he would just wait, taking this piece of knowledge back to his Bentonsport.

That was all he could do.

If, however, the two women were one and the same, he had fences to mend. He must, somehow, try to reconcile and help her see what could lie ahead while, at the same time, convincing her he was not out of his mind. He'd have to ask her to open herself to the possibility of going back in time with him while understanding this far-fetched notion might be impossible.

And he'd be fortunate if she would even speak to him.

Chapter Twenty-Three

Christmas carols played from the radio. Sarah, standing side by side with Lani at the kitchen counter, heard a knock at the door.

"Come in!"

Richard stood at the door, appearing dumbfounded.

"Aw, quit your gawking and come inside." Lani waved him in. "We may not be a pretty sight under all this flour, but we're what you've got."

Sarah suppressed a smirk. Lani was truly covered with flour. Sarah paused to pour him hot coffee. "What brings you out this morning?"

He rubbed reddened hands together, then warmed them on the cup. "The desire to have coffee with two attractive women."

"Well, warm up a bit, and then we're putting you to work. I don't trust you at baking." Lani pointed to her left. "But you can certainly box."

He slugged his hot coffee as the music played before Lani gave him a job.

"See, just set them in so they are barely touching. That way, they won't shift all around and break. Then place a piece of this paper between each layer and leave enough room at the top for Bubble Wrap, okay?" Richard nodded as he washed his hands.

"With you right here at my side," Richard joked, "I might just be able to manage that. Say, did you all hear a new antique shop is opening in the old house up on Riggs' Hill? They say a man from Chicago bought the place and hopes to have it stocked and open by spring."

"Pretty soon"—Lani bent over, rolling out a new batch of cookie dough—"everyone will be looking toward spring, planning for store openings, busy crafting. It seems we never have a slow season here."

"That reminds me." Sarah drizzled icing on a tray of cookies, each with a different design. "We should organize a group to help Caroline with all her preparations this spring. The baby will have just arrived, and she'll start off the year behind if several of us don't get together to lend a hand."

"Speaking of Caroline," Richard chimed in, "I was thinking, if the roads clear by tomorrow, I'd be happy to drive whoever wanted to accompany me to see them. Have either of you heard any news?"

Sarah rested the frosting-piping bag in a cup and scooped the frosting from the bowl into the bag, pushing the frosting toward the tip. "When Thomas and I were there ..."

It was the first time any of them had brought up his name.

She swallowed. "I'm hoping no news is good news. I keep an eye out for lights in their house or some other sign Bill has come home, but so far, nothing. I don't want to bother them, but if I don't hear from them tonight, I'll call tomorrow."

"Well, as I was saying," Richard continued, "I'd like to check in on them, and I imagine, if Caroline is feeling at all well, a few visitors would do her good."

"Well, count me in." Sarah pulled the bag of frosting from the cup and twisted the end.

"Me, too," Lani added. "Caroline needs visitors, and I'll need to get away from these cookies."

As she said the word *cookies*, someone knocked at the door. "Come in," Sarah called out.

The door edged inward. Thomas peered around the side.

THE PLAN WASN'T A GOOD ONE, BUT IT WAS THE BEST Thomas could come up with on short notice. He'd use his remaining two and a half days to reveal the truth to Sarah. He'd begin by trying to make amends for the thoughtless way he had responded this morning.

"Thomas," Richard beckoned, "come, join the cookie brigade. I could use a hand boxing the finished product. Lani keeps staring me down. I'm certain she thinks I'll destroy a whole dozen if she dares look away."

"Yes," Sarah said, her voice steady, carefree, almost jovial. "Join us."

"Thank you." He tried to steady his voice.

At least she hadn't thrown him out. Her whole demeanor had changed. She seemed at ease, even somewhat perky.

He drew in a deep breath and let his shoulders relax, glad to rejoin his friends and be in Sarah's presence without conflict. But her easy manner ... had she truly recovered from what he'd said?

He washed his hands and, under Lani's direction, joined the cookie operation, serving as a helper wherever needed. Careful not to mention any unpleasantries, he kept an eye on Sarah for hints of her thoughts. There were none.

The hours passed with Richard's witty stories. Christmas carols from the box on Sarah's counter filled the intervals. On the hour, a man's voice spoke from it, giving the news and weather report. If he could stay in this Bentonsport forever, he'd never get used to music and voices streaming out of boxes.

At four o'clock, following the weather report, Sarah turned down the sound. "How many dozens have we completed?"

"Let's see." Lani dried her hands on her apron as she walked to where Richard stacked finished boxes. She counted them once, then once again. "One hundred and ten dozen here, not including those you are icing or the ones on the cooling rack or in the oven."

"I need 450 dozen. At what would you say, Lani? Twenty dozen or so cookies an hour? It's four o'clock now. If you all would be willing to help a bit longer, and if I stay up fairly late tonight, I ought to be able to finish half the project tonight, half more tomorrow ... I don't know. I may be able to get these delivered late tomorrow. If not, it will be Friday morning, and then I risk that storm."

"We'll get it done." Lani gave a firm nod. "And we'll have all day Christmas Eve to relax. We don't want to have anyone out traipsing around in the snow. Except for Thomas, I suppose. You still planning on leaving Friday, Thomas?"

"Actually, I plan to leave early on Saturday morning before anyone gets up, so I'll say my goodbyes on Friday." He met Sarah's penetrating eyes.

After she finished decorating a tray of cookies, she slid more cookies out of the oven. He grabbed an oven mitt to assist. She jumped, startled by having him move up on her so quickly.

"We need to go for a walk." He touched her shoulder. "I need to speak with you."

As her face flushed and she stood mute and frozen, he pulled out three cookie trays, placing them on the hot pads lining the counter. Then he picked up the first tray with a mitted hand and set it next to the cooling racks for her to transfer each cookie. A rhythmic thumping came from Lani, busy mixing up dough, while Richard stood gazing out the window, waiting for cookies to box and stories to tell.

Thomas cleared his throat. "If the two of you wouldn't mind, I'd like to take a break and take Sarah out for a walk, just to get outside for a few minutes."

"Good idea." Richard whipped around, smiling.

"Yes, yes." Lani wiped her brow. "We will manage quite well. You two go on out of here and get some fresh air now."

Outside, the sky was a bright silvery gray. The wind blew in biting gusts and then subsided.

"I wish we could go somewhere warm." He huddled deeper into his coat.

She stepped up beside him. "We could go to the inn. I'm certain Lani wouldn't mind. Or, if you know how to build a quick fire, we could go to the shelter house. There's a fireplace, and if you sit up close, it is plenty warm."

"Sounds like a promising solution." He tipped his chin up, already feeling better.

They walked to the shelter house, careful to avoid the ice patches shining on the road. Sarah brushed the snow off a bench as he constructed the fire, using the dry branches she had retrieved from a wooden box near the hearth. Then she balled up several sheets of newspaper stored beside the wood and tucked them between the branches. He frowned at the long smooth wand she had handed him. What was he to do with it?

"Oh, are you having trouble with that?"

When she wielded it, a flame appeared. She bent and lit each paper ball.

Thomas had no planned speech, no witty introduction. After several minutes, the bark began to crackle and glow. They sat on the bench as fire slithered through the logs.

"I wanted to be alone with you"—a slight quaver warbled his voice—"to apologize for what I said this morning."

She pivoted to him, the tip of her nose red, her cheeks a warm rose. His heart burned. He wanted to hold her, to kiss the top of her head and draw her near. But now was not that moment. That time had already slipped past. He took a deep breath.

"It was foolish for me to assume I'd never return here. After everything I've been through this week, it would be foolish for me to rule out anything again."

The wood crackled and sputtered. Sparks shot up into the chimney. "I've given this a great deal of thought, Sarah. I need—I mean, I would very much like—to spend a stretch of time with you. The things I have to ask you and tell you can't be rushed through. I need a solid, uninterrupted block of time alone with you just to talk, so you can better understand the situation."

Her eyebrows furled as she studied the fire. What was she thinking? After a long pause, she looked deep into his eyes.

"I've held up under truth my entire life. I would like to know the truth. But when can we talk?"

He gave her shoulder a quick squeeze. "That's why I started to panic when you were planning the next day and a half with the four of us together. No matter what, I do have to leave after Friday. I am all but certain of that. I love being with Lani and Richard, and you need these cookies delivered."

He took a long, deep breath. "But is there any way—please, Sarah!—we could spend time together, alone, just the two of us? I know it sounds rather forward, and trust me, I have never approached a woman in this manner. But my time here is so short." His words choked him, and he paused and cleared his throat. "And it is nearly over. I find myself needing to say things and behave in a manner I wouldn't dream of if I were back home."

"No, it's fine, Thomas, really." She gazed back at the fire. "I am quite flattered and taken aback, given our conversation this morning. The only block of time I know we'll have is if you're able to stay this evening and help me with these blasted cookies. Richard and Lani won't want to stay up late. I've had Lani on her feet most of the day. They'll want some sleep so they can help tomorrow. But, if you'd stay and talk and bake with me into the wee hours, that would be wonderful."

In one moment, Thomas thought this was wonderful, inappropriate, and necessary. Only here. Only in this time would he dream of accepting the offer of talking, alone, with a woman, into the night. A woman who made him lose words just through a smile.

"Good." He brushed his palms against his thighs, trying to

216

rub away some nervous energy. They sat side by side, warming their hands.

The embers were blackening under gusts of cold air. Standing, he offered her his arm. "We should head back."

She hugged it tight as they navigated the slippery walk.

He paused and touched her face. "Thank you, Sarah, for a second chance." He bent and kissed her. Softly at first and then embracing her in his arms, he kissed her more firmly, more passionately than he had ever kissed, more than he suspected she had ever been kissed.

And when he lifted his head, she looked more confused than ever.

Chapter Twenty-Four

The four friends continued baking until the clock struck seven. Sarah did a quick inventory. One hundred and seventy dozen. Two hundred and eighty more to go. Under any other situation, she would've sat and cried from exhaustion and the overwhelming prospect. But her mind was only marginally focused on the cookies, on their much-needed distraction, something to keep her centered as everything spun out of control.

"Richard, Lani." She washed her hands under the warm water. "Thomas has offered to stay late and help me bake the next eighty dozen. Why don't we stop here for the night?"

Richard stretched. "That would be fine. Give these old bones a rest. Lani. I'd be happy to walk you home."

"Well, I'm glad you'll be happy," Lani quipped. "Nothing like miserable company."

Sarah walked her guests to the door and hugged them. "Thank you both so much for everything."

"Don't be thanking us until the job is done." Lani wagged a gloved finger. "We'll be back tomorrow at say, um, eight thirty? Will that work for you, Richard?"

"That's fine. Good for you, Sarah?"

"Wonderful." And it was. So wonderful having such friends.

Lani looked him over. "Now, Mr. Thomas, I'll leave the door unlocked. You slip in and lock up behind you, okay? I want to let these poor tired bones rest hard tonight, so they can keep up with the cookie lady tomorrow."

AFTER RICHARD AND LANI LEFT, THE HOUSE QUIETED. With only the ticking of the clocks and the murmuring of Christmas music, Thomas helped Sarah tidy the parlor. He followed her to the kitchen and dried the dishes as she washed. They chatted about the task with lulls of quietness as they finished. All the while one question hung over him—how to tell her the truth?

As she set the dishes on the shelves, he stood behind her and placed his hand on her back.

She stilled. "I don't understand." Her voice came out low and small—almost childlike. "This morning, my heart shattered when you said you'd never come back. Then, less than four hours later, you come to my house as though the whole discussion never took place."

Without looking at him, she stared ahead, her arms crossed, seeming more perplexed than angry.

"This evening, you say you need to talk with me, and then you kissed me … you kissed me in a way that says you can't possibly leave. Thomas, just tell me what this all means, where this is going. I promise, no more tears while you're here. But this all makes no sense." Bracing both hands on the counter, she visibly steadied herself. "Which, in a way, makes your leaving even worse. I mean, what am I to think when you're gone?"

He sat on the stool across from her. Then he reached out and held both her hands. "I won't leave without you knowing everything I know and without you understanding what all this means. But I need time to explain so it does make sense. I promise. Is that enough?"

At her questioning gaze, he continued, "What would you think ... if it were possible for me to take you back with me?"

He hesitated only momentarily. "Come to my hometown, meet my friends, see what my life is like. I don't know, but if the opportunity presented itself now or later, would you come?"

"Now?" Her hands went limp. "It's Christmas, and there is Caroline. And, well, that's just two days away." She stopped and held his hands tighter. "But, yes, I'd love to visit you."

"Good." Smiling at her, he let his shoulders relax. They'd made some progress, small though it was.

Now all he had to do was convince her of a permanent visit. To Bentonsport. In 1869. He laughed to himself.

She bit her lower lip. "Did I say something funny?"

"Oh no." Still laughing, he managed to shrug. "I was just thinking of how different things are in my town, how different it would all seem to you, but how pleasant it would be for me to show you."

Her chin notched up, and she tipped her head, her eyes narrowing. "Thomas, I haven't lived in a town of thirty-five people my entire life!" She folded her arms across her chest.

This was heading in the wrong direction.

"Pennsylvania, I'm certain, is different from the Midwest, but it wouldn't be like another country."

"No." He stood up and drew her into his chest. "Not different in that sense. I'm sure you'd fit right in. But it's—well—just not the same."

She stepped back from him. One brow rising, she smiled at him.

Better to let that discussion drop. No point going any deeper now. Slow and steady progress is what he sought. Slow, as in one day.

"We better get back to work." With a long low breath, she crossed to the pantry for two aprons. She threaded the white one around her and held out his larger blue one.

"Have you ever wished," he began, trying to inch the conversation along without falling in a hole, "when you used the bustle oven and dressed in period clothes, that you could *actually live* in or even visit Bentonsport back in its early days—back in say, the 1860s?" He placed the cookie sheets side by side.

"Visit, oh yes!" She grinned as she tied her apron strings. "I'd give just about anything to visit Bentonsport when everything was new and bustling, when everyone was filled with hope about all it could become. Yes, it would be wonderful. But live there?"

As she smoothed her apron, he found himself almost stooping to see her face.

A smile crinkled up her eyes. "As much as I love that time period, I have to admit, I am a woman of modern convenience."

"Oh." The word rang hollow, despite his efforts to keep a neutral tone. "And how is that?"

"Well ... there is just so much I'd miss. My microwave, my old truck, my ovens. And those are just things. Mostly, I'd miss all the people you've come to know here, all my friends."

Pausing, Sarah inventoried her supplies, matching them to the recipe. "In terms of my things, I'd miss my radio most. So much of my day is spent here in the kitchen. I've never been much of a television watcher. I move around too much as I work, so I can't stare at a screen. But I listen to my radio, off and on, all day long. All types of music, talk shows, news, I can't imagine doing without it. How about you? What would you miss most if you went back?"

Her brows rose and her smile hinted at a kiss.

"You," he said, almost without thinking. He ducked his head, mainly from embarrassment, partly because he didn't know how she'd react. He could give no other truthful answer. He'd miss people, the ease and warmth of a morning shower, and yes, he

enjoyed the boxed music. But what he would miss most? Easy
—Sarah.

Her grin stretched impishly wide. "First, you flee, now
flattery." She folded her arms and rested against the counter.
"How am I to understand you in just two days' time?"

"I never claimed you'd understand me." He raised his hands.
"I only said you'd understand the situation."

"You sift. I'll start on the next batch." She handed him the
sifter. "Do you live close to your family now?"

"I don't. But we write each other frequently. And, of course,
we visit when we can."

"And call, right?"

"I'm afraid we still write."

As he sifted, she creamed together the butter and sugar, the
soft whoosh of a spoon against gritty sugar keeping time. "In
many ways, it is better to exchange letters than to call or email. I
often think our stories, you know, our everyday lives, will be lost
to history because they aren't being recorded. Rarely do people
print and save emails."

Pausing, she tapped the spoon several times against the bowl.
"So, what will historians look back at and use as our records?
Heaven help us if it's our television shows and movies. I'd hate to
think the people who follow us will think those shows in any way
reflect our real lives."

After two weeks of living here, even though they both spoke
English, he could only understand bits and pieces of what she
said. How would she adjust? Email? Movies? He'd be asking her
to give up so much more than that music box.

Hours of baking followed, filled with music and conversation.

"You know what I should do?" Sarah asked. "I should make a
batch of butterscotch milk. After we bake these last batches
tonight, we should mix up all the dough we'll need for tomorrow.
That way, I can clean up this mess, and we can focus on cutting,
baking, icing, and packaging cookies tomorrow. How does that
sound?"

"It's a good plan, but you've got to be exhausted. You were up earlier than any of us."

"I'm just starting to feel it now." She poured two mugs of milk into the pan and put it on a low flame.

Then she pushed up her white sleeves, now flecked with icing. "I'm sorry all this cookie baking has taken so much of your last days here. I can't imagine what you'll tell your friends back home you did on your vacation."

Pulling out the stool, he sat behind her. "I'll tell them I saw all of Bentonsport, took an internship in tinsmithing and baking, met some great people, and discovered a wonderful woman. A perfect trip, I believe, and they'll all agree."

She flashed a brilliant smile over her shoulder, her hair fluffing around her soft face. "Well, I have to admit your version sounds much better than 'I endured a blizzard, nearly broke my ankle, and wore an apron a great deal of the time.'"

They both laughed.

"Speaking of ankles," she continued, "I haven't asked you lately how yours is doing. It can't be good for it with all the standing you've had to do."

The oven timer chimed, and he opened the door to golden-brown cookies. "Actually ..." He removed three trays and slid another three in. "I don't notice it much. Now, it's just a dull ache. As for standing, this is nothing compared to what I do in the classroom each day."

After moving the two stools up to the counter, she poured the hot milk into the mugs. She plopped several hard butterscotch candies in each mug. When he dropped back onto one of the stools, she gave him a spoon. "Now, keep stirring until the milk looks amber and you can no longer feel the hard candies on the bottom."

Sitting close together, they stirred the milk into a light caramel brown. Then he raised his mug, and together, they said, "Cheers." He tested several short sips of hot, subtly sweet butterscotch milk.

Sarah blew across her mug. "Mmm ..." She failed to stifle a yawn. "I'm starting to fade. Yes, it is good."

She yawned a long, deep, dreamy yawn. "Maybe I should rest a while once we take this batch out. You could go back to the inn and sleep. You've got to be tired as well."

"Right now, I'm fine. But I've had more sleep than you."

They finished their drinks just as the oven timer pinged. She placed hot trays on the padded counter. "If I rest a bit, I can get up later and finish the dough and then turn in for the night. I just need a catnap."

Checking the clock, Thomas saw it was nearing midnight, but he wasn't ready to sleep. He wanted to stay right there, in her house, soaking up as much of her home—her world, the whole experience—as he could.

"I have a proposition." His ears tingled. Had he just said that? Shaking off the silly thought, he rested against the counter, his right leg crossed over his left calf. "Why don't you go nap? Really, I'm not tired. If you give me the recipe, I'll mix up some dough. When you awaken, you can take over, we'll continue our conversation and then call it a night."

"Thomas, this is your vacation. Your time off. I've already imposed on you too much." She brushed a lock of her hair off her face. She looked tired. Beautifully tired. "That's just asking—"

"You're not asking." He held up a hand, stopping her. Of course, she wasn't asking. Had she no idea how much she gave of herself to those around her? Caroline, Lani, Richard—they all saw it. But this magnificent woman didn't. "*I* am asking to do this for you. And you need rest. Please give me the recipe, and please get some rest." He smiled. "I won't substitute the salt for the sugar. I promise not to waste or ruin your ingredients."

"I'm not worried about that."

His grin deepened. "Prove it."

Rolling her eyes, she handed him the recipe. He took her warm hand and led her to the parlor. He placed two pillows against its arm, and she curled up on them.

His heart melting, he covered her with the quilt draped over the sofa back and kissed her forehead, the pert tip of her nose— but it wasn't enough. So, he brushed a kiss on her butterscotch lips. Wanting more, he eased back, and let his fingertips graze silky skin as they feathered her hair away from her temples.

"I want you to remember this moment, not the one earlier here today, okay?"

Chapter Twenty-Five

Thomas stood in the kitchen, gripping the printed recipe Sarah had given him, absorbed in his thoughts. This day, though still in the wee hours, he'd have to explain everything and offer her a choice.

Ignoring the instructions involving the mixer, he stirred the dough by hand. He measured, mixed, and rolled each finished batch into a large ball, then wrapped each in wax paper, placing them on the refrigerator shelves. Sarah would miss this contraption—the "mixer"—as well.

At two thirty, he finished the dough balls. He stacked them in the refrigerator's bottom bins, one atop the other, much as his students stacked snowballs to build forts. Beginning to tire, he didn't want to leave the kitchen in disarray. Sarah deserved to start her day with order before the coming chaos.

He padded into the parlor. He had thought of awakening her, but how could he discuss this with her when she was so exhausted? No, their talk would have to wait for the morning. Perhaps his dough-making now would open time in the afternoon. It would simply have to work.

The hallway light illuminated her, deeply asleep, curled up in her quilt with just a trace of a smile. Tendrils of honey hair wisped against her cheek, and he stood there, trying to imprint this in his memory. "Oh, Sarah," he whispered, folding his arms against his chest, "just give me this chance."

HE AWOKE THE NEXT MORNING TO A BRIGHT SUN, NOT the dim light of early morning. No sound coming from the kitchen, no smell of coffee or breakfast, he bolted up and examined the clock. It was nearly ten.

As he pushed back the covers, his head ached from the sudden movement after such heavy sleep. One glance in the mirror showed he needed to bathe and shave. As much as he would've liked to rush out, making up for the time he'd already lost, he had to look his best. Of all days, he had to make a good impression today.

After bathing and dressing, he shook his head and ran his fingers through the long curls his hair fell into when wet. He wore his white shirt and Bill's soft denim work pants, looking both dressed and casual.

At the table, his place was set. A piece of paper rested upright against his glass. Shoving his arms through his coat sleeves, he walked to the table.

Well, Sleepy, I was all prepared to shake you to make sure you were still in the land of the living, when Sarah phoned to say a little elf had worked in her kitchen making all the dough into the wee hours. Well, maybe not a little elf. Anyway, she thought the elf needed sleep. Join us when you're awake. I made you muffins, and there is juice in the fridge.

Lani

P.S. That was awfully dear of you!

He'd miss Lani. He didn't know anyone in his Bentonsport quite like her—firm, direct, sarcastic, and sweet, all at the same time.

He found the glass pitcher of orange juice and the plate of

wrapped muffins, drank a glass of juice, and stuffed a wrapped muffin in his topcoat pocket.

Outside, the sun was bright, and the wind was almost nonexistent. After knocking at her door, he waited to hear the familiar 'come in,' but instead, he heard Richard's low voice. He watched through the glass as Sarah hurried to the door.

It lurched inward, and she greeted him with open arms. "The shoemaker's—that is, baker's—elf has returned!" She gave him a quick hug, and her breath warmed his ear as she tiptoed to whisper, "Thank you, Thomas."

"My pleasure." His neck and spine continued to tingle from her warm breath. He sighed despite himself.

"But," she continued, walking back to the kitchen island, where Lani and Richard sat side by side, "you should have awakened me."

"You needed your sleep." He lingered inside the door and placed his coat and scarf on a hook. "I guess the same was true for me this morning."

"Yes," Richard said in his slow, pleasant style as Thomas claimed the stool across from him. "Fabulous what you did. The ladies have been baking and icing for the past two hours. All I've had to do is drink coffee and box."

"He means," Lani chimed in, "that's all we *let* him do. But there will be plenty of work soon enough for both of you. Sarah wants us to load these boxes into the truck today so she can drive them to Fairfield. Somehow, you men are going to have to figure out the best way to keep them from flying out of the back of her truck."

"Sarah, are you sure?" Richard asked. "I wouldn't mind having you load up my truck and then taking you up there myself."

"I don't—"

The ringing phone interrupted.

She picked up the receiver. "Yes, Caroline, yes. Oh, my, it's good to hear your voice."

After a few minutes, she said, "Oh, that is such good news ... Yes, of course, I'm going to come up there today. So are Richard and Lani. Thomas, too, right?" She gave him an arched look. "I wish you were here too. We've been baking up a storm. Lani, Richard, and Thomas have all chipped in, or I'd be at the bawling stage by now ... No, but I'll ask. Hold on."

She cupped the phone in her hand. "She sounds lonely. Bill is running some errands in Fairfield, and she's staring at the four walls."

"Did she say how she's feeling?" Lani asked.

"She said she's doing fine." Sarah beamed. "If she has no more pain, they'll let her come home sometime Christmas Day. But she needs visitors today. Thomas, would you be willing to deliver all these cookies with me this afternoon? I should be the one to deliver them, though—thanks for offering, Richard. If Thomas and I go to Fairfield, Richard, maybe you and Lani could visit Caroline sometime around noon?"

This was the opportunity Thomas needed—three hours alone with Sarah. His anxiety level rose, and he found himself flexing his hands. The moment of full disclosure was at hand.

Sarah firmed up the plans with Caroline and hung up.

"So, she sounds like the old Caroline?" Lani asked.

"She's a bit stir-crazy. But she sounds wonderful. You don't know how much you miss someone until they fall out of your life."

By noon, the remaining cookies were cooled and iced. About twenty dozen were left to box when Richard and Thomas bundled up to assess Sarah's truck. "You know," Richard began, "I've watched these boxes stacking up, and there's no way they'll fit in this truck. The Zimmermans have a delivery truck. They don't drive it themselves, but they hire an area farmer to pick up bulk shipments and deliver goods with it."

He ran his hand through his hair. "Part of me doesn't want to have to ask them for another favor, but ... maybe I should go over. Then I could take them a bale of hay later in the day as my personal thank you. My only concern is whether or not Sarah can drive the truck. It's not terribly big. How about you, Thomas? Have you ever driven a truck?"

"No," he answered too quickly. "I haven't, and I wouldn't want the Zimmermans' truck to be the first."

"Hmm, that wouldn't be a good idea." Richard frowned at his boots and scuffled the snow around them. "Well, no sense standing around here. Let's see what Sarah has to say."

When Richard explained, she cast Thomas a helpless, almost lost look. He wished he could comfort her, say he could do it for her. But he couldn't. At his silence, she frowned out the window and then back at Richard.

"A better idea"—Richard broke their awkward silence— "might be to have me drive the truck, with the two of you following me. We'll drop Lani off at the hospital with Caroline. Then Thomas can help unload all these boxes, and if either of the trucks has any problems, we'll have two men on hand."

Sarah's face lit up. "Richard, that's just perfect." And, clapping her hands together like one of Thomas's schoolgirls, she kissed his cheek.

Richard blushed. "Remind me to think of more good ideas."

"Now"—Lani planted her palms on her steady hips—"we don't need any more ideas. We need that truck. You and Thomas hike over and fetch it. Sarah and I will finish boxing and cleaning."

"Just a few more sips of coffee, and we'll be off." Richard hoisted his cup with a wink.

Sarah pivoted while surveying the room. Boxes lined the walls and clustered in stacks in the middle of the floor. "I can't believe we baked this many cookies!"

"My eyes don't believe it." Her voice flat, Lani used her forearm to wipe perspiration from her forehead. "But my back, fingers, feet, and nose all do. Cured me of any desire for a single cookie this Christmas."

Her eyes twinkled. "But you know it has been fun. Exhausting, but fun. But, Thomas, I wouldn't even try to describe your winter holiday to the people back home. No one would believe a man in his right mind traveled over a thousand miles to spend his vacation baking cookies."

"And when did I claim to be in my right mind?" He winked at Lani.

"And a good thing you aren't." Richard chuckled. "Or you wouldn't have stuck it out with this outfit for so long. Let's go get the truck and deliver these cookies. I have a notion to ask Lani to dinner after we go see Caroline. I want to stay out of the kitchen."

"Well, I have a notion to accept," Lani said. "Having someone wait on me sounds good. You two go on now. We'll be cleaned up and ready when you get back."

Thomas lost track of how many times he'd crossed the bridge to Vernon since he arrived—almost hard to believe he'd have to go back to using a ferry. He should look around, memorize the details. In just a day and a half, he'd be home, and memories of this Bentonsport would fade.

"I'd like to share something with you, Thomas." Richard stilled at the bridge's crest. He reached deep in his pocket and withdrew a red velvet box. With his large calloused fingers, he opened the lid. Inside, recessed into the velvet, winked a gold band with a single oval diamond. "It's my Christmas gift to Lani, um, that is"—he swallowed—"if she'll have it, have me. On Christmas morning, I plan to ask her to marry me."

"How wonderful. Congratulations." Thomas gave Richard's shoulder a quick shake. "I guess I didn't know ..."

Richard laughed. "Don't congratulate me yet. She hasn't said yes. I don't know if I have a chance, but I want to take that chance. And, in large part, Thomas, I have you to thank."

"Me?" Thomas's shoulders stiffened. "I've never been married. For that matter, I've never asked—"

"No." Richard waved away his words. "It's been watching you and Sarah. Reminds me of my younger days."

As they stomped through well-trod snow toward the Zimmermans' home and store, Thomas breathed in the familiar fragrance of woodsmoke.

"The two of you remind me time is short. You need to grasp hold of happiness, of love, if the chance comes. I'm sorry you won't be here to learn the results, but perhaps I could call you or write?"

"I'd sure like to hear from you." Thomas kept his head down, watching the steam of his warm breath. "But I have no doubt things will go well for you and Lani. I only wish Sarah and I could have the same result."

"If you feel that way, Thomas, then don't give up." Richard cupped him on the back. "Just keep at it and don't give up."

After Mr. Zimmerman gave Richard the keys, they drove down the steep hill into Bentonsport.

The women carried the boxes out, and the men stacked them inside, securing them with shiny ribbed straps against the truck walls. Finished, Richard latched the back door with great ceremony.

"Well, we are almost done. Lani, why don't you ride with Sarah and Thomas to the hospital so I won't have to steer through the parking lot? I'll wait at the roadside before the hospital until you drop Lani off. Then off to Fairfield."

Sarah, Thomas, and Lani climbed into Sarah's truck and waited for Richard to start down the road, then followed him.

"It'll be good to see our Caroline again." Lani strapped herself into a front seat much the way Richard had secured the boxes. "Even better to get her home. Storm or no storm, we could help her more if she were close."

"It will be wonderful," Sarah chimed in. "And even more so when the baby comes and we all have it to spoil. Just the other night, I dreamed I was baking—of course—and Caroline was sitting across the counter from me sewing. And there on the counter was the baby, sound asleep in a pumpkin chair. I don't know if it was a girl or a boy, but the baby had become part of our world. It was amazing and wonderful."

Leaning his head against the seat behind him, Thomas closed his eyes. Would this scene unfold for her? Or, by any miracle, would she be in his Bentonsport this spring?

They entered the hospital parking lot and dropped Lani off at the front door. As she left the truck, she turned back. "Now remember what I said about keeping a close eye on Richard. He always plunges ahead, so sure of himself, and God love him for that. But one day he'll bite off more than he can chew. We are both getting older, though we won't admit it, either of us. So, just keep an eye on him for me, okay?"

"We won't let him out of our sight, Lani," Thomas answered. With that, Lani patted his cheek, shut the door, gave a quick wave, and entered the hospital.

Sarah circled back to the highway and slowed as she approached the delivery truck. Soon, they were following Richard again.

"Well, for once, Miss Sarah." Thomas shifted to face her in his seat, folding his arms across his chest the way he did before a school lesson. "I have a new secret to share with you."

She flicked her gaze to him, then back to the road.

"Now you can't say a word," he lectured in a scolding tone, not unlike Lani's. "I wasn't told I couldn't tell you, but then again, I wasn't told I could. So, not a word, right?"

Her lips curved up, her eyes sparkling, that one deep dimple winking. "Yes, of course, not a word."

"Richard is proposing to Lani on Christmas Day." And here he was gossiping like the women back home.

"What?" She jerked her gaze back to the road. "Richard and Lani? You're kidding ... Oh, my. How did you find out?"

"Richard told me on the way to get the truck. He said he made the decision after watching us."

"Us?"

Just as when he formed a useful lesson, he watched his words, leading himself where he wanted to go. "He said time is short and you need to grasp hold of happiness where you find it. He also didn't want to run the risk of losing Lani."

Her grip tight on the thing they called a steering wheel, she focused on the road ahead. But surely, she was thinking too. She said nothing.

"When he said that, Sarah"—he lowered his voice—"I knew I, too, needed to take a chance. I needed to risk everything and explain why this whole matter between us is so strange. Why we keep getting entangled in words and misunderstanding. It's because I haven't been fully honest."

She bit her lip and inhaled a noisy breath, her whole body stiffening.

"I haven't been fully honest because, quite frankly, I've been too afraid. Afraid you would think I'm crazy. Afraid you'd think I was mad, because if you told me what I'm about to share with you, I would think you'd lost your mind."

He paused, swallowed hard, and licked his lips. "And that is why it has been so difficult for me. Why I've had to weigh my words and hold back so much when what I want to do is hold you and reassure you I care so deeply for you."

Two tears traced shiny paths down her cheek. She reached up to wipe them away.

"Oh, Sarah." He exhaled a long breath clogging his throat, then pushed the rest of the words out. "Sarah, this is so hard. I wish I could end right here. We could be happy right here at this moment. But time keeps ticking away, and truly, I have to leave early Christmas morning. There is no turning away from that."

"But ..." She braved a glance at him, her expression softening, something pleading in her eyes. "You asked if I could visit, and of course—especially after what you just said—of course, I will come and spend time in your world."

He touched her arm. "No matter where that is?"

"You said Pennsylvania, right? And that's not oceans away."

LISA SCHNEDLER

Richard slowed the delivery truck as they entered Birmingham. She braked each time the speed dropped, keeping an even distance from the delivery truck.

"I said I was from Pennsylvania. That's true. Throughout all this, I've been so careful not to lie to you, and I haven't. I'm from Pennsylvania, but I don't live there now. In fact, I haven't lived there for more than a year."

"It doesn't matter where you live, Thomas." She glanced at him. "If you believe you and I—that is, if *you*—believe this relationship has a chance, I'll visit you wherever you live. What? Is it a dangerous place?"

He laughed. And oh, how relieved he was to laugh! "No." He smiled at her. "It is perfectly safe, an occasional prank by one of our children, but other than mischief, no, no crime."

"Well, that sounds nice. Do you want me to guess where it is? Is it some sort of place I wouldn't want to go?"

Thomas sat up straight, his hands flexing into fists and then relaxing. "Sarah, I'm certain you'll love it. I'm certain everyone will love you. And, no, you can't guess, because it's beyond comprehension."

Puzzlement crinkled her forehead. Then she shook her shoulders loose. "Okay, then I give up. Where do you live?"

He breathed in deeply, so deeply it was audible.

Without looking away from the road, she reached over and squeezed his hand. "It's okay, really."

How soft her words were! If only he could believe them.

"I'll come—no matter where it is. So don't worry. Promise you'll meet me, and I'll come."

"I'll be there, but ..." He peered out the window, unable to look at her. "I live in ..." He tried to say *Bentonsport*, but the word stuck in his throat. He chastised himself for not just saying, for not just blurting it out. "Sarah, I live in Iowa."

"Iowa?" She jolted, and the truck lurched sideways before she corrected it. "You live right here in Iowa?"

He couldn't answer. So he nodded.

"I don't understand." Her voice was shaking. "All this time I have fretted over you leaving ... and you live here, in Iowa? Why haven't you told me?"

Now he had to choose his words carefully. Each one mattered.

Before he could say anything, she blurted, "Tell me, please, what would be so terrible about you living in Iowa? You're not married?"

Married? "Of course not, I wouldn't—"

"Engaged?" she continued. "Or serious about someone else?"

"No." How could she ask these things? "I've told you before —there is no one else, Sarah."

"Then what?" She lifted her hands off the wheel and up in the air, but then returned them.

"I live in ... Bentonsport." He said it. It was out, and with it, all the breath left him.

She twisted her hands on the wheel, gripping it until her knuckles turned white. Then she gave a little peek his way, a hopeful curve to her lips. "You mean you're moving to Bentonsport?"

"No," he said in a flat voice. "I live there now."

He waited, but she said nothing. Nothing.

Finally, she inhaled deeply. "Where in Bentonsport do you live?"

"The academy building."

"Thomas ... The academy building is owned by a professor in Des Moines. He opens it a few times each year. The rest of the time, it's empty. Are you saying you live at the academy when no one is there?"

Was she angry or confused? Probably both.

He clasped his hands between his knees. "I'm not some vagrant, a hobo who hides in vacant buildings. I live in the academy all year. It's my permanent home."

They entered Fairfield. Richard moved the Zimmermans' truck over to the side of the road, put his arm out the window, and waved her ahead, signaling her to take the lead.

"Right." She spoke as if things were normal. "I forgot. He doesn't know where we're going."

Nor do I. This wasn't going as planned.

"We're here." How dull, how distant she sounded.

They turned into the driveway. Richard stopped the delivery truck just behind her, opened the back of the truck, and called out, "Well, that was an easy trip."

"It was?" Sarah muttered just loud enough for Thomas to hear, then jumped from her seat.

He sat for a moment before getting out. Praying? Thinking? Hoping? He wasn't sure he could manage even one of those.

"Well, folks." Richard patted them each on the back. "We made it, cookies safe and sound. Sarah, you can relax now and enter the Christmas spirit."

"I hope so." She didn't look at either of them

Her customer—what had she said the woman's name was? Mrs. Michelle Barkley greeted them, her face lighting up when Sarah introduced herself. "You got them done?"

Sarah motioned to Richard and Thomas. "We got them done."

"You are an absolute angel." Mrs. Barkley gave Sarah a long hug. "I can't tell you how this brightens our Christmas, brightens our employees' Christmas!"

"It was a group effort, an unbelievable group effort, but we had lots of fun. This is Richard."

When Sarah stepped aside, allowing Richard room on the porch, he stepped up and shook Michelle's hand.

"And this is my friend, Thomas," she continued. "They were troopers, as was my friend Lani."

After they unloaded the cookie boxes into a pantry room lined with long deep shelves just off Mrs. Barkley's kitchen, Mrs. Barkley handed Sarah an envelope. Presumably, it held the money she owed her.

"Thank you. You've been more than generous," Sarah told her. "I'd be happy, grateful to help you at any time."

Sarah gave her a quick hug, and everyone said goodbye, then headed back to their vehicles.

Richard paused. "Why don't the two of you go on to the hospital? I'm going to take the truck back to Zimmerman, and then I'll pick up my truck and meet you."

"Thanks, Richard." Lifting onto her toes, Sarah planted a kiss on his cheek. "I couldn't have done it without you."

After Richard assured her he'd enjoyed it, she climbed into her seat, not letting Thomas help her. So he hurried around to his side. While he strapped himself, she cleared her throat. "Thomas, I'm trying hard to understand you, trying to understand this whole situation, but—"

"But I'm not making sense. I'm not making any sense because what I have to say is unbelievable. And, I'm afraid, it only sounds worse, more ridiculous, if possible, when I try to tell you what has happened to me, who I am, in small pieces. So"—he sat up as straight as he could—"as hard as this will be, I'm going to tell you the whole story straight through."

He cleared his throat as Sarah turned onto the road, her face frozen in serious lines.

"I was raised in Pennsylvania. But I moved to Iowa when I was offered the position to teach at the Bentonsport Academy. I accepted the position in 1868. I have taught there now for just over a year."

Her face tense, taut, she didn't look at him but stared ahead at the back of Richard's truck, fixated, almost motionless.

If only he had some hint as to what she was thinking behind that mask. "Nearly two weeks ago, I was home in bed when Pastor Lockhardt came to my door and continued to knock until I answered it. He seemed almost giddy, breathless from his walk to the academy. He proceeded to tell me he had a dream—almost a vision—that I would be taking a trip to a Bentonsport."

He took a deep breath. "He said a special gift awaited me there. He told me to make my discovery and to remember time was short because, on Christmas Eve, I would return home, and the door to this experience would be closed for good."

His mouth dry, he paused to wet his lips but didn't want to lose his momentum. "I went back to bed. Truly, as I am sure you feel right now, I thought he was delusional or at least had a bad dream that made a huge impact. I went to bed, and when I woke up the next morning, I found myself at the inn, under Lani's watchful eye and care. And the rest you know."

Still staring straight ahead, Sarah said nothing. He could see the muscles along her jaw.

Finally, he couldn't stand the silence any longer. "Please, Sarah ... say something. I'd rather hear what you have to say than imagine or guess what you're thinking."

She clenched her teeth, opened her mouth. Then she tightened her lips and drove in silence.

"I'm just trying to decide," she began, in a monotone, "if you're doing this to spare my feelings, you know, to make me dislike you, to make me think you're nuts. Or if you're playing a practical joke on me. And, if that's it, given all we've been through, I don't think it's funny. So, no, I don't believe it, and quite frankly, Thomas, I don't think you believe it either. And I don't think you're crazy. But perhaps mean—or cruel—would be a better description."

The words pierced him, twisted, and lingered. He would have much preferred she thought him mad, some delusional maniac who concocted a story involving time travel. In her place, he would've had similar thoughts. But mean? Cruel? In all his thinking and planning for this moment, he never considered this response.

"So, which is it? You're a nice man who's done a dumb thing to spare my feelings, or you're a jerk who's fooled me over the past two weeks, only now to show me the nasty person inside you?"

She glared at him, causing the truck to swerve from the road and skid across the gravel roadside. Thomas grabbed the wheel and tried to steer to the middle, causing the truck to fishtail.

"Let go," Sarah screamed, slapping his hand off the wheel, slowing the truck, and bringing it under control. She drove onto a side road, turned off the engine, and placed her forehead in between her hands on the steering wheel.

"Break my heart, Thomas," she said, "but don't kill us."

Tears streamed down her cheeks, long streaking tears. Her nose began to redden like when she showed up at the inn after Bill had threatened to chance driving through the blizzard. That time, she'd held onto Thomas through her tears. Now, as he reached toward her with the back of his hand to wipe them away, she recoiled and again crumpled against the steering wheel.

"Sarah"—his voice quavered—"for two weeks, I've tried to keep this from you. I thought on Christmas Eve, I'd be able to slip out of town, out of your life. But, as our feelings moved from friendship to ... to much more, I realized that would be, as you put it, mean or cruel. I never imagined by telling you the truth, I'd evoke the same reaction. Of course, I thought you'd think me mad, out of my mind, but never mean or cruel."

She reached down under her seat, unearthed a box of tissues, removed several, and blew her nose. Her left arm rested against the window, and she bit down on the back part of her thumb. She stared out the windshield, and occasionally, involuntarily, she shook her head. Lost in her thoughts—thoughts obviously not in his favor.

STARTING UP THE TRUCK, SHE TRIED TO LOSE HER thoughts by driving, a futile effort. She clenched her teeth and clamped her hands on the wheel, needing to get to the hospital, sit, and visit Caroline. With her thoughts such a blur, she didn't trust her driving. She kept losing track of where she was, what landmarks she passed, only to snap back, look around, and wonder, *How did I get here?*

Easing the truck into the hospital parking lot, she then turned off the engine. She was just reaching for the door when Thomas grasped her shoulder and touched her chin, turning her face toward his.

"Sarah, please," he whispered, desperation tightening the voice she'd once thought so charming. "Just think back. What did you think when you first met me?"

She jerked her face to the window, too angry to think back on happy times.

But he persisted. "No, Sarah, think, please. What did you think when I walked into your house?"

What had she thought? No need to think. She remembered the moment well. Despite herself, she smiled. "I thought you were handsome, strikingly so."

He couldn't be blushing, but he was, as he glanced down, clearly uncomfortable.

"I thought you were easy to talk to, you know, fun, interesting. But ... there was something odd about you. The way you were dressed, your hair, your speech, and, of course, the money you used. It was as if you had stepped out of the ..."

She stopped short and caught herself before saying *past*. His eyes met hers. She sat, steadying her breath. A mixture of confusion and fear replaced her anger.

Wanting out of the truck, she was desperate to walk around, breathe fresh air, and see Caroline. This was too much, too confusing, too outrageous. She fumbled with the door latch, somehow unable to make it work.

Then she slowed down and forced her fingers to comply with the rote action. She climbed out, and they walked side by side up the hospital's main hallway, neither saying a word. She stopped at the nurses' station and asked which room Caroline was in and was directed to Room 210.

With the door ajar, Lani's voice drifted out, then Caroline's laughter. When Sarah knocked, Caroline called out, "Come in, come in."

Propped up in bed, blankets folded over her rounded middle,

Caroline glowed. Lani sat in a straight-backed chair just to the right.

As Sarah walked over, some of the numbness left. She perched on the edge of Caroline's bed, leaned over, and hugged her. "You look radiant."

Concern momentarily darkened her friend's glow. Caroline could surely tell she'd been crying. But she said nothing and squeezed her hand. As she did, she turned to Thomas, huddling against the wall.

"She's right." He sounded so pained. "It is good to see you."

"I feel so good, so much better. And I owe so much to all of you. I keep reminding myself I only have to wait two more days to get home—two more, that's all. And then I can sleep in my bed, make hot tea, sew, skip over to Sarah's. I can have my life back again."

"And me mine," Sarah murmured.

"Well, you can forget about skipping," Lani chimed in, having sat quietly for too long. "I was listening to the weather report on the way over here. Today is supposed to be glorious, cool, in the upper thirties, and no wind. And we have the same forecast for a good part of tomorrow.

"But, then, just so none of us gets too disappointed, wishing for our white Christmas and all, the snow starts Friday afternoon and doesn't let up until Christmas afternoon. No, not skipping weather, but it will be pretty and white." Lani arched a brow at Thomas. "That may make it difficult for you to leave us."

Sarah bit her lip to keep herself from saying, 'Not as long as there is pixie dust and magic.'

"We'll play it by ear," Thomas said. "It seems that, since I arrived here, I never know what to expect."

When she looked over at him, he stared back knowingly. Suppressing a shudder, she turned back to Caroline, not wishing to reenter her fog of thoughts.

"I had a late lunch with Caroline," Lani said. "A nice nurse ordered me a tray, but how about the two of you? I bet you haven't eaten all day."

Sarah eyed her clasped hands, flexed her fingers, and meshed them together again on her lap, aware of Thomas, his eyes revealing his troubles. Despite his crazy tales and unknown origins —yes, despite her anger—she was still smitten with his ruffled good looks, his charming style. He wasn't a cruel person, wasn't deranged, but just what *was* he?

"I haven't had anything except a slice of toast this morning. I somehow forgot about eating. How about you?" Again, she braved looking his way.

"Now that you mention it, I haven't eaten all day. I placed a muffin in my pocket earlier this morning, but it's still there. I haven't had a chance to think about it."

"Well, maybe you two should go get a sandwich or something downtown. It's only two thirty now, so you couldn't get a tray of food here for another hour and a half. Lani and I will be fine. Right, Lani?"

"Well, you can add Richard to that list too, I hope," Lani said. "He should've been here by now."

"He'll be right along," Sarah said. "He was going to return the Zimmermans' truck, pick up his own, and come. But I don't want to leave you, Caroline, when we just got here."

Caroline smirked. "It's not like I'm going anywhere. Go eat and come back. If you're feeling terribly guilty, you could bring a cup of tea for me. A hot cup of Earl Gray from Cups and Plates sounds wonderful."

THOMAS WATCHED THE TWO WOMEN VISITING, remembering the first time he intruded on their time together. He'd thought Sarah's hair resembled a boy's and been charmed, even that first day, by her description of Bentonsport, his Bentonsport, and—

That was it. A chance, an inroad. He would ask her for a chance—beg her for the opportunity—to let him show her his Bentonsport through his eyes. He'd describe in the minutest detail, the Bentonsport she could only see in shadow. He'd make her believe with her heart. And hope her head would follow.

"Sounds good." Sarah folded her arms. "So, are you ready?"

"I am."

Chapter
Twenty-Six

S arah chatted about their brief visit with Caroline as they drove out of the parking lot, each trying to be on their best behavior.

"So," she said, "what are you in the mood for? Pizza? Sandwiches?"

"Why don't you choose? But ... can we go someplace quiet where we can eat and talk?"

Letting a deep breath fill her lungs, she drummed her fingers on the steering wheel. Could she take much more of his talking? Whether she could or couldn't, they couldn't leave things where they were. "How about pizza in the park?"

"Sounds great." He relaxed into the seat.

She went into the restaurant to order this pizza and returned to the truck empty-handed. "Twenty minutes until it's ready. Let's go for a drive."

The roads were clear. The sun shining through the windows was bright—nearly too bright. She flipped the radio on low.

"I am sorry I said the terrible things I did," she began. "I was —actually, I still am—taken aback by what you said. I was expecting something else, something that would've hurt still, but something more like 'Sarah, I'm married,' 'Sarah, I have a girlfriend,' 'Sarah, I'm a priest'—really, almost anything other than 'Sarah, I'm the Ghost of Christmas Past.'"

Thomas twisted in his seat to face her, several curly wisps of hair blowing from the heater fan. "I've put myself in your place a hundred times. I asked myself how I would feel if someone showed up at my home, I got to know them well, and then they proceeded to say they were from the Colonies or neighbors of George Washington or anything like this. I'd be ready to show them the way to the asylum."

He turned toward her. "But all I want is a chance, Sarah. You owe me nothing—you've given me so much already. That said, I'm begging you for a chance to let me show you, through my eyes, my Bentonsport."

She squinted as the sun's rays shone brightly through the window. Her hands loosened against the wheel.

"Remember when you told me all about the Bentonsport's beginning years? Let me complete the picture for you. I can tell you things the books won't give you—about the people, what they are like, what we do, the day-to-day stories of my Bentonsport. If you still don't believe me, at least you'll have a better picture of the town you—*we*—love."

Sarah drove down the Pittsburgh road. "Give me a moment to think, Thomas. I just don't know what to think—what to say."

Had she filled him with her tales until he could see himself there? No, a rational person didn't jump to such crazy thoughts. He didn't seem crazy. Odd sometimes, but not crazy. So how did he begin to think these strange thoughts? Sometimes people's thinking was altered through shock or a sudden blow to the head.

She slowed the truck. A sudden blow to the head? Thomas had held his head when he fell on the bridge. He'd complained of a headache. Perhaps it all went back to that fall. Twisting her grip on the wheel, she thought of how to suggest this idea but stopped.

Thomas believed his story. She had to create doubt in his mind. If she could get him to that point, she could mention the fall and show him how this didn't make sense. She could suggest perhaps he'd suffered a concussion. If she could get him to accept this possibility, they could seek help.

Hmm ... No one knew Bentonsport's history better than Richard—no one. She'd agree to listen to Thomas's story on one condition. He'd go with her to Richard's house. After she heard his tales, they could visit Richard, and somehow, she could show Thomas the inaccuracies of his stories, not outright but subtly, through conversation with Richard.

Thomas would hear the truth about old Bentonsport from someone he trusted, and maybe he'd see he was confused. And, maybe, through that, there'd be the hope of helping him.

"Okay." She lowered the radio's volume. "I'll listen to all you have to say about Bentonsport, if you agree we can end the day on a cheery note with hot chocolate at Richard's. Deal?"

He might have thought it an odd request, but Thomas agreed.

They grabbed their food and ate outside at a picnic table. Sarah was lost in her thoughts. In so many ways, he approached the simplest things like a child. If it weren't so crazy, she could almost force herself to believe his story. But he obviously suffered some type of amnesia or delusion.

But if that were true, who was he? She shuddered.

"Cold?" he asked and, when she nodded, he moved closer to her, wiped his hands on a napkin, and put his arm around her.

Why couldn't he just be normal?

"We better go." She eased away from him. "Cups and Plates closes at five, and I don't want to forget tea for everyone."

THOMAS STEADIED THE TRAY HOLDING THE CUPS AS HE walked around the truck and set it on the roof. He opened the door, reached up for the tray, climbed into his seat, and shut the door without spilling a drop.

Caroline was still propped up on pillows, but this time, Bill was to her right, sitting somewhat sideways with his feet on the floor and his arm draped over her. Lani and Richard flanked the bed, Richard telling one of his stories. He cut it short when they entered. "No, don't stop, Richard," Sarah protested. "We're just here to hand out tea."

"You probably saved the day." He laughed, thanking her as she passed one cup to him. "They've heard this story several times before, but it's a good one."

Tap-tap.

A nurse entered carrying two trays.

"Is this a good time?" she asked softly.

Lani, who must have been sitting quietly for too long, stood. "Any time is a good time for food, especially when someone is eating for two. And we have been jawing at this poor girl long enough."

Caroline protested as Sarah, Thomas, and Richard followed Lani's lead by putting on their coats. "Now, you eat and get some rest, darling, so you can come home for Christmas."

"Thomas, I don't know if I'll have a chance to see you before tomorrow night." Bill stood, stepped over to Thomas and embraced him. "If not, I want to thank you for all you've done for us. You're a good friend. If you decide to come back for a visit, you have a place to stay with us."

"And now you rob me of a paying guest," Lani teased and clucked her tongue.

When Sarah asked Richard if she and Thomas might stop by later, around nine, for hot chocolate and conversation, Richard beamed, noting he'd welcome the company.

Caroline motioned Thomas over. He reached for her hands, but she hugged him instead. As she pulled him closer, she said in a whisper Sarah strained to hear, "Please try to come back, Thomas. We will miss you so much. I'm so grateful for all you've done for us. And no matter what, I promise Sarah will be fine."

Thomas clenched his teeth. He looked down at the bedsheets

and stood when Caroline released her grasp. Sarah moved between them and enveloped Caroline in a hug.

"Oh, you goose," Sarah teased, "it will be so good to have you home."

Then they followed Lani and Richard out of the room. She stilled as Thomas took one last look back. Bill was returning to his space on the bed with Caroline. Like two birds in a nest. And it appeared as though Thomas took a mental picture.

Chapter Twenty-
Seven

T homas, elbows on the counter and head resting on his hands, marveled at how quickly Sarah could do anything in this kitchen. Just about everything in this world was so easy. Coffee streaming down into the pot in just minutes. Trucks speeding you to and from adjacent towns. How would she give all this up?

"Why don't we take the mugs with us?" she asked. "They'll keep our hands warm, and we can come back for a refill if we'd like."

"Or if I get long-winded," he teased.

As they walked, the air held only the faintest hint of woodsmoke, unlike the smoke-laden air back home.

He reached for her hand, and she entwined her gloved fingers around his. He stopped just before Front Street to sip his coffee. "Close your eyes for just a minute and step back into Bentonsport with me."

She scrunched her eyes shut and exhaled—she was trying. She really was. He hadn't believed she would.

"Now, take a deep breath. Can you smell it? The woodsmoke is thick. All the homes fill the air with smoke, day and night, this time of year. Now open your eyes. See, the streets are dark, lit only by the glow of lamps in windows lining the streets and hillside. As the night progresses and the townspeople turn down their lamps and go to bed, the night becomes black, and the stars hang low in the sky."

He led her down Front Street. "So much here, Sarah, has been lost. It's hard to know where to begin. You can't imagine how shocked—no, sad—I was when I arrived. Before I came here, if anyone had asked me what Bentonsport would look like a hundred or more years in the future, I would've said it would be grand, large, developed. Not like this ... nothing like this."

Sarah pressed her palms flush against the coffee mug. Such sadness in his voice. He meant it. This was no act. Clearly, this man, in his own mind, lived in the past, the grand past of Bentonsport. But *why?*

"Here." He interrupted her thoughts. "We'll start at this familiar building."

The Odd Fellows' Hall.

"Back home, this is the Macon and Augustus Renkopf's Building. They are cabinetmakers and undertakers. They have a profitable operation, though not a grand building, as you can see. But they make a nice income. I can't understand how this building managed to stay in such fine shape when so many others are gone."

"I know why." Sarah let the steam heat her face, breathing in the invigorating aroma. "It's always been in use. Richard once told me the building has, in many ways, 'housed Bentonsport.' It has been a furniture factory, a newspaper office, even a dance hall. But what preserved its future was when the Odd Fellows bought the building and used it as their meeting hall."

"It's a shame they couldn't have purchased them all." He pointed to the other side of the road. "Across the street here on this stretch of land, there is a block of shops."

She'd always thought there had to be a row of buildings there. "If you look carefully, in the daylight, you can see depressions in the bank where I imagined foundations had been."

"There are—were." He corrected himself. "Right here stands a two-story brick building. It is the Tucksberry Picture Gallery, and next to it, Alex Carter's Butcher Shop. Some mornings, you stand in line to get into his shop. People come from all parts of the county because he is known for his fresh meats at a fair price."

The growing hum of a truck driving through town interrupted them. Goodness, how out of place it sounded!

"And, here, is Clark's Drugstore," Thomas continued. "People say Mr. Clark has a remedy for everything ailing a person except a broken heart, and for that, he has a ready ear. Next to it is Mr. Alexander's Shoe Shop. I can't say as I've ever purchased shoes here. I still buy my shoes back East, though these shoes seem fine."

They took another few steps. He did make the past come alive, as though she'd been transported back over a hundred years. Nearly every building had a story and a name of an owner, most unfamiliar.

"The McVinty Brothers have a leather shop here, one of the first businesses established on this part of the river. And here is the Hines Tailor shop, and next door, the Clement wood business."

He swigged from his coffee mug. He glowed with energy. In his mind, he was back home.

"Of course, the town's main employers are located up and down this side of Front Street." He motioned toward the river side of the street. "Here, where you have the rose garden, this is the foundation of the Browns' gristmill. When I saw this for the first time, my heart sank."

He shook his head. "You can't imagine this, but this is a five-story gristmill, a huge building, a landmark in the town. From here, all the way down to where the bridge now stands, large enterprises dominate the riverfront—the Brown and Moore woolen mill, the Greene Brothers and Bragg Paper Mill, and the Bentonsport Mills."

As they strolled down the road, he gestured, pointing out each building on the street—his street. If she didn't know better, she'd believe him.

"There are a few establishments here too. John Cox has his Tin Shop there, and next door is George Jack's dry goods store. Further down, there is a wagon factory and a sawmill. And beyond the bridge entrance is Calvin Tromley's stage barn."

She stood amazed as this unseen town unfolded, almost like Brigadoon, that mystical Scottish town that appeared only one day every hundred years.

"I was relieved to see a good part of the Greef establishment is still standing, and in some ways, looking better than it does now —or I should say, then. But these are just the buildings, Sarah. I'm not giving you a picture of the town, of my life there." He tapped his now-empty coffee mug against his thigh, appearing deep in thought. Then, taking her arm, he brightened. "Come with me."

In silence, arm in arm, they walked up her street. Even as she wondered where he was taking her, she straightened her shoulders. This part of the evening was all his. Her coffee was cold, but she finished the last sip.

Around the bend and up to the academy drive, he stopped. "I'd let you in." A wry twist flatted his lips. "But I don't think my key would work."

He couldn't be serious. But he was.

Shivering, she tried to laugh it off. "With our luck, someone would see you, assume we were breaking in, and have us arrested. We'd spend Christmas in the poky."

"For just a few minutes, pretend you're with me." He set down his mug and clasped her upper arms, giving her a squeeze. "It's Bentonsport, and it's the year 1869 ..."

Sarah swallowed hard. There it was again—1869. If this were possible in any way, this man was well over a hundred years old—

1869. She turned the date over in her mind. What did she know about 1869? Very little. The Civil War was over, but just barely.

"I know it's hard to imagine, but let me show it to you, okay?" His voice came breathy, pitched high. He slid his hands free from her arms and grasped her chin, turning her face up. "You know it in your head. You told me all about Bentonsport, my Bentonsport, that first day when I sat in your kitchen. Remember? Now, all I ask is that you let me add the color."

With a deep breath, he scooped up his mug. "It's a wintery day, like today, and nearly Christmas, only it's morning. School is on break, and I'm restless, anxious to get out and about. I've decided to run some errands. Won't you join me?"

He bowed, tipping his cap. She gave him a curtsy and looped her arm through his. They walked down the road, her hand through the crook of his arm, holding securely onto his forearm. His whole demeanor seemed to change. He stood taller, more relaxed. As though he had stepped out of one world and into another.

They turned down her street, and he stopped and grinned broadly. "The first task is to decide whether we should walk briskly down the street, heads facing downward in hopes Mrs. Carrington hasn't seen us coming. Or face our fate bravely, realizing she's been watching us since we first came into view and shall be greeting us shortly."

"What?" Sarah couldn't help giggling. "I have no idea what you're saying."

"Caroline and Bill's house." He swept his hand grandly toward it. "As innocent as it may appear, inside sits Virginia Carrington and family. She has a heart of gold—I've no doubt. But she is the biggest busybody, and in my case, she has a mission."

"Wait." She had him trapped. She slid her hand free and faced him. "Caroline's house was built in 1869 for the Greef family. Who is Virginia Carrington, and what mission is she on concerning you?"

"The Greefs built the house." He relinked their arms. "But they have not moved into it yet. The Carringtons moved into the house when it was built because the Greefs hadn't yet sold their current home and, as the town ladies like to say, just aren't prepared to make the move yet. The Carringtons sold their home and are in need of a place to reside while their new home is being completed, so the Greef home is theirs for the coming year."

He patted her hand on his arm. "As for the mission"—a mischievous lilt brightened his voice—"the same ladies will tell you, in hushed voices, that the headmaster of the academy will relocate if a suitable bride is not soon found. Mrs. Carrington has taken it upon herself to find the woman whom she believes is the right one for me."

After staring hard at Caroline's house, he turned back to her. "So, this spot officially marks my danger spot, the spot at which Mrs. Carrington prepares to pounce, generally greeting me at the end of her walk. So, do we walk quickly or stroll?"

"I question that she would find me a suitable match," Sarah quipped, finding her footing back in his world. "I say, heads down, and let's make a run for it."

They walked briskly past Caroline's house, laughing like schoolkids. Then they slowed and stood in front of Sarah's walk. "Ah, safe."

Once they'd set their empty mugs on a stump in the middle of her lawn, Thomas put his arm around her shoulder. "Your house is known even in my Bentonsport as the Montgomery House. Mrs. Carrington once told me your house is one of the oldest homes in Bentonsport. Now, in my Bentonsport, it's owned by an elderly widow, Mrs. Cresswell, who still bakes pies and cakes. She is a member of the church I attend."

He sailed through the description, leaving nothing to dispute. She knew nothing of Rosanna Cresswell, only that the name did appear on her abstract. And, likely, the house would be owned by someone who enjoyed baking. No other house in town had a bustle oven covering one entire wall of the summer kitchen. She wished he'd known the Montgomery family, the original owners. But he said he knew of the house nearly twenty-five years after it was built. The Montgomerys no longer lived there.

"I attend the same church as you, the Presbyterian Church on the hill. And it is very much the same. Even our ministers are similar, and you—like everyone else in town—would love Pastor Lockhardt. He came to the academy and told me of the vision he had of this trip. I am certain he is anxious for my return to see what I have discovered."

"What will you tell him?"

Thomas was silent so long that she distracted herself, watching him tap his foot against the stump.

"That depends a great deal on what happens during my remaining time here." His soft answer fogged the air.

The wind blew, and they each drew their coat up around their necks. Thomas tied his scarf tighter, then guided her toward Front Street again.

"Wooden boardwalks run the street's entire length. As you walk down the planks, you hear the soft hollow sound under your feet. When many of us walk these planks at the same time, we create a cacophony."

They walked arm in arm down the dirt road to the wooden walkway fronting the shops to Greef Store. "Careful, we're surrounded."

"Surrounded?" Sarah twisted, looking around her. Where was he going with this?

"It's nearly Christmas, remember? The Greefs encourage the children to come and look at the new toys, and they hand out candy canes and mugs of hot chocolate. Whenever I come down here, on days like today, I'm engulfed in children sharing their Christmas lists, telling me what new toys have arrived, or just chatting. I'm pretty familiar to them."

Sarah squeezed his arm. She could see the whole scene, the busy gathering of children, noses pressed to the glass, and Thomas in the middle, listening nodding, teasing. Somehow, it didn't seem too distant or so far-fetched.

"Ernst Gentry, a retired farmer, stands on the corner there, over by the inn, and serenades all us with carols on his fiddle. As you walk toward the inn, the storefronts are decorated with greenery and wreathes."

A gust of wind blew cold, and Thomas held her closer. He made the town sparkle, and she wanted more.

Farther down Front Street, they stood on the corner *with Ernst Gentry* as he played his fiddle. "If you look up the street, there is a one-story stone building."

"The Mormon House?"

"That is what you and others here have called it." He squinted toward the building, studying it. "But in the world we are in today, it is a fine two-story house. Here, the upper floor is strangely missing. Mrs. Carrington told me it was once used as a dormitory for the workmen who built many of the brick homes here in Bentonsport, perhaps even your home. Today, the Macon family lives in the house and uses the back part of the building as their wagon factory."

He glanced up and down the street, then reached for her hand.

"Let's cross over to the inn now, which today is the Phoenix Hotel, and before that, it was the Ashland House. The hotel is known for its fine food and is the first stop for people who come to Bentonsport by train and get off at the depot just down Front Street or arrived by steamboat and dock over here. The crew assists the passengers with their bags to the front of the hotel."

He looked off in the distance. "It's sad because the steamboat traffic has all but stopped in my town. Everyone is taking the train. Still, the Phoenix is nearly full at all times, and many of us come on Sundays for our after-church meal."

Steamboats, trains. He was describing a unique time in Bentonsport. Thinking of the railroads reminded Sarah of a piece of trivia Richard had shared. "Do you recognize the building there, next to the inn?"

Thomas drew closer and circled it. She could see him puzzling over the structure, squinting, trying to recognize some detail to jar his memory. After a few moments, he shook his head. "No, I don't. All I know is it has been added to the hotel."

"It's the old Bonaparte Train depot. The couple who bought the inn back in the sixties had it brought here and rebuilt it next to the inn. They ran it as an antique general store and sold candy and ice cream to the visitors."

He cocked his head and smiled.

"Do you recognize it now?" Sarah asked.

He chuckled. "You have to understand, Bonaparte has always been a proud and prosperous town. If the Meek brothers were alive today, they would be disgraced at the thought of the town depot sitting in Bentonsport."

"If they'd have seen how Bonaparte was deteriorating back when the train station was hauled here," she teased, "they probably would've left town."

He threaded his arm around her waist and bent his head toward her. "Sarah, I could tell you so many more stories. About my students, the merchants, the townspeople ... so much I could share. I know this is impossible to believe, but if you could just —*somehow*—trust I'm not mad. This whole affair is as strange and awkward for me to live as it is for you to hear."

And looking straight into his eyes, she reached up, smoothed a lock of his hair, touched his cheek. "I don't think you're crazy. At this point, I'm not sure what I *do* think, but I *know* you're not crazy."

"How about mean and cruel?" He put his arm around her waist and pulled her close as if trying to hold onto something he couldn't.

She frowned, taken aback by the question.

"Remember, in your truck today," he added. "When I told you where my hometown truly is?"

Ah. That. "I was confused and angry. I'm still confused, but I'm no longer angry. You're anything but mean and cruel."

He held her close, rocking side to side.

Tearing up, she swallowed hard. *So not the time to cry.* Instead, she rested her forehead against his wool jacket and breathed in his unique scent of smoky clove—a smell uniquely his—and she loved the aroma. Perhaps it was the smell of too many trips to the Greef Store. She smiled and held onto the moment.

Then she stepped back and breathed deeply, knowing this was something she couldn't hold onto either. "Why don't we go to my house and drink another cup of coffee before we visit Richard. We told him we'd stop by tonight, and I don't want him to stay up too late for us, though I'm sure he would."

At her door, Thomas held the screen door open for her as she fumbled through her keys in the darkness. She opened the door, reached behind it, and flipped the light switch. The kitchen full of light, they pulled off scarves and coats and hung them on the hooks. This pattern already becoming so familiar—their life together. She couldn't imagine that, in a night and a day, it would all be gone.

She poured coffee into their mugs. Before sitting with Thomas, she phoned Richard and told him they'd be over in about a half hour.

At this point, he'd given her nothing in all he'd told her that she could probe with Richard. Everything he'd said fit the stories she'd heard.

"So, what made you decide to leave Pennsylvania and move halfway across the country?"

Thomas leaned forward and sipped his coffee. He set the mug on the counter and cupped his hands around it.

"Sometime after my thirtieth birthday, I began to feel wanderlust. My boyhood friends had married and were involved in their new lives. My mother and sisters continued to suggest local eligible women I should court."

Sara, intrigued, sat back a bit. He looked far away.

"But it wasn't just that. Several of my friends and acquaintances headed out West, and they were sending letters to family and friends with stories of new towns developing, new opportunities. It sounded like what I needed, and I began to make plans to move. But I wasn't sure where I wanted to go."

How she knew that feeling. That restlessness, like the life you were living wasn't a good fit. That same feeling led her here. She set her mug down and rested her chin on the backs of her hands.

"My great-aunt took pity on me for the needling I got about being single and thought a change would be good for me." He sat up straight, flexing his fingers. "She received a letter, weeks before, from friends of hers, the Moore family. They'd moved from our town to Bentonsport, and Mrs. Moore mentioned the local headmaster of their academy had resigned. Without my knowing, she wrote Mrs. Moore and gave a very, I'm certain, unbiased opinion of her nephew's abilities."

Thomas winked at her. Sarah loved this. She loved this man. And he was leaving her.

"They asked me to write a letter detailing my interest in the position, and about three weeks after submitting my letter, I was offered the position. I relocated here shortly after."

"I can't imagine leaving everything you know based only on stories, having not even seen the place where you'll live. What did they say to inspire you to move?"

He leaned forward. "A number of things." He turned the mug in his hands, peering at the imprinted Queen Anne's lace flower on its side. "Tales of people finding great success in starting new businesses, of creating new homesteads, making new friends, and finding new love. But the story that made the difference was the one the Moores told of Mr. Freeman."

Sarah tossed the name over in her head. Freeman. Freeman. She couldn't remember hearing any stories about a Mr. Freeman.

"The Freeman family came to Bentonsport just after the Moores arrived. The townspeople were horrified when men went to call on Mr. Freeman and discovered he was a slave owner and had brought his slaves with the family to Bentonsport. The town was an antislavery town."

His expression intensified. "With the men and women so angered, prominent citizens decided to call on Mr. Freeman and give him a choice. He could either free his slaves and help establish them as free residents of Bentonsport or move to one of the southern states sanctioning slavery."

This might be it. Thomas may have just gone one story too far. Certainly, were it true, Richard would have told this story over and over again.

"Well, Mr. Freeman was angered, of course." Thomas smiled. "But he didn't want to leave the town to which he'd just relocated his family. So, he followed their guidance. He freed each of his slaves—not only freed them but also provided for each, ensuring they had a small acreage or money to get started.

"Several of his slaves became merchants in town and are widely respected. Others have become farmers. In fact, one of Mr. Freeman's slaves is buried in the Bentonsport cemetery and kept the Freeman name."

"Interesting." She finished her coffee and set her trap. "I've never heard that story before. I wonder if Richard has. You wouldn't mind sharing it with him, would you? And speaking of Richard," she said cheerfully, "we better head over to his place before he starts to wonder about us."

They walked through the cold night air. The stars hung large in the sky. Small electric candles shone in windows along Front Street, with greenery decorating window boxes and trimming doors and windows. They crossed the bridge, which was lined with paper bags filled with sand, an unlit candle in each.

"Tomorrow night, we'll all meet at the bridge following the Christmas Eve service and light the candles, welcoming the Christ child to our world," Sarah explained. "We started the tradition four years ago when a foreign exchange student from Mexico lived with Pastor and Mrs. Turner. Normally, they head south for the winter, just before Christmas. But that year, with the foreign exchange student staying with him, they stayed in Bentonsport the full year. "

Sarah pulled up the hood on her coat. "The Turners found out this was a Mexican tradition, to celebrate the birth of Christ by lining the streets with luminaries, lighting the way for the Christ Child. We thought we'd make her feel more at home, and following church on Christmas Eve, we lit the luminaries and sang Christmas hymns as we crossed the bridge. We found it so meaningful we've repeated the tradition each year. You'll be able to join us tomorrow night, right?"

"I wouldn't miss it!"

Richard's house glowed, awash with lights. A wreath hung on his door.

"When I got home tonight, I realized I hadn't done much in my own home in terms of decorating." He took their coats and scarves. "So, I bought a wreath from the Zimmermans and cut down that little tree over there from the back woods. I just started decorating it when you called, Sarah. So, come now, sit down. I have the hot chocolate. It's ready over there in the Thermos on the table."

They sat in his cozy parlor, and Richard filled their mugs and passed one to her. "So, what have you all been up to since leaving the hospital this evening?"

"Well, we drank coffee and strolled around Bentonsport." She blew the steam from atop her mug. "I hadn't realized how much of Bentonsport's history Thomas knows. He was entertaining me with many stories."

"Well, Thomas," Richard said, "I wish I'd known that. I would've swapped tales with you much earlier."

"Yes," she jumped in, not wanting to be sidetracked from her mission. "Several of the names he mentioned, I remember from tales you've told. But one story, in particular, intrigued me. Something I never heard before. Thomas, why don't you tell Richard the story of Mr. Freeman?"

Sarah ducked her head, a cringe coming over her as she led a sheep to the slaughter. Too dramatic. More like leading the sheep to the shearer.

Relating the Freeman story with great ease, Thomas punctuated it now and then with a sip of cocoa. Richard followed along, forehead scrunching at first but then nodding, encouraging. Thomas ended the story by noting the burial of one of the Freeman slaves in the Bentonsport cemetery.

Richard leaned back in his chair. "My, I've never heard that one before. See, Sarah, you can teach a man something regardless of age. I know the location of the Freeman graves in the cemetery. What is interesting—and supports this tale—Thomas, is the Freeman stones aren't all together in one plot. They are clustered together, but in two *separate* plots."

This was not going well. Thomas had drawn Richard in. Sarah stared at Richard, waiting. He had to find some point to dispute.

"I always assumed they were different families, or worse, estranged families. But your story ... The Freemans who'd been slaves were probably still on good terms with their former slave owner but located their plot away from his immediate family to emphasize their independence."

Richard clapped his hands once, then rubbed his palms together, obviously pleased to have a new story to add to his collection. Sarah exhaled, blowing a wisp of hair that had fallen over her eye. Why would Richard accept the story at face value? Why didn't he question Thomas more? But that wasn't Richard's nature. He accepted people as they were, believing what they told him to be true unless he knew otherwise.

"Where did you hear this story, Thomas?" The man clapped his hands together again.

Sarah half expected him to hug Thomas. His smile was as broad as Sarah had ever remembered seeing.

"I wouldn't think your friends in Pennsylvania would swap stories of our little town."

As Thomas paused, she tried not to stare. But really, how

would he maneuver out of this corner?

"I heard the story from a friend of my great-aunt's. It intrigued me about this town on several levels. First, that people would hold so strongly to their values that they would confront a situation they considered evil. Second, that a man who was accustomed to owning slaves and benefited from their labor would value a town enough to not only relinquish the slaves but also ensure he provided for them."

Thomas took a long sip from his mug. "And, lastly, that these slaves would not only embrace their new lives but also give back to the town that helped secure them their freedom." He looked at Richard, his fingers forming a steeple just at his chin. "To me, it's a true story of redemption. And I was anxious to learn more about such a town."

"Well, Thomas." Richard tilted as far forward as his large frame permitted. "I consider that your Christmas present to me and our town. It's always good to learn the town you love has a heart even bigger than what you believed. What do you think, Sarah?"

She bit the side of her tongue. "It's a wonderful story. I was just surprised we hadn't heard it before." She sipped her cocoa, watching Richard.

"That's the beauty of history, my dear." Richard laughed.

Did he have to be glowing?

"People move from place to place, my dear and our stories go with them. And, once in a while, someone will come back, carrying with him a story we ourselves have forgotten. It is almost like having a visit with someone from our past."

Thomas, who had just taken a sip of cocoa, began to cough and sputter. Sarah, having lifted her mug, set it down and handed Thomas a paper napkin from the table. Their eyes met, but she averted hers. She'd had enough talk of visitors from the past. She wanted proof, some sliver of proof.

After finishing their cocoa, they thanked Richard and parted.

He called after them, "Enjoy the moonlight. What a lovely

night."

As they walked, Sarah tugged at her gloves, and Thomas, at her side, cleared his throat. "Do you believe me?"

Sarah stared up at the stars. The cold air stung her eyes and cleared her thoughts. "I feel confused, overwhelmed, and tired. Earlier today, I felt betrayed and angry. Now, all the many things I feel have left me strangely numb."

Not wanting to be in physical contact with Thomas now, she stuffed her hands in her pockets and kept her eyes focused forward. Eye contact might derail her.

A deep, long, audible breath lifted his shadow. "I'm being honest with you, Sarah. I've never lied to you. What else can I say to convince you?"

She stopped and forced herself to swallow, once—twice. *Honesty? Okay, here was honesty.* She began walking again.

"These past two weeks ... I've been falling in love with you. I don't believe in love at first sight. I don't believe in quick romances. In that sense, I'm fairly old-fashioned."

She stopped and faced him straight on. He had to understand *her*.

"But I do believe, when the right person comes along, something deep inside lets you know to proceed and tells you that you can let go. For me, Thomas, that's a huge step. I'm protective of my heart." In spite of herself, she touched her heart. The gentle pressure felt good. Like a sling, like support.

She started across the bridge, the water beneath them flowing away, leaving her, like everything she'd ever loved. Her arms crossed over her chest. The pain was almost unbearable.

"Maybe it's because I lost my parents at an early age. But, when you told me you were leaving, I felt like my heart was caving in."

She swallowed hard. But the tears came anyway, first warming, then chilling her cheeks.

With gloved fingertips, he wiped them away, tears welling up in his eyes.

"Oh!" She grasped his upper arms. "No, don't start to cry. Please, I'm okay. I'll get through this. You see, Thomas, some people could fool themselves into believing that, when someone says they're leaving, they'll come back. I hear that optimism in Lani's and Richard's voices when they encourage you to visit in the summer."

She hesitated. She was speaking now to her own heart as well as his. "But when those I love have left me—my parents and my grandmother—they haven't come back. They *can't* come back. So, when someone tells me they won't be back, I believe them ... you."

Steadying herself to get through this, she rubbed her gloved hand up and down the metal bridge railing.

The moonlight turned the river silver, and hunks of ice flowed by. Another time, this would have been romantic, the churn of the water, the crackle of the ice, the silver-tipped gentle waves. But not tonight. It was a needed distraction.

"So, I've been so sad." Her breath came out in a long gust, and the release felt strangely good. But, as the cold air she inhaled pierced her chest, she struggled to continue.

"I might have found the right man for me, someone who shares my interests and my beliefs, and after two brief weeks, he tells me he's leaving."

Drumming his hands against the rail, Thomas stared straight ahead. She could tell he was listening. What was he thinking?

She kept her eyes on the steady, stable moon.

"But love gives you this tiny crack of hope. When my parents died, a part of me thought one day they'd come home and tell me they weren't the ones in the accident. Sounds stupid, huh?" She gave a self-effacing shrug.

He laid his hand on hers, but their gloves withheld the warmth.

"But those cracks of hope let just enough light in to brighten the darkness, so you feel you can breathe, you can survive."

She waved up at the sky. "Just like the stars on a moonless

night. They give the sky enough light to overcome the night's true darkness." With a tissue from her pocket, she wiped her face.

He brushed his eyes with his glove.

"So, when you said you were leaving, I held on to this hope that maybe, just maybe, you'd grown fond enough of the town, the people, *me* to find a way back." She traced a finger along the rail, wiping away the ice film. "What is hard now is, if I could force myself to believe your story, all hope would be gone. And, even so, I want to believe you. But, if I apply an ounce of thought or reason to it, I can't. Does that make sense?"

He rubbed his brow, then placed his hand atop hers again. "Of course."

Sensing him looking at her, she kept her gaze forward.

"I told you, if this matter were put before me, I'd never believe it."

She wiped her nose with her tissue, then shoved it in her pocket.

"So ..." She rotated her hand until it clasped his, then squeezed hard. "No matter what I believe, I lose. If you're from a different era, you'll never be back. I'll wake up on Christmas, and you'll be gone forever. If your story isn't true, I still believe you'll leave. In that case, I'm in love with someone who I don't even know and who truly doesn't even know himself. And that"—she fought the tremor in her voice—"is not only sad, it's also scary and empty."

There was a long pause.

"My turn?"

Still staring over the bridge, she nodded. She couldn't speak anymore anyway.

"When I first came here, I tried my best not to have an impact on this era because it's not mine. But one can't associate with people without impacting them and without having them impact you."

He cleared his throat. "All I can say is I'm a man, and I'm weak. You drew me to you as I've never felt attracted to anyone in my life. It became impossible not to want to spend time with you. But spending time with you was a terrible mistake—for, in the end, we'd both be hurt. Especially you, because I knew all along I was leaving, and you didn't."

A vehicle crossed the distant bridge, casting a beam that pierced the horizon as it drove down the road. Thomas watched, appearing deep in thought until it moved out of sight.

"My thinking changed because of something that happened to me the day you asked me to leave your home, the day I first told you I wouldn't be coming back, remember?"

It seemed long ago.

"After I left your house, Richard came to the hotel looking for Lani. We talked for a while, and I agreed to help him take his sleigh back to the barn and the horses to the Zimmermans. As we passed the cemetery, I surveyed the stones, almost absentmindedly, and recognized a name. Sarah, I can't fully describe that moment—the shock, seeing the headstone of someone whom you know well. Someone who is very much alive."

The wind was starting to kick up, and she tightened her coat and pushed away from the rail. They crossed the rest of the bridge and down Front Street.

"I should have stopped there and diverted my eyes, but drawn in, I continued to survey the names on the stones. In the back row, on the second stone from the end, there is a square stone with an inscription that—" He lost his footing and slid forward, then stopped. "On the top, in large letters, is the name Barton."

He resumed walking, though at a slower pace. Her heart was beating so fast she was struggling not to pant.

"Under the name are two names in smaller print. Thomas—Teacher, Father, Husband, and Friend."

She didn't want this discussion to continue. The veins in her head throbbed, and she rubbed her temples to ease the pressure. How could she talk with someone discussing his own headstone?

"With the inscription of teacher, I knew it was mine. Snow

covered the dates, and I was glad for that. That is more than any person has the right to know."

Death ... tombstones ... Thomas ... teacher ... The words flooded her head, and she wobbled, woozy. Thomas steadied her, placing his arm around her shoulder as though knowing what he had to say would be even more difficult.

"Sarah." He pressed the name into her hair. "Let's go sit down, either at your house or in the rose garden."

The air chilled her. It—or something else—was causing her to shake inside and out. But she didn't want to go inside. Somehow, the cold air and wide-open space almost absorbed his words, allowing her to breathe. "Let's sit over there." She motioned toward the rose garden.

They sat amidst the rose bushes that were nothing more than stalks. He grasped her hands in his.

And they just sat, breathing in the night.

Then he wrapped both arms around her, and she leaned into him, grateful for his solidity even if she couldn't feel his warmth. "You remember I said there were two names on the stone. Remember?"

She nodded and shivered, feeling all at once cold to the core.

"The other name on the stone is 'Sara,' and under the name, the words *cherished wife, devoted mother, now home.*"

She tried to make sense of this. But how?

"What does it mean, Thomas? You're going to marry someone with my name?"

His breath warmed her cheek.

"It can only mean one of two things," he said, his voice slightly higher but soft and warm. "Either I will leave here and, at some point, meet another woman named Sara whom I will marry. I know of no Saras presently in my town. The only other explanation I can come up with—and, Sarah, this is my deepest hope—is that somehow the Providence that brought me here and will take me back home will allow you to come back with me."

As much as she tried, she couldn't get her breath. His arms

held her like a vise, and she pushed them off her and sat up, her hands gripping the seat of the bench.

She lowered her head and took several deep breaths and, despite her best efforts, shook her head. "No, no—"

"It seems impossible. But already so many seemingly impossible things have happened here." He tipped up her chin and sought her gaze. "I have given this a lot of thought. I believe the only way it could happen is for you to be open to coming home with me."

Sarah slumped forward and held her head with both hands. She couldn't think.

Here she was, almost Christmas Eve, with this wonderful man. She should be happy. They should be wrapping gifts, listening to carols, driving around looking at the lights on display. Instead, they were discussing tombstones, his leaving, their breakup, or stranger yet, her leaving everything—*everything*—and somehow slipping back in time.

Shuffling her feet against the snow-encrusted flagstones, she wanted to go to bed. The cold and the darkness now were adding to her depression. She needed to sleep through this strange night and awaken to a new day. A completely new day.

"Thomas." Her shoulders sloping, her voice reflected her weariness. "I wish I could think of the right response, the right thing to say. But I am just so sad, so deeply sad, and so tired. We both understand where things are between us. I couldn't have been more open with you if I were talking just to myself. In your own way, you have been too."

She wiped a lock of frozen hair from her cheek, rubbed her hands together, and confessed why she'd gone to Richard's. "I saw it as perhaps your first step back to me, to here."

After retrieving the crumpled tissue from her pocket, she dabbed her eyes and blew her nose.

"When we were walking the streets tonight"—his voice was hesitant, and his body rocked—"when I was telling you all about my town, my people, there were times you seemed to believe me."

"It's because you're so convincing!" She whipped around, her hands fisting, her temperature rising. "I find myself being sucked into your fantasy. But, when I come back here—back to my world, back to reality—there is nothing of your world to hold onto. Just stories I've heard from others, only with more flesh. The tale of the Freemans, I'll admit, was extraordinary, but how do I know—and I don't want to hurt you by saying this, Thomas —but how do I know it's not just a wild embellishment?"

"Didn't Richard confirm the story, describing the location of the tombstones in the cemetery?" He stood and began to pace. "Do you think Richard is gullible? A fool?"

"Of course not." She stood in front of him, arms crossed, blocking his path. Her voice sounded full of gravel—nasty, brittle —but she didn't care. "But Richard isn't being asked to believe what you're asking of me. He's being told a tale and is asked to believe one story, not the full story. He has no reason to distrust you."

"And you do?" Thomas jabbed.

"Not you, Thomas, but the tale. The story. I once had a friend who had an uncle her whole family called The Liar."

"Well"—he thrust his arms toward the sky, then lowered them quickly—"that's flattering."

She touched his arm, his wool coat stiff against her gloved fingers. "Her uncle was a nice man who lived an ordinary life, but he had this ... ability to convince himself he'd done extraordinary things. He told her family he'd served tea to the pope with his own hands."

As Thomas looked at his shoe, his heel gouging a brittle patch of ice, she tried to regain her composure.

"Honestly." She cleared her throat, her voice softening. "No one in the family disputed his accounts because it was futile. He believed them. How do I know you didn't read articles and booklets on the history of Bentonsport? When you visited the cemetery, you could've seen the Freeman stones and concocted this story."

She clasped her hands together. His jaw muscles twitched, and his lips pressed white. He sat back down, shifting on the seat as if ready to spring up and stomp away, but she couldn't hold anything back. Not now.

"I don't know if you are in fact Thomas Barton. What would stop you from picking a stone with a Sarah on it and concocting this whole story before walking into my home?"

When he sprang from the bench, she stumbled back. She'd pushed him too far. She reached for him, but he shoved her hand aside, resuming his pacing but with a more deliberate stride. She dropped onto the cold bench. He stopped, his voice steady and hard, his arms punctuating his words in smooth slashes.

"Are you so impressed with yourself that you think I would come halfway across the country, find out about you, a girl named Sarah, walk up to a cemetery to seek your name—this, without having even met you!"

She recoiled as he stabbed an accusing finger in her direction.

"And concoct, as you put it, an identity, search the county, with no truck as you have, for appropriate clothing, somehow locate period money—all to deceive you?" He ran his hand through his hair. "You think my story far-fetched?" He planted his feet and dropped his head toward her, thrusting his finger forward. "Review your own!"

Sarah rose. She swallowed and licked her freezing lips. Her story was as out of line as his. "Thomas—"

"No." Looking down, he ran both hands through his hair. "I don't want to say anything else tonight. This has been a long stressful day. We'd best end it before this discussion goes any further—if it can."

And he walked out of the rose garden, up Front Street toward the inn.

Sarah started to tremble. At any other time, his civility would have trumped his anger, and he'd have walked her home. In confessing all of her thoughts, every last one, she might have lost him a day sooner.

275

Chapter Twenty-Eight

Winter's silver morning shone through Sarah's lace-paneled curtains. She lay on the bed, half-asleep, listening off and on to the radio, trying to convince herself to get up.

As she walked home alone last night, she thought her emotions were so raw she'd never rest. But, in the warmth and familiarity of her home, she felt heavy with sleep. She hadn't wanted to think about the matter anymore. She showered and collapsed onto the bed, promising herself she'd sort matters out in the morning.

And here morning was—cold and overcast, the weatherman's promise of the sun occasionally breaking the bleakness seeming as impossible as everything she faced. Friday's forecasted snow had moved to tomorrow, Christmas Day.

Today would be complicated enough without snowy weather. Tomorrow, after Thomas had left, she'd look forward to the snow and a white Christmas, especially if Caroline could make it home. She would need a friend tomorrow. She needed one today.

She wrapped herself in her thickest robe and padded down the stairs barefoot to make coffee and clear her head. The coffee on, she tugged a stool up to her kitchen island and sat where she could watch the birds fly back and forth from the tree to her feeder in their early morning ritual. She should dump the ice from the birdbath and fill it with fresh water, but she didn't want to go outside. Not yet. Not after spending so much time walking Bentonsport the night before.

She got up, poured her coffee, and sat back down, her head in her hands. She breathed in coffee's steam. There was no plausible explanation for who Thomas was, what he knew, or where he was from. Her explanation was as ludicrous as his.

If only he'd confided his beliefs early on. But she was beyond that now. They talked with the same ease, laughed at the same stories, loved the same town, related to the same people, and shared the same faith. They'd become a couple. And, now, they had less than twenty-four hours together, if that.

She pivoted on her stool, remembering the day he walked in, the period clothes he wore, the old money he tried to spend, the Amish outfit he bought. Oh, she and Caroline were so startled. She'd confided in Caroline that there was something strange about this man.

She sighed and stared back at the birds. They seemed so carefree. As she swung her feet back and forth, her leg scraped against something under the counter.

"Oh no!" She hopped to her feet. The baskets she was to hand out today, each awaiting a loaf of bread.

"Well, I know what I'm doing this morning," she muttered as she fumbled in the left-hand drawer for her well-worn family recipes. Reading the Christmas bread recipe, she calculated the four hours the loaves required.

Oh well, she needed to keep her hands busy. She combined the oats and boiling water, enough for five batches or twenty loaves, setting the timer for the twenty minutes the mixture would "rest."

She dashed up the stairs and pulled on a pair of jeans, a black turtleneck, socks and clogs. She paused, one foot still wiggling into the stiff leather, and plunked onto her comforter. How different her life would be tomorrow! She'd no longer have the warm anticipation of Thomas's visits. Her old life would return, along with its emptiness.

If only Caroline were here. But ... *would* she tell Caroline even if she were here? Probably not. The whole thing was too painful and weird. And she somehow felt protective of Thomas, like a loved one you keep inside so no one knows how deranged they really are.

Downstairs, she put each of the five balls of dough into its own greased bowl, turned them once, and set them aside, covered, to rise. They'd need an hour and a half. She'd have time to eat and decide how to spend the rest of her day with Thomas. That is, if he'd see her.

THOMAS AWOKE EARLY, AGITATED AS HE FACED THE day ahead and marking each moment as one in a series of lasts. The last time he would awaken in this inn, take a hot shower, and dress in casual work clothes to go about his daily business. Every activity chronicled another *last*.

How depressing to spend his time thinking this way. Better to remember *firsts*. The first shower he'd taken and his difficulty comprehending how the contraption worked. The first encounter with outspoken, always opinionated, warmhearted Lani.

And then Sarah, that blonde, impish, beautiful woman who opened herself to him as a rose opens in warm weather. She fragranced his life as no other woman had and, as he now believed, no woman again could. But could a rose such as this thrive in his world? Or, once transplanted, would it wither and die?

So many memories. The boyish young woman behind the counter. The lovely woman who baked cookies, threw snowballs, and played the piano like a concert pianist.

Their long, intimate, late-night conversations, moments only possible in her Bentonsport, but moments that allowed them to grow close quickly. And their first kiss, her lack of resistance letting him know her feelings matched his.

No thinking about the painful moments interspersed throughout these two weeks. Plenty of time later to review what he'd done wrong. For now, for this last day, he wanted only to redeem their relationship, set matters right, and leave it open—how did Sarah put it? The 'crack of hope' that this would not be the end.

He'd asked too much of her. Asking her to believe the impossible without experiencing it. Asking her to leave behind a known world for one she hadn't seen.

Hadn't Pastor Lockhardt asked the same of him just two weeks before? Now, he was asking someone to believe the same type of impossible happenings from a man she'd known for less than two weeks.

He'd been tested and failed. How could he ask more of Sarah? But, without this from her, where was the sliver of hope?

After toweling his wet hair, he dressed in Bill's clothes, which were now so familiar, folding the cuffs of the work shirt. So how was he to spend this last day? The Christmas Eve service and last walk across the bridge would fill his night. But what should he do with the fifteen hours between now and then?

He wanted to spend them with Sarah. It didn't matter that they'd quarreled last night. They were wrestling with far-from-ordinary issues, and they'd done a good job.

He donned the jeans, his socks, and shoes.

If the burden were his to carry, the decision his to make ... If the choice were open to him—to go back to his world without Sarah or to stay here with her—what would he decide?

He would stay. The decision had become simple.

What was it Pastor Lockhardt had said? The door would be closed for good? But was there any chance—*any* chance—he could choose to stay?

This sliver, the 'crack' of hope, was all he had. This would be his gift to Sarah. Along with his book of hymns from the Greef

Store, the tea strainer, and tea, he'd give her the knowledge that, if he could, he would stay. He'd choose her.

He would wrap the gifts he'd bought. He'd apologize for asking the impossible and give her the gifts. He could leave the other gifts with Lani for Bill, Caroline, and Richard. He scanned the room for an old newspaper to use as wrapping paper. Not finding one, he toweled his hair one last time, shaking out the remaining dampness, and did what he'd done here every morning. He went downstairs to see Lani.

Stirring something on the stove, Lani had already set his place. She answered his good morning halfheartedly. "I must admit I'm just a bit down, knowing you're leaving after today and all. We'd all feel better if we knew you'd miss us enough to come back."

He sat at the table, and she poured his coffee and spooned oatmeal into his bowl. "You know, Lani, I'll do everything I can to do just that, okay? So, no more fretting. We won't allow it today. If missing all of you can bring me back, I will be back sooner than you want. Now, on to happier subjects. What are your plans for the day?"

"Well, I'm going to Richard's to see the tree he decorated." She put the pan and coffee pot back on the stove. "He's pretty proud of it. He called me first thing this morning and invited me to come have a look. My guess is he's anxious for company." She placed a yellow bowl filled with brown sugar in front of him and a pitcher of cream.

"Then we'll do what we've done during the day for many Christmas Eves." Warming her hands on her coffee cup, she sat at the table. "Before the late service, we'll deliver presents Richard has collected from the Bentonsport merchants to the nursing home and county home residents. It's the best way to enter the Christmas spirit. You're more than welcome to come with us, but I suspect you have another place to go."

Thomas stirred his hot cereal, then tested a bite. "I hope to." It was smoother, creamier, but blander than he was used to. "I picked up a few gifts for her, Lani, but I'm afraid I don't have any newspaper to wrap them. Could I trouble you for some?"

"Why, I'll even let you have some pretty wrapping paper." She tousled his hair and squeezed his arm. "If you turn to the left at the top of the stairs instead of going to your room, there is a teeny room, almost a closet. You'll see a table set up with wrapping paper, ribbon, scissors, tape—you name it. From time to time, I help some of the shopkeepers gift wrap items for special occasions."

The clock in the hallway struck the half hour. The machine that washed the dishes hummed. He soaked in every detail of this scene to take back with him.

"I forgot until I was going through the freezer today that Sarah left a bag of frozen knishes for you here after our potluck. Said something about you wanting to try them?"

He laughed over their discussion about his lack of adventure in the food arena. Maybe he'd take them over to Sarah's house and show her he'd set a new course.

"Thanks, Lani. I might take them to Sarah's. I'm not sure what my day holds. In any case, I will see you at services tonight and afterward at the bridge walk, right?"

"And a special night it will be, for all of us, I hope."

He mounted the stairs two at a time, anxious to get on with his day. He retrieved the gifts from his room and found the wrapping table, the festive paper an improvement over the newspaper he used. He wrapped each gift, beginning with the book of children's stories and nursery rhymes for Caroline. On the inside cover, he wrote:

Merry Christmas. These are stories to share with your little one this spring. Make sure to add the story about the snowy day he or she wasn't born, in December. It's one I'll never forget. I will also never forget your kindness. Thomas.

He taped the ornament on top.

Next, he wrapped Bill's pipe holder and drafted a note on a scrap of wrapping paper.

You will be surprised to learn I didn't make this myself, or perhaps you won't. I only work in tin! Thank you for your friendship—even giving me the shirt off your back. God bless you and your special family. Thomas.

He set these aside and turned his attention to Lani's hand-forged rose. He rolled the rose into the paper, sealing the ends.

To a special lady and good friend, to grace the table we shared so many days. Christmas Blessings—Thomas.

For Richard, he wrapped Pastor Lockhardt's Bible, including an explanation of the Bible's history. He enclosed two of his old bills, the paper money in which Richard had shown such interest. And next to the bills, he wrote:

Please consider this my wedding present to you and Lani. I hope your Christmas is blessed with an answer of yes. Thank you for your friendship. Thomas.

The whole experience was bittersweet. Giving gifts to those he would never see again. The pleasure of giving, the pain of ending.

The remaining gifts were for Sarah—the tea, tea strainer, and his hymnal. He debated removing his inscription in the hymnal, with his name and the date, afraid she might think he was in some way trying to conjure up evidence from the past. In the end, he left the inscription.

It was what it was, and he'd let it stand with no comment. When he finished wrapping Sarah's gifts, he paused. What should he write on her card? After a great deal of thought, he bent over the paper.

If the choice is mine, I choose you. If I can stay or return, I will. My greatest Christmas wish is to spend it with you. Love, Thomas.

He nestled her gifts in the bag and laid the others on top of his bed. He carried the bag of gifts downstairs. When he stepped into the kitchen to get the knishes and say goodbye to Lani, he paused by a note on the table.

See you tonight—don't forget the knishes (however you spell that word).

He tucked the note in his shirt, knowing he'd be glad he kept it when he returned home. Knishes in the bag, he set off for Sarah.

SARAH FINISHED DRESSING AND RETURNED TO THE kitchen to check the bread timer. She couldn't believe she'd forgotten the gifts. How could she forget twenty baskets? She'd never forgotten to get the gifts ready. She'd better wrap Thomas's presents. After prepping the breadbaskets, she'd go to the inn and apologize for insulting him. Perhaps, he'd accompany her to distribute her baskets. Afterward, she could give him his gifts.

Since it was Christmas Eve and his last day here, surely he wouldn't hold a grudge. She retrieved his packages from a bag stacked on top of her gifts for Caroline, Bill, Lani, and Richard. She would hand-deliver the rest tomorrow.

First, she lifted the cookie tin, then the photos with the snowball 'splat' and her misspelled name. She laid them aside, unwilling to detract from the photo by adding the final *H*. Her fingers touched hard plastic, and she drew her hand back. The CD.

She'd forgotten this gift. Cookies could be eaten in any era. Photos could be viewed in any time period. But CDs? What would that gift signify to Thomas? That she didn't believe his story? No, the CD would not do. But what could she substitute?

It was 9:38. Sullivan's was open until noon. So many of their times together had involved music, from baking with the carols on, to singing at the piano with the nursing home visitors, to caroling familiar hymns.

The music box. The one with the Bentonsport-like church. Perfect. It played "Angels We Have Heard on High"—the song she and Thomas sang in their unexpected duet. Absolutely perfect.

Thirty minutes remained on the timer. Enough time to get the music box, have it wrapped, and give the bread its final kneading. She laid the cookies in the tin and set it on the stairs as a reminder to finish his gifts when she returned.

THOMAS HURRIED UP THE WALKWAY OF SARAH'S HOUSE, gifts in hand, and knocked on the door. No answer.

Waiting a few moments, he then knocked again. Still, no answer.

A sense of dread filled him. Her truck was gone. What if she'd decided to leave town for the day after last night's conversation? They had made no plans, other than the Christmas Eve service and the walk across the bridge. The lights were on in the kitchen. Maybe she'd just dashed out to run an errand or visit a friend.

He'd let himself in as far as the kitchen and leave a note on the island. He tore a scrap of paper from the top of his paper bag and found a pen on her counter.

Sara, I stopped by for a visit and to give you something. Please get in touch when you return. Thomas

Just as he shut the door and headed down her walk, a vehicle turned onto the road. He exhaled a loud breath, his shoulders slackening.

Sarah waved. Good sign. At least the morning wouldn't begin badly. She hopped out of the truck, carrying a sack.

"I hope you don't mind. I let myself in, just as far as the kitchen, so I could leave you a note. I was hoping you hadn't decided to leave for the day."

Her hands hung at her sides, and she cocked her head. "I had no plans for the day other than going to the inn to see you. That is, until I happened to glance at the shelves under my kitchen island and discovered I'd forgotten to bake the bread I put in my gift baskets every year. So, my morning will be spent right here. I would love for you—that is, if you don't have any plans—to come in and keep me company?"

"Better yet, I'll help." He held the door for her. "As I recall, we're quite a good pair in the kitchen."

A forced smile hardened her face. "Thankfully, bread doesn't require as much work as cookies, at least not once the loaves are in the oven."

They set their bags on the floor under the coats. She retrieved their aprons, handing him one.

"I have the ingredients all mixed, and the bread has risen once. I need to give it its final kneading and separate the dough into loaves." She dusted the island with flour and began punching down the dough in each bowl. Thomas followed her lead.

"I'll set the timer for one hour." She swept a wisp of hair from in front of her face. "This isn't an exciting way to spend your last hours here, is it? Is there something you'd like to do, Thomas?"

"This is how I wanted to spend my last day. I don't mean baking. I mean spending time alone with you—if you would see me."

"Listen ..." She set her dishcloth on the island and took several steps toward him. Sadness—no, regret—etched her springtime green eyes. "About last night, I want to apologize."

"No." He held up a hand. "I'm the one who should apologize. Do you realize, Sarah, that just over a week ago, I was in your place? And I didn't even give Pastor Lockhardt's words the slightest thought of being true. And this, of a man for whom I have the highest respect, the greatest admiration, and the deepest friendship."

He grasped her slender hands. "I expected more, so much more of you. To believe a man you've known for less than two weeks? To trust him enough to give everything up and step into a world you can't possibly imagine? I must have been crazy. And I am sorry for asking."

Looking up at him, she tightened her grip. "I don't know what to believe concerning you. Nothing makes sense. So, for our last day together, I have decided not to question or doubt you. I can't say I can fully believe your story, but I don't want today to be quarrelsome."

He wrapped his arms around her, and they stood in a comfortable embrace, feeling the sweet sensation of joy and pain that accompanies all moments that are wonderful yet knowingly brief.

A fter a few minutes, still holding her in his arms, he pressed his cheek to her hair, then tipped his mouth to her ear. "I brought something for us to share."

He separated from her and lifted out the bag of frozen knishes. "Now, in case you were wondering, that isn't your Christmas present. I just wanted to share this adventure with you too."

"Mmm, this is a delicious adventure."

She arranged the knishes in a circle on a plate and fit it in the microwave. As the small rolls rotated on the glass tray in the box, she made a pot of tea. When everything was ready, she poured tea into bright poinsettia mugs. She turned the music-playing box on low and set the knishes between them on the island.

She reached for the first knish and held it up for him to try. "The adventure begins."

And he took a large bite. The heat, array of deep spices, and damp but crisp crust filled his mouth. This was wonderful.

At a lull following the baking, Sarah excused herself and finished wrapping his gifts, placing each under the tree in the parlor.

Then they donned their outer garments and, both carrying

five baskets over each arm, set out to deliver the gifts. "I hang them on the door handles." Sarah walked as close as the baskets allowed them. "That way, no critters will get into them if they sit there long. But, usually, people come and go so often on Christmas Eve that they find them quickly. Even those who are pretty much shut-in will find their baskets when they get their mail today."

The streets seemed bright with anticipation. Wreaths decorated doors, and garlands draped many a fence. As their arms emptied of baskets, they strolled arm and arm down the gravel road. And he thought to himself how much some things change and how little others do.

All the conveniences of life surrounded them here, the trucks and cars, the light streaming through windows at night, but the essentials of life continued. Expressions of love, gifts, and holding hands remained. Friendships, the peace and joy of the season, were still abundant, and for this, he was grateful.

"Quiet?" Sarah nudged his arm. "I'd ask what you're thinking about, but perhaps I don't want to know."

He squeezed her hand. "Only happy thoughts now."

And she was glad. Moment by moment, she had to remind herself—*Don't rush this and don't look ahead. Take it moment by moment so you can remember it all.*

By two o'clock, they'd delivered all the baskets. When they returned, the mailman had filled her box with cards and letters and left packages on her doorstep.

They hung their coats and scarves on the hooks. He sat at the island while she heated tea. As the mugs turned in the microwave, she leaned against the island next to him. "Well, nine hours until church starts. We have a few choices of things we could do between now and then."

She wanted time to talk with him and enjoy his company. But

not long periods of dead time to cause them to think too deeply and begin to mourn the loss of each other much too early.

"My time is yours." He nudged her with his shoulder, then rested his chin on his hands. "I'll do whatever you'd like."

"Well ..." She traced one finger on the marble. "I should make Caroline's homecoming special. Bill is a wonderful guy, but ... I'm sure the house needs to be tidied."

The microwave pinged. She carefully removed the steaming mugs and, with a steady hand, placed one in front of Thomas.

"I thought it would be nice to have a Christmas casserole waiting in their fridge so all they'd need to do is pop it into the oven. It's not a noteworthy way to spend our last hours together, but we'd have the time together and help two good friends."

"It's brilliant." He toasted her with his mug. "After Lani described what she and Richard would be doing today, I felt guilty not doing something charitable. Back home—in Pennsylvania, that is—we always visited the orphanage on Christmas Eve. We'd take oranges and knitted mittens and scarves and toys. We always felt better about opening our gifts on Christmas Day after giving presents to the orphans. There is no orphanage in Bentonsport—at least there isn't in my town ..."

Sarah shook her head—no orphanage in her town. She wasn't certain there were still orphanages in America. Foster homes, boys and girls schools, but she had not heard of any orphanages.

"So, when I moved to Bentonsport"—he paused to drink his tea—"I sent money home to help my mother with the gift expenses. But it's not the same as going and helping."

"We could start by making two Christmas casseroles, one to put in Caroline's fridge and the other for us to share tonight. If we're out of there before five, Bill won't find us. We can come back here to play a few games and eat. I have a few gifts I'd like to give you before we head off for church, okay?"

"I have yours in there." He motioned to the bag near the door. "Caroline's and Bill's gifts are back in the inn. I had thought Lani could give the gifts to them, but if we're going to their home, we could collect them before we head over."

"Sure. We'll tuck them under the tree so they'll have them tomorrow."

When they reached the inn, the lights were on. "We're in the kitchen," Lani called out.

"Nap time at the nursing home and the county center." Richard, sitting at the table, hoisted his coffee mug. "So we decided to have a snack, though a nap also sounds wonderful."

"Too much to do to be napping today," Lani scolded, her expression soft. "Just have some more coffee. We'll perk up. Join us, Sarah, Thomas."

They looked at each other, and Sarah nodded. They had plenty of time.

"So ..." Richard held the mugs up as Lani poured the coffee. "What are you two up to today?"

Sarah settled next to Thomas. "We were coming here so Thomas could pick up a few ... things." She stopped short of saying "gifts," not knowing if Thomas had gifts for Richard and Lani, then explained their plans.

"Well, bless you for thinking of that." Lani pressed a hand to her red blouse. "It never occurred to me, but of course, that's a perfect Christmas gift. And to do this on your last day together makes it an even greater gift."

Sarah cradled the warm mug between her hands. "I hate coming home to an untidy house. And I don't like to think of her sitting around in one on Christmas Day, or worse yet, feeling she has to clean it. Besides, we'll make it fun."

Thomas smiling back at her made her cheeks warm. Could she say anything they did together was fun? No, better not.

"We'll eat and then be off to services," he added.

"Speaking of the service," Richard chimed in, "I spent my morning going over my message for tonight's celebration. Took a bit of time, but I'm ready now. How about you, Lani?"

"As ready as I'll ever be." She topped off everyone's cup. "I'm reading the Scripture, so I don't have to improvise. For a bunch of amateurs, we do a fine job."

After they finished their coffee, Thomas excused himself, returning with a bag that surely contained Caroline's and Bill's gifts. Then, bundled up, they headed out.

In Sarah's kitchen, he shed his coat, then stepped behind her to help her off with hers. The weight of her wool coat lifted off her shoulders, and she slid her arms loose, then grew still. The back of his hand grazed her neck, his fingers cold and his touch shivery. He drew in a deep breath as if savoring her, and her knees weakened.

She couldn't have moved if she wanted to. Never wanted to. He discarded the limp wool, letting it slip to the nearby bench, and they just stood there. His face pressed against her hair, their breathing and the ticking clock the only sound.

"Sarah ..." Grasping her shoulders, he turned her to him. He kissed her forehead, her cheeks ...

Then, finally and with great anticipation, she tipped her lips to his. She held on to his arm to steady herself. "My," she said, feeling somewhat flushed, "that was nice."

He wrapped both arms around her—how well they fit. "Come back with me. Let's not let this be the end if there is any way to prevent it."

She stood back from him. The sun streamed in the windows in long golden panels. They still had many hours ahead, no reason to risk any deep painful discussions. Not yet.

"It's time we start cooking." His hand in hers, she led him behind the island. In unison, they put on their aprons. "Okay." She tied his strings in back. "I know just the recipe."

When they finished the casseroles, she planted her hands on her hips. "Done."

Thomas helped her tidy the kitchen, then hung up their aprons. The clock struck the half hour.

"Four thirty." A sigh whooshed past her lips, ruffling her

bangs. "This day is going fast. We'll never get Caroline's place done by five."

"Why don't we go over and see what needs to be done." He shrugged. "Then go back after Bill returns to the hospital for the evening."

"It'll push us into the evening." She swiped loose hair away from her forehead. "But it'll work."

They crossed the frozen ground to Caroline's. Sarah knocked twice and then used her key. They hung their coats on the kitchen hooks. With the few dishes on the table, in the sink, and on the countertops, Bill had been eating simple meals.

Mail stacked like fallen leaves on the dining room table in the large sunroom. Glasses littered the end tables. The Christmas tree, somewhat yellowed, looked dry.

She returned to Thomas in the sunroom. "I hate to say this, but the tree has to go. It's the saddest Christmas tree I've ever seen."

"We have time to cut down another. Is there a place nearby where you cut your trees?"

"We always go back behind the church to the acreage Richard owns," Sarah said. "Richard doesn't mind if we cut down the pine trees. He plants new ones each spring, a renewable crop."

"Do you have a saw?"

"In my shed. Richard always helps me. We could call him if you'd like."

Thomas laughed. "I think we can manage."

By the time they retrieved the saw, the sun had set, and the sky was dark gray with night's onset. Bill drove up. He was hurrying toward the door and didn't see them in Sarah's backyard, Thomas with the saw in his hand.

As soon as Bill went inside, they slinked past, arms around each other, heads bent down against the cold. They ascended the snow-covered hill. Deepening dusk obscured the trees, but they settled on a five-foot pine.

With Thomas sawing, Sarah held on to the trunk, steadying it as it gave way.

"Okay, we're ready," he called out.

She let go, and the tree fell forward.

"If you can steer the front," he told her, "I can get the back. Just lead and I'll follow."

If only it were so easy.

She'd forgotten how heavy a five-foot tree could be. Sometimes carrying, sometimes dragging it, they turned onto her road, both red-cheeked, somewhat out of breath. Bill's truck was still parked outside.

"We'll put it behind my house," she whispered. "Then let's go in, have something to drink, and thaw out until he leaves."

They were just finishing their drinks when the clock struck six.

"I hate to say it." She picked up his empty glass. "But we'd better see if Bill is gone. If we work quickly, we'll still be time for us to eat and relax."

He moved to the window while she strode to the kitchen. "Bill's truck is gone."

"I'll put our casserole in the oven and set the timer on my cell phone so we can keep track of the time."

Thomas entered the kitchen as she dried the glasses. "Do you need any help?"

"Um, you could take the extra casserole and sauce out of the refrigerator and grab a sack of rolls from over on the counter." She slid their casserole into the oven.

As they entered their friends' dark kitchen, she flipped on the overhead light, then took the containers of food from him to the refrigerator. She didn't need to clear a bare space for them.

"Well, it looks like I'll have to go to Bonaparte," she said, shaking her head. "No milk, no eggs, no juice. Nearly nothing."

She shrugged her shoulders. "I'll get a load of laundry and the dishwasher started. Then I'll slip out and buy groceries and come back to help you with the tree. How does that sound?"

"You're the best person to drive the truck," Thomas said, half turning to her with a sly smirk. "Which makes me the best person to take down the tree."

She filled the dishwasher and put the laundry in the washer before he had taken down the top layer of ornaments. By the time she returned from the gas station with two sacks of groceries, he had half the tree ornaments off and lined up on tables, couches, and chairs.

She poured two glasses of eggnog she'd purchased and gave one to Thomas, then held hers up for a toast. "Merry Christmas."

"God bless us"—he clinked his glass with hers—"every one."

"Ah." The sweetness was wonderful. "Dickens."

"The words are etched in my brain after the children's play."

"I bet you miss them?" She let a hint of question into her voice.

"It's always nice to have a break from the students." He gave her the ornaments as he removed them from the tree. "Especially at this time of year when they're nearly frantic, anticipating Christmas. But after the New Year, when the days are gray and cold, I'm always ready to get back to teaching. Like these ornaments, the children are bright lights in an otherwise gloomy time of year."

Standing next to him, breathing in the scent of pine and his warm, spice-laden fragrance, she showed him how to take down the lights. "They're strung in and out of the branches like this." She moved her hand in the motions of an upside-down *U*.

She loosened the final strand, and he helped her take the tree outside. Together, they removed the stand and braced the tree against her shed. They retrieved the fresh tree, secured it in the stand, and lugged it inside.

"Let me get these pine needles up off the carpet before we set up the tree in the corner." She returned with a vacuum, and as she sucked up the needles, he frowned at the machine. This was no act.

She dismissed the thought. Plenty of time, starting tomorrow, to ponder all these things. They positioned the tree, and she gave him the light strand and began to pull the wire, snaking it in and among the branches.

"I better go check our dinner." She gave him the end of the lights. Minutes later, she returned to the sunroom. "I put our dinner on warm, so we still have some time. Let's plug them in and make sure we don't have any bad bulbs."

She scooted behind the tree and plugged in the cord. The tree glowed with soft yellow lights. She climbed out from behind it.

"Beautiful," he said. "Absolutely beautiful." He bent down and kissed her.

They finished decorating the tree and readying the house for the arrival of their friends. After surveying the results, she rested her head against his chest and took a deep breath, the roller coaster of emotions starting all over again.

"Come home with me tonight, if that is possible."

The clock struck seven times. *Only a few short hours left.*

Chapter Thirty

S arah set her best table: Christmas china, long tapered candles, lace tablecloth, and linen napkins. She positioned the casserole in the center of the lace medallion and asked him to say grace.

Carols played in the background, filling the silence between conversations. They talked of close family, of past Christmases, and of special friends.

"I'd like to give you your gifts," Thomas said after they'd finished eating.

Smiling, she lowered her napkin to the table. "Why don't we go into the parlor, by the tree?"

He retrieved his bag of gifts from the kitchen. They sat side by side on the couch, each engulfed in the moment's bittersweetness. The gift opening was the beginning of the end. This was their last time alone together.

"You first." She offered him the stack of gifts. First, he opened the tin of cookies with her for-future-orders information.

"That's just in case you're ever near a phone." She smiled a rather painful smile.

Next, Thomas discovered the photo series and laughed out loud when he reached the end. "How in the world were you able to put this together?" he asked, reading it several times over, amazement softening his face.

"The wonders of modern technology." She tried to swallow and then swallowed again. It hurt. Everything hurt.

"Sara. S-A-R-A. I've seen that name before. In fact, not long ago ... in a most, well, unusual spot." He smiled at her.

Not wanting to revisit cemetery stories, she quickly added, "Mine is spelled with a final *H*. I ran out of time putting the letters in."

"Sara ... Sara-h. They both sound the same to me ..."

"Yes, the *H* doesn't add much. You can call me either one." She winked at him. Dear heaven, she loved being with him.

He unwrapped the last gift, the music box, and as he lifted the lid, "Angels We Have Heard on High" filled the room. His mouth tightened in an almost pained expression. He breathed deeply. He understood. Their love of church, of beautiful carols. Their one duet. "They're perfect," he said after a few moments, his fingers following the lid's raised pattern.

Setting the gifts on the floor, he retrieved his bag. She first opened the tea and tea strainer. A good choice. She went through a lot of tea in the winter. She folded back the paper on the last gift, the book of hymns, and read the inscription.

She swayed slightly, and her head tingled as his shadow world began to seep into hers. "Your hymnal?"

"It was so strange, Sarah." He seemed cautious about selecting his words. "I was searching for gifts at the Greef Store. Yes, it is— that is, *was*—my hymnal. And ... I wanted it to be in good hands."

Sarah's hands trembled as she lowered the book to the cushion next to her. Her breath came in short snips, and she steadied her gaze on the clock, regaining her composure. As she turned back, Thomas held out a card. She eased open the envelope and read his message, a tremble moved up her arms.

If the choice is mine, I choose you. My greatest Christmas wish is to spend it with you. Love, Thomas.

"Oh, Thomas ..." And the moment overtook her. She'd been

strong, so strong all day, but the strength was gone. She wiped a tear from her cheek. "Do you think it is possible? Even somewhat possible? Could you stay or come back?"

"The fact that I'm here means anything is possible." But his lips pressed tight, and furrowed brows conveyed his doubts. "But my staying is not at all what Pastor Lockhardt described. He told me I would return to my home and the door to here would be shut. But, Sarah, if I am the one who can choose, I'll stay."

The tremor deepened to shaking, her teeth almost chattering. He was hoping for the same commitment, that, if the choice were hers, she'd leave all this behind and enter his world. She stood and paced in front of the tree, staring at her feet, willing them to keep going in small, firm steps.

He stood and grasped her shoulders, stopping her. Then he held her face. "It's okay. I understand. It's okay." Such pain lurked behind his tender look.

"I can't lie to you, Thomas, or to myself. I just can't make the same commitment. But, Thomas, I pray—yes, pray—you'll stay. And, if you do have to leave, my ongoing prayer will be that somehow you return."

"If I do leave, Sarah, and if much time has passed"—his thumb stroked her chin, then grazed her lips—"please don't continue to wait. I can't stand the thought of you spending your days here in some false sense that I might be back. If I do leave, the chance I'll be allowed to make this journey twice is ... not good." He kissed her hair. "But always know that, if the choice is mine, I do choose you. Sara—no *H*."

He released her as the clock began to strike, and she counted the chimes to herself, Thomas wincing at each one. Ten. Ten o'clock. Soon they'd be leaving for church. Soon they'd say goodbye.

They returned to the couch, holding each other as though they could stop the time from passing, stop the inevitable events. They held hands, fingers locking and unlocking. They kissed. But mostly, they held each other, trying to imprint the night in their minds so, for the rest of their lives, they'd remember these quiet last moments. Soon, the hour had passed. She was the one to stand.

"It's nearly eleven." She offered her hand. "We should go."

He wrapped her in his arms, this time, holding her so tightly she thought she might faint. Without a word, he let go. They gathered their coats and scarves. He put his gifts from her into the bag he'd brought, and they left for the church.

THE CHURCH WAS AWASH IN CANDLELIGHT AS A FEW stragglers, Thomas and Sarah included, made their way up the steep stone steps. At the halfway point, she could see Richard through the open door, ringing the bell from the vestibule.

In past years, her heart had welled with the joy of the season. But this year, the bell sounded forlorn as if tolling a funeral. It must echo the listener's heart. Closings her eyes, she snuggled closer to Thomas, who put his arm more tightly around her.

Nearly fifty people joined them in church, residents and family and friends. Thomas and Sarah sat in the second pew from the back, and a young woman handed them the song sheet.

Lani began the service, reading the Christmas story as told by Luke. Though Sarah tried to concentrate, her thoughts were moving from the Scripture to Thomas, from tomorrow back to the Scripture. With such familiar reading, she easily picked up the story as her thoughts moved back and forth. Thomas stared straight ahead, a calm, almost determined expression hardening his face, like someone who knew his fate and had decided to walk out and meet it.

The congregation sang "Away in a Manger" and "O Little Town of Bethlehem," which had always been one of her favorites. Then Richard gave the message. He stood in front of the audience, not wanting to appear in any way priestly. He greeted everyone and then began.

"I developed my message tonight after reading the different accounts of the birth of our Savior as told in the Scriptures and meditating on them. The message that nearly leaped off the pages to me over and over again was *fear not*."

A baby cried from behind Sarah, likely someone's visiting grandchild. A woman's voice stilled the child, and the church grew quiet.

"I had never before realized how many times the words *fear not* are associated with the birth of our Lord. In Matthew, the angel tells Joseph, 'Do not be afraid.' In Luke, when the angel appears to Mary, his first words are 'Do not be afraid.' Zacharias, in his prophesy after the birth of John, says, 'Grant us that we, being delivered from the hand of all who hate us, might serve Him without fear.' And the shepherds, who came to worship the Lord, were told by the angel, 'Do not be afraid.'"

The clock chimed one short *bonggg*, signaling the quarter hour.

"But how many of us, after this miraculous event, are still afraid to turn our lives, all our affairs, over to Him? How many of us worship this wonderful God, our holy Savior, and yet are afraid to say, 'Lord, Your will, not my will'?"

Richard stopped and surveyed the church, a warm grin rounding his wide cheeks.

"So tonight, I'd like us each to think about the gift we've been given, the gift of a Savior, One who can reconcile all sinners to God. We should meditate not only on our love but also on our trust in Him. As the wise men sought Him, as the shepherds left their fields to greet Him, let us pledge to let Him lead us— wherever He would have us go—and let us 'fear not,' for we have a Shepherd who will guide us."

Spreading his hands forward, then bowing his head, he said, "Let us pray: 'Christ child be born in us today. Be our Guide and Shepherd, and let us follow, fearing nothing along the way.'"

Lani distributed the candles, and the congregation sang

"Silent Night" as the flame was passed from candle to candle. As the last candle flickered, the congregation continued to stand.

"Let us go forward into the night, replacing all fear with joy, just as here we are replacing the darkness with light," Richard said.

One by one, the worshipers raised the wax guards to shield their candles from the wind and left the church to process to the bridge. As they walked, they joined in singing "Joy to the World." Thomas and Sarah, arm in arm, held up their candles. She forgot her sadness, for who could feel sad in such a moment of beauty?

At the bridge, Richard coaxed Sarah and Thomas forward. "Why don't the two of you lead our procession? I thought we would sing 'Angels We Have Heard on High' and conclude with 'Hark the Herald Angels Sing.'"

The children scurried ahead to light the luminaries lining both sides of the bridge.

With the final candles glowing, Sarah and Thomas linked arms and started the procession, singing in perfect harmony. The air, cold and sharp, blew across the river and over the bridge. Their candle flames flickered. They sang on, smiling at each other just like their first duet. At the end of the bridge, they stood, holding their candles, while the rest of the group passed on either side of them.

When all finished gathering, Richard said, "We will conclude our service with 'Hark the Herald Angels Sing.' When we reach the front end of the bridge, please extinguish your candles in the pots of sand there. Merry Christmas, everyone! Our Savior is born!"

SARAH'S ARM LINKED IN HIS, HER WARMTH AT HIS SIDE, Thomas led the group back across the bridge. They glanced at each other as they sang. Gratitude relaxed him and brightened his step. This was the perfect ending. He couldn't feel his own sadness when surrounded by such joy.

When they extinguished their candles, his heart beat in his throat. This was it. The end he had longed for just two short weeks ago. And, now, he didn't know how to say goodbye.

"Well, Thomas." Richard's hand clapped on his shoulder. "Lani and I left a gift for you upstairs. We're hoping you'll have good cause to use it and soon. We've enjoyed your company these past two weeks." The men embraced.

Stepping up next, Lani planted a kiss on his cheek. "Just in case you get in after I've gone to bed." Her eyes brimmed. "We'll miss you. We certainly will."

He hugged Lani. "I'll miss you as well." And he would.

Richard clasped Lani's hand, and together, they walked toward the inn.

"Well," Sarah began.

"I left my gifts in the church," Thomas interrupted her. "Would you walk with me to collect them?"

"No, Thomas." She stared deeply into him. "You see, I am bad at goodbyes. I told you once before, I know how permanent they can be. Let's say goodbye here, in the open sky, where I won't feel so terribly alone."

His heart ached under her penetrating stare. She was right. It was best to end right here. There would be no easy way to end this goodbye, and long goodbyes hurt all the more.

As he cupped her chin in his hand, her eyes closed, and one moonlit tear shimmered down her cheek. He closed his eyes and kissed her softly, then more firmly, and softly again. His arms around her and lips pressed into her hair, he whispered, "Always remember, Sarah, if the decision is mine, I choose you."

Head down, she nodded and turned for home. She walked slowly at first, then quickly, without turning back.

There was nothing more to say. It was over.

He entered the church, which was black against the dark

night. He groped just inside the sanctuary door and located his sack. After picking it up, he pulled the heavy church door shut.

Not wanting to alert Lani, he crept into the inn. Avoiding any more goodbyes, he padded upstairs, laid his coat across the bed, and switched on the light. He found the gifts he'd wrapped for Lani and Richard and placed them on the bedside table where she would find them in the morning. He glanced around the room, making sure everything had been packed, then tucked his gifts from Sarah in his bag and snapped it shut.

Next to his large bag, he discovered an envelope. "Thomas, Merry Christmas! Lani and Richard."

Inside he found a voucher for a round-trip train ticket, good for anywhere in the United States. He sighed. Too much sadness. Cold, alone, somewhat scared, and suddenly exhausted, he lay down to think and covered himself with his coat. Drained, completely drained, he surrendered to slumber.

SARAH COULDN'T STOP THE TEARS. SO MUCH LOSS ... her parents, her grandmother, and now, Thomas. She ran up the stairs and threw herself on her bed. The phone rang, but she couldn't compose herself to answer it. After four rings, the call rolled over to her answering machine. Richard's voice gave a muffled message downstairs.

Richard? She wiped her eyes. What could Richard want now? Tonight? She grabbed several tissues, hurried downstairs, and hit the *Play* button.

"You might not be home yet, but I keep forgetting to tell you. Hopefully, you'll have a chance to tell Thomas as well. Anyway, I went prowling through the cemetery, and I found proof Thomas is right. About the Freeman slave owner and all. One of the Freeman stones, the one in the back of the cemetery, had a strange marking that said—"

The message cut off.

Said what?

The phone rang again, making her jump. She cleared her throat and lifted the receiver.

"Sarah!"

She winced at the cheer ringing in Richard's voice.

"You must have just come in. Anyway, I left you a message, but I got so long-winded. ... And this can wait until tomorrow, honey. I just thought, if you were still with Thomas, you could tell him. I decided to follow up on that story about the Freeman slaves, remember?"

"Y–yes?" She tightened her grip on the receiver, the plastic warm and slick in her sweaty palm.

"Well, the Freeman stones, in the back of the cemetery? One of them has a marking I don't recall having seen before. The marking is USNT. It turns out USNT stands for United States Negro Troops, the African-American men who fought on the Union side in the Civil War."

The joy of discovery tinged his voice. "None of the other Freeman stones in the front section of the cemetery have that marking. There are a few colonials, but none marked USNT. So, you see ... Thomas's story is correct. That's all, honey. Let Thomas know for me, and merry Christmas."

"Yes." The word clogged her throat. "Merry Christmas, Richard."

Dazed, she stood by the phone, her Christmas tree glowing in the background, Thomas's hymnal resting on the coffee table. What had she been asking for? Just one small sign, just one indication there was any truth to Thomas's story? She made her way up the stairs to her room.

It was early Christmas morning. Tomorrow, she'd wake up, alone, as she had every Christmas morning since her grandmother's death. She would pad around the house, listening to music, winding clocks, feeding birds, and killing time until Caroline came home.

Thomas would be gone—for good. But gone to where?

Could it be possible he was allowed to slip through time just for a few days? Could she even remotely consider doing the same?

Her thoughts swam, leaving her queasy. She lowered herself onto the soft easy chair. She'd always considered herself a lover of adventure, but the adventures she enjoyed each had boundaries, parameters, like knowing where she was going and when she'd return. Slipping through time into some unknown black hole—well, it was terrifying!

Fear. It was too common to her. The little girl who thought her world had ended when her parents never returned. Fear. The grown woman standing at her only living relative's bed and watching her slip away. Fear. The tears came again. No need to stop them now. No one was here.

What did the angels say time after time in the Christmas story? 'Fear not.' 'Do not be afraid.' But how could she not be afraid? How could she decide what to choose—if the choice were hers—and in just one night?

She stood up. Her body moved with her thoughts. She didn't have to decide. She would leave it up to God. She'd respond as Mary, Joseph, and the shepherds responded when faced with life-altering decisions. She'd turn her will over to God. If God wanted her to go to a strange land, in a different time, she'd go. She would follow, but she wouldn't charge ahead.

She dropped onto her bed, her back against the headboard, and wrapped the bedspread around her. If she were taken to Thomas's world, what would everyone think? Lani, Caroline, Richard, Bill—they'd be in a panic, thinking she'd been kidnaped or harmed in some way. She unwrapped the quilt, then crossed to her desk for a pen and paper and wrote as she thought.

After writing 'Dearest Caroline,' she put her pen down. *What* would she say? How could she explain falling in love with a man from the past, time travel? They'd fear for not only her safety but also her sanity. No, she'd have to be truthful but vague. She toyed with the pen and tried again:

I left with Thomas to follow a new dream. I might not be able to return for a long while, if at all. You've been the sister I never had, and I'll love you deeply—always.

She wiped tears. Staying was hard—but leaving was harder.

But, as sisters, what I leave behind is yours. Use what little there is to help bring up my goddaughter or godson and let her know her auntie loves her (or him!) dearly. Time is short. Trust I am happy. Love, Sarah.

Having folded the note, she tucked it beneath the pen on her desk. She was tired, so tired, but not afraid. She'd given her will over to God. In His will, all would be well.

Downstairs, she turned off the kitchen light and entered the parlor where she and Thomas had sat just hours before. She laid her head on a pillow, intending to rest for just a few moments before changing into bedclothes. But soon, she was in a deep sleep.

Chapter Thirty-One

The sun shone through the windows in long bright planks. Thomas awoke to children's voices screaming and squealing outside his window. He opened his eyes in the comfort and solitude of his room. The stove in the corner was fully stoked, the room warm.

Alone. He jumped out of his bed and put on his robe. He was alone. He was home.

He opened his window, and cold air blew back at him. One young boy, pulling a sled up the academy hill, heard the window open.

"Merry Christmas, Mr. Barton. Good to see you're home."

Lowering the window, Thomas waved. He got back into bed, under warm covers, and sat upright, pillows propped behind him. More than a hundred years ahead of him sat a beautiful woman, alone in her home, sipping coffee and watching the birds at the feeders. And here he sat, alone in his room. What was he to have learned from *that*?

A rapping came from the door below. He shoved his feet in his slippers and shuffled to the stairs. "Coming," he called out, hoping not to find a wild-eyed Pastor Lockhardt. He was not ready for another adventure.

Jimmy Perkins stood on the stoop. The young boy tipped his hat. "Morning, Mr. Barton. Pastor Lockhardt told us we were to keep an eye out for you, and at the first sign you were awake, we were to tell you to meet him at the church. That was about an hour ago, but I imagine he's still there, being it's Christmas and all."

Thomas nodded. "Please tell Pastor Lockhardt I'll be over shortly."

"Yes, sir," the boy called back and ran down the walk.

Upstairs, Thomas poured cold water from the pitcher into the bowl and splashed his face, remembering the pleasant shower just the morning before. What would he tell Pastor Lockhardt? What had he learned?

He warmed the water on the stove. Pastor Lockhardt must've thought to start it for him last night, anticipating his arrival. As he shaved, he thought about Sarah's Bentonsport. How completely different it was from the future he thought his Bentonsport held.

He could tell his friend the legacy of their Bentonsport was not in buildings, not in material wealth, but rather in relationships between people, the dreams they kept dreaming, the community they were forming. The Bentonsport of the future continued to be a place where people came to make their dreams come true.

After dressing in a freshly pressed white shirt and dark-gray trousers, he brushed his hair back, and his long curls fell to his collar. He was in need of a haircut.

The air was cold and crisp, but the sun was bright and, in a strange way, warm. The sledding children made long snakelike paths up and down the hill. A chorus called out after him as he walked down the path, and he stopped and waved to all of them.

"A blessed, merry Christmas, children," he called out as though they were sitting in front of him in the classroom.

"Merry Christmas, Mr. Barton!" In unison, they gave the singsong reply.

How would he describe the painful, sweet lesson that, despite short, spiky hair, short skirts, pants, and a strange way of speaking, people were people? Goodness of the heart and virtue of kind deeds were as prevalent in the future as today. Pastor Lockhardt would want to know people's faith stood the test of time.

All this was true, but none of it conveyed his deep, deep sense of loss. Before he left, he'd known something was missing in his life, known he lacked a companion, lacked the intimacy he saw in the married couples he interacted with daily. And the loneliness had been real, but it had come and gone like a veil draped over his life and then lifted.

This was different. Something had been cut out, removed from the center of his life, and he didn't know if he'd ever be able to fill the cavity. His heart and soul ached for someone he had no way to reach. But despite this pain, he wouldn't have foregone the experience. It had been a gift, a priceless gift. And it held memories he would play over and over again. Richard. Lani. Bill and Caroline. And Sarah—oh, Sarah!

He reached the stone steps, the steep climb he and Sarah had made just the night before. They'd held onto each other, realizing every step took away from their last time alone together.

The church doors were closed. Should he knock? He'd never knocked on the church doors before, but he'd never come there as a visitor alone with the church closed up.

As he was preparing to knock, Pastor Lockhardt stepped out, clapped him on the back, and then embraced him in a bear hug.

"Thomas, my good, good friend. My, my, it is so good to see you. Come in. Do come in."

They entered the vestibule, and Thomas hung his coat on a coat rack near the door. "It's good to see you too. It's good to see all of Bentonsport again." Yes, it was all here. The mills and stores, the industry and hope—all here but Sarah. He steadied his voice. "I have so much to share with you. So much."

"Yes," Pastor Lockhardt said, laughing. "And I have something for you. A gift."

He walked in front of Thomas, placing his hand on the

sanctuary door. And, just as he did, from inside, Thomas heard the beginning of a familiar song. He stopped as the words rang in his head, each following the piano notes—"Angels We Have Heard on High."

The pastor grasped his forearm and winked. Then he opened the door wide and ushered him toward Sarah at the piano.

"Merry Christmas, Thomas!"

The End

About Lisa Schnedler

I write cozy fiction, set in small towns you'll want to visit, with characters who soon will become your friends. They have certainly become mine.

I find joy in serving Jesus, loving my family, and writing about good people you will want to meet. I also serve through my work, Christian Life Planning ministry, blog, and podcast.

My life is about serving Jesus, loving my family, and writing about good people you will want to meet.

I am married to my best friend and love of my life. Together, we have served churches in small towns people love to visit.

I have this great family—three grown children, married to my "additional three kids," six grandkids, and two parents who love the Lord and put a solid foundation under all of us. I am a pastor's wife—and we have served churches for more than 30 years. My husband and I recently opened a Christian Learning Center, "Cornerstone," offering free classes and gatherings to help Christians learn and form friendships.

I am blessed in my professional career and have worked as a hospital president for more than 30 years.

I love to make new friends! Visit my website to learn more. https://www.lisaschnedler.com

You may like ...

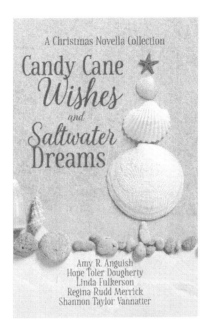

Candy Cane Wishes and Saltwater Dreams

A collection of Christmas beach romances

by five multi-published authors.

***Mistletoe Make-believe* by Amy Anguish** – Charlie Hill's family thinks his daughter Hailey needs a mom–to the point they won't get off his back until he finds her one. Desperate to be free from their nagging, he asks a stranger to pretend she's his girlfriend during the holidays. When romance author Samantha Arwine takes a working vacation to St. Simon's Island over Christmas, she never dreamed she'd be involved in a real-life romance. Are the sparks between her and Charlie real? Or is her imagination over-acting ... again?

***A Hatteras Surprise* by Hope Toler Dougherty** –Ginny Stowe spent years tending a childhood hurt that dictated her college study and work. Can time with an island visitor with ties to her past heal lingering wounds and lead her toward a happy Christmas ... and more? Ben Daniels intends to hire a new branch manager for a Hatteras Island bank, then hurry back to his promotion and Christmas in Charlotte. Spending time with a beautiful local, however, might force him to adjust his sails.

A Pennie for Your Thoughts by **Linda Fulkerson** —When the Lakeshore Homeowner's Association threatens to condemn the cabin Pennie Vaughn inherited from her foster mother, her only hope of funding the needed repairs lies in winning a travel blog contest. Trouble is, Pennie never goes anywhere. Should she use the all-expenses paid Hawaiian vacation offered to her by her ex-fiancé? The trip that would have been their honeymoon?

Mr. Sandman by **Regina Rudd Merrick** — Events manager Taylor Fordham's happily-ever-after was snatched from her, and she's saying no to romance and Christmas. When she meets two new friends—the cute new chef at Pilot Oaks and a contributor on a sci-fi fan fiction website who enjoys debate—her resolve begins to waver. Just when she thinks she can loosen her grip on thoughts of love, a crisis pulls her back. There's no way she's going to risk her heart again.

Coastal Christmas by **Shannon Taylor Vannatter** — Lark Pendleton is banking on a high-society wedding to make her grandparent's inn at Surfside Beach, Texas the venue to attract buyers. Tasked with sprucing up the inn, she hires Jace Wilder, whose heart she once broke. When the bride and groom turn out to be Lark's high school nemesis and ex-boyfriend, she and Jace embark on a pretend romance to save the wedding. But when real feelings emerge, can they overcome past hurts?

Christmas Tree Wars

by Delores Topliff

Christmas is meant to be a time of goodwill, but there's no peace between two neighboring Christmas tree farmers involved in a longstanding feud. Can this year be different with a bit of holiday romance tossed into the season?

When the financial planner son and forestry major niece of feuding Christmas tree farmers come home to help their families in crisis, it takes Christmas tree wars to a whole new level. As the young people seek success by competing to provide a national Christmas tree, romance fills the air and connects them like mistle to toe.

Scrivenings
PRESS
Quench your thirst for story.
www.ScriveningsPress.com

Stay up-to-date on your favorite books and authors with our free e-newsletters.

ScriveningsPress.com

Made in the USA
Middletown, DE
26 November 2022

15779225R00181